The Spun Sugar Hole

by
Jerry Sohl

Simon and Schuster
NEW YORK

Second printing

SBN 671-20874-8
Library of Congress Catalog Card Number: 73-139661
Designed by Irving Perkins
Manufactured in the United States of America
By H. Wolff Book Mfg. Co., Inc., New York, N.Y.

True sanity entails in one way or another the dissolution of the normal ego, that false self competently adjusted to our alienated social reality; the emergence of the "inner" archetypal mediators of divine power, and through this death a rebirth, and the eventual reestablishment of a new kind of ego-functioning, the ego now being the servant of the divine, no longer its betrayer.

—R. D. Laing,
The Politics of Experience

The
Spun
Sugar
Hole

I

PETER HARTSOOK lifted the curtain and got off the thought train, feeling at once terribly vulnerable. It wasn't easy coping with the outside when the inside was so safe and beautiful. It didn't help when Mr. Hochdruck was waiting in the shadows nearby. Of course being out had never been exactly easy, with or without Mr. Hochdruck, but Peter was finding it more difficult all the time and he knew that some day he just might decide to stay inside and never again come out.

He saw the day was bright with sun, it was warm, and he liked that, so he allowed what he could of the outside to come through to him. He twisted his head, his neck cracking from disuse, seeing birds chattering and chasing each other in the elms and bushes, squirrels making noisy nuisances of themselves as they scurried along branches. All that he saw was in shades of gray, not at all like the vivid colors inside. He wished he could see bright things again, not these depressing grays, this drab world. He wished, too, that he could be like these live things he saw, free and simple and responding, filled with raw smells, feelings, wetnesses and drynesses.

He was not aware of Father Bischoff's approach. Father Bischoff examined him from several angles, saw the glimmerings and decided to sit down beside him. Peter had no chance to retreat to sanctuary before the priest started talking.

"Have you heard from the Council fathers?"

Halfway in, halfway out, Peter wondered why the man thought that he, Peter, would do anything so overt as to contact Father Bischoff's people. Then, because he wasn't all the way in, he became unsettled by Father Bischoff's presence. He tried to get the rest of the way in and, being unable to, he

9

started to panic. How could he wrap himself in foil with the man sitting right there watching him?

Father Bischoff was saying, "I suppose you're one who thinks the Council fathers don't echo the ancient accents of all that's past, that they are pretty good guys."

The priest leaned close. "For your information, Dimpled Brain, they're not. They're barnacled. And I mean *barnacled*. They won't listen to me, only to ethereal music." Father Bischoff turned to view the trees ruefully. "I've tried to tell them, but they speak only in terms of ecclesiastical discipline."

Peter was beginning to adjust the mantle despite Father Bischoff when the priest said, "A divine friendship, that's all I want. Can't they see that? How can I talk of love and never kiss?" Father Bischoff lowered his eyes like a penitent, studied the ground for a long moment. "I've said my Mass devoutly, but they evidently don't believe me. I don't doubt God's being. He is not dead. I've talked with Him. But they don't believe that either. They don't even believe I feel Christ's presence in the Eucharist."

Father Bischoff stood up, faced the direction of Italy. "You bastards are barnacled!" he cried out angrily. "Reactionary! Do you hear me? He told me and He ought to know. You want to know what else He said? He said He will bring the walls down any time I say. So watch yourselves, old men. I'm warning you."

Father Bischoff sat down, his hand absently wandering to his crotch and staying there. "I'm not boiling with sex, Peter," he said quietly. "It's just that I want fulfillment. Is it a sin to want fulfillment?" Dreaming of fulfillment, Father Bischoff's eyes glazed.

In the ensuing silence Peter managed to wrench the cloak about him, and when he came out of it, Father Bischoff was gone. So were the squirrels and most of the birds, and the sun was behind the trees.

Then came Charlemagne walking as if he had an urgent message to deliver, which was the way Charlemagne walked, and seeing that Charlemagne had discarded his shoes, Peter looked away, for when Charlemagne was barefoot it was harangue time.

Charlemagne sat down facing him, hissing that he didn't look well. "Aren't you following the regimen I prescribed? You're going to have to eat good red meat if we're going to get out of here." He brought out two cloth bags of marbles, put them on the ground, rested his feet on them, flexing his toes and massaging his insteps. "Can't have weaklings on the trail, Alcuin."

Peter slid sideways into his shell because he didn't know what "Alcuin" meant and he didn't like being called something he didn't understand and there was a threat there somewhere. As he floated along narrowing, curving corridors, the word "Alcuin" reverberated until it became "Alcoa," and because that was a metal like steel it became "Al Capone" and "Chicago" and suddenly in color there was Frank Sinatra singing my kind of town Chicago is, and there were the other six hoods, all for one and one for all, and he and Marcella were seeing it, the theater was musty and empty, and it was the kind of movie he and Marcella used to go to all the time because Marcella thought a movie was better at a movie than it was at home on the TV screen even if it was in color.

Charlemagne punched holes and pulled him out. "It's tonight, Peter. We're getting out of here tonight."

Peter stayed halfway in.

"Don't worry about the attendants. They're not such a bad lot. You hear everybody griping, but where would we be without them? Who'd tuck us in at night, eh, Peter? But they're blind, and what makes them blind is they have problems of their own." Charlemagne stopped talking because what he said amused him and he laughed.

As for the attendants, Peter never locked eyes with them. They intruded, and he was never sure how much of him they were seeing, which was the way it was with Mr. Hochdruck, who stood around in dark places and looked like a vulture waiting for him to give in. In spite of his calling him Alcuin now and then, Peter liked Charlemagne.

"Saw the good padre with you a while ago. He's going with us." Charlemagne talked on about the plan for escape, his lips so close Peter could feel his breath.

Yes, he did like Charlemagne, and he guessed it must be because he could slip away and Charlemagne would let him, not jabbing him with an elbow to bring him back as some of them did, or shouting at him or shaking him as if there was something wrong with him. And if he refused to come out, Charlemagne wasn't offended. In fact, Charlemagne was always interested in where he'd been on his trips.

"Are you with us?" And when Peter did not answer, Charlemagne put a hand on his arm. "Peter?"

Peter shuddered, drew away. He could not stand to be touched.

"Do you hear me? It's tonight. You, me, Father Bischoff and Andros. We'll lace our helmets; our hauberks will be all agleam."

Peter was beginning to adjust his shroud so he wouldn't have to listen any more when Charlemagne said quietly, "Nobody knows. Really. You can believe me, Peter. I know there are problems, but they're not entirely insoluble. Put your faith in me." Charlemagne laughed. "Hell, it's the grass roots, that's what's important, and that's what we'll be doing, grass-roots work, right down where the people live. Do you realize how abominable their health is?" Charlemagne worked in physiotherapy under Herpes Zoster and Salma Gundi and it was well known what a good job he did there. "I'd like to take some of the others along, but they're not interested, and there's so little time, nothing can be done without organization, generalship, so we have to be careful. I'm against the draft. It must be volunteer through and through. An unwilling army loses the war. Alcuin, the trouble with the world is there isn't enough anarchy."

Charlemagne went on about reforms, the development of natural resources and the order of battle while Peter quietly covered himself until Charlemagne's voice was only a buzzing in his ear, and suddenly he was in the outhouse again pressing to defecate while a bee zoomed about angrily.

Inside the outhouse the air was limp, heavy and dead, old spider webs sagged, and the sun beat down on the old wood, the knotted, gnarled, unpainted wood. Outside was Marcella, in the corn rows, in the arbor, in the vegetable garden, somewhere in the house with her mother and father, and they weren't married yet, he and Marcella; he was merely visiting them. It was the kind of day when the least exertion left the skin greasy and heavy with sweat, the leaves on the elms were motionless and the wooded ravines lay simmering in the summer heat, the chickens were quiet, cats found shaded corners to sleep in, or lay under the porch, their gimlet eyes half closed, watching for wandering rodents foolish enough to brave the heat. Only the ants were busy, making long lines across the scorching cement walk to the house, impervious to the searing sun. And inside the outhouse there was the sickly sweet stench of feces and lime. And the bee, the damned bee, wanting to get out, and the door and its latch out of reach. Didn't it realize it was safe inside?

2

Dr. Therin Sheckley walked the long corridor with Dr. Nathan Tillheimer wishing the director had not picked this time to accompany him to the doctors' lounge. He had a lot of thinking to do and didn't relish the intrusion.

They turned in at the lounge door, Dr. Tillheimer opening it and saying, "After you, Doctor." Always polite, Tillheimer was. Old Worldish. Therin could do without it.

Inside, Dr. Tillheimer said, "I'll get the coffee," and Therin went to the john.

Under the harsh fluorescent lights, after he had urinated, Therin examined his face in the mirrors above the basins and saw how pale he was. Well, why shouldn't he be pale, knowing guilt when he felt it, his palms being wet with it most of the time these days? The strange thing was that he'd rather not be rid of the guilt, and he wondered how this could be.

He thought how easy it would be just to go ahead, throw Minnie out, confess everything to Elizabeth, live in the backlash from that until it was over, and then he could once again lend his body and mind to his patients.

But he could not break it off because he was having too much fun with Minnie. Then he thought wryly: If half of me is here and the other half is with Minnie, what's left for Elizabeth, my wife of record?

His trouble was he was letting himself become too absorbed with his problem rather than his guilt, and he knew he could go on forever in thought spirals, guilt chasing thoughts about guilt, peristalsis cramping his gut, crippling his efficiency, all of it becoming a problem which, because it was a problem, had to be solved because it was beginning to crowd everything else out, his work, his colleagues, his patients, and now even Dr. Tillheimer, his superior.

Pretty soon, if he kept on like this, it was going to become apparent to everyone that something was wrong. He could hear them. What the hell's happened to Dr. Sheckley? Have you seen him lately? So pale and preoccupied. What's eating him, anyway?

And Dr. Sheckley replying loftily, not what but who.

He turned, pausing to think and remember before going out. Little Minnie in her miniskirt, just about the cutest thing he had ever seen (or did he have to convince himself of this in order to perpetuate the relationship?). Surely the best thing that had ever happened to him. Or maybe the worst. It all depended upon whether you were Dr. Therin Scheckley or Mrs. Therin Scheckley. And that cute little nympho Minnie not getting hurt at all. How was that possible? Was she really smarter than he?

Thinking about it was solving nothing, so Therin forced his mind from it and opened the door.

As soon as Therin was handed his coffee, Dr. Tillheimer said, "How's that new patient, Le Moyne?"

Berylwood, a private sanitarium, was not overpopulated because it was expensive, and so patients were still new by Dr. Tillheimer's reckoning even if they'd been there for weeks.

Therin said, "I'll do a workup in a few days. He isn't due for Staff for another week or so."

Tillheimer nodded. "What I meant was, does he fit in with the group?"

"Yes. I think we've got him catalogued right, but I've never had a patient like him."

"Oh?"

Therin wished he hadn't made that opening, mostly because he was not all that sure about Charles Le Moyne. But he said, "He's got good ego strength. It gets out of hand once in a while, that's all."

15

"He wants to play therapist perhaps?"

"Something like that." It was more than that. Therin wasn't quite sure what it was, but he didn't want Tillheimer interfering. "I can handle it."

"You'd better."

Therin looked at him sharply.

Dr. Tillheimer's leathery face broke into a broad grin. "We'd all better, eh, Doctor? Otherwise they might lock us in."

Therin laughed politely. There were few locks at Berylwood. Patients would have had a tough time trying to do a thing like that.

After coffee, Therin walked out into the bright sunshine and grounds of Berylwood, the neatly manicured lawns, curving walks, feeling a little better. He always liked strolling about the place because it was well kept up, and its low, vine-covered buildings made it look like anything but a sanitarium.

Immediately his problem infiltrated his mind again, Minnie and Therin, eros invading libido, two zodiacal signs moving into conflict in the vault of the heavens. He had not known he could be so vulnerable, such easy prey to mischievous dark blue eyes and a miniskirt.

It was his own fault, though. One day, on his way home from the sanitarium, he found Minnie standing by the side of the road looking forlorn, a waif in a brief skirt, her eyes tremendously large in her pretty face, so clear, so innocent, a saddle-bag over her shoulder, the smooth skin of her face reflecting the amber of the late-afternoon sun. His first thought was: What child is this left alone to fend for herself in a hostile world that might not appreciate her innocence? His second thought was to stop the car and rescue her from what might have been.

But it really was the other way around. Minnie had actually rescued him, though he did not know it then, seeing only the flashing eyes, even white teeth in a smile, and white thighs as she got in and he started the car. She said nothing, turning to lean against the door to examine him, while he did not dare take his eyes off the road, enjoying a growing nub of excitement that suddenly ran to censure, for he knew it was true each man does that which he must. Did he really *need* this child?

Her not saying anything discomfited him. That, plus the examination. Dr. Sheckley, so long the observer, now the observed. What the hell did she think she was doing? Because of the unease her silence and scrutiny was creating, he said, "I'm Dr. Sheckley."

"My name is Minnie. My friends call me Minnie the Pooh."

And so he'd taken her home to live with him and Elizabeth.

Therin had more than once tried to learn her real name, but she cleverly avoided revealing it. Instead, with the incredible precocity and directness of the young, while he would be trying to pin her down on her age and origins, she would con him into examining his entire life structure or defending his stance in the world. It was not that she was reluctant to talk about herself—she readily admitted she was an escapee from a hippie commune—but when he wanted to know *what* commune *where*, she was off on another tack, saying she felt she had transcended such things, there was more to life than a simple sharing.

"Isn't that true, Doctor?" Her smile was so sweet.

Therin, who had a penchant for classifying things, decided that Minnie was a devotee of what was called in the jargon privatism. The reason, he believed, was that she preferred feeling over thinking, was absorbed in herself and had absolute faith in the inviolability of her inner workings. A clear-cut case. Even without considering the fact that she was also articulate, subjective, possessed extraordinary self-confidence, was happy by herself, and always exhibited a healthy sameness. That merely cinched it.

But Therin was confounded to find that she was more than that, exhibiting symptoms (after all, aren't all actions symptoms of one thing or another?) that, while they did not betray his original diagnosis, certainly complicated it. She started to look at him with inordinate warmth. And if that wasn't unsettling enough, she began to exhibit a kind of romantic self-centeredness that made it impossible for him not to like her, for he always thought of himself as a free soul, a romanticist, somewhat self-centered (though sheltered would have been more like it). So, before he knew it, he had seduced her. Or had it been the other way around? He wasn't sure. Isn't it true, Doctor, that women select their sexual partners despite anything and everything a man might think or do?

His involvement with Minnie had rendered him disoriented. No doubt about it. He knew Elizabeth was looking at him oddly these days, and for the first time in his marriage he found himself unable to relate to her.

Therin sighed with the weight of reflection, saw that his steps had taken him nearly to the entrance to Berylwood. He turned, taking a different path, one which would take him around behind the administration building to his small office where he knew a patient was already waiting and wishing he had the courage to cancel the rest of the day so he could really work things out in his mind.

He came upon three patients from his morning and afternoon group.

Charlemagne sat on one of the white benches that were scattered about the grounds, his bare feet resting on two identical bags of marbles, a carpet roll at his back. He kept working his toes and arching his back.

Father Bischoff was nearby on the grass under a tree, working his beads with quiet intensity.

Andros was chinning himself on one of the lower limbs of the tree.

Therin looked around for Peter but did not see him.

Charlemagne regarded him coolly. "To whom do you owe your fealty, sir?"

"Where's Peter?"

"Having visitors." Charlemagne smiled. "Care to join these troops?"

"I'll see you all later this afternoon." Therin walked on.

"Men for their lords great hardships must abide," he heard

18

Charlemagne say, and he wondered if the remark could have been directed at him.

Therin rather liked Charlemagne and he knew it was because Charlemagne was cooperative and cheerful most of the time, though he was often given to oblique utterances and fustian outbursts. Charlemagne's real name was Charles Le Moyne, and he would admit to it under stress, which Therin considered unusual in a patient of his type. Charlemagne suffered that the Saxon invasion had not yet begun, though he continually assured the group that great plans were under way and that this would be merely a prelude to a larger conflict which he, Charlemagne, would lead.

Andros, whose real name was Scott Kleinschmidt, claimed he was run by a tiny extraterrestrial, an E.T., who had landed on Earth and picked Scott from among all humanity to inhabit, invading his bloodstream and reaching Scott's precentral gyri to run his Earthling from this vantage point in Scott's brain. Scott, who insisted everyone call him by his E.T. name, Andros, and would never answer to Scott or Mr. Kleinschmidt, was therefore not responsible for anything he did or said. This was, of course, very convenient for Scott Kleinschmidt/Andros, but it was the way he had to be.

Father Bischoff's real name was Howard Petersen, and he had once been a dedicated altar boy at Chicago's Church of St. Stephen on the West Side. Like Scott Kleinschmidt, he would not even turn if called by his given name. He was the focal point of a battle of good vs. evil, both views his, both views exposed, neither disinhibitioned, all encased in the flesh of the late Howard Petersen, now pirated for his hieratical enslavement and Father Bischoff's imperfect contrition.

Therin's steps took him to a bench where Peter Hartsook sat by himself in the sun looking not at all like part of the world, staring vacantly across the grounds. What time he did not spend in silent absorption, Peter spent looking for hidden microphones, for it seemed he thought he was being spied upon.

Therin stopped in front of the bench.

"Hello, Peter," he said.

Peter did not move. His eyes blinked now and then. Sometimes his eyes moved and focussed, seeing things that weren't there. But most of the time he was like this, lost in an inside world.

Therin sighed and moved on.

3

Urinal—Entree Numb 1

I Peter Heartsick being sound all way thru solid like rock do and hereby make the following disposition position a suggestion from Doktor Shekel and here I am at the urinal

I further and farther depose it will be an ill wind this wind for what other purpose except for info from this unobdt svt that is not otherwise unanswerably available

Your electronics are not good enough genitalmen because my squelch controls operate at peak efficiencies all the time more than 24 hours the day

We are receiving you loud and clear and the RF I get tells me Over and Under youre not even straight line I get harmonics like a regular player and my tuned circuits show me your cleverness but it is not enough

Just like the coroner and the policemen who came after they saw it all on TV and said I killed Marcella

This is a lie

Marcella is a loyal person which is more than I say for you any time I know what big liars you are

Peter Heartsick

4

THERIN SAT back in the chair behind his desk, alone in his office, staring at the door through which his last patient departed, knowing he should be up and moving across the grounds to the little room off the day room where his group would now be assembling, yet still sitting, in no mood to go.

In a way, he envied his group. All they had to do was report here and there. They had no responsibilities. Their world was created for them by others; all they had to do was try to fit into it. No, that wasn't right. He must stop thinking like that!

He let the vague sounds of the outside come in to him. A shout. A truck starting up. A radio playing somewhere. Someone walking by.

Therin hadn't helped his last patient, he knew that, and he wondered why he persisted when his mind was elsewhere, elsewhere being Minnie. What was she doing? Watching TV? Playing his sound system twice as loud as it should be? Elizabeth didn't enjoy it and neither did he, Minnie's musical taste being mostly rock, though they never criticized her for it. Surprisingly, Minnie and his wife hit it off well, far better than he thought they would.

"It's a palace!" Minnie exclaimed when she first saw the house, which was fifteen miles from Berylwood. Therin, unused to rash enthusiasms, thought she was putting him on. But Minnie, he discovered, was full of such breathlessness and reckless response and seemed beyond guile. He reasoned later that it must have been the contrast between what men of craft had wrought and the crude, drab and drafty teepees of the commune.

He remembered how electric her long black hair was at that

moment, flashing a demoralizing violet in the alternate patches of setting sun that came through the elms along the street. He remembered, too, how it had seemed strange that he should have brought her home, but he had not asked her where she was bound, and she didn't want to know how far he was going, and so they ended up in front of the most unlikely place, his home, with Elizabeth staring out at them from one of the front windows.

Perhaps it was his brash behavior in bringing her home that demolished Elizabeth's objections before they could be voiced. Or it could have been the innocence of it. Anyway, Elizabeth, being a good Christian woman with ascetic forebears, took Minnie in as her own and set to work restructuring a character transmogrified by the hang-loose ethic. Elizabeth was, as far as Therin could see, completely unsuccessful. Elizabeth spent hours with Minnie, but Minnie was only partly there, given to nodding rather somberly now and then, her eyes far away, lighting when they saw Therin (but not lighting too much later when they came to mean so much to each other for fear Elizabeth would see). It wasn't that Minnie had no stances; it was that she was unswervable. Several times, cornered by Judeo-Christian logic, Minnie simply replied that she did not believe it. It should have been clear to Elizabeth that Minnie would have defied even divine fiat.

Therin thought that he might counsel Minnie, that what he'd say would be more pertinent than that old stuff from the *Reader's Digest* and the Bible that Elizabeth was spouting. After all, he was a psychiatrist and certainly more capable of nursing an injured psyche than Elizabeth. That was why, alone in his study one night a few days after Minnie had been taken in, Elizabeth out to one of her churchwomen's meetings, he was happy to see Minnie come in. There could not have been a better time; he hadn't wanted to flaunt his mastery of such things in Elizabeth's face, so he had held off. But this was the time. Except he had not taken into consideration Minnie's flashing Mediterranean-blue eyes, her glowing cheeks, her disarming smile. And so he discovered it was *not* the time for counseling;

it was time for exploration, one body by another, and the amazing thing was he hadn't a moment's doubt or hesitation, it was so natural, so direct, so necessary, so *good*. In fact, he felt so euphoric afterward he went to bed, had a fine night's sleep, and didn't start to feel guilt until the next morning when Elizabeth was preparing breakfast for them.

In the days that followed, his guilt increased each time he had sex with Minnie until it reached the saturation point. As for Minnie, she evidently didn't feel the slightest bit reprehensible, which only made him feel worse because it should have been the other way around. After all, who knew more about guilt and dealt daily with its myriad manifestations, Minnie the Pooh or Dr. Therin Sheckley?

Which brought him to considering: Dr. Therin Sheckley and His Relationship to His Environment, Notes on a Changing Moral Pattern, and: A Study of Dr. Therin Sheckley—Factors in the Easy Fracture of a Life Style. There was no explanation, unless one considered Minnie's modality, her appealing amorality, her complete lack of inhibition, her total letting go. The plain fact was he was even better able to accommodate Elizabeth sexually, which surprised her and disturbed him.

And now he realized that, guilt-ridden though he was, he did not want anything to change. Not even the guilt. But he knew all things change, with the possible exception of Minnie, who seemed to feed off the relationship, yet seemed unaffected by it. *He* had changed. He knew that he was hooked on Minnie, that she held options on his emotions, and now he felt not only guilt but also a tinge of fear.

When they came up to Peter sitting on the bench, it was Charlemagne who reached in for him, saying, "Time to go, Peter."

Peter wrenched from inside to outside, heart lurching. "Time?"

Father Bischoff looked morosely across the broad sweep of lawn.

24

"Come on, Peter," Andros said, standing on one foot, then on the other. "Come *on!*"

The afternoon encroached and Peter tried to adjust to it, shifting about, stretching, finally getting up.

Charlemagne waited with him so he could get all the way out, the other two walking on.

Peter thought that was nice of Charlemagne.

They had been quiet in the room for nearly twenty minutes.

Peter stood rigidly at the window looking out and seeing only God knew what. Andros sat backward in his chair, chin on the back of it, looking absently across the room. Father Bischoff fingered his heads, moved his lips. Therein watched Charlemagne, who had been drawing something with a stubby pencil on a pad of note paper.

Charlemagne, finished now, looked at what he'd done, viewing it from a number of angles.

Therin could see it was a drawing of a scepter and a crown, very elaborate, very ornate.

"None in the sun so glitters to the view," Charlemagne said. "And none shall snatch it away."

"Whose scepter and crown is that?"

"Carlon's, of course." Charlemagne regarded Therin with vitriolic scorn. "Didn't you get taught anything where you went to school?"

"And you are Carlon?"

Charlemagne turned to the others, pointing to Therin. "The prosecution is leading the witness."

Andros yawned, saw Charlemagne's sudden glare, explained: "Andros has never experienced an Earth spring. He's very impressed."

Charlemagne snorted. "An E.T. with spring fever is something I never heard of. You might tell him he's a little late for spring, if he's still there."

Andros was in his mid-twenties and he was often intimidated by Charlemagne because Charlemagne was nearly twice his age and knew how to rattle him. Now Andros looked sharply at Charlemagne to see whether to take offense. "He knows all about you, Charlemagne. Every cell. All your workings."

"Does he know the names of my brothers?"

"He knows everything."

"I have no brothers."

Father Bischoff looked up from his rosary. "If Andros is so smart, then how come he doesn't get you out of here?"

"Because he's not a nonsequitur like you."

Father Bischoff colored. "He should be quoined down. The key should be turned to crush him down, really pulverize him, make him one-point, even less."

Andros turned to Peter. "He likes you, Peter. Says you remind him of the Residents of the Rear Rim, and those are good worlds. The stratum happens to be nonjudgmental." When Peter did not turn or indicate he had heard, Andros went on: "He says for you not to worry. He can spot a bug within a mile."

Peter turned, startled, blinking rapidly.

"There are no bugs in here," Father Bischoff said as if he knew. "I know because I've looked."

"No fair stealing from Peter," Andros said.

"Not even type lice, Bent Brain."

Charlemagne said, "Andros is the only bug I know."

"Andros is no bug," Andros said vehemently. "His size is measured in millimicrons."

"Is that him saying it, or is that you? As if I didn't know the answer to that one."

"For your information, control was long ago relinquished to Andros."

"Millimicrons. That would put him in the class of a bacteria. Or is that bacterium?"

"Don't be barnacled," Father Bischoff said. "That's like asking how many bacteria can sit on the head of a pin."

Andros held up a palm, as he always did when he felt in a bind. Father Bischoff groaned and Charlemagne took off a shoe and massaged his foot, for they knew what was coming. Andros

26

said, with appropriate pauses: "A pledge of evil . . . often overcomes . . . the strong. . . . In this world . . . nothing is softer . . . or thinner . . . than it is."

"Doggerel," Charlemagne said. "They're not real poets where Andros comes from."

"That sort of thing goes on all the time in the upper reaches of Paradise," Father Bischoff said airily. "And, I might add, with better effect."

"Andros," Andros was saying, "is from the fourth planet of the star Acheron in the Pleiades in the constellation Taurus, and I might say he's vexed by the trend of the conversation in this room."

Charlemagne said, "It seems to me he could have picked a better brain to inhabit."

Therin shifted on his chair as they went on, hacking at one another, and he did not try to stop it. It was, he knew, a form of touching, a way of getting close with words and still remaining insular. After a while it stopped and they sat silent again.

Charlemagne got up. "I have heard that the Merovingian kings are weak. The *missi dominici* imparted that piece of information to me. As a result, I believe they will be pushovers."

"All you choirs of the just," Father Bischoff said, nodding. "All you holy patriarchs and prophets."

"Litany, latiny, gluttony, it's all the same, isn't it?" Charlemagne moved to Father Bischoff.

"I am a priest. I am a priest now and forever. I chose the priesthood. I embrace the priesthood. But, gentlemen, I want you to know I did not choose celibacy."

Charlemagne said scornfully, "Did you choose wine, financial drives, real estate, golf, poker and bingo? And why is it they're always raiding your games? Do you do your own laundry?"

"Be merciful, spare him."

"You have to buy a gambling stamp for a thing like that, Padre. A federal gambling stamp."

"From your anger, deliver . . ."

"I am not angry, sir."

"Then you are barnacled."

"I am muscled and tendoned."

"Hopelessly encumbered, encrusted and squandered, sir, that's what you are."

Charlemagne laughed. "How wrong you are! I am osteologized, myologized and syndesmologized, an intricate working together of four hundred muscles and two hundred and six bones, same as you."

"Purgatory for all. That's my platform, sir." Father Bischoff impaled him with a stare. "As far as I am concerned, you are not even Charlemagne."

"Why do you say that?"

"Everybody knows Charlemagne is dead. If I am not mistaken, he died in the year eight hundred and fourteen."

"How can I be dead if I'm talking to you?" Charlemagne shook his head, squinted at Father Bischoff, then walked around him, Father Bischoff suffering the inspection without moving. Finally, Charlemagne stopped in front of him, glared down at him. "Are you an inquisitor of the kingdom, a majordomo, or what?"

"I am a priest."

"And a rather simple priest, it seems to me." Charlemagne suddenly turned, walked away, saying in a loud, strettolike voice: "I am Carolus Magnus Incarnate, King of the Franks and Emperor of the West, crowned by the Pope, ruler of all the Romans."

Father Bischoff lowered his head. "*Utuque simblatus imibus erte servum es. Carborius ingalo ex uturque californium patellego sum.*"

"Father, I can give you absolution, if that is what you desire, and it seems to me it is."

"*Profundus quondrum influxorium cogitabitis conjunctivitis nequaquam ubiter regia.*"

It was suddenly quiet.

Therin turned to Peter, who had returned to the window. "Peter, is there anything you want to say to us?" But of course there wasn't.

"Peter's defluxed," Andros said.

"What does that mean?"

"It has to do with his inner magnetism. He told Andros about it. It seems his primary circuits aren't tuned with his auxiliaries, resulting in crumbling and flaking off."

"That still doesn't explain it."

"I'll confess I don't know, but Andros does. The reason he brought it up is he thought he'd help out, explain a few things, seeing how everything's getting bogged down around here." He turned to look at Charlemagne, who still stood before Father Bischoff. "He also had judgments about these two, considering Charles's impersonation of an apotheotic reliquary. Don't ask me what that means either. The words are not part of my computer banks."

"Andros is the only relic I know," Charlemagne said. "And the name is not Charles."

"A shipwrecked relic," Father Bischoff said. "The heaviest type sinks to the bottom in any case."

"I am not even a joint king any more, even though I will admit to being the son of Pepin the Short. You see"—and he moved to stand before Therin—"Carloman is dead."

"Sit down," Therin said.

"You are Charles Le Moyne," Andros told him. "Andros saw the patient registry."

"A *nom de guerre*, my good man. There were spies here then."

"Spies?" Peter said in a shrill voice, turning from the window, frightened. "Here?"

"Not any more, my dear Alcuin. You need have no fear here in the palace."

Andros squirmed uncomfortably in his chair. "Andros doesn't like it here."

Therin asked: "Where would he like to be?"

"Ask Charlemagne."

Charlemagne's eyes flicked to Therin. "The name, as I said, is Charlemagne, and we will defeat the Avars, let there be no doubt about that. Even now relentless wars against the pagan

29

enemy are being prepared for, to pave the way for the Carolingian Renaissance. I thought I had explained all this."

"What does Andros mean?"

"He had reference to the coming struggle, I believe. The incipient battles."

Father Bischoff expressed doubt that Charlemagne could conduct a war from where he was standing.

"It will not be so, friends," Charlemagne said. "When the time is ripe, I will set you all free, and in doing so become your liege lord."

"You mentioned freedom before," Therin said. "And escape, too. Are you serious?"

"Of course, Doctor. Aren't you? Must we wait for the king's trumpet to sound?" Charlemagne shook his head regretfully. "Doctor, sir, unless your attitude changes, I'm afraid we will have to leave you behind. It is unfortunate. You are a good doctor, but a poor spy for the Lombards. We all wish we could confide in you, don't think we don't." He looked around guardedly, said in a lowered voice, "But we must keep our escape plans secret until the final hours." He smiled. "And I might add, Doctor, those final hours are approaching."

5

PETER KEPT sliding in and out of the here and now because Charlemagne was talking escape in one corner of the recreation room. He was sweating. Even old Hochdruck seemed to be tense, which was unusual, sitting where he was on the window sill, taking it all in. Peter envied him his evanescence. It was late afternoon.

"It's not even a matter of superior generalship," Charlemagne was saying. "But don't misunderstand me. There's to be generalship if we need it." Charlemagne had taken off his shoes and was wriggling his toes; his feet were on the bags of marbles. He twisted and rocked in the big armchair against the carpet roll he adjusted now and then. He said it kept him young, cracking his spine the way it did.

"Andros doesn't like the idea of going out in the middle of the night," Andros said. "There ought to be some generalship, like knowing where we'll be going."

"Don't worry about it. I'll come in, wake you if I have to."

"There will be no need to wake me," Father Bischoff said. "I plan to pray all night." He turned to Andros. "I'd suggest you do the same."

"Andros has no need of prayers."

"Now is not the time for religious frou-frou," Charlemagne said rather sharply.

"Locks shall fall for the righteous."

"This is a holy cause, Father. But even so there are no locks to monkey with. All we have to do is keep to the bushes and then walk fast past the administration cottage to the entrance. Could anything be more simple than that?"

Peter felt waves of alarm at the thought of sneaking any-

was so overpowering that solid objects began to waver. He made them hold. He was able to do that now and then. Had Charlemagne, Father Bischoff and Andros gone on without him? The diffraction grating and all the little reticules moved toward him to blot out everything, he started to get sick to his stomach, the weakness he had been hiding fled to his muscles and sweat began to pour out. It was *Angst* time, and it started to wring out his intestines. He knew he would have to flee.

But he did not. It was as if Charlemagne was there, holding him, talking to him. And as he thought about Charlemagne, the spell passed. He'd have to thank him for that. But why should he? After all, wasn't it better in the outhouse than here? There he was unassailable and he could ignore the knocking, just look at the farm, which wasn't always hot and full of the sounds of locusts. There were times when it was cold and there wasn't a sound, except imagined ones, like the screaking when the elm tree grew while he watched. Or the sighing of the wood when the house leaned to the east, very precariously. Or when there was laughter from nowhere, which was often, and could have been from the world he'd left rather than the outhouse one (it couldn't have been Hochdruck because he never laughed any more). Or the tinkle of the corn rows when they turned violet and the tassels became a brilliant cerulean and sounded like a mighty carillon when the wind blew.

He knew the farm was not stable, though the outhouse was. From the small crescent in the outhouse door he saw the most unlikely people come to sit in the swing, to laugh at him, knowing where he was, or to leer, point weapons they never fired, people like Charlie Gummerman, one of his uncles, looking sharp and chipper, lean, mustached and capable in his uniform, carrying a carbine in the crook of his arm. Or Franklin Delano Roosevelt with cape and cigarette holder, actually a blowgun, swinging slowly, Secret Service men in the shadows behind, pushing him.

He sat very still in the hush in the recreation room feeling the seat of the chair with his rump, the back with his shoulders, the slight movement of air through the room with his cheeks. He heard the banging of pots and pans in the kitchen, the clinking of silverware. He was really here, and he could feel his blood and heartbeat, and that, plus everything else, told him this was the real thing.

He saw the copy of *National Geographic* on the nearby library table where Andros must have left it, still open, the worn foldout page almost torn free and draped over the side of the tabletop. It was a page he had once stared at for a long time. Remembering, he felt his flesh crawl, for it was Frank Borman's photograph of the earth rise taken on Apollo 8's journey to the moon.

Peter left himself sitting to levitate about the room, trying to decide whether to think about it or not. He kept turning to examine himself as he stared at the photo, thinking how thin he looked, how pale, and then zooming through the ceiling to look down at himself still sitting, staring quietly at the picture, his astral self the only thing alive.

When last he had stared so at the Borman photo he was in the shop. He had taken the magazine with him that morning, was thumbing through it while the boys were busy in the back, talking in loud voices so as to be heard over the sets they were running to see if trouble had been corrected, which was the way it was in the mornings.

As he, on that day, gazed at the foldout sheet depicting the earth rise in color, it came to him with a sense of shock that all that is man was on a blue marble hanging in a black sky, a tiny ball that whirled slowly through limitless night. As he became more engrossed, the sounds of the shop receded, and it began: a sensation in his stomach, a pressing down, an encapsulation, a feeling of being frozen in a cube of lucite, so crushing was the knowledge of man's triviality, compressed as he was on that ball floating beyond the moon's horizon.

On that blue planet, probably undistinguishable in the cosmos, was all that man is or was, and if some irate God wished to, He could easily remove, with the flick of His little finger, all of everything that everyone ever knew.

And then he knew man for the microscopic pipsqueak he is: puny, imperceptible, petty, insignificant, and unimportant.

He remembered how the thought ate at him: that man was very much like Peter Hartsook himself, so eminently disposable, dependent only upon celestial caprice, on earth yet only because of divine whim . . . or oversight.

Lowly, obscure and worthless, hardly meriting obliteration, that was Peter Hartsook. He had thought that! Even then. If Peter Hartsook should ever do anything, it would, in the long run, amount to nothing, and be restricted, like humanity itself, to this miniscule blue-and-white dot that circled endlessly one of the stars of one of the systems in one of the universes.

He recalled how he had raised his eyes from the picture, looked up into the rows of television eyes which stared at him from the floor, all new sets, all waiting to be sold. They were there, of course, because they were not yet in homes where buyers would look at them when the shows were coming in over the air.

It was then that a large truth was suddenly revealed to him: *They were Spy Eyes. And They were watching him.*

Shaken that day (and since), Peter realized he had stumbled on to something Bigger Than Life, a glimpse of the Master Plan, and he also knew that, in that moment of thinking it, he was Marked, as are all men who discover God's Secret. Having done so himself, he suddenly felt equal to God, and so feeling, he knew he'd have to be careful, for if What He Knew were to be imparted to humanity at large, Everything Would Stop, and The Experiment That Is Man could be continued no longer. God could not allow it. Omnipotent, if He allowed His Secret to be shared, He would no longer be omnipotent. Therefore, *Peter would have to pretend that he had not discovered any Secret.* He knew that God could not read minds, else he would have already been struck down. He knew He did not know that Peter was aware now that men die when they reveal in some way that they have stumbled upon the Secret: that life has no meaning, that life is a charade perpetuated by Him, beginning and ending nowhere.

36

It was so obvious, it had seemed to Peter it was a wonder no one had figured it out. Before there were so many people in the world, there were Spies. No doubt every neighborhood had one or two. Perhaps They were even able to make Themselves invisible in order to penetrate homes where such Secrets might be revealed at times of relaxation, festivity or meditation. He was sure it was so. But with the increased population and its incessant moving about, it must have been clear, even to the all-pervasive Mind, that it would be impossible to keep track of everyone at once. That was where radios came in—and, later, television.

Peter could not help admiring the ingenuity of God and his minions. Radios that worked both ways: sending music and news and comedy, all very innocent, and at the same time hearing everything that went on within range, and recording it in the Master Unit where it would be readily available any time He or They wanted it. Yes, Spying in living rooms and bedrooms, and now, with the transistor, Spying from inside pockets, cars, boats, purses, shops and everywhere man was.

And how much more clever He was with television! Now the listened-to could also be The Watched, scanned for Betraying Facial Expressions and mannerisms that might reveal Foolish Attempts to Hide Something. Even during *Laugh-In*, while eyes were glued to the set, It was watching the viewer, alert for Signs that would give away the Thought-About Something.

That was why They took Marcella away. Came in and took her and then accused him of her murder just to try to break him down, make him disclose What He Knew.

He knew They had tried to extract Something from her. Then, failing that, what else could They do but send him where They did, where he would be under constant Surveillance, where They sent all those who had discovered Something, to have people like Dr. Sheckley try to ferret It out.

Well, They were getting nothing from him.

6

It was after eleven o'clock when they found Peter in the men's toilet on the cold floor between two urinals, propped up with pillows from the day room, the journal he'd been writing in on his lap. He'd finished his entry and was sitting there mute. He didn't even look at them when they came in.

"Of course," Charlemagne said. "Of course. The lights are out everywhere else, he wanted to write, so here he is. Can you hear me, Peter?"

Father Bischoff said, "You can see he is missing his robe of grace. If he had a full pardon he wouldn't be doing things like this."

"Speak for yourself," Andros said, deciding to relieve himself in one of the urinals. "You are nothing but a gathering point for reprehension."

"No recriminations, please," Charlemagne said, moving to Peter, shaking his shoulder. "Peter. Peter? It's raining outside. The trip's off."

Father Bischoff said at least Peter was dry, which was more than he could say for the people who'd been looking for him.

"We're not going," Charlemagne said to Peter. "Do you hear? We're not breaking out tonight."

Peter's eyes flicked, moved to Charlemagne, who repeated what he'd said. Color came back to Peter's face and he turned to stare at Andros' penis.

"You're making me nervous," Andros said, hurrying to finish, then zipping his pants. He flushed the urinal. It was such a sudden, loud noise Peter was startled and he shook, almost dropping his journal.

Charlemagne helped Peter to his feet. "A good campaign is

one that adapts, and that's generalship. We'll break out some other time."

"What time is it?" Peter asked in a thick voice.

"Time we were all in bed," Father Bischoff grumbled. "And I haven't even started on my prayers."

Charlemagne laughed with a cheerfulness no one else felt. "All things are possible. Large wars are won despite minor defeats. *Il n'y a que le premier pas qui coûte.*"

"Andros knew we weren't going," Andros said, very superior, as they started for the door. "His sensors picked up the storm miles away."

Peter shuddered.

Charlemagne would have put an arm around him but thought the better of it.

7

Urinal—Entry No. 23

I see I have perfected shunt circuits unequaled in performance. Even God cannot penetrate. My mind would short out
before I would say.

Thank you Dr. Shekel and all your hirelings for my starting
in this urinal business where its always light. Its not as good as
Andros poetry doggerel Charlemagne says but I enjoy putting
down what leaks from the shunt. Already Im on 23 and safe
here as you see and I get better continually eternally fraternally
like all boxes on the back shelf which are always where the real
stuff is and hardest to get.

FYI you will never destruct me in five seconds because Ill be
gone doggone gone really hes got it doped out in generalship I
dont know just when but Im looking forward not backward
or at least trying to.

Hochdruck watches as I write well did you learn anything
you couldnt reach Shekel & Co anyway because he doesnt stay
here at night.

In the power of the shunt
Peter Heartsick

8

THE DAY at Berylwood usually starts with wearisome routine, beginning with the knowledge that breakfast is, after all, the reality and not the golden dreams of the night before, except if the dreams were filled with terror, in which case breakfast is a welcome reprieve.

For Father Bischoff, Andros and Peter the thoughts of near-adventure the night before paled this day, the food and the talk. With Charlemagne they sat together, as they usually did, a kind of territorial imperative, surrounded by an insulating area of empty chairs and tables, and they could see Charlemagne was filled with something that threatened to come bursting through.

"No time like the present," he said at last. "It's not raining any more." While they were happy that he'd finally got it out, again they waited, half-eaten breakfasts beginning to become lumps in stomachs, muscles tightening against the knowledge of just how it was to be done.

"The inspectors of the kingdom will move out right after breakfast," Charlemagne said. "Right under the noses of the enemy."

"God help us," Father Bischoff said.

"They'll see us going," Andros protested. "In the daylight they'll stop us. That's no good."

"Not if we look as if we're sauntering about the grounds in a blood-stimulating after-breakfast walk. We do that sometimes, you know."

Peter's face had become pasty and he looked as if ready to fly to the far country. Charlemagne said, "Stay with us, Peter." Peter blinked and swallowed. And stayed.

Charlemagne went on: "We'll walk right through the gate and rally our forces just west of the entrance."

"There's no gate," Andros pointed out.

"Then we should have no difficulty going through it." Charlemagne surveyed them and decided they were all still with him. "Salvage nothing. As God's vice-regent, with apologies to you, Father, I promise you everything you will need. There's generalship behind all this."

"Let us hope so," Andros said.

Father Bischoff was able to get off only a short prayer at bedside, gathering his rosary, breviary and assorted knick-knacks from his dresser and drawers and stuffing them into his pockets. Andros shoved several handkerchiefs and a few old letters into his pockets. Peter inserted his journal deep inside his pants next to his stomach and found he had to walk rather stiffly as a result. He took nothing else except an old suit coat he was fond of.

And so they gathered after breakfast at the roadside just outside the grounds, the smell of frying bacon from the kitchen lingering wispily in the air, suddenly uncomfortable with one another, eyes probing eyes for reactions, for fear which might send them scurrying back to sanctuary, or for courage and affirmation which would move them on out. If an attendant had appeared, they surely would have turned and strolled back to the grounds.

As it was, they stood undecided, even Charlemagne, upon whose shoulders lay the responsibility for their being where they were.

Andros said movingly, "Andros says we are all history in the making."

Father Bischoff, shifting his weight in the thin morning mist, said, "I offer me, not for myself, but for the good of all mankind."

Taking heart, having seen them so desperately groping for commitment and wanting not to go back, Charlemagne told them to join hands. Father Bischoff and Andros did so at once, and Charlemagne put his hands over theirs, looking to Peter, who stood staring at the six hands so joined and not moving to put his where theirs were. "A table with three legs is rickety," Andros said. But Peter stood transfixed.

Then Charlemagne said something wonderful, very quietly, their hands still joined: "We all understand your aversion to touch, Peter, but we're going to be together, a *Gestalt*, we've got a great work to do, and we're going to have to touch one another. So there's no reason for you to behave this way, no reason whatsoever. None of us is bugged, we have no radios, no concealed electronics of any kind, and I, Charlemagne, will personally vouch for Andros and Father Bischoff. Andros isn't interested in spying. He just wants to see the country, and, God willing, he will. And Father Bischoff is seeking his own salvation."

Father Bischoff shook his head. "Apotheosis, that is what I am seeking." Then he added, "If that is possible."

"I intend to appoint several saints when the time's right," Charlemagne said, "but right now we have the problem of Peter's nonparticipation."

Father Bischoff, eyes glowing from the mention of saints-in-the-making, turned to Peter, his eyes wet with emotion. "Please, Peter."

So, being needed, Peter allowed his hands to be added to the others', rejoining the world of touch, all hands now encompassed by Charlemagne.

Charlemagne said solemnly, "Let us in this way recognize that we are liegemen, one to the other, bound so in this rite of homage, and I, Carlos Magnus, King of the Franks, also known as Carolus Augustus, Emperor of all the Romans, as your liege lord, do promise to protect you in life, avenge you in death, maintain and reward you."

Father Bischoff raised his swimming eyes to heaven and said with heavy emotion, "*Aureolatis delphinium, quod petibas sum, capito mentholatum, icthyosaurus plurubus est.* Amen."

After a long moment, Charlemagne said, "Thank you, Father," and they withdrew their hands and started off down the road.

They had walked barely a mile when it started to rain, and they suffered it and moved on despite it, as if, once moving, they were irreversible. But when the rain came on even harder, they broke and ran, suddenly demoralized, not knowing where they were dashing, only why, eventually reaching a culvert, where they huddled together like wet kittens, looking out with solemn eyes at nature's untimely treachery.

"It is a Sign," Father Bischoff muttered. "We must go back."

Charlemagne agreed that it was, indeed, a Sign. "But not a Sign to go back, Father. A Sign to go ahead, for He is showing us that the road ahead is not easy; He is testing our mettle."

Then it stopped and Charlemagne told them it was time to move out like good troops, and they did, climbing the bank to the hard road, drying out while they walked in the fresh-washed air, Father Bischoff inhaling deeply and exhaling rapturously as if he'd never breathed before, Peter slogging along with wet feet, head down, face full of nothing, trying to keep up with Charlemagne, who was trying to stay right behind Andros, who insisted on staying on point in unfamiliar territory.

It was when the sun left them for good, when it started to rain again, the sky giving up a steady, thin drizzle that showed no promise of slackening, that Charlemagne spied a garage, an old garage set well back from the road, a good fifty feet from a farmhouse, and told them they would stay there until it was over.

The air beyond the opened garage door was laced with fine rain that was given to shifting this way and that, like curtains rustling in the wind. It had been coming down for some time now but nowhere near so heavily as the sudden early-morning shower that had caught them on the open road.

They could neither go back nor on until the rains stopped. Yet they did not fret, perhaps because Charlemagne did not fret; they had been patients and were patient, used to long periods of inactivity. Or perhaps because they had suffered so from exposure to compulsive counters, hebephrenic reciters, obsessive washers and other forms of mania, had witnessed the gamut of madness at such close range, they now sat in wonderment that they should miss it. Whatever the reason, they were not depressed or cynical but were willing to see what the hours or days would bring.

In the junk under a workbench, Charlemagne found two old dusty folding cots. Andros helped him set them up, wanting the experience, and then went to stand at the wide entranceway to look out at the rain. In the gathering chill Peter sat on one cot, Father Bischoff and Charlemagne on the other.

Father Bischoff said, "I could have fallen in love a dozen times." It was the voice to the line of thought he'd been following.

"Why didn't you?" Andros asked the rain.

"I was never able to let myself go."

"Andros believes in total letting go. That is why he is here. He abandoned the Krepifs entirely when he moved out and away. They were absurd, anyway."

"The Krepifs?" Charlemagne asked.

"I know now I was wrong," Father Bischoff went on. "I should have done something. You see, I want to be a man, not an ideal. A father, not a father image."

"We should all be what we want to be," Andros said. "There's no other way around it, believe me."

"That is exactly what we're all about," Charlemagne said. "For one thing, celibacy has built a wall between the clergy and the parishioners."

"Amen," Father Bischoff said, crossing himself.

"The Cana Conferences are a hollow mockery, always have been. The blind leading the blind."

"Amen."

"I tell you, Father, I intend to carry out sweeping reforms. These Council fathers of yours had better watch it."

Father Bischoff blinked to hear such talk.

45

"I believe a priest should live close to the laity," Charlemagne said severely. "The closer the better."

"Yes," Father Bischoff said, eyes glowing.

"I shall tell my seneschals there will be love-making after all feasts. There will be wine from pewter mugs, meat from fatted calves, bread from the broad sweep of grain fields."

"A holy banquet," Father Bischoff said dreamily.

"Not at all," Charlemagne said with a trace of irritation. "A flat-out, simple banquet with frank emotions, innocence and abounding in good cheer. There will be no holy overtones. None at all."

"We who are sinners will be heard," Father Bischoff said.

Andros turned from the entranceway. "I don't see how you can call yourself a sinner if you never did anything."

The priest looked down at his hands in a kind of abject mortification. "My sin is wanting to."

"Even without the O.K. from the Council fathers?"

"Are we speaking of omission or commission? I have done nothing." Father Bischoff looked miserable because he hadn't.

"They're imperious," Charlemagne said helpfully. "It's morally inhuman what they've done to you and those like you."

"One day I woke up to find my oath of celibacy no golden path to God, just to solitude. I had to cut myself off from life."

"What do the Council fathers do with their hard-ons?" Andros wanted to know.

"Same as me," Father Bischoff said mournfully. "Or sin in their minds if they don't." He looked out at the rain drearily. "It's dwarfed manhood, that's what it is. I'm a minikin manikin."

Andros turned back to the very edge of the rain. After a while he said, "The people, they'll be coming home, Andros says. He has drawn a bead on the house, says it's occupied. There are people living in it, I think he means. Yes, he says there's no one there right now."

"Any fool can see that," Father Bischoff said.

"He's merely reporting what Andros thinks," Charlemagne explained. Turning, he said, "Tell Andros thank you." He

46

leaned over, squinted up at the sky. "It's getting late and they'll be coming home all right. We must be ready for them."

Peter started shaking, muscles in his legs, arms and neck jerking in small spasms because he was afraid. Even when he tried to wet his lips with a dry tongue his jaw trembled. Charlemagne, seeing the incipient vacancy in the eyes, moved to stand before him at the cot so Peter would have to look up at him, speaking his name sharply and ordering him not to leave them. He was rewarded as recognition fought with abandonment, but the agitation got worse. Then Charlemagne stepped to him with some authority, put his hands on Peter's shoulders. A look of horror won out in the eyes and Peter drew away.

"Peter," Charlemagne said gently. "Homage. We swore, took the oath. Remember?"

Peter stared at him. Outside it was so overcast the day turned dark and rain started to fall more heavily again. Charlemagne said, "We were to have fealty, one for the others."

Peter nodded, but it was a jerky nod, one of miserable and trapped helplessness.

Charlemagne stood before him a long time, shutting off Peter's view of the rain, then bending over to watch Peter's eyes, which were alternately bright and dull. When they were bright, they were full of pleading. Suddenly, as if something secret and silent had passed between them, Charlemagne stepped around, put his hands on Peter's shoulders and started a gentle massaging of tightly turnbuckled muscles.

Peter winced and stiffened at the first touch, Charlemagne watching him closely to thwart withdrawal, then working with the cushions of his fingers through the thick cloth of Peter's coat. The knots of muscles began to dissolve and Charlemagne relaxed a little himself, saying, "Without you, Peter, there is no campaign, no reform." His hands were kneading, then pushing. "No record can be made without Alcuin, the Duke of York."

Later, Charlemagne, rummaging around in junk in a corner of the garage, among old paint cans, moldy rags, rusty angle irons and wood scraps, found an electric heater. They closed the garage door and got it going.

It was nearly dark when Andros said, "Andros is hungry."

Charlemagne, stretched out on one of the cots, opened his eyes, stared at the roof for a moment to consider it. They had not eaten since breakfast. He said, "We will fast this day."

Father Bischoff, who was standing to one side of the workbench with his rosary, whispering to it as if to a lover, turned to say, "The Lord will not suffer the soul of the righteous to famish." Seeing that this changed nothing, he went on: "It doesn't matter what the Council fathers think, bastard intermediaries that they are. I think this matter can be taken up directly with Him." He turned and proceeded to do that.

Andros said, "Andros isn't sure he will continue to lodge in a human lacking essential ingredients, such as food."

"Ask him to consider it an experience," Charlemagne said. "Tell him a hungry man is a better fighter, provided the battle isn't too long. Bloated troops are no good at all. And if Andros is really curious as you say he is, tell him the body will take care of itself."

"Fat goes first," Father Bischoff said, having completed his intercession. "Everybody knows that. But is there any criterion in cases of sexual deprivation?"

Andros frowned, and the rumblings of his empty stomach could be plainly heard. "Andros tells me he is still hungry."

Charlemagne sat up, eyed him severely. "Tell me something. Wouldn't you say hunger frees the body from encroaching precipitations?"

"Andros doesn't know, having such little access to human physiology."

"Consider fasting a penance," Father Bischoff said. "Forty days of fasting were nothing to Jesus."

"They all fasted," Charlemagne said. "The whole kit and kaboodle, Elijah, Moses, Mohammed, Buddha, and all the rest. But I'll tell you something you don't know. Old Herpes told

48

me they treated syphilis that way in ancient Egypt. And with good results, I might add."

Andros, who had been sitting on a tool box, got to his feet, put his hands in his pockets and strode to the garage door to stare out through the crack between the door and the jamb. "I've never missed a meal." Then, a moment later: "Except one."

"What one was that?" Father Bischoff asked.

"The one before the operation."

"What operation?"

"I can't remember, I've done so many."

"You?" Charlemagne eyed him severely again. "You have a certificate for that sort of thing?"

"Andros was a surgeon on his own planet, among other things."

Charlemagne lay back. "Nature provides feast and famine in order to maintain balance. I recommend fasting to help one regain possession of the mind."

"Someone's coming," Andros said suddenly.

Instantly Peter began shaking, the red and yellow marrow of his bones vibrating as Charlemagne and Father Bischoff moved to the crack to peer out.

"It's them," Andros said.

Peter was unable to hold back the shriek he uttered, at the same time getting up, vacant-eyed, face full of panic. In a moment, before he could give vent to the scream in his throat, Charlemagne moved to him, clapped his hand over his mouth. They struggled and fell to the floor. When Peter quieted, he stared up at Charlemagne's eyes, stopped trying to breathe through his mouth and started to breathe through his nose.

"They're getting out," Andros said.

The bone marrow began to turn to jelly again, but Charlemagne tightened his grip. "Cut it out, Peter. You be quiet." When Peter stopped shaking and started blinking and tried to nod, Charlemagne took his hand away, got up and moved off.

49

Peter lay where he was, his clothes damp from perspiration.

"Jesus," Andros said. "All those kids."

Peter lay, wetting his lips, not moving. Charlemagne came, sat on the cot nearby, grinned down at him. "It's the family. They parked by the house because it's raining. Probably think they closed the garage door when they left. Man and wife and a half dozen kids." He leaned closer. "You all right?"

Peter nodded.

9

TUESDAY MORNING Therin was feeling better. He had decided to do nothing about Minnie, absolutely nothing, and he was relieved to have come to a conclusion at last.

His first two hours had gone well. He was able to send both patients out the door with some hope and ambition. "It's the same old world out there," he had told one of them. "It's the same place it has always been. It's you that's different."

It was true, too.

He looked at his watch. It was 10:35. He had walked briskly through light rain to the room off the day room where the morning session should have already started. Where was everybody? No Charlemagne, Father Bischoff, Andros or Peter. At least one of them should have hurried there, perhaps to explain that the others had been caught in the rain and would be along directly. But there was no one.

It began to rain more steadily, so he went to the window where Peter usually stood. It was pouring down. Perhaps, he thought, they're having fun with me. But he didn't think it was very funny. They shouldn't do things like this. It was probably Charlemagne. He was always up to something.

After ten more minutes had passed, he knew they weren't coming, any of them.

Therin left the day room, returned to his office to see if they could possibly have gone there, then started searching. He asked attendants and aides if they had seen them, still not alarmed, taking a look in the dining room, the bungalows, where they had obviously spent the night, the laundry, the grounds, the road, the store, rooms, cars and the library. Nobody had seen them.

He had no alternative. He went to Dr. Tillheimer's office. Tillheimer was surprised to see him, asked him to come in and sit down.

"Doctor," Therin said, not taking the offered chair, "four patients are missing."

Dr. Tillheimer stared at him in surprise. Then he turned to look out his window at the rain. "No one in his right mind would pick a day like this to skip out of here."

Therin was a bit shaken to have it put quite like this, and for a moment he thought Tillheimer was joking. But the doctor was not.

Tillheimer plucked a pen out of his desk set, poised it over a pad. "Who are they?"

When he told him, Tillheimer raised his eyebrows and said, "That Le Moyne. You were talking about him yesterday. Do you think he's behind this?"

"I don't know, Doctor. They were all right yesterday." He remembered Charlemagne's warning about escape plans, but he did not want to get into that with Tillheimer.

Tillheimer sighed, picked up the phone. "One is bad enough, but *four*." He shook his head.

The report was made to the sheriff's office and to state police headquarters. Then several aides and attendants went out in cars with Therin and Dr. Tillheimer and they made a sweep of roads in a ten-mile area around Berylwood. It proved fruitless. Since no cars or trucks were missing, it was assumed the men had taken off on foot, yet not a single person they talked to had seen four men walking in the rain.

"I don't understand it," Dr. Tillheimer said, shaking his white mane of hair when they returned late in the afternoon. "After all we do for them, they would rather face what's out there. It doesn't make sense."

Therin thought the men might return for dinner, and they stayed to see, but the men did not come back. Therin was all for calling relatives at once, but Dr. Tillheimer said it could be done just as easily on Wednesday, and he was right, Therin thought, because it would give the men time to go wherever they were going, which might be home.

10

It stopped raining late, though a blustery wind came up and sent sprinkles from mothering trees heavy with wetness spattering on the garage roof.

Inside, on his cot, Peter moved restlessly, sliding in and out of sanctuary, wondering, when he was out, why he alone should not be asleep. He knew he should have been demolished by the previous fifteen hours, yet here he was, wide-eyed, his mind clear and his body full of spirit when he was out, which he had been most of the time since the others had gone to sleep. Perhaps it was because he had not eaten; yet he reasoned that it should have been the other way around, he should have felt weak and numb.

He turned so as to see the bright effulgence of the heater, wondering if it would provide enough light for him to make a journal entry. He'd taken the journal out, saw it was none the worse for wear and rain, and he had his ballpoint pen, so he was set, but he kept putting it off, fingering the journal and listening to the wind and the fall of stray water drops on the roof.

He moved his shoulders and saw Father Bischoff in the adjacent cot and wished he were as relaxed and snoring. He heard the sharp, knifelike crackling sounds nests of newsprint made, and he turned to see Charlemagne and Andros stirring in the paper beds they had made. One turn, both turn. He was surprised to see how small and helpless Charlemagne looked lying down. And he hadn't realized what bushy eyebrows Andros had. Also, from this angle, he saw the protruding hairs in Andros' nose. Marcella used to be very strict about such hairs in Peter's nose; she was forever snipping them. She was also a great blackhead popper.

He put a hand up, fingered his nose. There were hairs there, all right, as he expected, and he was distressed. That was proof she was gone.

He shifted his position and glanced to Father Bischoff again, seeing he must have gone to sleep saying his beads since his rosary was hanging from an outstretched hand, as if he were offering it to some invisible person.

Sitting up and swinging his legs off the cot, Peter felt pleased with the cozy warmth of the garage. He wished he'd kept his watch so he'd know what time it was, but he'd thrown it away because it had stopped working. The truth was, it had stopped working because he could not remember to wind it.

To hell with it. What was time, anyway, but some relative thing, different to different people, something you could never be certain about. To a clock a minute is immutable. So much for the aphorism of the day.

Yet it was true that people use and experience time with great disparity. When he was a child, he had found time to be a viscous thing, like warm tar, slow and unyielding; it was always an eternity from breakfast to lunchtime. But lately, and he was thirty-six, time had become telescoped, especially at Berylwood. He could not even recall when he had been taken there. He knew he hadn't been there as long as Father Bischoff, but he wasn't sure about Andros. Charlemagne was a relatively late comer. All in all, the Berylwood days were like tapioca, each grain being different but all of them together a homogeneous mass, gray and not very interesting, and he was glad they were over.

Peter turned his head and was startled to look straight into the eyes of Mr. Hochdruck. He had forgotten Hochdruck was sitting there at the very edge of the workbench, arrogant, severe, damning, saying nothing but looking emaciated, hypnotic-eyed, thin-lipped and ascetic.

He looked away. Since Peter would never really talk to him, why the hell did Hochdruck insist on spying on him? Why did he keep turning up in odd corners? Sometimes right in the sessions with Dr. Sheckley, on the grass outside the window, to be there when Peter looked out. Always trying to catch Peter's eye.

Old Hochdruck hadn't always been so quiet. When Peter first met him in the jail/hospital, Peter thought he was a police officer. A plainclothesman. Peter was sitting on the jailhouse/hospital bed trying to figure out how to deal with his Accusers, being dazed by all that had happened, shocked by their insinuations, when Hochdruck came in. Peter had not heard the cell/room door open, but there Hochdruck was, looking fresh and efficient, dressed in a natty business suit, smiling and saying, "How do you do, Peter Hartsook? My name is Hochdruck," as if that explained everything, and he moved to sit on the high, white hospital/jailhouse bed near Peter.

Peter said nothing. By this time he'd already become familiar with Them and Their operations, and for all he seemed, Hochdruck could have been one of Them.

"I've been sent to advise you," Hochdruck said. "Of course you realize They're trying to frame you. That's why I'm here to help." His smile was dazzling.

Peter needed help, there was no doubt of that, but more than that, he needed to keep his mouth shut. He knew if he said anything to Hochdruck, and Hochdruck worked for The Other Side, then his goose would be cooked and nothing would matter any more. Besides, the room/cell was probably bugged, by both the doctors/police and Them. All the more reason to keep his mouth zippered up. Still, Peter yearned to converse with someone, and the man must have sensed that because he went on as if the decision had already been made and Peter was going to tell him everything.

"Good, good," Hochdruck said, getting off the bed and pacing the room, though Peter had said nothing. "I'm glad we understand each other right at the start. You see, once the wheels start rolling, it's hard getting them to stop, justice being what it is, protecting the people as well as the individual. And right now as an individual that set of wheels is rolling right over you. And their inertia is something terrific."

Hochdruck paused for effect, moved to Peter. "But they can be stopped, Peter, just like anything can be stopped. Look what they did to Niagara Falls!"

Hochdruck snorted, turned away. "But of course it won't be that simple, though I'll try to make it as easy on you as I can." He got out a gold cigarette case, extracted a cigarette, lighted it with a gold butane lighter, then produced a secretary's notebook and No. 1 pencil sharpened to a fine point. "Don't try to tell me the whole thing at once. Bits and pieces will be all right. Start anywhere."

Peter hadn't smelled cigarette smoke or felt the wafted air that a moving body stirs.

Hochdruck's pencil was poised, smoke curling up from his lips, his eyes on Peter. "Every minute is precious. You must start now if we're going to save you."

If he had smelled smoke, Peter might have said something. Or if he had felt moving air. As it was, he said nothing. Hochdruck didn't think much of his silence, came to sit near him again, talking to him like a father. "Peter, my boy, you're making a big mistake, clamming up like this. They'll nail you for sure, you keep this up. Now how about it? Be a good boy, start with the most insignificant detail, if you want." Again the pencil was poised.

Even when the jailers/attendants came, took his temperature, his pulse, and asked him questions he never answered, old Hochdruck never left the room. He just waited patiently until they were through, then started all over again. There was never any communication between him and Hochdruck or between him and the police/doctors. The closest they ever got to him was when one of them asked him what it was he looked at at the foot of the bed, what did he see down there, and then made a notation in a notebook when Peter did not answer. But the question revealed to Peter it was as he thought, Hochdruck was one of Them. It was disappointing to think They would try to fool him with such a clumsy trick.

After that he ignored Hochdruck. But Hochdruck kept trying. First, he sent Mr. Schmerzen, a bullet-headed Otto Preminger type, complete with accent, much heavier than Hochdruck's.

Schmerzen's technique was the sympathy ploy, the I'm-here-to-grieve-with-you routine, and he was given to much groaning and grunting and rolling of the eyes, as if he were in pain, which was a secondary gambit. And, as with Hochdruck, Peter wasn't sure at first whether Schmerzen was straight or not until Schmerzen said he'd feel a lot better if Peter would talk to him, Schmerzen was sure it would take his mind off his aches and pains.

He really tried, Schmerzen did, far into the night, even after the jailers/attendants came in and made him take his pills. But in the end old Schmerzen gave up, moving over to the side of the room where Peter saw Hochdruck must have been standing all the time. They were still talking in soft voices when Peter fell asleep.

And then there were Drunter and Druber, the fat twins. They were real clowns with red noses, rosy cheeks and vests that barely covered their abdomens, buttons about ready to pop, looking like Jackie Gleason at his heaviest. At first Peter thought they were a couple of harmless drunks the police/doctors had thrown in with him. They kept laughing and jumping, doing tricks, trying to pull the bedclothes off Peter, trying to get him to laugh with them, enter into it, say a few things offhand, offguard. But in Peter's estimation this was by far Their weakest try, and he was not in any way even remotely moved to say anything. In fact, he felt sorry for Them and thought if he were They he would have been far more resourceful.

Hochdruck saw it was no good, came and got Drunter and Druber after several hours of nonproductive horseplay. They protested, but in the end agreed to go since the only way they had of working wasn't getting anywhere. Hochdruck came back to sit on the bed and tried to work up a little sympathy for himself, but Peter didn't buy it.

The last endeavor, before Hochdruck stopped talking for

good, was a series of threats wherein he said Peter would die unless he opened up. Peter figured Hochdruck was pretty desperate, and he was really worried for a while.

He was terrified when Hochdruck produced a red-hot poker and came at him with it, a satanic scowl on his face, demanding that Peter talk. Peter backed against the wall and was about to give in and speak out when, at the last possible moment, he realized that, though the poker looked red-hot, it was giving off no heat. So he stood still and let Hochdruck ram it through him. He never felt a thing, though he was fairly dazed for a while. The jailers/attendants came in and put him to bed.

Hochdruck's next move was straight out of Poe: a swinging ax suspended from the ceiling. Peter woke up to it one morning, finding Hochdruck also standing by the bed, his eyes filled with a kind of mad hilarity.

Hochdruck told him it was his last chance. If he didn't tell him what he wanted to know, the pendulum blade would be lowered, inch by inch, until it cut into Peter and caused his death. For a moment Peter was paralyzed with fear as he actually saw the metal coming lower, light gleaming from its razor-sharp edge. Then, remembering the previous incident, he knew it would not hurt him. When he ignored Hochdruck and got up off the bed, Hochdruck was angry.

Hochdruck's last try was sealing the room with tape, then starting a machine which began to exhaust the air. Hochdruck laughed hideously, if not convincingly, and in spite of himself Peter began to feel faint and out of breath. When Peter, with great effort, ignored Hochdruck, he was able to breathe normally again, and Hochdruck retired, defeated.

For two days he didn't see Hochdruck; then the man came to sit around, glaring at him. Eventually this became Hochdruck's stance, and Peter was subjected to it continually. For all he knew, Hochdruck was there even when he was asleep. It was unnerving, finding Hochdruck on the toilet bowl when he went to pee, or knowing Hochdruck was slithering across the floor just to get into his field of vision. He knew it was a game, an attempt to wear him down, and so he was determined not to let it. His relationship with Hochdruck, therefore, dissolved into something resembling a stalemate, and as long as it stayed that way, Peter didn't worry.

Peter got up from the cot, walked past Hochdruck at the workbench on his way to the window, thinking he might go outside. Staring out at the drenched farmland now only dimly visible and listening to drops of water hitting the garage roof, he remembered other rains, pelting rains on the outhouse roof, the hollow, *thunk*-ing sound it made on the old wooden walls and roof, the elm-tree limbs becoming dark-wet, puddles forming on the hard clay ground of the barn lot.

It occurred to him that he never left the outhouse when he took refuge in it, but right now he was free, he could go or stay, just as he wished.

He found the thought frightening.

He shuddered, turned, moved back to the cot and the warmth of the heater.

I I

Garage—Entry No. 24

Well weve done it were out except somebody should have stayed there I mean Hochdruck.

As you can see were in the garage even though it stopped raining its still wet outside but its night too and the others are asleep. If it wasnt for the heater I wouldnt be doing this but Im enjoying it its something to do better than doing it back there even though I know what the heaters for a spy thing as if I didnt know. Ever once in while rain from trees drops on the ceiling its scary because I dont expect it I keep forgetting its going to happen.

Marcella liked rain.

Im not doing this in the urinal since there isnt any here and I didnt anyway except the whole outside so Im doing it in the garage which is a true fact and real.

Well thats all for now Im going to turn over and sleep like a leaf to be ready for tomorrow whatever day it is Im not sure of the month.

Peter Hartsook
Agent in Charge

12

THERIN LEARNED that the men had not returned when he got to his office Wednesday morning.

He was at once disturbed anew. He had spent a sleepless night worrying about them, hoping that somehow they would find their way back to Berylwood and that things would go on as they had.

Their departure was a crushing rejection of him; their not returning only made it more complete and damning. Had he been such a bad therapist that he drove them to the outer world? He could not, of course, believe that he was, yet their continued absence made it seem so. Where had he gone wrong?

There was the possibility that they had returned home. Patients were always doing that. But as he picked up the phone to make the calls he knew they were not headed home and he could not explain why.

Therin called Marietta Le Moyne in Oblout first. There was no answer. He made a mental note to call her later in the day.

He called Gunther Hartsook in Price, was told by a woman there that the elder Mr. Hartsook was at the television shop. Therin called him there and related the information and asked him if Peter had returned home.

"No," Mr. Hartsook said, "Peter has not come home. When did he leave there?"

Therin told him, then asked him if he had any idea where Peter might have gone.

"No," Gunther Hartsook said. "But Peter's in no condition to be going anywhere."

Therin agreed, told him they were doing all they could, the

state police were on the lookout and perhaps there would be news soon.

Mr. Hartsook said he would telephone relatives in Mountbury to alert them to the possibility they might be seeing Peter. "He grew up in Mountbury," he explained.

Therin next called Andros' parents in Wood Park. Mrs. Kleinschmidt answered the phone and became instantly hysterical. It took some time to quiet her, explain the situation and listen to her offer of help. He did elicit a promise from her that she would call in the event Andros showed up.

He waited a few minutes before making the final call, trying to compose himself. Why should these four men move out? Was Charlemagne really responsible? Had he planned it? Remembering Charlemagne's warning to him, Therin wished he'd spent more time with him; he simply did not understand the man.

He knew Andros, Father Bischoff and Peter. They were schizophrenics and as such they had their delusional systems, all with positive referents, all of them external, which made treatment easier since he used them to initiate the necessary changes in their personality structures.

He castigated himself for not seeing what was happening with the group. It was easy to see now that Charlemagne had replaced him as a positive authority figure, that the men were relating more to Charlemagne than to Therin, that Charlemagne had been more supportive. That was why he was able to lead them out of Berylwood, if that was what he had done, and it seemed reasonable that he had. It was a sticky, dangerous situation for the patients.

As he made his last call he wondered if he would ever live it down. Oscar Petersen, who owned the Petersen Type Co. in Chicago, where Howard had been an executive before he adopted the role of Father Bischoff, was upset but promised to cooperate if his son came home.

Therin had no sooner hung up than the phone rang shrilly. Hoping it was good news, he picked it up.

It was Elizabeth.

"Therin," she said in such an annoyed voice that Therin, in a state himself, almost hung up. "I thought Minnie was coming back with the car."

He looked at his watch. At the same time, with a sickening wrench of his stomach, he thought: When sorrows come, they come not single spies. . . . Minnie had driven him to the sanitarium so Elizabeth could have the car. "She should have been there an hour ago."

"Well, she's not here!" Then, shrilly: "What am I going to do?"

13

As soon as Minnie saw the four men walking single file along-
side the road looking cold and all hunched over, she knew who
they were because she had overheard Therin say something
about them to Elizabeth the previous night. They were the escapees from Berylwood, no doubt about it, and the moment she
saw them she felt she could bawl because they looked so miserable and alone, like wilted flowers.

She didn't stop even though her eyes stung with tears but
kept on down the road, flicking her eyes to the rear-view
mirror to keep them in sight and slowing down.

She had driven Therin to work and they had said nothing all
the way from the house to the sanitarium, at least nothing important, just stuff like it's clearing, isn't it, it may warm up,
don't you think, but through it all she could feel his churning
and her own discomfort. It was like they were both down.
When she let him out and started back, she had tried thinking it
out.

She decided something was happening to them, and it was
about time something did. The way it had been was phony, it
wasn't right, the whole set-up, and she wondered how she
could have conned herself into accepting it. It wasn't supposed
to turn out that way. With all that love, all that giving, all that
cooperation (and let's be honest, it was on both sides), it had
finally come down to the hard embrace of silence.

She had thought, when she first met him, that this was something she had been looking for all her life. If a psychiatrist didn't
understand you, then who the hell could? God knows he scared
her at first (she thought he could look right into her brain, not

really, but sometimes she wondered), but then she saw that he didn't know what love was (how could that be?) and the disillusionment started. What did they teach shrinks these days?

She knew he knew lust (God, how they both delighted in *that!*) but he didn't know about sharing, that was for sure, for he never shared himself completely with either Minnie or Elizabeth. He had never heard of water-sharing or nesting, and he had obviously never considered a threesome. He was simply not with it. He preferred keeping his women in tight little boxes (to be opened only when used), allowing them to mix only superficially. Elizabeth seemed to prefer it that way, and for Minnie's money she was the more three-dimensional for it. At least you knew where you stood with her.

Minnie didn't like the way she was having to bend to fit, and so she was becoming unhappy, more so each day. Not that it had been such a terrific trip to begin with.

Therin had caught her at a bad time (or was it a good time?), she'd just been through a lot, a succession of real bummers, and at twenty-five she thought she'd better ride it out with him for a while; it would give her time to get her head straight, find out where she was at. Except she still didn't know. She didn't mind Elizabeth's crappy sermonizing; it gave her something to think about. And disagreeing was at least doing something, taking a stand against shit in general, but she didn't think Elizabeth, who couldn't have been more than ten years older than she, had a corner on The Way, Jesus Christ notwithstanding.

Let's face it, Elizabeth never in her whole aseptic goddam life experienced a gangbang or a freakout or lived macrobiotically for six months with a clammy-skinned friend to end up skinny as a straw and just as fragile.

Elizabeth had yet to hear of Rod McKuen and probably would be corny enough to like him if she ever did. She would probably think Airplane was a heavier-than-air craft. What could you expect from a dame who had bathroom color schemes and blue in the toilet bowl? She was so concerned with soap, living as she did in the flickering glow of her television set, dragging her ass off to bed after the late show to dream stainless dreams, she didn't know man was a prisoner of his concrete castles, breathing belched exhaust poison, was a planet plunderer, killer of wildlife, despoiler of lakes, rivers and seas, bigoted bastard man both black and white, yellow and red, drowning his brain in drugs, shattering his eardrums with electronic bombast and depersonalizing sound assaults.

To Elizabeth all was gold whether it glittered or not, Lawrence Welk had no belly button, God Bless America and Man was essentially Good. It was Little Women and the missionary position. And for all that Minnie was genuinely sorry for her.

On the other hand, the friends Minnie'd had, the scenes she'd been making for nearly six years after dropping out of college and all that SDS crap, were nothing to brag about. She'd been part of the bullshit revolution, dropping pills and acid, taking uppers and downers, saying she was dropping out of everything but dropping out of nothing, living in the same room with garbage hunters, and with pincushions who shot up a dozen nickel bags at a throw, made threadless embroidery of their arms, legs, necks and anywhere they could get the needle in. Minnie'd never shot up, but she didn't put them down.

Oh, yes, she fell in love weekly (sometimes daily), wore soiled bras with frayed straps or no brassieres at all (mostly no brassieres at all), hardly reading anything but going to rock concerts and movies to be pawed at and looked at, touched, tickled and licked, owning virtually nothing, not even a bottle of mouthwash, drinking too much wine, smoking too much pot, sitting in too many drafts, clutching too many unidentified bodies.

It had been all she could do to beg money to get the Pill for twenty-five days of no anxiety. So what? What was the difference between communal sex and the suburban orgy? Everybody was on the same trip, the white-shirt short-sleeve wonders of the straight nether world and the freaks outa sight who did nothing but get high, blow their minds and then sit around talking about dope until they came down and went out to find some more.

It was the same, sauce or speed, the same hierarchy, the same pecking order, only the objects of value were rearranged. Both classes sat in their own shit; one simply consumed and left his waste everywhere, the other produced and polluted his world with worse than fecal matter, which, in reality, was not waste at all. But feces, which had organic value, were processed to valuelessness.

One day she woke up to see in a burst of insight that she was all wound up with nowhere to go that she hadn't been. She'd become a thing, an object, not a person. A rolling, rounded stone with no distinguishing marks or characteristics, no remarkable mannerisms or interesting observations to make.

She suddenly knew she could no longer abide the sweaty bodies, the unwashed hair, halitosis, excuses, funky clothing, so she flushed down the garbage disposal all the values she'd had and walked away from the scene, maybe never to be with it again, or maybe to open up like a spring beauty, she didn't know. She would simply do what *she* felt for a while, not what *they* felt. And if this didn't work out, she'd think of something else.

She had felt settling down was part of the square world, yet she sometimes wished she could, for then the struggle would be over: It would be downhill from there on out. And even as she thought it she knew it was a bunch of crap. Minerva St. John, she told herself, you damn well know if you move in for a day and stay a year, it's because you love *it*, or *him*, or *them*. And when love goes out the window, so do you. You *know* that. If you don't like the heat, then get out of the goddam kitchen. Now, is that what you're going to do?

She had reached this point in her thinking when she saw the men, and having gone past them for a few blocks, she still didn't know what she was going to do about Therin when she turned around to go back. She slowed the car, then stopped it half a block from the advancing men, watched as they came up.

They looked drawn and tired, and her heart went out to them again. There was a young man in front, a dark-haired, rather good-looking young man with intense eyes and a good build. He was wearing a sloppy blue sweater with stains, a pair of thin slacks and old off-white tennis shoes that had seen better days. He couldn't have been more than twenty-five. He was followed by a stocky man between forty and fifty, a man with graying hair, ruddy complexion and a cherubic face. He was smiling even before he saw her. He had on an old brown corduroy suit that was a bit worn and loafers Minnie was sure would not serve him much longer. Then came a man in a blue suit coat, old brown trousers, baggy and wrinkled, and scuffed black shoes, walking bent forward, absorbed in himself or the ground, unaware of her. He was lanky, needed a shave, had a sensitive face. She could not guess his age. The fourth man walked erect, wisps of what little blond hair he had left undulating as he stepped along the shoulder. He seemed happy in his windbreaker, denim pants and brown suede shoes, though he looked older than that, and he regarded her curiously as they neared the car.

Minnie knew it was dangerous, stopping the way she did, letting them get near her, four lost, crazy men, lunatic-asylum escapees, but she could not just let them be, that's all there was to it.

When they were within twenty feet of her, they stopped, and Minnie was shocked to see the emptiness in the eyes of the third man as he looked at her. Then, even as he stared, his look of emptiness changed to fear. She half expected him to turn and bound off like a frightened deer.

The second man, the Smiler, came toward her.

"Morning," he said in a surprisingly pleasant voice, which helped ease some of her tension. When she took no chance but responded with the same word, he looked at the car. "Nice car you've got here."

How to treat them? Like babies? She decided to play Mother. "Get in," she said.

He smiled. "You're going the wrong way. Besides, I can't leave my troops just standing there."

He was crazy, all right. Troops! That ragged trio? "I mean them, too. And I'll turn around."

"Really?" He seemed amused. For the second time she thought of the danger involved, even though she figured she'd handled some weird ones in her time. She couldn't tell what he was thinking, and she found this frightening. He said, "Where would you be going?"

She couldn't tell him she'd be taking them back or they'd never get in. "Where do you want to go?"

"Well, now, that would be very accommodating, Miss."

"The name is Minnie." There could be no harm in their knowing her name.

"Charlemagne here. Allow me to introduce my entourage." How he did go on! *Charlemagne*, yet! He turned to the others. "That's Andros." Andros did not move but stood scowling, studying her. "And that's Peter." The fear flared again. "And that's Father Bischoff."

"Get in," she said, wanting to get them in and on their way. When they were, she turned the car around, not sure how she was going to get to Berylwood traveling in the opposite direction but knowing she'd manage it somehow.

"I suppose you wonder who we are and where we're going," Charlemagne said, once they were under way. He had taken the front seat, directing the others to sit in back. "It so happens we are on a holy crusade. That is why the good Father is with us."

"I see." Charlemagne was as batty as they came, she decided as she worked out in her head the route that would take them in a rectangle of roads back to Berylwood.

"Excuse me," he said, "I should have told you right off how beautiful you are."

Now it comes, she thought. Off into the woods to be raped by four kooks.

"You are, you know."

"Thank you." There was a flush of broken fragments of memory, round faces, thin ones, boys with live lips, boys with

70

thin ones, dry lips and cracked, and many of them had said she was beautiful. Few had meant it, the words spilling out coldly, ritually. She had the feeling Charlemagne meant it. Well, there are worse things than being raped by somebody who appreciates your good looks.

"In fact," Charlemagne said, regarding her profile solemnly, "you must be the daughter of Desiderius. Why did you stop for us?"

"The daughter of who?" If she kept talking and kept him talking maybe he'd forget what he was after.

"King Desiderius. You see, he is our first campaign. We shall seize all his possessions and I shall be crowned King of Lombardy. And of course I will marry his daughter. One cannot argue with history, Minerva."

She glanced at him sharpy, convinced now he was a clever old coot and not so off in the upper story as he seemed. She wondered how he could have guessed her real name, though it was common enough. When she was a little girl her mother, who was given to fits of melancholy sitting on cold radiators wishing they were warm, told her Minerva was the goddess of wisdom, that she would not be beautiful forever, it was wisdom that counted in this life. Her mother also confided that men say they want beauty but what they really want is brains— brains to see what a man wants done, brains to see how he wants it done, and brains enough to do it just that way.

"Father Bischoff is no anachronism, believe me," Charlemagne said, settling down in his seat. "A warrior priest is not unknown to Christian history. Isn't that true, Father?"

"That is true, sir." Father Bischoff's voice was deep and resonant, as a good Father's should be.

"Father Bischoff is a rare priest. He goes through no intermediary in his prayers, no Mary, mother of God, no saint. He goes directly to the Big Man Himself."

"That is also true, sir. But beyond that it is also true that celibacy is as bitter as the priesthood is sweet."

Now it comes, she thought. This time for sure.

71

"Can you see that, Miss?"

"The name is Minnie, if you are allowed to call me by my given name."

"All things are possible. Tell me, do you have any influence with the Council fathers?"

Minnie turned and was startled to find Father Bischoff's nose an inch from hers. She turned back quickly. "I'm afraid not."

Charlemagne sighed. "Father Bischoff seeks his other half as he wanders half a man."

"I want to be a whole man so that I can be a whole priest. Then God will be to me a whole God." He sat back in his seat as if he had said it all.

Minnie flicked her eyes to the rear-view mirror, saw that Father Bischoff had indeed got it all out, then looked at Andros, the hint of a smile dancing about his mouth as their eyes met. She felt warmth there and in herself. A harmonic of sorts. My God, Minerva, she told herself, one from the loony bin yet! The warmth did not cool. After looking at the road for a few moments she shifted her head, saw that Peter's faraway eyes were fixed on passing corn rows.

"What about your other two friends? What do they do?"

"They are brave men, rash, provocative, almost arrogant sometimes, but always intensely loyal. Open as the day, those two."

Minnie had to laugh, the description being so contrary to what she saw. Charlemagne seemed a little hurt by it, turned to view gravely the onrushing road for a long moment before saying quietly, "The world is full of blood and grief and death and naked brutality. And so we go forth to pit ourselves against the forces that make it so."

Only the crazy ones have hope, she thought. Where are the sane heroes who were supposed to right wrongs?

Charlemagne said, "*Dieu! Que le son du cor est triste au fond des bois.*"

Minnie didn't know what to say or think. A deranged man who spoke French? Was it possible?

Charlemagne sighed again. "Yes, Minerva, they don't know

72

it yet, but no one will forget us, just as no one has ever forgotten the horn of Roland, for it still sounds through the Pass of Roncevaux."

She had no idea what he was talking about, but she had to confess she was fascinated by it.

Charlemagne went on, speaking of the tragedy of the times, the tragedy of life itself, saying that people were, at best, children of hopeless, unrewarded toil.

"And sometimes," he said, "I think life is nothing more than a series of minor assassinations, the slights and innuendoes provided so gratuitously by others."

"That's true," she said.

"We each live a life in which we need an interpreter to understand the other person." He turned to her. "Do you believe that, my dear?"

"Yes," she said, grooving with it.

"Then tell me why that should be. How can that be when we are speaking the same words, the same language?"

She laughed and said she didn't know. She made two turns to the right, finally making the third as Charlemagne spoke of polarization.

"There are no shades of gray any more; the nuances have vanished. A man must either be white or black. Which brings us to the question of what happens when a black man wears the white hat."

She laughed again. They were on the road to Berylwood now. She didn't know whether any of them would recognize the road or what they would do if they did. The most difficult part would be driving into the grounds. She had no idea what might happen then.

"In our forthcoming campaigns," Charlemagne said, "we will engage in no small battles. When we do engage the enemy we shall do battle valiantly and well. And, unlike history, which forgets foot soldiers and remembers only the generals, in our battles even the lowliest participant will be memorialized."

As Charlemagne continued to speak in his peculiar way, Minnie was held to a silence, a sadness beyond her power to evade, seeing his brightness dulled and becoming colorless and conforming and probably complaining, and visions of electric shock, insulin and wet packs flashed through her mind, bits and pieces she'd read about. She felt an incipient nascent joy there in the car and she did not want to see it die.

"There is a universal electric brain that is devouring us all, Minerva. Bit by bit, cell by cell, name by name. When are we going to be free, completely free, unbridled, unhobbled by conformity, reason, guile, duty, manners and all the other corrosive things flesh is heir to that hurts itself and other flesh?"

She could not say it.

"Never," he said for her. "Never, Minerva, if we never do anything about it, never if we do not don those bright helms with gold and jewels gleaming, the shields and coats of burnished mail and those lances from which the pennons wave."

They rode on.

Charlemagne said quietly, "Why are we as afraid to live and afraid to love as we are afraid to die?"

Tears sprang to Minnie's eyes. She suddenly felt out of place in the world she had made for herself.

"You forgot to turn in back there," Charlemagne said.

"I know," she said, laughing giddily, feeling suddenly inflamed and free.

Charlemagne settled back in his seat.

Minnie saw birds coupling in flight, the grain in the fields silvering in the wind, swaying in the meadow in a delight of its own movement, fecund and ripe with promise.

14

THE DAY was growing warm, the sun seeking to suck up such rained wetness as had not yet seeped into the soil. It was flat country, monotonously flat, but rich farmland given to fields of barley, rye and oats that already danced in the rising heat.

"For Father Bischoff," Charlemagne was saying in response to Minnie's query, "it's a matter of vastation, and his problem is keeping himself from being consumed in the process. Not so with Andros. He is not quite sure whether or not he approves of us. In fact, I think the whole world is on trial there."

Minnie caught Andros' eye in the mirror.

"Andros observes," Andros said. "The report date hasn't been set yet."

Minnie said she could confess to nothing so rare as being possessed by an E.T. or having a passion for ecclesiastical approval. "By contrast I feel rather insignificant."

"You're you," Charlemagne said. "And that's important to us all."

"You haven't said about Peter."

"Peter?" Charlemagne turned to look at him. "Peter leaves us now and then, goes on private trips. But he likes us well enough to return."

They passed miles of barbed-wire fences, areas where daisies encroached on pastureland, everything green and yellow except the sky, which had become filled with haze.

They had been traveling for about an hour when Minnie said suddenly, "I forgot to tell you, this car isn't mine. It belongs to Dr. Sheckley."

While Charlemagne blinked in surprise, Andros leaned forward to inspect the dash. "It's a good car."

"It is nowhere good enough for our purposes," Charlemagne declared. "We will have to abandon it."

Minnie was shocked. "*Abandon* it?"

"We'll buy another."

"But how can we do that?"

Charlemagne shrugged. "How does one do anything?" He looked out at passing scenery. "Actually, it's a matter of generalship, the whole thing, from beginning to end. Every campaign is that way. And every successful campaign is the result of acute and superior generalship."

Minnie asked him to clarify that.

"There is nothing to clarify," he said. "The fact of the matter is we're going to Oblout."

"Oblout?"

"I have a castle there."

"Is that in the United States?"

"I'm surprised you don't know where Oblout is, being a bright young woman so full of all the right vibrations."

"I'm new to this part of the country."

Whereupon Charlemagne was able to tell her a few things about the Midwest, the terrain, industries, complexes, banks, other lending institutions, population densities, demography in general and geographical determinism in particular.

When he finished, she said, "You seem to have a wealth of information at your fingertips. What did you do . . . ?" She did not go on.

"Before Berylwood?" He laughed. "Before the cincturing incarceration? Well, Minerva, I'll tell you: I was unhappy. Not that I was exactly joyful at Berylwood, but the contrast was powerful and effect-producing. Actually, it has been useful, all of it, and it has resulted in this hegira. We were all marking time. Now we are starting to stretch our legs and minds. On the other hand, as La Rochefoucauld said, it is easier to be wise for others than for oneself."

"I believe that."

"I think it is more eloquent in French. Would you like to hear it in French?"

76

"No."

"I should have said it in French first. Then you would have asked what it meant and I would have told you."

"I wouldn't have asked. I think it's rude to go around spouting things in languages others don't understand."

"I suppose that's true. Sometimes, though, a person gets carried away. Surely you would forgive an old man his penchants."

"Look, if you really want to say it, go ahead."

He said he did, and he did. And as soon as the last word had been uttered, Father Bischoff, who had been waiting, said rather loudly, "*Seroptimus oblatus algonquinis est. Consodit donizetti et pirandello sum.*"

Minnie laughed and shook her head. "That's delightful!"

"It's natural in the padre's case," Charlemagne said, "although I don't think there's a missal that covers it."

"It's really weird, but I loved it." She glanced at Andros, who met her eyes again in the rear-view mirror. "What does Andros speak? Besides English."

"The music of the spheres," Father Bischoff said.

"Andros," Charlemagne said, "has been trying to master our language."

"He's learned it," Andros said with some vehemence. "And he's mastered it." Then, very superior: "Actually, Andros knows all languages."

"Does he know French?"

Andros blinked, rescued himself by holding up a hand, palm forward. Father Bischoff grimaced; Charlemagne sighed. Andros said, "Fifteen mittens are fine . . . tightened tympani are beat . . . but a jogged jugular . . . comes from tight shoes." He grinned at Minnie.

"Thank you," she said.

"Doggerel," Charlemagne said sourly. "Andros has yet to grasp our prosody."

"I liked it," Minnie said with a smile, her eyes caroming off Andros' in the mirror.

They discussed other matters, such as whether the written word is of value, if a person who is nothing but soul can be happy, what happens if one is surfeited with being surfeited, and, beyond the population explosion, what will happen when there is no more room to bury the results of that population explosion. Charlemagne felt that language, whether written or spoken, hinders the free expression of the psyche since feelings transcend one's ability to communicate those feelings, and he opted for touch and caress. Minnie was more generous, taking the position that language is a necessity but it should be only an adjunct to what each man is and serve him the way he wants it to, just as music does. Charlemagne said he was going to make everyone live below the ground so the surface of the earth could be kept as a garden; no more tall buildings, only deep ones, and the material excavated would be used to fill in where needed, making hills where there was nothing but flat land, and he said, "We will make mountains out of molehills."

"And there will be no more feeling of guilt if you're not consuming," Minnie said.

"Yes." Charlemagne would have gone on, but the mention of consuming reminded Andros how hungry he was and he broke in to say so.

Minnie looked at him in the mirror and remarked that he even *looked* hungry; perhaps they should stop somewhere.

"We haven't eaten since yesterday morning," Father Bischoff announced.

Minnie's eyes darkened. She pulled the car over to the side of the road, stopped it and regarded them all with a look of solemn intensity. "You should have told me," she said. "Why, you must be starved!"

"Actually," Charlemagne said, a little sheepish, "we're fasting."

"That's no good. You've got to eat."

Charlemagne tried to explain about fasting, but Minnie would not hear of it, and Charlemagne, who was hungry him-

78

self, told her he thought it was time their fast ended anyway, except they had no money, and they weren't really attired for restaurants or cafés even if they had.

"You talk of generalship," Minnie said. "I don't see much evidence of it."

"Don't sink the ship because it needs a little calking."

"La Rochefoucauld?"

"Nobody's perfect."

"I'm sorry." Minnie looked healthy and suntanned and sorry as she placed a hand on his arm. "I do think you've done remarkably well to have come this far." She turned to start the car. "But you *do* need to eat."

"We will. There's a treasury to be plundered."

"I won't be a party to anything criminal."

"In my entire life I have never done anything illegal."

"I don't believe that."

"As I said, nobody's perfect. But if we do get something to eat, I'm sure we'll all be able to think better."

"Surely God is watching over us," Father Bischoff said as Minnie, her dark hair splashing about her shoulders, walked to the car for the salt she had left there. Father Bischoff held his breath, watched her miniskirt.

Andros said, "You couldn't do it."

Father Bischoff turned on him hotly. "Don't be such a barnacled boob. I love to look at beautiful women. A mother and her child is a breathless work of the Creator."

Andros, better able to control his own agitation, said, "I don't see where you got a child in there unless it's wishful thinking."

Charlemagne said gravely, "Minnie is a beautiful person."

They politely waited for Minnie to return before starting lunch in the shadow of several great gray oaks just off the road in a designated rest area, a carved-out slice of what passed for grass maintained by the highway department and populated by two new redwood benches and a picnic table. A few hundred yards beyond was a cemetery which looked cool even in the hot sun, and farther on was an orchard and beyond that a pasture. In the other direction lay silent corn rows, unwavering and green on this windless day, stretching as far as one could see. From across the road somewhere came the bleating of lambs, the sound drifting thinly through the hot bright silence.

"Yes," Father Bischoff said, "she is beautiful." He added hastily, "And not just because she bought the lunch."

Peter, also greatly affected by Minnie-in-action, bit his lip and looked away, his eyes panicky.

"Beautiful," Andros said, "even by ABC standards."

"ABC standards?" Charlemagne turned to look Andros full in the face. "That's a new one. Is it a union, a network or something from the computer banks?"

"The Troika planets, A, B and C. The best from each is sent once a year to compete for Miss ABC. Andros was a judge one year."

"I thought there were four planets in your system," Charlemagne said. "I remember your telling us Andros is from the fourth."

"That is true," Andros replied, unflustered. "Those on the fourth planet do not enter the pageant, limit their participation to judging only. There are even various classifications of judging."

"I imagine," Charlemagne said dryly.

The redwood table was already spread with a cloth, plates of barbecued chicken, potato salad, cole slaw, rolls, butter and coffee. As Minnie returned and sat down with the salt, Father Bischoff, who could not hold it any longer, leaned forward to blurt out, "I am not seething with sex, but I want you to know I long to experience its mystery and fulfillment."

Minnie turned to look into Father Bischoff's eyes in a long-sustained gaze of growing gravity, and it was suddenly very quiet at the table. "You should," she said.

Father Bischoff leaned back, beaming. Andros snorted huffily as he picked up a piece of chicken. Peter's frightened eyes lost themselves in the trees.

As Father Bischoff helped himself to the potato salad, he said,

" 'I am the vine, you are its branches. If a man lives on in me, and I in him, then he will yield abundant fruit.' " He paused with the salad. "I believe that. But I don't want to be a vine without any grapes."

"Pass the potato salad," Andros said.

"Pollination is divine," Minnie declared, looking a little intoxicated at the thought as she opened the cole-slaw bucket. "Like slow, warm rain. That's divine, too. The warm smell of the person beside you in bed. Sharing. All we do openly, caringly, is divine."

Minnie had been watching Peter and saw his absorption in the cemetery. She asked him what he was looking at.

"The cemetery," he said.

She smiled. "Do you realize that's the first thing you've ever said to me?" When Peter said nothing, she said, "You keep looking. Why?"

Peter turned with the drumstick he'd been chewing on and the look in his eyes was like lenses shifting. His eyes suddenly jumped to a place behind her. She turned; there was nothing to see there. When she turned back, Peter had got to his feet and was moving away. He set his plate on an old tree stump nearby, sat down and stared at the fields as he resumed eating.

Minnie asked Charlemagne what that was all about.

"He's a victim, Minerva. As are we all."

Father Bischoff reached for another helping of potato salad. "That is true, my child."

Charlemagne said, "You have your Council fathers."

"Not me," Andros said, gnawing a breastbone. "I've refused to be victimized, villified or vasectomized."

Charlemagne snorted. "What do you call what that little mite does to you that sits in your head?"

"He's not a dissembler. I know he's there."

"But you said you've let him take over your body," Minnie said. "Isn't that being victimized?"

"It's an honor," Andros replied loftily. "For all we know he could have started computer programming."

81

Charlemagne said, "Andros doesn't know how long he's been here—in the world. It could be centuries."

"He's heavied over on that point," Father Bischoff explained. "Sopturated."

"We don't have to impress."

"It's all right," Minnie said, turning to look toward Peter. "It's Peter I'm worried about."

"He leaves us now and then."

"Even when he's here," Andros said.

"Where does he go?"

"The outhouse," Charlemagne said with a tired sigh. "It's his jury mast, vent plug and safety valve."

Minnie had no way of knowing that Peter had already decided she was one of Them when she sat down to share the tree-stump table with him. All she saw was that he continued to eat and did not look at her, only at the fields across the road. He could have told her he was looking at the fields because they did not zoom up all out of proportion like the gravestones and were not covered with flecky gray stuff, but he said nothing.

She did not know that he thought They were getting desperate because they were using a woman, or that she was feminine without being frail, fetching without being beseeching, that the way she walked in her miniskirt upset him, made him want to leave, draw the cover over. Yet he couldn't leave. He had discovered he really didn't want to.

She only sensed his agitation. "You don't have to say anything, Peter. I'll love you just the same."

They ate and she saw where his eyes were, so she said, "That's just ground haze over there. Not smog. I know because that's the way it used to be in Los Angeles when I was a kid. Hazy, not smoggy." He darted a quick glance at her, so she smiled, saying, "Yes, I was a kid in L.A. In fact, I'm a native Californian." She laughed. "Somebody had to be born there, for God's sake! . . . Have you ever been there?" Charlemagne, Andros and Father Bischoff, at the nearby redwood table, waited with her for the answer, but it never came.

Minnie lost herself in recollections for a few moments. Then: "You'd love it, Peter. It gets to you, like a narcotic. There's no death there."

Seeing his shudder, she said quickly, "I mean there's no winter, no black branches against cloudy skies. It's alive, the whole state, even in winter. Something doing all the time." She was happy to see the paroxysm pass.

Later, when they had finished, she slipped her hand into his and said, "You should see the ocean sometime, Peter. Make a point of it. Long, wide beaches. Wild ones. And south of San Francisco at Davenport Landing there are beaches with walls behind them, walls of color, bright reds, blues and yellows. You just wouldn't believe it."

She studied his profile; she had no idea he was scanning her every word. "It's never the same, Peter. Caves, spray, anemones, sandpipers, driftwood, jellyfish. Wouldn't you like to see all that? What about a beached ship they've filled with cement? It's there for all time, and that's the idea, I think. What about the London Bridge? The *Queen Mary?*" She laughed. "We've bought their rummage, Peter. Don't you think so?"

She turned to look across the road with him. "Really, though, you could spend your life in California without watching television once, not even knowing it's there, and not thinking either, but standing ass-high in history or goggle-eyed at such inanities as the biggest picture in the whole fucking world, to coin a phrase."

Peter went pale and started to shake.

When he suddenly became aware of her hand in his he went into the tunnel and didn't come out until they were in the car and nearly to Oblout.

15

FROM THE air on a clear day Oblout looks like green-dyed sponges set on an architect's model display table, surrounded by neat-as-a-checkerboard squares of what are really townships, farms and smaller parcels. The sponges are elms, for the most part, and at a lower altitude one can see, through the protecting trees, the bright white buildings of Oblout University, the county courthouse, shopping malls and peripheral residential areas. Farther out there are several industrial plants, low and wide, set so as to blend with the land. There are also cemeteries, parks, man-made lakes, golf courses and country clubs, but one gets the impression that they are merely adjunct to the real purpose of the area: the treeless farmlands that stretch out of sight in every direction where the business is the production of corn and soybeans.

Oblout is hoary with history and tradition, and many things are simply unspoken of there. Though there is the mark of today (television antennas and tract homes), it is more that technology has been accepted only as a supplement for what has been standard for generations. There are monuments and plaques dedicated to the valiant, to the fallen in skirmishes and wars, from an Indian uprising of the late 1700s to the Vietnam dead. The architecture is bastard, a conglomeration of ancient and mid-Victorian, with daring little Frank Lloyd Wright. The houses in the older section are staid, gabled, bay-windowed, ornate, some with mansard roofs, most having been reconstructed inside and out, but usually with a nod to keeping the old and colorful, such as elaborate inlaid mantels; efforts to seal basements completely against seeping from the springtime rising of the water table have been to no avail.

The city has been successfully bypassed by throughways, which may be the reason Minnie never heard of it, but she could not deny it existed when the sign plainly stated that it was there, right in front of them, and when she asked Charlemagne, "A castle *here?*" he did not change expression, which was one of tense expectation, but replied, "A man's home is a man's castle," and a few minutes later they drew up in front of a white house with a deep, wide porch bare of rugs, chairs or growing things.

It was a boxlike, high-ceilinged two-story house with three bedrooms and a study (a former bedroom) and bath upstairs, a front hall, living room, dining room, kitchen, bath and pantry downstairs, all the rooms large and the furniture sturdy. The woodwork had been painted many times, and the way the big doors had come not to fit showed that the house had settled considerably.

For some time they sat quietly in the car, being witness to Charlemagne's anxiety as he shifted in his corduroy suit, peering out at the windows. Then he got out and told them he'd go in himself; they would have to wait in the car; yes, he knew it was warm and it was going to get warmer, but he'd be as quick as he could.

When they protested, Charlemagne leaned forward to speak to them, putting a hand on top of the car but jerking it back because it was so hot. He spoke, then bent forward at the middle. "What is ours must be taken; the enemy must not be left to rise again in bloody rebellion."

Before he could go, Minnie said, "Charlemagne, I think we'd all feel better if you told us exactly what you're going to do."

"This is no sacking of a helpless city," he said. "This is the beginning of our holy crusade." With that, he was off, up on the porch and peering in one of the front panes. He tried the door; it was locked. He came down the steps, turned to the walk that ran through a gate to the rear of the house.

The men were used to waiting, waiting for the doctor, the attendant, for medication, for lunch, time to go to bed, so the minutes did not lie as heavily upon them. But they did on

85

Minnie. When it became almost stifling in the car and they ran out of things to say and started stirring uncomfortably, Minnie got out and told them to stay where they were; she'd go see what Charlemagne was up to. But when she moved up to the porch, she saw that Andros, Peter and Father Bischoff were already out of the car, yawning and stretching on the parkway.

She saw the mailbox next to the door. It was labeled LE MOYNE. She went to one of the front windows as Charlemagne had, looked in and caught a glimpse of corduroy, and a few moments later he opened the front door and saw them all.

"Come in, come in," Charlemagne said.

It was cooler in the house, and they welcomed the change. Charlemagne told them to enjoy themselves, this was his house, there was beer and Coke in the refrigerator, there should be cookies, the makings for sandwiches, they were to make themselves at home. As for himself, he would continue his search.

When he moved to go, Minnie went with him and asked him what in the world he was looking for.

He stopped at the secretary desk in the living room. Some of the drawers had already been upended on the floor, the contents lying about. He opened it, began going through the pigeonholes. "I have decided," he said. "We're going to California."

"California?"

"I heard what you said to Peter and must confess I've always had a hankering to go there. I once had a student from Pasadena. He was an expert in dirigation. He was the anomaly of the physiology department."

"You were a teacher?"

"In the past. All is past." Charlemagne worked at opening envelopes and boxes of knickknacks and letting what was inside fall on the desk. "What we must do is work toward what will be memory. No one wants bad memories."

"You still haven't answered my question."

"I'm looking for a passport."

"But you don't need a passport to go to California!"

Charlemagne did not seem upset by this news, and Minnie stood watching and waiting, but when he did not seem about to react or volunteer any more information, she went to the kitchen, where Andros and Father Bischoff were drinking beer. Peter, who did not like new things, sat alone at one of the stuffed seats in the breakfast nook looking pale and uneasy. Minnie poured a glass of Coke for him and for herself and sat down beside him, but he would not touch his.

Even as they sat they could hear Charlemagne rummaging around upstairs.

"A man searches," Father Bischoff said, looking at her. He was sitting with Andros at the kitchen table. "What does he seek?"

"I don't know," Minnie said. "He said he was looking for a passport, but I don't believe that."

"Andros sees," Andros said, "but he can't go into his mind. He could, but there is a Federation Ukase against it. He says he's not permitted to interfere in the lives of people in the colonies."

Father Bischoff snorted derisively. "He's interfering in your life, isn't he?"

"It's an honor, sir."

Later, they moved about the house. Peter looked in corners, under tables and rugs and behind pictures for bugs and kept clear of the television set. Father Bischoff said he could find no Bible. "Without a Bible there cannot be peace in this house," he said. "Or to those who dwell herein." He also stated that the absence of a crucifix was demeaning to the occupants. "I am surprised at Charlemagne. I had assumed he walked in the newness of life. I shall have to speak to him about the Second Mystagogical Catechesis. He can learn something from St. Cyril of Jerusalem."

It seemed to Minnie, judging by the frenetic way they were acting, they must be pretty wrought up, even Andros, who remarked, as he strode quickly about, that this was the first time he'd been in an Earthling's house, and he was finding it extremely interesting. He would file away in the computer banks all that he saw, to be reported to the Triumvirate on the Fourth Planet when he returned.

Minnie thought it was a comfortable old house, well lived in, and in one of the bedrooms, on a dresser, she found a photograph of a woman, head and shoulders, in color and in a gilt frame. The woman was a brunette, about thirty-five, with an orchid corsage on what looked to be the upper part of a formal gown. Though her eyes looked cold and her lips thin, Minnie thought she was rather attractive. She brought the photograph to Charlemagne, who was in a closet in another bedroom, emptying boxes of papers on the floor.

"Who is this?" she asked.

Charlemagne, who had worked up a fine sweat, paused to dab at his face with a handkerchief as he looked.

"The enemy."

When Minnie said nothing, he went on: "Her name's Marietta. Marietta Le Moyne." And when Minnie just stared at him, he said, "She's no proem. She's the whole text. At least that's what she thinks she is. An impossible woman to live with. She doesn't soar. Just root-hogs. Even when there's plenty to eat." He took the frame and regarded the photograph neutrally. "She'd make a lousy queen. I wish I'd have known that before I married her. But she saw the impending hostilities and would not be liegeman to me. No Holy War for Marietta. Not unless she could lead the troops herself. And she has no generalship."

"She's your wife?"

"I said so, didn't I? But make that *was*, Minerva." He handed the frame to her. "I have transcended the judiciary and have, by my own decree, severed the relationship." He turned back to the pile of papers on the floor. "She thinks otherwise. That is why she must surrender her sureties. When I have power, I shall send her back to her father." After a moment: "Maybe I'll do nothing. That would be even more insulting."

Charlemagne was certainly making a mess of the house the way he was strewing things all over, emptying drawers on beds, boxes on the floor. Minnie decided not to say anything. After all, it was his castle.

When Charlemagne found what he was looking for, he let out a shout that brought them running—even Peter—to where he was in what was Marietta's bedroom upstairs. They nearly collided with him as he came out the door.

"She thought she hid it where I'd never find it," he said, exultant. "Right there in with the panty hose." He laughed. "Oh, she thought she was so clever." He did not say what it was but turned his now almost beet-red, happy face to Minnie. "The keys. Let me have the keys."

It took Minnie a moment to realize he meant the keys to the car. "They're in the car."

"That's risky," he said, but he didn't look unhappy about it. "I'll be back shortly." He started down the stairs, humming.

Minnie went to the railing. "Shouldn't I drive you?"

He didn't stop. "This is a secret mission, a vital one for us all. Take care of things here. I leave you in command." Then he was out the door.

They moved to a window to watch him drive away; he looked very chipper as he did so. When he was gone, Peter sat down heavily in an old armchair and stared at the opposite wall.

Andros turned from the window, frowning. "He shouldn't have done that," he said in a voice edged with the panic he was feeling.

"He's a free agent," Father Bischoff said. "He has nothing to lose but his soul. Perhaps we could offer up a prayer."

"He's the commander-in-chief," Minnie said, half believing it. "A commander-in-chief wouldn't desert his troops."

That seemed to put some of the marrow back, and they moved out of the room, leaving Peter staring at nothing.

Minnie stood at the kitchen window with her coffee, feeling very comfortable about things. Father Bischoff was in the backyard on a bench under a tree with his beads, his wispy hair rocking in the breeze. She was amused. She had driven them all out when she turned on the radio on the shelf over the sink, and she had let them go. It was a good station, the one she'd found, and it gave out with a good rock beat. She wished the radio had more bass, though, the kind you feel rather than hear.

When she'd turned it on, Father Bischoff threw up his hands and left, Peter scuttled out of the room like a frightened rabbit, and Andros gave her a look of surprise before he cut out.

It had been a long time since she'd heard any good rock. Elizabeth hadn't liked that kind of music, though Dr. Sheckley's rig was one of the best, being built for it. It could really blast. Janis Joplin on his woofers and tweeters was really something else. She sounded like cascading gravel falling into a washtub, which is the way Janis Joplin should sound, and when she closed her eyes she could see Janis giving out with her wild beast style, the way she socked her violent sensuality right where it did the most good. It transformed Therin's living room, big as it was, into nothing more than a sardine can. It really did.

She missed rock, probably the only thing she missed since she came east. California was days that had strangled her with expectation, but now she knew they were really enormous caves of emptiness. Sure, there had been lassitude and there had been rush, but she'd been nothing but a bright leaf in a gulleywasher, crashing here and there, and then left lonely in a tidepool of ambling uneasiness, nowhere. And so now she was here, and that was someplace else, and Therin's car was out there somewhere, Charlemagne riding around in it. She hoped there wasn't a stolen-vehicle report out on it. Therin wouldn't do that. Or would he? She really didn't care.

She was happy. Even if they were all crippled. Maybe she was a cripple herself. But who the hell cared? Not her mother or father, sister or brother. She was a big girl now (though she felt like twelve, really, she didn't feel any different). She dug Charlemagne. He lived by his nerve endings, and he didn't have to have anything to turn him on. And that was fine for a change. Who needed it? The other way it was hark, hark, the nark and being hassled day and night, and busts are bummers.

Besides, there was Andros, and she felt things for him (how did he ever get on that E.T. kick?), and she knew it was reciprocated. After a while you get to know things like that. And she felt real concern for Father Bischoff; she wished his Council fathers (or somebody) would do for him what he wanted. And Peter. Poor, dear Peter, so little-boy lost, so in need of love. She was really getting wound up with the four of them, but she didn't mind. She guessed what she was really feeling was being needed, and she hadn't felt needed for a long time. It felt good.

Minnie sipped her coffee and started to move her body in time with the rock beat. Yeah, there was raw animal in that sound, and she liked that. For a change, anyway. She had to smile. Father Bischoff was doing his thing out there under the tree and she was doing hers in the kitchen.

She heard a creaking sound behind her, turned away from the window. Andros was standing in the doorway looking at her. Despite his stained sweater, sloppy tennis shoes and baggy slacks, he was a good-looking fellow. Reminded her of James Garner. She could tell by the way he was standing, the way he was looking, he was feeling the music, too. She gyrated toward him, put her cup and saucer on the table, did a little undulating dance before him.

He stared.

"Come on," she said, tossing her head so her hair would flare, keeping the beat, harder now.

He was entranced, genuine pleasure overriding his brooding eyes, brightening them.

She closed her own eyes, let the music come to her, take her. It was highly polished hard rock now, with some real wild-fingered guitar work, and she knew her hair was twirling, her body moving. She cold feel it. It went on and on.

Then it was over, the announcer was a cutdown, and she opened her eyes, went over, shut him up.

Andros was still staring.

She smiled. "You like?"

He came into the kitchen. There was a lot of color in his face.

"Well, *do* you?"

He smiled through his flushed face.

She picked up her coffee cup. He was a dear thing, all right, but there was a big fight going on somewhere underneath those broad shoulders and she wished she knew how to help him win it. She took a sip of coffee, found it only lukewarm. "I suppose Andros is going to make a report to the Triumvirate about it." It wasn't exactly fair, but she couldn't just let it die out there nowhere.

Andros wet his lips.

He was still with it, but there was still that struggle inside. She decided to be quiet and see how it came out.

Andros' eyes flickered to her legs, her miniskirt, waist, bosom, then her eyes. He swallowed and did not seem able to look away. His face got redder. He was hunched up now, hung up now, his forehead a sheen of sweat. He just stood there.

He had dark intensities she suddenly wanted to explore and she heard her own intake of breath over his labored breathing. Well, he was no freaked-out sex nut, no sadist, and for that she could be happy. Sure, he had his spermy dreams and she had hers, just like everybody, but in a thing like this there isn't supposed to be a stalemate. If it came to that, they were both at fault. She moved to him, put a hand on each shoulder, found him trembling. She looked into his eyes, deep, and wondered where he was, really, and wanting to be there with him.

He blinked furiously.

Then he pulled her to him so roughly her neck cracked.

The coffee went sailing.

16

Mr. Bostwick was polite but firm in the matter of the withdrawal. He sat confidently in his ball-bearinged swivel chair on its green vinyl pad on the thick rug behind his glass-topped desk in the middle of a row of other, smaller desks, looking very much like a bank president, which he was. He smiled benignly at Charlemagne.

"Actually, Mr. Le Moyne," he said, "we could legally require you to give us notice for a withdrawal that large. Of course we would not want to do that."

"Of course not." Charlemagne returned the smile and, seated to one side of the desk in a comfortable chair with cushioned arms, he lifted one leg and put it over the other. There was no crease to adjust.

"It's all there in fine print in the passbook."

"Yes."

"And what isn't there is in the bylaws of the bank itself."

"Mr. Bostwick," Charlemagne said, "I had no idea I could possibly embarrass the Bank of Oblout. I had assumed it was one of the more stable financial institutions of the city."

"Oh, it is, it is," Mr. Bostwick hastily assured him. "But I don't think any bank would want you to walk out into the streets carrying—" he referred to the savings-account passbook—"twenty-three thousand, five hundred sixty-seven dollars and seventy-five cents."

"Twenty-three thousand even," Charlemagne corrected. It's there on the withdrawal slip. You see, I'm leaving the five hundred and sixty-seven dollars and seventy-five cents for seed."

"That is wise."

"It will be withdrawn only in the event of an emergency."

"Emergency? I had the feeling there must be some kind of emergency right now. Otherwise why should you—"

"But I see no difficulty in the campaign."

"Campaign? Did you say campaign? Are you entering the political arena by any chance, Mr. Le Moyne?"

"In a way, Mr. Bostwick, and it's not just by any chance. Actually, it's a holy crusade, and it's by plan."

"I see." Mr. Bostwick studied the passbook. "Ah, it seems to me I remember someone telling me that you've been somewhere, out of town or something for a while."

"I think it's fine the way you keep up with the whereabouts of your depositors. If I may guess, I would say Naughty Marietta's caught your ear." Charlemagne looked soulful. "It's too bad we couldn't have done it together."

Still examining the passbook, Mr. Bostwick said, "At least you have a joint account."

"Of course. Marietta and I feel joint tenancy places the survivor in a more favorable position should either of us die."

"Yes."

"And of couse neither of us intends to do that. Do you, Mr. Bostwick?"

"Do I?" Mr. Bostwick looked at him blankly.

"Intend to die."

"Oh," Mr. Bostwick grunted. Then he said jovially, "We all have to go sometime, don't we, Mr. Le Moyne? But confidentially, I plan to hold on as long as I can."

"That is wise," Charlemagne said.

"Don't you?"

"Don't I?"

"Plan to hold on as long as you can?"

"Of course."

"Well," Mr. Bostwick said, returning to the matter at hand. "Miss Prescott wouldn't have referred this to me if your request hadn't been a little unusual."

"Mr. Bostwick, I sense in you a certain reluctance to give me my money."

"Reluctance?" Mr. Bostwick laughed shrilly, nervously, and heads at Paying and Receiving, New Accounts, Time Payment Loans and Trusts turned toward him. "It's your money, Mr. Le Moyne, isn't it?"

"Is it?"

Mr. Bostwick straightened in the chair, then leaned toward Charlemagne to say in a low voice, very intense: "You will get your money, Mr. Le Moyne, believe me. It is just a matter of how it is to be withdrawn. As I have said, it can't be all in cash."

"Don't you have that much money in the bank?"

"Yes, of course," Mr. Bostwick hissed. "But if we went around to all the tellers and took everything they had, I doubt we would come up with much more than twenty-three thousand. And then how would we conduct the rest of the business day?" He withdrew a thin gold pen from a gold desk set and wrote on a pad. "I suggest you withdraw, say, five thousand cash—we can easily accommodate you there—and make up the balance with cashier's checks in any amount you like—say, three for five thousand and one for three thousand."

"Eight thousand cash, with three checks for five thousand each, would be more like it."

"Mr. Le Moyne, let me assure you the Bank of Oblout is here only to serve you. If you want eight thousand cash and three cashier's checks for five thousand, you shall have it." Mr. Bostwick got to his feet. "We'll get to work on it at once."

Charlemagne did not get up but eyed Mr. Bostwick severely. "Mr. Bostwick, are you by any chance Semitic?"

"Semitic?"

" 'With what measure ye mete, the same shall be meted unto you.' It's an old Hebrew moral axiom."

"That's very interesting."

"Isn't it, though? The Semites were earlier civilized than the Aryans, you know. They were and are to this day a counting people. Their sense of equivalents and reparations remains strongly rooted in their genes."

"I'm sure," Mr. Bostwick said, fiddling with the passbook

and withdrawal slip. "Would you care to accompany me so this transaction can be completed?"

"Money in inexpert hands is a danger in human affairs. It is freedom and power, privacy and leisure. It is also unfairly distributed."

"Please, Mr. Le Moyne."

Charlemagne got to his feet. "I will, of course, do something about that."

"About what?"

"The unequal distribution." He put a hand on Mr. Bostwick's shoulder. "But you needn't worry. I'm sure there will be a place for you. An inspector of the kingdom, perhaps. I'll let you know."

"Ah . . . that's very thoughtful of you, Mr. Le Moyne. Now, if you please."

"Of course," Charlemagne said, moving with him.

Peter was in ferment. He was sitting on a blue-and-white throw rug on the varnished floor of the front bedroom, his back against the bed, his eyes tightly closed, trying not to think of Minnie.

Still, the images came: Minnie as she looked when he first saw her in the car, large blue eyes filled with empathy; Minnie calm and cool in the car driving right past Berylwood, her eyes meeting his in the rear-view mirror and seeming to say she was ready to understand, ready to listen; Minnie sitting on the grass in the sunshine, her legs tucked beneath her, eating chicken at the stump, holding his hand, talking about California, telling him he didn't have to say anything, she'd love him anyway.

He forced his eyes open, looked out the window high in the wall, seeing the sky, a network of branches and leaves, a few cotton clouds. There was color there. Most of the time when he returned from The Other Side, where it was often rather dazzling, it took him a while to see color at all, even faintly. It was as if, as in a television set, his color-intensity control wasn't working right. And if he was on The Other Side very long it sometimes took hours for him to recover. Not that the displays where he'd been were always so brilliant and sparkling; he never knew what he'd see when he looked out of the outhouse, what kind of a day it would be. Once he'd gone there and arrived in the middle of a thunder shower.

Continuing his concentration, he decided there was now no distortion in what he was seeing: the window was square, the branches outside weren't at all grotesque, and the clouds were rounded puffs of perfection. Come to think of it, things had been pretty much what they were supposed to be since the picnic. He'd actually enjoyed the scenery, and Oblout reminded him of Mountbury, where he'd grown up, with its white buildings and predominant greenness. It must have been much more confining than Minnie's California background. And there he was, thinking of Minnie again.

He had almost talked to her when she poured him his Coke. What would have happened if he had? He remembered how he felt about Charlemagne when Charlemagne first started to talk to him, how he didn't answer at first. He knew Charlemagne couldn't be one of Them because some of the things he'd said to him were pretty dangerous, such as where he went when he went away (the outhouse), what he was thinking about at specific times (the outhouse and environs were more real than life) (plus a few references to Them) (and the latter just happened to slip out).

As he'd thought before, Minnie, if she was truly one of Them, could not have been a better selection for the job, but now he began hoping she was not, and as a result he was tempted to talk to her. When she'd asked him what he was looking at, and he'd said, "The cemetery," that could have been a mistake. He realized he'd have to be on his guard. But only if she was what he feared. If she was not one of Them (God, how could he tell for sure!), then wasn't all this caution denying him the pleasure of a relationship he wanted?

He sighed, suddenly realized Mr. Hochdruck hadn't been with him for a while, and he was grateful for this small favor. Or was Mr. Hochdruck not there because They thought Minnie could take over from here on out?

He had run directly to this room when Minnie turned on the radio so loud. He really didn't mind that kind of music, but she turned up the volume so high it panicked him and he had to do something before he broke down and said something, so he got as far from it as possible. Even up here he did not escape entirely, but at least he could endure what he heard. He guessed the speaker cone must have come free from its anchor, the way it rattled and shrieked. From their reactions, he judged Father Bischoff and Andros must have felt the same way.

He knew about the upstairs because he'd been through all the rooms, and he felt less uneasy in the one he was in.

One bedroom was a woman's, probably Charlemagne's wife's. Charlemagne had mentioned her several times at Berylwood, though Peter could not now remember her name. He only remembered how surprised he was to learn that Charlemagne was married. Perhaps it would have never come up if Dr. Sheckley hadn't asked Charlemagne if he knew why his wife didn't visit him. Charlemagne said he didn't know why, but he didn't care, if that was what Dr. Sheckley was getting at. Then Dr. Sheckley asked Charlemagne if he had written her, and Charlemagne said he hadn't written to anyone, he was expecting Peter to take over that chore, which upset Dr. Sheckley even more. Then Charlemagne, who seldom got angry, raised his voice in protest because Dr. Sheckley didn't try to understand about Angilbert, his counselor, and Einhard, his secretary, and the establishment of the school at Aachen.

Yes, that bedroom was hers, all right, the lived-in one with the double bed and the electric blanket, the perfume on the vanity, the room with the cleaner mirrors, the one with the magazines, crossword puzzle books and jewel boxes, the one room Peter felt alien to on sight.

On his tour he'd found which bedroom had been Charlemagne's. It was smaller than his wife's and had a double bed but little else except for a dresser, on top of which stood a photograph in a gold frame; there was very little in the closet. The photograph must have been of Charlemagne's wife, and Peter found he did not like the way she looked: severe and judging. He felt like an intruder, an intruder being watched, so he didn't linger.

The third room was a study, three walls lined with books, a small desk in front of the window, a globe, several chairs, and convenient lights, obviously Charlemagne's. He did not feel comfortable there. The books, mostly on history, depressed him. They made him feel there was so much he didn't know and so much he ought to.

The room he'd settled on was the least of all evils. It was practically bare, only throw rugs on the floor, an unintimidating picture ("The Blue Boy" reproduction) on the wall, nothing at all in the closet (except hangers) and a small, antique-looking dressing table stuck next to the only window.

The radio sound from downstairs stopped, and now he heard some moving around in the house. He guessed Father Bischoff and Andros must have felt it safe to go back to the kitchen for another beer. He thought of joining them but decided not to, but when Mr. Hochdruck came in smirkingly to invade his field of vision, he changed his mind. Peter knew Hochdruck couldn't read minds, so it was all bluff on Hochdruck's part, so Peter ignored him and got to his feet.

As he moved out of the room he suddenly missed Berylwood and its certainties and routine. Here it was up to him and he didn't like it; mostly he guessed he didn't like not knowing what was going to happen next, where they'd be the next hour, what the real plans were, if there were any. But that wasn't the worst. It was Minnie, the way she had stirred him up, made him become aware of his body. If he were in Berylwood right now he'd simply go to his room and not be home to anybody, just ignore everything and not worry about Minnie because he wouldn't even know she existed to worry about. But if he were at Berylwood there was always the possibility They would have sent her under the guise of an attendant or an associate or something.

There was no one in the kitchen. No sound, either, except

the low humming of the Dutch electric clock on the wall. He saw a plastic cup on the floor. He picked it up, put it on the table. Where was everybody?

Peter went to the window, saw Father Bischoff in the yard on a bench, his back against a tree, his eyes closed. He looked so completely relaxed Peter envied him. His first thought was to go out and join him, but then he thought the better of it. Let the good padre sleep.

Where were Andros and Minnie? Neither of them was anywhere downstairs. He was on the point of seeing if they could be sitting on the front stoop when he heard sounds from upstairs. Bed springs? One of them must be up there taking a nap. He went by Mr. Hochdruck, who stood at the foot of the stairs, an arm around the newel post and looking very superior.

When he reached the top of the stairs he saw that the door to the big bedroom was closed, and he could hear the rustling of cloth and the bed springs. Well, that settled that. Andros wouldn't be in there. But Minnie couldn't be asleep. Not with all that noise. He went to the door. What in the world was she doing?

He felt he couldn't call to her, and he didn't want to knock. She probably had a book from the study and was in there reading it, in which case he could go in.

Minnie cried out.

Peter opened the door.

Marcella was on the bed with Andros and neither had a stitch on. When they saw him they smiled.

Marcella and Andros smiled!

Peter felt his bones turning cold and brittle. He wanted to flee but found he couldn't. Bile came up his throat, his hands and feet felt raw, his eyes hurt and his breath commenced going in and out, fast, and he was losing control. He began to feel so terrible he started shouting. He went into the room crying out at Andros and his wife, making angry, animal sounds, and they shrank back on the bed and went out of focus. A series of violent colors started flashing and he was beginning to flit in and out of a place he'd never been.

No, it was the room. It started to change size. Now it was an enormous room with stained ceilings twenty feet high and Marcella and Andros were on a tiny bed in a corner, and the dread started, the horrible, flesh-crawling kind of dread that cold-sweated the skin as the ceiling came down crushingly as if to press the life out of him, his heart jackhammering as he lurched out of there just in time, to stand in the hall gasping, then staggering to the stairs, which were at the top of a thousand steps that wavered down, down, down somewhere. He grabbed for and found the balustrade and stumbled down all thousand, eventually reaching bottom, crying hoarsely now, tears steaming his eyes.

"Peter!"

Marcella, he saw, was at the top of the stairs, a blanket around her nakedness, her face white. Andros was at her side, gaping down at him as he zippered up his pants.

Peter rushed headlong into the downstairs bathroom, closed and locked the door.

"Oho, Peter!" Mr. Hochdruck said.

Peter stared at him in the bathtub, where he stood hanging on to the shower-curtain rod, grinning evilly. Hochdruck knew! Hochdruck knew all the time!

"Ho, ho, ho!" laughed Mr. Hochdruck.

Peter's hatred fulminated. "Shut up, you!" he bellowed at Hochdruck.

"Me?" Hochdruck asked with sweet innocence.

"Shut *up!*"

"Go ahead, go to the outhouse."

Peter tried, but he couldn't make the connection, and his blood began to congeal coldly.

"This is real!" Hochdruck said with shrill joy. "You saw! You saw!"

Peter picked up the wastebasket, threw it at the repugnant face. Hochdruck sidestepped nimbly.

"Naughty, naughty!"

In his raw hatred, Peter rushed to do violence to Hochdruck, but Hochdruck jumped away.

"Here I am, Peter, darling," Hochdruck said in the bathroom mirror. "You can't reach me here."

With a cry of rage Peter picked up the bathroom scales and threw them with all his might at the mirror. The glass shattered, the scales falling first to the sink and then to the floor.

Peter did not hear the pounding on the door.

"I'm here, Peter," Hochdruck said, emerging from the toilet bowl. "Up from where you've been."

"By God," Peter said, advancing on him. "By God!"

"By who?" Hochdruck said. "I didn't catch the name."

Peter ripped down the shower curtain and tried to throttle Hochdruck with it, but Hochdruck managed to escape at the last possible moment. He then tore the medicine chest from the wall and threw it at Hochdruck, who stepped aside.

"It's no use," Hochdruck said. "It's no use at all, Peter. Guilt will out."

"You son of a bitch!" Peter screamed, trying to reach him. Hochdruck moved quickly, smoothly. Peter's inertia sent him into a small white table. It fell on the floor, all the bottles and things on it clattering and smashing on the floor.

Hochdruck laughed. "It's no use, Peter!" he cackled with huge enjoyment. "Better give up!"

Peter's legs felt like lead-filled boots, and he sank to the floor, breathing hard and beginning to cry. Then he was wrenched with sobs.

Suddenly he was in the outhouse, down through the holes into the corridors beneath. He locked the intervening doors and crept into a corner and put his palms hard against his eyeballs.

It was safe there.

He didn't even hear the pounding on the door.

17

CHARLEMAGNE HEARD the pounding and crying as he got out of the car, so he hurried up the steps and into the house. He snapped to a stop in the hallway, rooted in surprise by what he saw.

Minnie was clad in a blanket which she had trouble keeping around her shoulders with her left hand as she struck the bathroom door repeatedly with her right fist. Tears stained her cheeks and she kept calling out, despairing: "Peter! Please!"

Andros, clad only in his paper-thin slacks, had one hand on the doorknob, one palm and shoulder against the door, pushing; his face was red and sweated with effort.

Father Bischoff, who stood placidly to one side, was making the sign and speaking in an orotund voice: ". . . that by the grace of the Holy Spirit you cure the illness of this sick man and heal his wounds; forgive his sins, and drive away from him all pains of mind and body. In your mercy give him health, inward and outward, so that he may once more be able to take up his work . . ."

"For God's sake," Charlemagne said as he broke forward, "what's going on?"

They turned to stare. Then Minnie wrenched to him, embracing him and pressing her head to his shoulder, saying through sobs, "Oh, Charlemagne!" and "It was awful!" Charlemagne, touched by Minnie's reaction, raised a hand to stroke her hair, then faced Father Bischoff, saying, "What happened?"

"It's Peter," Father Bischoff said neutrally, as if that explained it all.

"It's quiet in there right now," Andros said, "but a minute ago he was wrecking the place."

"He may be dying," Father Bischoff said darkly. "We must save his soul from the clutches of sin."

"He locked himself in." Minnie sniffed back more tears. "Then things began to crash inside." She shuddered.

Charlemagne left her to go to the door to call out to Peter. There was no response.

"It may be a case for Extreme Unction," Father Bischoff said with a mixture of urgency and hope.

Charlemagne put his shoulder against the door, motioned for Andros and Father Bischoff to do the same. Minnie watched them with round eyes as together they hit the door. She winced when it broke open with a splintering crash.

Inside, Peter was sitting on the toilet seat, his face white and waxlike, his eyes like glass. He was facing the opposite wall, his hands curled in his lap.

They moved in on careful feet, avoiding the glass shards and debris, stepping around the table. Minnie ran the last few steps recklessly to kneel before Peter, taking one of his hands between both of hers and massaging it. She looked up at him. "Peter . . . Peter." Tears began again.

Father Bischoff put a hand on Peter's head and said harshly, "May any power that the devil has over you be utterly destroyed."

"He's all right," Charlemagne said after a hasty appraisal, mostly the feeling of his pulse and a palm to his forehead. "He's gone to the outhouse, that's all." He looked around at the wreckage. "What a mess!"

"But why?" Minnie looked into Peter's expressionless face as if she thought she could find the answer there. "Why should he wreck things and then leave us like this?"

"I don't know. He never did anything like this before that I know of." He looked to Father Bischoff and Andros. They shook their heads. He turned to Minnie. "What are you doing in that blanket?"

Andros moved away with embarrassment, but Minnie said without qualms, "Andros and I were in bed together."

"Oh." Charlemagne looked around, took a few steps, kicked aside a large piece of glass. It skittered along the floor. He shook his head. "What a mess!" he repeated.

Father Bischoff, who was staring at Minnie in shock, said, "Did you hear? Did you hear what she said?"

Charlemagne snorted. "Let us not be pernicious. We've got to move out. There isn't even time to clean this up."

But Father Bischoff moved to Minnie with concern. "Would you want me to hear your confession, my child?"

Minnie blinked at him blankly, then said rather sharply, "No."

"It would remove any fragment of sin . . ."

"I'm sorry." She was more equable now. "I didn't mean to be so curt. It's simply that I don't believe in it—sin, I mean. I just do what I do and try not to hurt anybody." She regarded Peter's immobile face anxiously. "For some reason I seem to have hurt Peter."

"Then may the Lord have mercy on your soul."

"Stop picking on her," Andros said with some belligerence.

"May the Lord have mercy on your soul, too."

"Andros has no soul. On his planet—"

"You had one before you let that microbe take over. I'd hate to see what shape it's in right now. All bent and wrinkled, probably."

"You're jealous!"

"Stop it!" Charlemagne said from the bathroom door. "There isn't time for argument. To the showers with everyone."

"Showers?" Father Bischoff said askance.

"Cleanliness is next to Godliness, Father. You ought to know that."

"I don't want to take a shower," Andros said, beginning to sulk. "Andros doesn't like showers."

"We've lots to do. Minerva, you can be first. The shower's upstairs."

Minnie got to her feet, moved a few steps toward Charlemagne. "But what about Peter?"

"We'll clean him up."

"That's not what I mean!" She turned to regard Peter anxiously. "He's just sitting there. How can we do other things when he's like that?" She looked around at them all. "Doesn't anybody care?"

"What would you suggest?" Charlemagne asked.

"I don't know," she said miserably.

Charlemagne came to her, put his arm around her. "I said he's going to be all right and he will be. Believe me, we've seen him like this many times. He'll work his way out of it sooner or later. Now don't worry. Promise?"

"All right." She left his embrace, then for the first time noticed his new clothes, and she moved off a few steps to view him better. "Why, Charlemagne, you've—you look wonderful!"

"Clothes opens doors," he said, preening a little, pleased. He was attired in a new gray plaid business suit of stylish cut, black buckle shoes with an Italian look, and a dark gray shirt with a pale-blue tie. "Would you like to see something else? Come on."

He led them to the front window, pulled back the curtain so they could all see a nearly new black Lincoln Continental parked at the curb. "Behold!"

"I don't understand," Minnie said. "Isn't that rather fancy?"

"If I could have bought a used Silver Cloud, I'd have done it, but Oblout affluent gravitate to Cadillacs, so there are no Rolls. This is the only one of its kind available." He looked out at it proudly. "There's style, Minerva. Class. You might say it befits our cause."

"What happened to Dr. Sheckley's car? I hope you didn't try to trade it in."

"Oh, nothing so foolish as that." Charlemagne let the curtain fall. "It was abandoned in the parking lot of a supermarket and the keys were sent to Dr. Sheckley at Berylwood." His mood suddenly darkened and he looked at them all under severe eyebrows. "I've been busy in the field in some necessary rear-guard

106

action while you've all been playing games." Then he brightened, smiling as if he'd been joking. "However, I am happy to report that the treasury has been plundered as planned, and though there aren't four hundred mules with gold all charged, there is enough to sustain us on the march to the Land of the Miwok. And let us hope we remain as fearless as they." He raised his hands and clapped them. "Now upstairs, Minnie, and I mean right now. Chop-chop."

"Are you sure Peter will be all right?"

"Quite sure."

Minnie turned. "Andros?" She held out a hand. Andros was hesitant, so she grabbed his arm and started with him toward the stairs.

"And there isn't time for any hanky-panky," Charlemagne warned.

"Two can wash faster than one," she said gaily, flinging the blanket aside as Andros fell in with it and they raced up the stairs.

Father Bischoff looked after them enviously. Charlemagne took his arm, saying, "Now let us see what we can do with Peter."

Father Bischoff shook his head. "She doesn't believe in sin." He would have stayed where he was, lost in his fantasies, if Charlemagne had not tugged him away. As they started for the bathroom, he said, "In a way, she's lucky. She can live a life of sweet innocence and do anything she likes."

"God is love, Father. Minnie is only doing her part."

At the bathroom door they looked in on Peter, who had not moved. Father Bischoff shook his head. "There's nothing we can do for him, except pray."

"We can do more than that. We can clear an area and bathe him." When he saw Father Bischoff's repugnance, he said, "Has he sinned, Father?"

"All have sinned."

"Then we'll wash him as if we were removing accumulated layers of sin."

Minnie and Andros found it good in the shower, a preliminary run of warm water to wash away road dust and body film, then the gentle lathering of one body by another, interpersed with tender kisses that threatened more than once to incinerate them but which they turned off lest they did actually reach kindling temperature. Laughter, the show of white teeth and I-dig-you eyes and smiles, giggles, a feeling of soft flesh and hard flesh, intakes of breath and sighs, glory and warmth and a sense of being alive: two animals playing. And then the roaring cascade of water that washed away the lather and sorry to see it go, a sudden pressing together under the water, Andros playfully turning it to ice needles and the resultant scream, and then the warmth again, eyes closed, the water running everywhere.

Then there was the drying with the biggest towels Minnie could find, and more giggles and kisses that inflamed again, to be averted before the holocaust, and then they were standing there, Minnie saying she hated to put on what she'd been wearing but there didn't seem any way out; she didn't want Andros to put on his old sweater or the dirty slacks but didn't see a way out of that either. But she did find some underthings for herself in Marietta's room and some clean underwear and socks for Andros in Charlemagne's.

When they came downstairs, they found Charlemagne and Father Bischoff at an impasse. They had succeeded in undressing Peter, but they could not get him in the tub of warm, sudsy water they had prepared for him.

"He's like a bag of cement," Charlemagne said.

"We were afraid we might hurt him, drop him in there, maybe drown him," Father Bischoff explained.

"With Andros now maybe we'll be able to do it." Charlemagne turned to Andros, but Andros was staring at Peter's penis, and Charlemagne asked him why.

"He was examining mine yesterday," Andros said. "His is nothing special."

"This is not a class in comparative physiology. Come on."

Andros moved around, took Peter under his arms, Father Bischoff taking his feet and Charlemagne helping around the rump. They hoisted him over the edge and gently lowered him into the tub. Peter was like a pliable manikin and offered no resistance, no reaction. Andros helped keep him upright.

"Minnie," Charlemagne said, "would you do the honors?" He gestured to the waiting soap and washcloth.

"Second one today," she said cheerfully, falling to the task while Charlemagne rounded up some lathering soap and a safety razor.

When Peter was safely out of the tub and on the toilet seat, Charlemagne shaved him, and when that was over and his clothes put back on, with some help from what little of Charlemagne's wardrobe remained in the house, they stood back to look at him.

"He looks good," Minnie said.

"He does," Charlemagne said. "The cleanest I've ever seen him. Now the only problem is getting him to the car. But that will have to wait until Father Bischoff and I have our shower."

"I'll just get into the tub here," Father Bischoff said. "I'm not a communal shower-taker like some."

Andros grinned. "You don't know what you're missing, Father."

"No," he said sadly, "I know exactly what I'm missing."

Later, with Andros holding Peter under his arms and Father Bischoff and Charlemagne on either side of him, they got Peter to the car and into the back seat. Minnie crawled in beside him, Andros taking the seat beside her. Charlemagne got in on the driver's side, Father Bischoff taking the seat beside him.

"We're off," Charlemagne said, turning the ignition key. The engine purred smoothly.

"May God be with us," Father Bischoff murmured as the car pulled away.

18

THE LINCOLN CONTINENTAL whispered along the highway to the big city in the late afternoon, and Minnie sat holding Peter's cold hand and wishing she knew some way to get through to him. Sometimes she spoke to him, telling him everything was all right, but he sat there like a statue, his eyes unseeing, his lips not moving. He never swallowed. At least she hadn't caught him swallowing. It was as if he were asleep with his eyes open.

She thought she might have been happy if it weren't for Peter. He looked so alone, so absolutely helpless, so apart from everything. She kept asking Charlemagne if he thought Peter was still all right.

"He's fled the world, Minerva. He's not with us right now."

"If he's not with us, then where is he?"

"In the outhouse, probably."

"You've said that before. Just where is that?"

Charlemagne blinked at her in the rear-view mirror. "Look, did you ever have one of those spun-sugar Easter eggs? Look through the decorated hole in one end and what do you see? Fantasy land, that's what. A magic, supercolored world beyond belief, full of strange shapes and weird things. Well, that's what Peter's seeing."

Maybe so, she thought, maybe so. "But does he hear what we're saying?"

"He's in a state. When they're like that sometimes they hear, sometimes they don't."

"Why did he react the way he did?" Charlemagne had said Peter was married, so why the big thing about finding them doing it? Why was that such a grabber? Hell, Puritan America is dead, but maybe it's not buried yet, was that it? Better Peter should go off his rocker thinking about atomic-gas-germ war-fare, good old CBW, mayhem from the school lab, or the fouling of the sweet air, the water and soil.

"Look at it this way: middle-class morality, middle-class shock." Minnie thought it rather unkind, since Peter was right there beside her and might be hearing. But Charlemagne went right on: "A recurring phenomenon occasioned by conditioning. To avoid it in the future, I intend to abolish the normal taboos of sexual behavior and thereby create a more moral people. There will be no hypocrisy."

"The Council fathers be damned," Father Bischoff said bravely and immediately bit his tongue.

"Mark," continued Charlemagne. "We will no longer be a society of received manners and ideas. We shall each of us search for and reach fulfillment in his own way. The Society for the Liberated, I will call it."

Minnie smiled wryly. It was a fine thought, but she doubted it would come to pass for everyone. There were too many anchors, too many foot-draggers. But she had to admire Charlemagne's thrust and his over-all quest for reformation.

Father Bischoff turned around to rest an arm on the seat back and look at her. "I want to apologize. I do not think the body is a source of evil."

"I'm glad to hear you say that, Father."

"It's so difficult, veering away from the established order of things."

"Right on."

"I have, in fact, been giving the matter a great deal of thought."

"He masturbates," Andros said suddenly.

"Shame on you," she said. "So do I."

"You do?" Andros stared at her in amazement.

"Don't you?"

Andros reddened, dropped his head forward to stare down at the car floor. "Andros wanted to know how it felt, so I did it."

"It's sterile and unsatisfying," Father Bischoff said like a man who knows. "I seek a woman who longs to love God as I do, who longs to give of herself as I do."

"You can't have Minnie!" Andros leaned forward to glare at Father Bischoff. "She's mine!"

Charlemagne laughed. "Yours or Andros'?"

"Look here," Minnie said with some heat. "I'm not anybody's. I'm my own woman. Not chattel."

"The superwoman," Charlemagne said gleefully. "She's been born and she's with us. It's a two-edged sword from here on out. No more double standard."

"You could have laid a woman any time you wanted," Andros told Father Bischoff. "Why didn't you?"

"You're an agitator, that's what you are," Father Bischoff said, flaring. Stammering, cheeks blowing out: "You—you are full of all sorts of shitty frictional psychology."

Andros laughed. "Notes from a curdled celibate." He turned to Minnie. "He's crazy, you know."

"Look who's talking," Father Bischoff taunted. "A kid with a bug in his head."

Andros reddened, then raised his hand, palm forward. But Father Bischoff, knowing what was coming, turned around, facing forward, saying in a loud voice, "I don't want to hear any shitty poetry," and stuck his fingers in his ears.

"If a bigger bug won't bagel . . . better a bitter bugle should." Andros beamed at Minnie and sank back to the seat.

"Doggerel," Charlemagne said. "Right on time."

They were quiet and the scenery floated by in quiet splendor, and Minnie wished again that Peter would join them, see the world and share himself.

It was a state, Charlemagne said. Well, she'd had no experience with states, though she'd had an uncle, Uncle Earl Hamilberg, who she'd heard just sat in the same chair in the state hospital at Camarillo for twenty years, never speaking, lost in his own world, until he just withered up and died, and she often wondered if he died because nobody talked to him, let him know they knew he was there. Maybe finally Uncle Earl just gave up the ghost because he was convinced he didn't exist any more.

Everybody runs away, only some run farther than others. Herself, she'd run away from college, dissension and riots, and had hidden herself among the hippies because she could no longer face the doomsday fears and the plastic world gutted by guile, the world where one hand didn't know what the other was doing. The Indians were right: The white man did speak with forked tongue. All the time. So she'd tried it. She'd slept with a stranger tonight, many nights, too many nights, and she couldn't go home again even though she'd found the commune just as full of bullshit as the university, the revolutionaries and Philosophy 101.

She knew she could never speak to her parents again. No doubt they still believed there was a shining promised land there somewhere at the end of the rainbow and the President was taking them and everybody else there where beauty and justice would reign triumphant. They'd believed it every time there was a new President and she guessed they'd continue on that way until they were dead. She didn't hate them. In her way she loved them. But she couldn't stand to see them and crush their dream. Their—delusion? Talk about Charlemagne, Father Bischoff and Andros! There were so many things that, for her parents, simply did not exist. They weren't concerned about dehumanization, mechanization, depersonalization. If it were possible for her to ask them about it right this moment, they'd probably look bewildered and hurt and her mother would ask, "Just what do you mean, Minerva, dear? De-what?" So who was to blame? What was to do? Better let them have their plastic dreams and I'll have mine.

Then she thought: If my parents are deluded and I won't go back to them, what in God's name am I doing riding along with four deluded gentlemen? She understood that people who were in the asylums were, for the most part, sane and couldn't be told from other people except if you pushed the wrong button.

Well, that was true and yet it wasn't true. Peter had gone over the edge, but Father Bischoff and Andros were pretty much the same most of the time.

Andros seemed like a child in many ways. Maybe he just never grew up. No, she remembered, feeling a pleasant tingle in her cheeks, he was grown up, all right. Maybe his mother never paid any attention to him. Father Bischoff. What about him? Scared to death of the Council fathers. Sometimes she thought he was more afraid of himself. How was Therin trying to cure them?

Charlemagne. She was having doubts about him. His brain seemed twisted, all right, but he was sharp. He knew things her professors had never known. Was he really insane? She couldn't, for the life of her, think of him that way. Maybe she'd never pressed the right button.

She looked past Peter's unmoving profile out past the fences and trees to a lonely cemetery on a hill, and she thought: The most beautiful places left in this country are the cemeteries. They are uncluttered and green, and they are given tender, loving care. And then there is the silence, the wonderful silence, just the soft soughing of the wind in the trees and the gentle buzzing of bees and the chatter of birds. Of course there was a reason for the silence. They were usually far removed from the American pyramids, the freeways.

Soon maybe they'd be gone. Where are we going to bury all the dead?

The only sure thing in this world is change; the old things were passing, like the scenery, old ideas, old ways, old people. Now it was the era of the four-letter word, and love was one of them, probably the most important, race was another, and unfortunately hate was a word, too. Why did people get so uptight about words? For the same reason doctors study disease and not health, Charlemagne had said.

And he was so right.

"Are you sure you'll be all right?" Charlemagne asked Father Bischoff in the early evening in the parking lot of Le Comte's, one of the more exclusive, larger department stores in the city.

"I am not an altered rubric, if that is what you mean," Father Bischoff replied without conviction. "I have been properly sanctified." It was evident he was terrified to stay with Peter while Charlemagne, Minnie and Andros went into the store. "I shall pray the entire time you are gone."

Charlemagne was doubtful about the arrangement, but as he'd said, he did not know what to do with Peter; he did not want to leave him alone in the car in his state, and he did want Minnie with him. "I confess I don't trust my own judgment in buying clothes," he had said. "It was always Marietta's province."

"But the clothes you bought for yourself are tasteful," Minnie pointed out. "They're just right for you."

"An old friend, Spencer Perkins, did the honors in Oblout, but I didn't want to make any more purchases there."

"Peace be with you," Father Bischoff said as they moved off.

"Andros doesn't like this," Andros said petulantly, dragging his feet as they neared the store. Charlemagne had made it plain the clothes he'd be buying would be for Andros.

"How does he know he doesn't like it?" Charlemagne asked sharply. "He's not doing it yet. Come on."

Minnie linked her arm with Andros' and they were able to move on.

Just inside the door on the main floor was what looked like several acres of toys and games, and Andros was instantly struck dumb by the sight of it, and he moved like a person hypnotized from row to row, aisle to aisle, his eyes round and bright with his wonder. Le Comte clerks, with the radar indigenous to such terrain, kept a wary eye on the young man in the stained blue sweater.

"He was a deprived child," Charlemagne said as he and Minnie followed him, to see Andros disappear beneath a counter in pursuit of a mechanical racing car he had inadvertently started.

"How do you know that?"

"I saw his case history."

"How in the world could you ever do that?"

"By looking at it."

They moved around the aisle corner to find Andros emerging from under the counter with a large robot. He set it up in the middle of the aisle, pressed a button. The robot started off, saying, "Earthmen, you are doomed" in a deep, rumbling voice.

Several clerks were converging on Andros, who was oblivious to what else was happening, having eyes only for the robot, which was saying, "Earthmen, you are doomed," over and over, walking in a waddle straight down the aisle.

"Young man," a saleswoman said severely, "what do you think you're doing?"

"We are doomed," Andros said with a laugh. "Didn't you hear?" He started after the robot, saw a large, wicked-looking weapon on display, labeled COMMANDER CORKIN'S FAMOUS DEATH RAY WEAPON, and, in smaller letters, "Space Ace's famous laser beam carries three light-years—disintegrates anything it illuminates." Andros snatched it off the display rack and hurried after the robot, stopping once to fire it. A bell inside the gun clanged shrilly, a fast-pulsing light came from out of the barrel, and Andros shouted gleefully "Gotcha!" and continued after the doom-saying robot.

Andros' way was suddenly blocked by a large man in a dark suit with a carnation in his lapel and wearing a stern face.

"Look out!" Andros said, and when the man did not budge, he raised the gun and fired it in his face.

The floorwalker fell back against the counter with a gasp, Andros moving on to the waddling robot, shooting spectators on the way and laughing wildly.

Everyone—salespeople, the floorwalker, Charlemagne, Minnie and the spectators—came on Andros and the robot at the same time, the floorwalker taking his arm in righteous wrath.

"Andros doesn't like that," Andros warned him, his eyes beginning to cloud with anger.

116

"Andros? Who's Andros?"

"An extraterrestrial," Andros said before jerking his arm away.

"Let me have that," the floorwalker said, reaching for the death-ray gun.

Andros obliged, firing it in his face again.

"Excuse me," Charlemagne said calmly, moving to the floorwalker. "I can explain this."

"You do that," the floorwalker said, mopping his forehead with his handkerchief. "If you are responsible for this . . . this . . ." He could not find words to describe Andros. "What's the matter with him, anyway?"

"A comparison shopper is all," Charlemagne said. He turned to Andros. "It's over now. Return the gun, please. We're through here."

Andros gave the floorwalker the gun, but the floorwalker was not satisfied as Charlemagne took Andros' arm. "Just a minute there, you two."

Charlemagne turned to regard him coldly. "Does the name Gallimaufry mean anything to you?"

"Gallimaufry? I'm afraid not."

"Just as I thought." Charlemagne produced a small notebook from an inside pocket. "What is your name?" He now withdrew a ballpoint pen and prepared to write the name.

"I'm not required to give you my name."

"Then you are in trouble and when Gallimaufry gets the report . . . Well, I can't promise anything. I suppose you don't realize that even at this moment with a zoom lens and parabolic reflector this entire scene is being videotaped?"

"I don't believe it."

Charlemagne said, as he wrote in the notebook, "Credibility stability: negative."

Salespeople had begun to move off at the beginning of the hassle. Few remained. The floorwalker's face didn't have to be saved any more. "Look, I don't know any Gallimaufry or any videotape thing, whatever that is—"

"It's a wonder they wouldn't let you in on the security system. How long have you been employed here?"

"Let's forget it, shall we?" He tried to smile. "My name's Harrison, and I'm sorry all this happened."

"No more sorry than we are," Charlemagne said, making a few more notes. He snapped the notebook closed, regarded Harrison with disdain, said, "They'll be in touch," and took Andros' arm with one hand, Minnie's with the other and moved off.

In the men's department they had more difficulty with Andros.

"May I help you?" a clerk who looked very much like De Gaulle said as he approached them. He was all manners and had a thick accent.

"We want a complete outfit for this young man," Charlemagne said, indicating Andros, who stood looking back toward the toy department. "Nothing tailored. It must be ready to wear."

"Of course, Monsieur," the clerk said, taking Andros' measure visually and appalled by what he was wearing. "I can assure you Le Comte's is more than equal to the task. This way." He bowed slightly in Old World elegance and indicated they were to follow him.

Charlemagne and Minnie selected item after item for Andros to try on, but he liked nothing, exhibiting a vast indifference to tapered shirts, blazers, sports coats, crushed-velvet things, flared slacks.

The clerk, in his frustration, after a disapproving look to Charlemagne and Minnie, who had not asked Andros' preferences, asked Andros, "Perhaps Monsieur would like to make his own selections?"

Andros clearly had not considered this. He blinked several times, then moved around making choices. He ended up with a glittering gilt suit, a metal belt, outrageous dayglo pink slacks and crimson moccasins.

The clerk looked as if he were going to be ill.

Charlemagne then said to him, *"Il s'agit d'un problème spe-cial ici, vous comprenez, Monsieur?"*

The clerk's tired eyes sparked to life. *"Bien sûr, Monsieur."*

"Malheureusement mon fils est un peu fou. Ne l'écoutez pas, il faut l'habiller proprement."

"C'est dommage," the clerk said, shaking his head sadly and regarding Andros with mournful Gallic eyes.

"Il faut être ferme."

"Je comprends," the clerk said, rising to the challenge. *"Je le traite comme s'il était le mien."*

Andros was demolished by the clerk's gentle but firm insist-ence, submitting but protesting, throwing glances of help me to Charlemagne and Minnie, who retired from the arena to watch the clerk, who clucked and nodded and shook his head as he tried one thing and then another, sometimes pursing his lips, standing back now and then to judge the effect.

"What in the world did you say to him?" Minnie asked.

"I told him Andros was my mentally ill son and that he should dress him so he doesn't look that way."

Minnie shook her head, then she studied him through nar-rowed eyes. "You tame a floorwalker, you speak French, you know so many things I don't . . . I don't understand."

"Don't try, Minerva." He gently patted her hand.

"You're not like them—Andros or Father Bischoff or Peter. I've been meaning to say that to you."

"Of course I'm not. Everyone's different."

"Charlemagne, you're not insane."

"Of course I'm not insane. Are you?"

"Don't go getting me off the track. I mean you're playing it all like a game. You're putting it all on."

"Then I must be insane." He smiled. "After all, isn't that what insane people do?"

"I wouldn't know. All I know is you change. You shift gears all the time. When you're with me you're different from the way you are with them."

He laughed, put a hand on her arm, squeezed. "I love you when you're so serious."

"Don't change the subject. There are the case histories you know about, the way you handle people—"

"I'm merely adjustable, that's all."

"Chameleon-like. You seem to know what everybody wants."

"Is that bad?"

"No, but it's not the way an inmate of a private sanitarium would act."

"Are you a doctor now, Minerva?"

"And there's more, there's something more I feel, the things you're doing . . ."

"Of course there's more. There's the holy crusade, for example."

"Is there? Is there *really* a holy crusade?"

"I would be disappointed if you didn't think so. We're going after the Holy Grail, remember?"

"Now you're playing games with me again."

Charlemagne's eyes lost their devilish glitter and for a time he seemed more interested in the deep blue of her eyes than in answering, but in the end he said, "I'm not playing games, Minerva. I'm—what?—living, I suppose, just like Father Bischoff, Andros and Peter, and like you, too. Does it matter how we do that? Shouldn't it be done with a certain levity, abandon and hope? Shouldn't we soar a little in the process?"

"Charlemagne," she said, shaking her head and smiling at the same time, "you have the damnedest faculty for being able to convince me of anything."

His eyes left her face, became moody as he looked off. "The world should be made up of Minervas."

The clerk brought an abject Andros to them. He looked uncomfortable in his expensive tan shoes with heel cleats, light brown trousers of good weave, wide leather belt, dark brown tapered shirt with matching tie. The clerk, who had a pinstripe deep brown and black sports coat over his arm, now proceeded to put it on the suffering Andros, patted it in place and stepped away, pleased.

They looked at him, nodding. Minnie said, "Andros, you look like a movie star!"

"I do?" He walked to a three-way mirror and looked at himself, his spirits rising until he finally smiled as he turned back to them. "Andros thinks I do, too."

"Don't get any fancy ideas," Charlemagne said. "We can't lose a good soldier."

Before they left the men's department Andros owned more slacks, sports shirts and sweaters, shoes and even the crimson moccasins, a special concession, and this pleased him. Charlemagne, who had taken Peter's measurements, also purchased a comparable wardrobe for him, sending it all out to the car with Andros.

The people in the toy department held their breath until he was out the door.

The De Gaulle-like clerk held up the stained sweater, the old tennis shoes and thin slacks.

"Incinerate them," Charlemagne said.

The clerk looked happy at the prospect.

Andros joined them in the women's department, where he watched himself in his new clothes in mirrors and inspected the merchandise and salesgirls while Minnie and Charlemagne were waited on by a bevy of saleswomen. Andros was particularly drawn to panty girdles, brassieres and the variety of lacy underthings, smiling as he was approached and inquired after, telling them all he was just looking, and receiving answering you-go-right-ahead smiles.

Minnie told Charlemagne she felt like Queen of the May with all the things he was buying for her, including three new miniskirts, three pairs of slacks, an ersatz fur coat (it looked like leopard), three pairs of shoes, two for casual wear and one for more formal occasions.

"Oh, Charlemagne!" she said as she held up one slinky gown

that was very expensive, a bias-cut hammered satin gown slit to the waist in back and fastened with rhinestone buttons. "When would I ever wear this?" It was simple and sexy and she betrayed herself by drooling over it.

"State occasions," he said, not batting an eye.

None of the clerks batted an eye.

She put it on and when she came out one of the clerks who had been hovering like a mothering hen said she looked exquisite in it.

"It's not me," she said. "I'm the earthy type."

"You think earthy," Charlemagne said, "but in that gown you look properly enigmatic and eminently available."

"Available?" She looked at him anxiously. "Really, Charlemagne?"

"Come on, Minerva, every woman wants to look available."

She turned to look at herself in a mirror and moved this way and that. "Well," she said, "up from the commune. Clotheshorse Minnie, I'll be known as."

There were also blouses, costume jewelry, plenty of hose, robes, pajamas, slinky things made from very soft, clingy fabrics like crepe and jersey, and there was a long-sleeved lavender chiffon Empire nightgown.

"But I don't even wear anything in bed!" she protested.

"Wear it before you go to bed."

"I hope wherever we go they have steam heat."

Still Charlemagne did not stop. He insisted she stock up on perfume and cosmetics, including a fancy traveling case with a mirror and a light that could be plugged into the 110.

"Where are we going to put it all? There isn't enough room in the trunk."

"There's enough room."

She bit her lip as she saw the packages piling up. "I feel like crying," she said. "My eyes are all steamed over. See?" She turned to him and he smiled. "Oh, Charlemagne, it's all so wonderful, I can't believe it. I never realized I'd be such a willing traitor to the self-denial I've been practicing."

"Asceticism isn't becoming to you," he said. "You look

pretty being seduced by the Establishment. So relax and enjoy it."

"I always do," she said, kissing him.

The clerks smiled.

Their last stop was not in any department at Le Comte's but many blocks away at Teremont Church Supplies, where, with some apprehension, they left Andros in the car with the still mute Peter, but Charlemagne insisted it be done; he wanted Minnie to accompany him and Father Bischoff.

Father Bischoff, who had seen all the packages they'd put in the trunk, the new outfits Andros and Minnie were wearing, said nothing as they got out but looked curiously tense.

When they reached the door of the supply house, he did not move to go in with them but stood still, looking through the glass doors, terrified.

"Come on," Charlemagne said, taking his arm.

"I can't!" he said suddenly, wrenching away. "I really can't!" He looked close to tears.

Charlemagne moved to him, looked him in the eye severely. "Are you Father Bischoff or not?"

"Yes," he said miserably, hanging his head. "I'm Father Bischoff, all right, but I can't go in there. The Council fathers—"

Charlemagne shook his head. "You're not Father Bischoff," he said with great disdain. "You're on no holy crusade or anything. You're just Howard Petersen."

Father Bischoff's head jerked to Charlemagne's, his mouth dropping open. It seemed for a moment he would take flight much the way Peter had, his mouth working, his tongue moving around, his eyes opening and closing.

"The rite of homage," Charlemagne said acidly, "that meant nothing. You owe no fealty, not to me, not to Andros or Peter, not even to Minerva."

"I do," Father Bischoff said in agony. "Oh, I do, I do, but—"

"But what?"

"They won't believe me, those people in there."

Charlemagne went to him, put a hand on each arm and looked up into Father Bischoff's troubled eyes, for Father Bischoff was taller than he. "I believe you, Father," he said gently. "I am your parish of one. Isn't that enough? And if it isn't, ask Minerva if she believes."

Father Bischoff turned tortured eyes to Minnie.

Minnie was choked up by what was happening, but she managed to say, "I believe, Father," and meant it.

"You see?" Charlemagne said.

Father Bischoff shut his eyes tight, tears leaking out at the edges, and for a while it seemed they had lost him, but when he opened his eyes they weren't the same and neither was he.

"Thy will be done," Father Bischoff said.

They moved inside.

"Let me introduce Father Bischoff," Charlemagne said to the white-haired man who moved to them as they neared the service area. The clerk eyed Father Bischoff's windbreaker, denim pants and brown suede shoes doubtfully. "The good Father's been away and he's lost everything, including his clothes, except for what he has on—all his clerical garb, everything. It was all he could do to keep himself together in the terrible place he was, and we're proud to say he was lucky enough to escape with his life. He needs a brand-new outfit."

The clerk turned to Father Bischoff with shock and admiration. "I'm sorry to hear that, Father," he said, then checked himself, coloring. "I didn't mean that the way it sounded. What church are you with?"

"Lately of St. Stephen's," Father Bischoff said grandly. "A fine old church, a wonderful parish. As it was, I was sent to do God's bidding in a more stringent area, as this gentleman has informed you."

"We're passing through," Charlemagne explained. "We're on our way to do holy work among the aborigines and don't have much time."

"Of course," the clerk said, blinking and unsettled. "Where shall we begin? Clerical apparel?"

"As good a place as any," Father Bischoff said. "I'll need shirts, albs, surplices. Cleric shirts for summer and winter, a cassock or two, birettas, capes, ferraiolos, collars and accessories."

"My, you did lose everything, didn't you?" The clerk got out a pad. "Let me put down your sizes. Have you been wearing Cathedral A or C, a Pontiff two or three?"

"I tell you," Father Bischoff said, putting a hand to his head in horrible recollection. "I can't seem to remember."

"It was terrible," Charlemagne said.

"I understand. We'll have to measure."

"He's lost weight," Minnie said. "It was such a harrowing experience."

"Of course. Were you wearing mostly black or gray?"

"Some gray and some black," Father Bischoff said. "I don't remember that either."

"We have some handsome shirt fronts of faille crepe with plain bosom and some with adjustable waistband." The clerk paused. "Perhaps we'd better get our heads together back here." He motioned Father Bischoff to come through the counter gate.

Father Bischoff nodded solemnly to Charlemagne and Minnie and went through to the fitting room.

19

THERIN REGARDED his image in the mirror in the small lavatory in Dr. Tillheimer's offices as he washed his hands, thinking, This face I see is the face of a man in love, but it doesn't look different from what it usually looks like except the events of the past few days have made it more haggard. Or is it the sweet anguish of being without Minnie that is giving it that gaunt look?

Situational preoccupation, aura fixation, temporary insanity, a reasonable animal desire to lessen the sexual distance between his body and hers, a desire to lessen the social distance as well—Therin had used these terms many times when trying to explain the phenomenon of love to distressed patients. Now he found the terms descriptive but not at all helpful.

The truth was: He loved Minnie. Minnie wasn't there. He felt awful because she wasn't there and he didn't know where she was.

He dried his hands and went to the desk Dr. Tillheimer was letting him use for the conference with Marietta Le Moyne, feeling very much like his image in the mirror. He had never in his life spent such terrible days. Tuesday had started as days that are strung out in a row begin, uneventful except for rain after breakfast, until the morning group when the defection of four of his patients was discovered, and followed on Wednesday by the tragedy of Minnie's disappearance in his car.

On Thursday he hungered more for the sight of Minnie than he did the car, but he refused to do what Elizabeth demanded: make a report of a stolen vehicle, naming Minnie. He would not have done that at this time even if he knew her last name. He was angered, shamed, and yet filled with his love for her, and he wondered how it was possible he could feel all three things so keenly at once.

And on Thursday Mrs. Le Moyne called. He had forgotten about her. She was outraged, and he couldn't blame her. Charlemagne had been there at the house, she said, and he'd wrecked the place. Not only that, the neighbors saw three men and a girl (*a girl!*) with him, "and God only knows what awful things they did here, the way this place looks."

He tried to explain that he had tried to reach her, but all the time his heart was racing. They were *all* in Oblout, *and there was a girl with them!* Could the girl be Minnie? When he interrupted her to ask questions, Mrs. Le Moyne became very curt and said she was coming up on Friday to see him; he'd better have some answers. Then she hung up.

Therin immediately advised the sheriff's office and the state police of this new development. He debated leaving Berylwood and going to Oblout to look for them (what you really mean is look for Minnie, don't you, Doctor?) and then reasoned this would not solve anything. He spent the rest of the day waiting for calls that never came.

Then this morning he received in the mail the car keys and a brief, scrawled note (not in Minnie's handwriting) informing him that he would find his car in the parking lot of Jack's Supermarket in Oblout. He called Elizabeth, but she was still full of righteous anger and said things about a girl who'd do a thing like that, bite the hand that fed her, etc. Therin did not bother to argue. He told her he would take a bus to Oblout and get the car that evening.

"You won't find her there, Therin," Elizabeth said, then severed the connection.

He sat holding the cold phone wondering at the meaning of those words. Did she know? Or was it that she thought he wanted to find Minnie to make her atone for taking the car?

Therin broke off the thought. It was Mrs. Le Moyne he had to worry about and he simply did not feel up to her, his mind being miles away with Minnie, remembering her blue eyes (maybe they were not true blue but he loved them anyway), the way she had about herself, alternating long, pensive looks of quiet intensity with moments of sheer shining delight, full of laughter, caprice, health, biting his cheek, and then becoming tremulous in his arms, so merrily alive, touching him, whispering in his ear, her breath on his cheek . . .

He checked himself again before he became too feverishly agitated and wondering why Elizabeth didn't seem to matter any more and knowing it was wrong and feeling terribly virginal and bewildered—and sad, too, because he was so hopelessly in love.

Where was Minnie? Had they kidnaped her? Was she in danger?

He realized he was sweating and the room was not that warm. He brought his mind back to the business at hand, picked up the folder on LE MOYNE, CHARLES. He must not be caught not remembering every aspect of the case, recalling his previous encounters with Mrs. Le Moyne with no great pleasure.

He had found her at their first meeting a headstrong woman with an ego strength that went off-scale, and he remembered wondering at the time how Charlemagne, whom he'd talked to briefly, could have ever married such a stern and demanding woman, but felt it must be that she had not remained what she was or that Charlemagne might have himself been responsible for the change (if there was any) in view of his behavior in more recent years.

She had recounted (and the routine Berylwood investigation had proved) that they had met at the University of Illinois when he was a graduate student and she was in her third year. They had married, she'd given up school and helped him by working so he could earn his doctorate without financial qualms. He'd taken a position at Oblout University in the history department, which she confessed she argued against because Oblout was a relatively small school and she had expected him to reach farther, and he was, at the time of his Berylwood admission, a professor of medieval history, which she thought was beneath him.

"Charles never advanced. He'd been passed over every time in favor of younger men. He was there for over twenty years and should have been head of the department at least, but he said many times he was perfectly satisfied to be where he was. If it hadn't been for the prize money, we'd have had no life at all." The prize money, the records showed, was fifty thousand dollars he had won on a television quiz show as an expert on medieval history.

"It was hardly fair," she'd told Therin, "since that's his specialty, but we took the money. That was twenty years ago and we've still got most of it. Charles simply never went anywhere, never did anything. He was just steeped in his subject, rooted in it." And when Therin asked her if he fantasized much about it, she replied, "Only twenty-four hours a day."

Therin was inclined not to believe Mrs. Le Moyne, but when she'd committed her husband for the ninety-day observation period, she'd had everything she needed, all legal and well documented. The crux of the report was that her husband was beginning to believe he was living in medieval times and that he was, in fact, Charlemagne (an ordinary enough delusion for him, considering his profession, though most people seemed to gravitate toward being Jesus Christ or some other well-known figure of power and authority).

Mrs. Le Moyne's position—and she stated this emphatically —was that her husband's insistence "on this ridiculous role" was embarrassing to her, a source of great pain and bewilderment, and Therin could understand that after his first conference with Charlemagne. He made no hasty judgment, however. He would have his report at Staff in ninety days.

Mrs. Le Moyne's report further stated that her husband was in the habit of inviting his students to the house, where, in the backyard, they would build and experiment with catapults, crossbows, weapons of siege and other armaments, all kinds of spears (the *escrime nouvelle* as well as the *escrime ancienne*, both with and without pennons and gonfalons which the girls in the classes made), swords, battle axes, maces and other instruments of destruction. Her husband insisted these forays actually gave his students the look and feel of medieval times, and Mrs. Le Moyne was willing to concede this, except that it seemed more evident to her that it was symptomatic of his illness.

The report delineated how several missent arrows were inadvertently fired, to be imbedded in the house walls, most of them so deeply they had to be broken off rather than pulled out. Once an old worn-out half-horsepower motor was placed in a catapult as a weight, but something gave way and the motor was sent arcing through the air to crash through the back-porch roof, down through a deck chair and on through the floor into the crawl space. Rather than try to get it out from where it finally came to rest, Charlemagne "at least had the good sense to repair both roof and floor."

The straw that Mrs. Le Moyne said "broke her back" was "the incident in Oblout Park." Charlemagne and one of his students, Carl (Burly Boy) Bingham, a six-footer who played end on the football team, one afternoon rented two horses from Carlyle's Stables, some chain-mail armor, swords, shields and accessories from Oblout Costumery, and proceeded to joust, being cheered on by his classes, some of whom were dressed in home-made period costumes and waving what banderoles were not attached to lances.

In the middle of the medieval pageant and jousting exhibition, Charlemagne suddenly turned his horse toward Burly Boy and shouted, "*A outrance!*" (To the death!), confessing later he suddenly had a violent antipathy toward Burly Boy, who he said never listened to his lectures anyway, and spurring his mount, Tencendur, with his sword, Joyeuse, whirling about his head, charged full tilt at Burly Boy, whom he called his hated enemy, Marsilion. Burly Boy was so terrified by the ferocity of Charlemagne's charge that he dropped his own sword and shield and sped out of the park at a gallop, Charlemagne in hot pursuit. They lost each other in automobile traffic.

Since the newspaper had been invited to send a reporter and photographer, the event was reported in vivid detail in the Oblout *Observer*. And this, Mrs. Le Moyne declared, caused her great shame and ridicule.

She said she was subject to more indignities, but when Charlemagne talked seriously of taking to the road to recruit an army to fight the Saracens, she gave up hope of his ever regaining his sanity and sought the aid of the people at Berylwood instead.

20

WHEN MRS. LE MOYNE entered the office, Therin rose to greet her. He was startled to find he hardly recognized her. Gone was the old coarse salt-and-pepper hair, and in its place was a chestnut wig that made her look years younger. She'd also had something done to her nose, and her face had been lifted. Unlike the dowdy things she'd worn two months before, she now wore a frilly white blouse and a velvetlike green skirt that ended inches above her knees. Of the old Mrs. Le Moyne only the reproachful look in the eyes remained.

She literally flounced in to drop into one of the chairs by Dr. Tillheimer's desk, and as she did so Therin looked toward her male companion, who stopped near the door. He was chubby, his eyes were large and brown, he was clean-shaven, pink-cheeked, and his face had a petulant air created, Therin decided, by the pouting fat lips. He was nearly bald.

"This is Mr. Colbert," Marietta Le Moyne said, waving languidly in Colbert's general direction. "Dr. Sheckley." She seemed so cool and collected that Therin felt a little unsettled. He didn't need any more trouble. Keep calm, he told himself, it may not be as bad as it looks.

Therin met Colbert's eyes. They reflected a mixture of distrust and disdain. He disliked him at once. On the other hand, he instructed himself, keep an open mind, Doctor. Colbert nodded. Therin said, "Mr. Colbert," pleasantly and sat down, hoping that the low-pressure area that had invaded the office would not blow up a storm.

Why did she have to come? Why was this Colbert person with her? His mind would rather be Minnie-occupied. Had Minnie, for example, left a note in the car? Perhaps there was something in the glove compartment, a cryptic message she wrote when the others weren't looking, slipping it in there, a note that would say, in essence, Help me, Therin, I love you, and perhaps giving some clue as to where they might be taking her. If they were taking her anywhere, if it was Minnie, if, if, if . . .

"Doctor," Marietta said, impaling him with such a cold glance all his thoughts froze. "Where did he go?" And when he stared at her blankly trying to guess what she meant, she went on, "Charles. It *is* Charles I came here to talk about."

"I don't know, Mrs. Le Moyne." He cleared his throat. Give nothing, take nothing. "I thought perhaps you might have some idea."

Colbert moved to stand behind Marietta, ignoring the other chairs in the room. My God, Therin thought, his eyes are colder than hers.

"Dr. Sheckley, I want to know why my husband was allowed to escape."

"Escape?" This would be easy. Explain it, ease them out. He leaned back in Dr. Tillheimer's chair. "Mrs. Le Moyne, this is not a high-security institution, not a prison. Your husband was not held behind locked doors."

"He should have been. You should see what he did to the house. He wrecked the bathroom, emptied every drawer. It's a wonder he didn't set fire to it."

"Are you sure he is responsible for all that? He did not impress me as the violent type."

"Just how did he impress you, Doctor?"

There was a strange eagerness behind her eyes. Therin said carefully, "I haven't completed my diagnosis."

She thought about that for a moment. "Just what is being done about finding him and returning him here?"

"We did what we always do in such cases. We listed him AWOL with the sheriff's office and the state police."

"Then they are looking for him?"

"They're on the lookout, yes."

"What will they do when they find him?"

"Notify us."

"They won't arrest him?"

"Why should they? He's broken no law." Therin sensed an acceptance of the procedure. A little shoring up of confidence might help. He smiled, shifted, put his elbows on the desk. If it all went as well as this, the end of the interview might be near. "The way we see it, when a patient goes so far as to walk out of here, it's a good sign. It means he is willing to accept the world out there on its terms rather than on his, and that's what treatment is all about."

"Brainwashing," Colbert said suddenly.

"What?"

"Brainwashing," Colbert repeated as if he knew unequivocally. "That's all it is."

"Mr. Colbert—"

"Mr. Colbert is a private investigator," Marietta said, as if that explained everything, turning reproving eyes to Colbert.

"I was not in favor of coming here," he told her.

Therin was unable to unravel the skein. "I didn't quite catch your meaning about brainwashing, Mr. Colbert." As Colbert's eyes met his he realized the man's face never changed. No emotion showed. The eyes were like fish eyes. Therin wondered if he ever laughed.

"You psychiatrists are all alike. You only understand things when you want to."

"I really don't follow you."

"Mr. Colbert!" Marietta said sharply.

But Colbert was not to be stopped. "Who do you get your orders from?"

"Orders?" Therin tried to forget the hostility to deal with the question. "Dr. Tillheimer is director of Berylwood, but the manner of treatment is purely up to me. He only advises when procedural questions arise."

"Doubletalk. You fellows are good at that."

Therin could feel his hackles rising, decided to say nothing, maybe Colbert would lay out his hand.

Encouraged, Colbert went on. "You take some poor man,

134

twist his mind, suck every bit of individuality out of him, bend him to your will, then push him out when he is no longer able to think for himself."

Mr. Colbert, Therin decided, was so far right he was out of sight, paranoid about paranoia. Easy does it with this type. "Mr. Colbert, it so happens—"

"You ever hear of that Commie—Pavlov?"

Therin, with masterful control, said, "The conditioned reflex is a simple psychological fact."

The brown eyes glowed with a kind of wild exhilaration. "You'd like to get everybody in here, wouldn't you, make them all alike, sheep! And the ones who won't bend, there's always electrical shock, drugs, isn't there? You can't fool me. You get to them one way or another."

"Believe me," Marietta said quickly, "Mr. Colbert is a good investigator. That's why I hired him."

"Is that a fact?" Therin said coldly.

The glow left Colbert's eyes. He turned away to look at the pictures on Dr. Tillheimer's walls.

Therin turned to Marietta. "Why did you bring him here?"

She did not answer at once, eying him speculatively, as if pondering the next move. "My attorney tells me you and Berylwood could be held legally responsible for what Charles has done."

Therin laughed. "For wrecking his own bathroom? That hardly seems likely." He did not tell her Berylwood would not like the exposure.

"Not for wrecking the bathroom but for not exercising due care while he was in your custody."

There was no doubt she meant it, but Therin felt he was on firm ground here. "Your husband isn't a package, a commodity, Mrs. Le Moyne. He's a human being with certain rights under the law."

"Then you must surely know, Dr. Sheckley, that a man with an unsound mind has fewer rights under those laws."

Therin found himself wondering if the prize money had anything to do with it. "You mean until his mental condition can be proved unsound, Mrs. Le Moyne. I think the term is by explicit evidence, not conjectural proof."

She wasn't fazed at all. "Papers are being drawn up making me Charles's guardian. The case will stand with or without your corroboration, from what my attorney tells me."

It must be the money. It had to be the money.

She went on: "Charles withdrew twenty-three thousand dollars from our savings account."

It *was* the money. He felt a twinge of admiration for Charlemagne.

"And if Charles isn't apprehended, I intend to sue Berylwood for that amount and more."

It had gone as far as he could allow it. He reached for the phone. "I'm going to call Dr. Tillheimer."

Marietta reached over, put a cool hand over his. "I wouldn't do that, Doctor." And now Colbert turned from the pictures and moved to them. She said, "With your cooperation I think we can dispense with Dr. Tillheimer."

Therin kept his hand on the phone and looked from one to the other. They wanted him to do something, probably something unethical, and he knew he wasn't going to do it. He should call Dr. Tillheimer.

"Speed is essential," she said. "If we can locate Charles before he spends the money, there will be no need for legal action."

Therin thought it out. The legal-action bit was pure bluff, he was sure of that. But speed *was* essential. If Charlemagne could be located, then Minnie would be, too, if they were together, and he was fairly certain they were. And putting aside Colbert's silly-assed view of psychiatry, maybe he was a good investigator, could do more than the police, especially if the runaways left the state. In that case, it would be wise to have someone on their trail. He thought about ethics, about Elizabeth, his own ambivalence. He also thought: Of such internal stresses are psychoses made. There had to be a way out of this, a reasonable way that could be rewarding to all, not that he was in favor of Mrs. Le Moyne getting the money back—it wasn't all hers anyway—but his need to have Minnie, to *save* Minnie, was important. He withdrew his hand.

"That's better," Marietta said, smiling, leaning back in her chair.

He would let her think she was convincing him of something, let her go on, see what she had in mind. He could always refuse to cooperate. He had nothing to lose.

"Now," she said as if she had the situation well in hand, "you told me when Charles was admitted you were going to talk to him privately and monitor—I think you said—what went on in his group. Isn't that right?"

"Roughly, yes."

"So you've been with him for nearly six weeks. I think that's fine, even if Mr. Colbert doesn't. We don't see eye to eye on everything. Anyway, Charles has needed someone to listen to him besides me, someone to help him see himself as he really is."

What was she babbling about? Where was she going?

"So you've heard him, you've listened to his crazy—yes, crazy—ideas. But I know you must have discovered he isn't always . . . off. Much of the time he makes sense and doesn't talk so . . . obliquely?"

"Mrs. Le Moyne—"

"Let me go on. What I was getting to is, considering all the time you've been with him or near him, he must have hinted at some plan, some purpose, some *thing* he was going to do. It may even have been very vague. Now didn't he do that, Doctor?"

Therin felt sorry for her. Evidently she had pinned some hopes on his being able to tell her what Charlemagne was up to. "Really, Mrs. Le Moyne, I'm not at liberty to discuss anything about your husband. It wouldn't be ethical. You should know that."

Marietta continued to smile sweetly, fetchingly. "Charles was really a good man, Doctor. Believe me, he was. A very *dear* man. It's just that—well, he was always so full of big plans. Most of them he never carried out. But now he's done something, and if you would just stop and think about it for a moment . . . It would surely help out a lot if you could give us a hint as to what his plans are."

Colbert said, "A man doesn't take twenty-three thousand dollars out of the bank for nothing. Not in my book he doesn't."

"There must have been *something*, Doctor." She was very intense, leaning forward. She almost whispered: "If you tell us, it will be, as they say, off the record. Isn't that right, Mr. Colbert?"

Colbert nodded.

It was ridiculous and Therin was tiring of it. They'd come up to Berylwood on a wild-goose chase and they were not only wasting their time but his. "Look, if it will make you feel any better, your husband never mentioned any plans. When he and the other three patients walked out of here—"

"Patients!" Marietta said shrilly. "You mean to tell me those other men with him were sick people, too?"

"Now we're getting somewhere," Colbert said, whipping out a notebook and hoisting his ample rump to Dr. Tillheimer's desk. "What were their names?"

"Get your ass off my desk." Therin was shocked by his own vehemence. It wasn't even his desk. He mustn't let Colbert get to him. As Colbert stood up, his demeanor unchanged, pencil poised, Therin said, "I'm sorry. It's been a hectic week." For something to do he blew his nose. "You must know I'm not at liberty to give you their names." Thinking of Charlemagne, Andros, Peter and Father Bischoff being with Minnie at the moment made him feel uncomfortable. Maybe he was overreacting. After all, Minnie was twenty-six, could take care of herself. Couldn't she? But would she be prepared for what she would encounter with these men? He supposed it was possible any one of them could become unstrung, highly disturbed.

Marietta was looking at him through narrowed eyes. "There was a girl," she said in surprising clairvoyance. "A girl in a miniskirt. Was she a patient, too?"

"No." His heart lurched at the thought of Minnie again. Could there be doubt any longer? It had to be Minnie. He sighed. "If it's the girl I think it is, her name is Minnie." They looked at him curiously, and he could understand their bewilderment. "She was staying with my wife and me. She dropped me off here in my car. They must have seized her and the car, driven to Oblout in it. I received the keys in the mail this morning. A note said the car was abandoned at a supermarket in Oblout."

Colbert, who had been scribbling in the notebook, looked up. "What's her last name?"

"I don't know."

"You don't know?"

"All she ever wanted to be called was Minnie. She said her friends called her Minnie the Pooh."

Colbert's fish eyes blinked several times. "You must be joking."

"I am not joking."

"She stayed with you and your wife, you say. And you never got her last name."

"That is correct."

Marietta said gently, "What did she look like?"

If Colbert was going to go looking for them, it wouldn't hurt to tell. "She is shorter than I, about five feet four. She has blue eyes, deep blue eyes." Yes, eyes that engendered rapport, mischievous eyes, eyes that he might never see again. "She has a lively disposition, dark hair. She was—yes, I would say most people would think her beautiful." Minnie, I love you. Did I ever tell you that? I mean really come out and say it? No, and I should have. "Very fine features. Twenty-six. Looks like Natalie Wood." Yes, she did, damn it. He'd never thought of that before. "And when I last saw her she was wearing a miniskirt." He remembered all too well how she looked on that final drive to the sanitarium, not knowing it would be the last look he'd have of her, perhaps even the last look of all time. Oh, dear God, no! Never to see that flashing smile, that little wave of her hand as he left her each day . . . With a catch in his throat he said, "She is a gentle, sweet . . . radiant person."

Marietta had been studying Therin's face. Now she said, "And you're hooked on her."

He blushed. "She's a fine person."

"And you want her back."

"I don't want anything to happen to her."

"And it was all right with your wife?"

Therin's blush deepened. "Was what O.K. with my wife?"

"The arrangement."

He stared at her, seeing only her equable smile.

"It was a delicate balance," Marietta said. "You and your wife and Minnie. Or didn't your wife know about it?"

"Now look here—"

"It doesn't matter, does it?" She had a broad smile now. "As matters stand you miss her and want her back. Or was all that blushing for nothing?"

Therin clamped his mouth shut, something he realized he should have done long ago. If he kept on, he'd founder, gunwales and all. He was sweating.

Colbert sniffed with great disdain. "I suppose you advocate this sort of thing."

"What sort of thing?"

"Marital infidelity."

"Certainly not."

"It's disgusting, if you ask me."

"What is?"

"You and her."

Therin got to his feet to face a cold and condemning Colbert.

Colbert said, "A case of moral turpitude, symptomatic of and contributing to the debasement of our times."

"You have a mind like a sewer," Therin said, grabbing the edge of Dr. Tillheimer's desk to steady and anchor himself. "It fits you."

Colbert was trembling. "How old is she? I think you said

twenty-six. Young and soft and probably innocent. And how old are you, Doctor? Thirty-five? Forty?" Colbert wet his lips. His eyes were beginning to glow again. "Did you do it right there in the house? With your wife home?"

Therin stood where he was, jarred by Colbert's reaction, then suddenly realizing Colbert was going into some kind of agitated state, the irises of his eyes vibrating with what was going on inside as he came undone.

"Slime," Colbert said, relishing the word. "Filth." He was breathing hard and there was sweat on his forehead. Suddenly he raised his hands. "Ha!" He dropped them. "Want to know why I'm a private investigator?" He put the hands flat on the desk, his face inches from Therin's. "I'll tell you why. Because of vile people like you, people who break down the moral fiber of our country, destroy the bulwark of our republic—the family. You taint everything you touch, you want coitus taught in the classroom, young minds degraded, you would destroy all that is good and pure. You have no God, no religion, no loyalty except to your gross and depraved appetites, your perversions, your sick desires."

Colbert's voice continued shrill, his eyes bugging out and the cords in his neck looking like dangerously tightened flesh-covered wires. "Don't think I don't know. Girls try to seduce me all the time, try to get me to do that filth, but I fight that, and I fight them, and I feel good fighting what's bad.

"You know what I like best? I like when a young wife hires me to get the evidence on foul persons such as you, and it's a matter of honor and principle with me to leave no stone unturned to get that evidence, Mister. I mean it. I put the guilty party—that's you—right where he belongs, make him pay in blood, grind him down, make him hurt, wince and cry out with pain, and it's only too bad his bones can't be broken, his eyes put out so he won't be able to see evil.

"And you know something else? I don't even ask pay in cases like that, it's reward enough, exposing the evil, the fetor, it's little enough to do, to right the wrongs in the world, the evil all around us, reaching for us, tentacles of evil trying to grasp us in our secret places, trying to violate us, pull us all down to where they are."

Colbert blinked because sweat was running into his eyes. He took his hands off the desk, leaving wet prints. He took out a handkerchief, unfolded it, swabbed away the sweat. Then suddenly he went backward, reaching for a chair and sinking into it, bending forward to cry into his handkerchief. "Oh, the evil," he sobbed. "The evil! It's everywhere . . . *everywhere!*"

Therin pushed himself away from the desk, went to the water cooler and drew a cup of water, moving to Colbert with it.

"Thanks," Colbert said, taking the cup in a trembling hand, sipping the water. He would not look at Therin or Marietta, his head slumped forward on his neck, staring lugubriously at the floor. "I'm sorry. I really am." He drank the rest of the water. Therin threw the used cup in the wastebasket, then moved to drop heavily into Dr. Tillheimer's chair.

Colbert raised his head, said to Therin, "I want you to know I've got nothing against you personally."

21

Fishing—Entry No. 24
   It seems when I write I don't leave
   I didn't understand that before
   Not that it matters
   One place is as good as another
   This is a fine spot Charlemagne has brought us to
   I don't know where it is
   Everything is all mixed up
   I know I lost weight
   I feel like I've been through something
   Something to do with Marcella
   Everybody has been good to me
   Sometimes when they are I want to cry
   I think if I could cry I would feel better
   Hochdruck doesn't think so
   I think so
   The sun is warm
   There are no bugs here

                      Peter Hartsook

22

PETER CLICKED the ballpoint pen, put it away, closed the journal. It wasn't exactly true about bugs; he'd seen some real ones: green treehoppers leaving egg scars, a black beetle foraging for caterpillars, a grasshopper on a spray of goldenrod, and noisy cicadas high in the trees.

Charlemagne and Father Bischoff were sitting on blankets on the riverbank, fishing. Charlemagne had taken off his shoes and had his feet on the cloth sacks full of the marbles he'd bought, his back against an old oak, adjusting his new carpet roll every now and then. They'd been sitting like that for hours, occasionally talking but not catching anything.

Peter had taken himself up from the water to spread his blanket on a shady spot under another oak, to sit and just be, listening to the lazy rush of wind through treetops up the hills. It was hot and still in the bottoms, the wind passing over. It reminded him of the farm. There were even Angus steers on a distant slope, grazing and chewing and snuffling. A mockingbird arced toward the water, then changed its mind and swooped up to perch in the top of a tree on the other side of the river.

Hochdruck was not there, thank God. Only that morning Peter had awakened in the motel, shaking and shuddering as he often did first thing. He found Hochdruck grinning at him from the foot of the bed. Peter turned away and saw Charlemagne standing at the window looking at him. He tried to stop his trembling, heard Hochdruck say, "Look at Charlemagne. He doesn't give a damn. He'd let you shake from now until doomsday. What the hell does he care?"

Peter ignored Hochdruck, had been ignoring him ever since the business in the bathroom when Hochdruck had got the better of him, but this time his silence hadn't stopped Hochdruck's mouth.

"We're going fishing," Charlemagne said.

Father Bischoff came out of the bathroom in his clerical garments. The night before, he'd wanted to sleep in them. Charlemagne solved the problem by telling him they were his security blanket; he could just as well put them within easy reach on a chair next to the bed. So Father Bischoff folded them neatly, kept an eye on them until he fell asleep.

" 'Simon Peter saith unto them, I go a-fishing,' " Father Bischoff said, viewing his splendor in a mirror. He started to hum "Shall We Gather at the River."

"That's a Protestant hymn," Charlemagne said.

"I have catholic tastes," Father Bischoff replied airily.

Charlemagne shook his head. "There's no arguing with the damned."

" 'And they had a few small fishes,' " Father Bischoff said, seeing to the tie of his cleric-collar shirt front. " 'So they did eat and were filled.' "

"An army needs a day of rest," Charlemagne said, moving to Peter. "We'll pretend it's Sunday."

It had been years since he'd been fishing. The last time was with his father.

"Charlemagne's not your father," Hochdruck said.

Peter got up and dressed while Charlemagne wrote a note for Andros and Minnie, who had taken the adjoining room. Hochdruck began to be abusive, wanting Peter to think about Andros and Minnie. "They're doing it, Peter. Right in the next room." Peter's agitation returned and he was glad when they left the Bartlettville Inn.

They had a late breakfast and it was well into the afternoon by the time they'd bought fishing gear in Bartlettville and, with proper advice, moved into the countryside, taking different roads as directed until they came upon the river. Charlemagne parked by the bridge and they started off along the steep bank, trying to avoid fronds of poison oak that hung into the trail, and wiping away drifting threads that oak-moth caterpillars had hung in the trees. At last they came to a bend where there was a gentle, grassy slope to the water's edge. Beyond it the woods thickened and bindweed made walls of the brush.

They busied themselves with brass barrel swivels, leaders and hooks, lines and sinkers, floats and bobbers, and Charlemagne optimistically set out a landing net within the reach of all. They tried lures, flies, nightcrawlers and doughballs, but they didn't even get a nibble. So they relaxed into the afternoon until Peter, tiring of it, moved to higher ground to make his entry.

Now the breeze in the treetops had stopped, the leaves were still, and a haze was spreading soft colors in the hills. Berylwood was another world, distant in time, and Peter expected his father to step out from behind a tree for room to fly-cast.

He supposed if he started to think about Marcella old Hochdruck would appear and ruin his thoughts, but he still hadn't figured out how Marcella got into Charlemagne's house or why she should have gone to bed with Andros. He'd been shocked, really shaken, when it happened, and Hochdruck was no help, and when he wasn't able to kill Hochdruck, he retreated into the outhouse and down farther than he'd ever been before, deep into the vaults into the small capillaries where there was room only for himself.

He had so shut off everything that he was later surprised to find himself in a car, Minnie beside him holding his hand and saying sweet things to him. He flitted in and out and he tried to withdraw his hand but something wouldn't let him. Then Hochdruck came to sit in the front seat between Charlemagne and Father Bischoff and started to taunt him so he couldn't hear what Minnie was saying. He went back to the outhouse where it was quiet.

When they were in the parking lot at Le Comte's he came out of it several times. Once he found Father Bischoff with him, another time Andros. Each time he went back. It was too frightening to stay out.

Since then he'd been better; he was able once again to ignore Hochdruck, who kept telling him what terrible people he was with and how foolish it was for him to have any feelings for Minnie since she obviously preferred Andros, then describing in elaborate detail just how they had sex. When Hochdruck did that, Peter got the shakes and the pictures started flashing, but he was learning to live with it.

One thing was clear: Minnie wasn't one of Them. If she were with the Other Side, Hochdruck wouldn't be making such an issue of it.

It wasn't Peter's father who stepped out from behind the oak, it was Hochdruck, and Hochdruck was saying, as he walked to Peter, "You've had it, Peter, baby. You've really done it. You've laid yourself wide open." Peter was tempted to ask him why the hell he thought he knew so much, but that was what Hochdruck wanted, so he didn't say anything.

Although Mr. Bostwick sat confidently on his ball-bearinged swivel chair on its green vinyl pad on the thick rug behind his glass-topped desk in the middle of a row of other, smaller desks, looking very much like a bank president, which he was, he was at the moment wishing he were something else. He prided himself on his memory of faces, words and deeds (to say nothing of figures), yet he could not recall for Mr. Colbert all of what Charles Le Moyne had said, and he knew he would have to answer to Marietta Le Moyne for this lapse, and he'd already had enough of Marietta Le Moyne.

He could have not given her husband the money. He didn't see how he could have actually physically not given him the money, but if he had not he would have escaped Marietta Le Moyne's tirade and threat of a suit when she found out about it. She should have had sense enough to do something about it legally before her husband ran away from Berylwood.

"He did say something about a holy crusade, but that's about all. Except he accused the Bank of Oblout of not having that much money. Which isn't true, I might add."

"Of course," Colbert said with pen poised above notebook. "Anything else?"

"He mentioned death."

147

"Death?"

"He said he wasn't planning to die and I told him I wasn't either." Mr. Bostwick fished around in his mind. "Oh, one other thing. He recited a Hebrew proverb, asked me if I was Semitic."

"Are you, Mr. Bostwick?"

"Certainly not." Because Mr. Colbert had asked him to tell everything, no matter how ridiculous, Mr. Bostwick screwed up his eyes and his brain with effort. "Something else. He said he was going to do something about the unequal distribution of wealth." Mr. Bostwick relaxed to smile knowingly. "Twenty-three thousand dollars wouldn't do much about that, I'd say."

"I guess not."

"When he left he said he was going to make me an inspector of the kingdom."

"What kingdom?"

"Don't ask me."

Minnie ran a curious finger around Andros' ear and was suddenly filled with the wonder of cells and cell division that in all its complexity made up an ear, pasted together in life and fed by blood, deceiving us into thinking an ear is different from an eye or a toenail or a penis (getting right down to it), an ear being something unto itself, soft and pink even on a man, and ready to bleed, like a woman.

Andros turned. They were eye to eye in silence, swimming in his maleness, her femaleness, naked before each other, not yet through, needing each other even once again, though loving each other with glances and whispers and soft breath, quickening with body joy at the awareness of this.

"That tickled," he said, lips tightening in a smile. "Why did you do it?"

"Why not?" She traced the lines of his eyebrows, sensing a fullness of emptiness, a giving to be a receiving at the same time, and she felt a finger sliding over the upper part of her breast, a finger making concentric rings around the nipple that popped out. "That tickles."

148

Andros laughed, drew her to him, and they no longer kissed with words and glances, and she closed her eyes thinking lips are the most sensual, the most sensitive part, touching, pressing, feeling, swirling. He pulled her so she was on top of him, and she gasped when he entered her again. He laughed. I give joy, she shouted to herself. I am given joy. The bed whirled and shook. They soared, flew closer to the sun than Icarus, then fell into the sea of rumpled sheets, perspiring and spent.

They were up early, when the sun was up, body hungry, the touch of each other draining away sleep, coming awake with blood heat and passion, wordless so early, so easy, so good, and doing it again right away, one more step into each other, no questions asked, no demands except glandular ones, the chemistry mixing again and again. And then laughter and giggles and glances and touches.

They went to breakfast in the motel coffee shop, not saying much but regarding each other, all the pores, moles, nicks, scratches, chicken-pox marks, bones, hair and manners not yet memorized.

And then back to the room, a peek into the adjoining one, seeing Charlemagne, Father Bischoff and Peter still asleep, closing the door gently, the demands returning, breakfast refueling, replenishing, and having at it.

A few steps bare about the room, watching each other, going to the bathroom, taking a shower, Andros shaving, then holding, inspecting and feeling what might have been missed before, smiling, touching, sharing.

Minnie lay still, conscious of him beside her, not seeing his head but the hair on his chest in a V down to his navel, a bare area, then more hair, hair on his arms and legs and knowing as good as this is it isn't all there is and happy that was so.

"You know, Mr. Colbert, it's really funny," Spencer Perkins said. "It was a booboo, mentioning it to Mrs. Le Moyne, I suppose, but hell, I thought they were going out there together, I really did. Besides, Oblout isn't that big and you always say hello to the people you know.

"Anyway, there she was in the bank waiting for Mr. Bostwick to get back from lunch, and I was making a deposit, and on the way out I said I was surprised to see her, I thought she'd be halfway to California by that time.

"Well, you know how she is. You don't tangle with Mrs. Le Moyne if you can help it. I knew I'd said something wrong when she got to her feet and looked at me with those eyes of hers and said whatever gave me that idea. So I told her Charles had been in buying a complete outfit and talking about the trip, what happened, didn't you go? You know how he is. No, if you never met him, I guess you don't.

"Well, the thing got started when he bought a few things at the store years ago, must be more than twenty years ago. I thought they were all right, but she raised hell, said they weren't stylish, they were a bad cut, they didn't fit, they were too expensive and from now on she was going to buy Charles's clothes herself. So ever since that time he never bought himself a damn thing. Until the other day.

"The funny thing is, when she started buying his outfits, he didn't like them at all, and one day after work I met him in the Columbine, you know, the place the college kids go, he'd go there sometimes, and I show up now and then just to keep my hand in, take out a few ads, get the feel of what they're wearing. Anyway, Charles was there looking gloomy until he saw me, then his eyes lighted up and he said over here, Spence, I want to talk to you, and he tells me this big plan of his. He says he won't buy clothes himself, he'll let his wife do it, all right, but it'll be different. Every time she mentions he needs something to wear, he says, he was going to say why don't you go down and see Spence, he knows my size. The kicker was, he'd come in and we'd go over the possibilities and he'd tell me what he liked, and the next day or two she'd be in and I'd steer her to the clothes he'd picked out. It worked like a charm and they were both happy. It was quite a game and I never let on. Hell, if that's the way to sell clothes, why should I kick?

"Everybody liked Charles, the kids, the other professors, and me, I liked him. Only thing is, he was inclined to be kooky, always saying things you never did understand. I wasn't surprised when she put him away, even though I thought that was going pretty far. Of course I didn't know how he was at home. Maybe he really let go there. I don't know. Anyway, I had no idea he was running away with these inmates. I was surprised to see him and was kind of edgy, knowing where he'd been, but he said everything was all right now, in fact, things were going to be different, California was calling, he wanted some clothes and he wanted them right away, ready to wear, they were driving right out. That's right, Mr. Colbert, California. He even showed me the car, the one you mentioned, a Lincoln Continental, and I thought hell, after all those years in Oblout those two deserved to kick up their heels, head west, maybe they'd get everything all settled between them.

"Well, Mrs. Le Moyne got pretty emotional there in the bank, saying my God, Spence, you know what he did? He drew out all the money and he's taken off with four freaks, that's what he's done. I didn't know what to say. I thought they'd gone through his prize money. Of course she wanted to know all about it, this California business, and I told her everything I knew. Hell, I felt sorry for Charles, but being in the condition he's in I felt I ought to help her, so I did. You never know about people, do you, Mr. Colbert?"

They lay side by side just after lunch, a bit lethargic, nearly dozing, happy.

"Andros," Minnie said. "Are you all Andros?" And when he turned, she went on: "I mean how much of you is Andros? And if he weren't there at all, would you be the same?"

He turned away.

"Does Andros push all the buttons all the time?"

"Andros enjoys," he said, kicking at the sheets with a bare foot. "You know that."

"Do *you* enjoy?"

Andros did not reply. Minnie turned to lie on her bare tummy, hoisting herself on her elbows so she could look down at his face. "Am I the first woman Andros has had sex with?"

Andros nodded. Minnie ran the tip of her finger along his lips. "Am I the first woman you ever had?"

"Andros doesn't want to talk about it."

"Tell him I want to know."

"No."

She studied his face and saw in the blanked-out eyes how far he had receded, and she wondered why. "Tell Andros I want him to give up control for just a little bit. After all, he needs a rest after all that button pushing he's been doing all day. Isn't that right?"

"Andros never rests."

"Why? Is he afraid?"

"Andros doesn't know fear."

"Then why won't he let me bypass him and talk directly to you?"

"Because he doesn't want to."

"He's afraid."

"No!" Andros turned his back to her.

Minnie lay down, started tracing designs on the broad back before her. "This way I'll never get to know you, you realize that?" When he did not answer, she went on, "I don't always want to screw just for Andros' sake."

Andros got out of bed, went to the television set, squatted there naked to fiddle with the controls. He looks like a big kid, she thought, an overgrown child, and yet he was a man, and she could not understand this. Sometimes he talked like an egghead, yet at the same time he did things that were positively childish.

She left the bed to go sit near him on the floor close to the television set, where he sat watching a Road Runner cartoon. Already his eyes were bright with interest. She ran a finger along his leg up to his inner thigh, continuing to stroke there, pleased to see the gathering tumescence of his penis. At first he did not seem to be aware of it, then he turned to her, lights going on again behind the eyes. He reached for her.

She scurried away and he came after her, catching her. They fell to the floor, faces inches from each other. "Andros?" she said. "Or is it you?"

152

The glow left his eyes, he rolled away and got to his feet, kicked the television set off, went to sit on the bed, frowning, looking down at his hands.

She got up and moved to stand before him. "Know what I think? I think Andros is a big bully."

Andros lifted his head, eyes flaring in anger. Before she knew what happened, his right hand came up from the bed and struck her cheek with such force she saw lightning flashes and almost lost her balance.

In a moment Andros was on his feet, gathering her into his arms. "I'm sorry," he said. "I'm sorry."

She laughed, tears welling. "That's good . . . That makes me happy."

He drew away to regard her with a puzzled expression. "Happy?"

She nodded, the tears running over. "Because it's you that's sorry."

23

"Now THEN," Charlemagne said, opening the gigantic Pheasant Room menu and running his eyes over the large number of offerings. Speaking above other voices, laughter and the clinking of tableware and utensils because the room was so crowded, he said, "An army preparing for a frontal attack needs something that will stick to its ribs."

They had been ushered into the room by a buxom Bartlettville Inn hostess who had met them at the door and steered them past the Dining Room and into the Pheasant Room, seeming to know right where they should sit. She was deferential to Father Bischoff, who walked so grandly he could have been on a holy mission (which was the way he'd been walking lately), and smiling at Andros, who grinned dazzlingly and had to be guided to a seat by Minnie. Peter was at first nervous and looked likely to bolt, but Charlemagne was so easy and breezy it was contagious, and so Peter sat down with some confidence.

"Oh, Peter!" Minnie said, putting a forearm beside his. "You're so sunburned!"

Peter's sun-reddened face flushed even deeper as he examined the two forearms, smiling and glancing shyly at Minnie.

"You and Andros," Charlemagne said, lowering the menu. "You should get out and get some fresh air. Might do you both some good."

"It can't be healthy, doing what they're doing," Father Bischoff said enviously.

"It's healthier than letting it shrivel up, like some people I know," Andros said.

"It's not shriveled up!"

Minnie smiled. "I should hope not." She was seated next to Peter, felt him tighten. She turned, put a hand over his forearm. He stiffened even more, so she took her hand away, shook her head. "Peter, I don't know what I'm going to do with you."

Father Bischoff said nastily, "If past performance is any guide . . ."

Minnie turned, regarded him for a moment. "Or with you either, Father." She smiled wickedly.

Father Bischoff looked panicky.

"All right," Charlemagne said. "Enough is enough. Let us get down to the business at hand." He lifted the menu again.

Later, after Charlemagne had ordered cocktails for everyone, assuring Father Bischoff the good Lord would drink with them if He were only there (though Father Bischoff didn't really need to be coaxed), he brought them to their feet to clink glasses. Every head in the room turned to them in surprise. He said, very solemn, not caring that others heard: "This is a state occasion. The opposition should be trembling because of our unshakable aplomb." They drank to scattered applause. Cameras flashed. "We shall overrun the bastions. The enemy will be decimated." They drank again, this time to louder and more general applause. There were more flashes from picture-takers.

While the others sat down raggedly, Charlemagne stayed on his feet to drain his glass, then looked around as if for a fireplace as room noises became normal again. He locked glances with a man at the next table, raised his glass in salutation, said, "To your health, sir," and managed to get one more drop before he sat down.

Minnie, who was getting some strange vibrations, said, "Charlemagne, I think we're in the wrong room."

As Charlemagne looked around, she pointed out that the dining room they'd been guided past was nearly deserted and this room was full, the people here were unusually chummy, there was an atmosphere of expectation, and most everyone was further along with the meal than they were.

"And look up there." She gestured to the far side of the

room, where three tables had been set side by side and people sat only on one side facing the diners. "I think we've landed in the middle of a club meeting."

"You're right, Minerva." Charlemagne laughed quietly, turned to Father Bischoff. "It's your outfit that got us put here, Father. For that you're going to have to deliver the benediction."

Father Bischoff beamed. "It will be my pleasure, sir."

As the waitress served them their dinners, Minnie said, "Animal, vegetable or mineral?"

Charlemagne blinked as he picked up his fork. "What's that, my dear?"

"This enemy of yours you keep talking about."

"This enemy of ours."

"Definitely animal?"

"Oh, yes."

"And two-legged, I suppose."

"Of course."

"Man being his own worst enemy?"

"You said it, I didn't."

"But *which* men, Charlemagne?

"Take a look around."

Father Bischoff said, "Sufficient unto the day is the ignorance thereof." He smiled as he chewed. "Just practicing."

"Andros says that's 'evil,'" Andros said, "and he suggests you look into your own heart."

"Small mind, small talk," Father Bischoff said sniffingly. "Andros' brain is the smallest there is, according to unusually reliable sources."

"Let there be no internecine warfare here," Charlemagne said. "It is too divisive."

"Andros doesn't understand man," Andros said, abandoning retaliation to butter a roll. "If he is his own worst enemy, why doesn't man make friends with himself and end it?"

"There is no more cunning adversary. It keeps him on his toes devising new ways to annihilate himself. You see, life is the cheapest thing there is on this planet. That is the way it is here."

156

"That isn't the way it is on Acheron."

"There are also myths here, such as the myth of man's superiority. But he isn't superior because he doesn't have the sense of a goldfinch, which limits itself to whatever is possible ecologically speaking and knows it would be death to overbreed. So you see, Andros, man has a lot to learn. If he is to survive, there must be a leveling off, a reversal of process, an end to plunder. And if he doesn't do that, nature will end him. We are all involved to see that that doesn't happen. In the words of La Fontaine, '*Aide-toi, et le ciel t'aidera*.' "

"I do wish you wouldn't do that, Charlemagne," Minnie said. "You know I don't understand French."

Charlemagne squeezed her thigh under the table. "That doesn't detract from its meaning, Minerva."

"Your hand is cold."

The Pheasant Room, rich food, being waited on, shrill talk, frozen smiles. A world I never knew, Minnie thought, munching her salad. People all dressed up, shaved, showered and powdered, and meeting to make noise, sweating with the heat and press of bodies but not worrying because their deodorant is good for twenty-four hours. Yes. Good, four-square with-it types. Or am I just jealous? Do I really want a life of nothing but pink curlers and mother-of-pearl earrings, Tampax and a blouse full of goodies, strawberry douches, nipples and face cream and dreams of gestation? God help me no. The commune was never as deadly as this; neither was the bloodthirsty militancy of the SDS. She felt she had not been premature in her determination. She wouldn't rather be writing Mother.

Once she had thought these were all dead people, the over-twenty-fives she had refused to admit existed (and she proved it by going to great lengths to avoid them). Now, listening and watching, she saw them as cop-outs, defectors, giver-inners, spineless wonders, and she wondered: Maybe they are really dead. Like Elizabeth. God, yes, she was dead. And Therin was dying. Maybe that was what was griping her about him. He was getting petrified and she was his last hope. Or was inverse ratio at work here? Maybe she was just more alive. She certainly felt like it, first with Therin, then with Charlemagne and the others, and of course with Andros when they did their wild animal thing.

Why am I judging the world? I don't even know these people.

A man at the head table rose, tapped a glass with a spoon for attention, telling everyone to go ahead, finish dessert, he'd get things started.

"Oh, Jesus," Minnie said.

"Right on, Minerva."

The speaker said he was John Terhune, the chairman, and those people sitting up there with him were members of the steering committee and founders of the movement. Then he introduced them one by one. Terhune, a balding, birdlike man with shaggy brows and piercing eyes that made Minnie uncomfortable, thanked everyone for coming; he knew they were going to make great strides . . . Minnie blotted out his voice as she concentrated on her prime cut *au jus*.

Then she realized he was talking about "tense lesbian sirens," "agonized masturbation scenes" and "eager nymphs" in an orotund voice, and she became hopelessly ensnared. What *was* this? She looked around, saw that everyone was caught up in it except Peter, who had started to shake as he tried to eat.

It was Sally Snyder, a large matronly type, big in all departments, who pinned on the label for them. She was introduced as the vice-chairman of the BPAF, and she coyly told her listeners not to let the "vice" part throw them, the Bartlettville Parents Against Filth was, of course, interested in vice and its obliteration, segueing into decrying an industry "which got its traveling money in the big cities so they can bring their filth to clean places like Bartlettville to exhibit it to our children," and she was roundly applauded for saying so, thereby being encouraged to go on.

Minnie found it hard to believe it was for real, but there was Sally Snyder on her own two feet saying she was pleased by the turnout, two weeks in existence and already the BPAF had

158

more interested people than she thought possible. "But to get back, Harold and me, we've got teens and we've got subteens, and I tell you there's a lot of raw stuff up there on that screen these days. And Harold and me, being here to do something about it, we feel like we're fighting the devil himself."

Minnie was appalled to see that even Father Bischoff applauded Ample Sally, and then she saw the elderly Edgar Bertacci, three tables away, so moved by the applause he forgot for a moment he was not at a revival and would have knelt at the head table, except he recovered at the last moment to turn and say, "I'm opposed to preversion of any kind, and I'll fight if I have to, I'm not so old I can't put my dukes up and give a good account of myself, and I surely would fight to keep it from happening right here in Bartlettville, this blessed place, it purely is God's last bulwark, and if it can happen here it surely can happen anywheres in this great and glorious country of the U.S. and A." He would have gone on, Minnie saw, but Terhune jumped up quickly, thanked him and Mr. Bertacci reluctantly moved off to find his seat.

The feeling of outrage Minnie had experienced at the outset diminished, and she was beginning to enjoy what kind of a show the good citizens of Bartlettville were putting on. She saw Mae Christenson, a large woman, too, struggle to her feet, wheezing a little, and when she got her breath she said, "It's a shame, a downright shame, all this nudity, all the filthy words, all the perverted affairs, all the perverted things they do. Why, they don't even wear bras any more! And that's just plain awful, sickening, and it's not right, and it's got to stop. Why, it's getting so I can't let the kids out of the house any more, except they might end up at the show, and God knows what they see there these days. *I* know. I've seen them, don't think I haven't, and I tell you you can't always tell by the name of the picture."

Terhune, finding a moment, went into the breach to dwell on the psychological traumas that result when kiddies are witness to the primal scene. "And it's not just that, my friends, it's pornographic studies of lesbians, homosexuals and group sex, too.

159

And I think you will agree with me that such things should not be seen in a clean community of God-fearing people like Bartlettville." It seemed to Minnie that Terhune had more than censuring interest in the erotic, the way he mouthed the words.

"While I don't go along with the theory that dirty movies are a Communist plot to undermine the morality of and totally corrupt our youth, though God knows that might be so, I do want to emphasize that at tender years the kiddies would be better off playing with tops, yo-yos and jacks and jump ropes, not watching people having sexual intercourse."

"My, my," Minnie said as, during the heavy applause, the waitress brought them their desserts. "Listen to the man."

"He jacks off behind the barn," Andros said.

Charlemagne said, "It's happening, troops. The Saracens are mustering strength. They would have us taken and fettered by main force and haled away to Aix to be doomed and done away with once for all."

"I'm going to utter a few words for the opposition," Father Bischoff said, moving to get to his feet.

"No," Charlemagne said. "It's not time yet for your benediction."

"It's going to be more than a benediction."

"No, Father. As a perceiver of the right times and places, I, your CIC, with proper generalship, do declare this is not it."

"The bastions," Minnie said hopefully.

"I know, I know." Charlemagne leaned back to hear more.

She glanced at Peter, saw that he was just sitting there, staring at his dessert, and she wondered what in the world he was thinking about.

A thin man at the next table was getting up. He looked natty, dressed as he was in a black suit and red bow tie, and smiling with empty radiance. "Everybody knows me." Not me, Minnie wanted to shout. "I'm Abe Mandel, your druggist. Everybody knows sex on the screen leads to experimentation by boys and girls. From there it's only a small step to degeneration and worse. It's only common sense that we should try to protect those innocent tots."

You left out the American Flag and Motherhood, Minnie thought wryly. An "Amen" from the Reverend Chancey Clittsfield made her turn to see the angular, white-haired clergyman rise to survey them all as if from a great height. "We're all children of God, let us not forget that. And let us pray that we're not too late to keep Bartlettville from becoming a Sodom and Gomorrah. There must be an end to this movie infiltration that makes such a hollow mockery of sacred institutions like marriage, and our prayers should be directed to this end."

"That's right," Lillian Praiseworthy, a pert housewife, said. "It's positively indecent. You'd think they never heard of it in Hollywood—marriage, that is. Worse yet, I don't think there's ever been a film marriage that's been a happy one, and having seen the films they put out, I can see why."

Minnie looked to Charlemagne, who was absorbed in listening to Mrs. Praiseworthy. "Hey," Minnie whispered, "aren't you going to do something? You know, like break it up, jar these people?"

"Minerva," he said, smiling, enjoying it, "they're building a trap for themselves. A self-righteous trap. They don't need any help."

If you'd do something, she said to herself, I'd love you for it, Charlemagne, for that is all I have to give, just me: Minerva St. John. And not just part of me. All of me. My heart, too, not just the fuzzy little thing.

24

THE BARTLETTVILLE PARENTS AGAINST FILTH meeting moved into its next phase, that of designing ways and means of thwarting the erotic invasion, and by this time the Pheasant Room was filled with cigar and cigarette smoke and Minnie was feeling edgy.

"Shouldn't we go?" she asked Charlemagne. "After all, if we're not going to do anything, sitting here is the same as agreeing with them."

"We are guests in the Pheasant Room," Charlemagne said pleasantly, dabbing at his lips with his napkin. "It wouldn't be right to leave these people where they are."

Minnie motioned to Peter, who had hardly touched his dessert and was sitting glassy-eyed. "I think Peter's already left us."

"I'm still here," Father Bischoff said, glancing to Charlemagne. "But nobody has noticed."

"You're still here because you think they're going to ask you to give the benediction," Andros said. "Well, I've got news for you, there's not going to be any benediction."

"How do you know that?"

"They're all going to work themselves up so much it's going to end in a screw circus, everybody screwing everybody else."

"You should be pilloried," Father Bischoff said heatedly, "with no one to intercede for you."

"You'd like that," Andros taunted. "An orgy would break your zipper."

"Pinhead within pinhead."

"Hold it down," Charlemagne said. Indeed, people were looking in their direction.

Terhune, who had been waiting, now resumed. "I do think the committee to preview films is a good idea, and I'm sure we can get the theater people to cooperate. It will be our neighbors alerting us to peril."

He went on, but first he passed around a paper and people began signing their names as committee volunteers. Minnie put her name down. A free picture is a free picture, she decided, and the committee'd probably go only to the sexy ones, and that was what it was all about, wasn't it?

"I think the committee thing is okay," druggist Mandel said, "but I think we need something stronger. How about an outright boycott of the theaters? Believe me, it hurts me as a businessman to have to suggest this, but I have the FDA to contend with, and you should see the paperwork when a doctor wants a patient on hard drugs. Why don't the movie people have something like this? Because they don't, they've gone too far. They're all sick out there and they're getting sicker."

And I'm going to be sick right here, Minnie said to herself. Unless I get up, tear off my clothes and do a wild sex dance, maybe pull John Terhune down on top of me, give the people something to remember us by. It was bullshit fantasy and she knew it, but she felt better having thought it.

Mae Christenson was saying, "There have been letters to the editor in the Bartlettville *Times*, but I don't think they've done a bit of good, except maybe get more people out to the movies."

So much for the power of the press. Next up: the judiciary. Terhune was asking attorney Arnold Gallagher if there was anything legal that could be done to stop the encroachment.

Gallagher seemed surprised to be called on, got up, twisted his face as he thought. "Well, John, I don't know. We might try to get an injunction to close the theaters, but I don't see how we could keep them closed; there would be only limited success with that maneuver, if we could get Judge Lamb to issue it at all.

"On the other hand, suits could be initiated by parents

against the theaters and the studios for psychological damages to their children. I don't know why somebody hasn't done that; I suppose it's too rough a row to hoe and there are just too many films and you can't sue each time.

"We could always have Sheriff Parsons confiscate the worst pictures, but maybe that wouldn't be good, considering it would be only temporary, and moves like that haven't been successful in other communities. I don't know."

Round and round goes the legal mind: if, but, considering, on the other hand, maybe, I'm not sure, I suppose, ending nowhere.

"Let's waylay the projectionists," Ample Sally Snyder suggested frivolously, and there was rewarding laughter. Minnie thought it was the best idea yet.

"You think that's funny," Reverend Clittsfield said, "but I don't. It's nothing to laugh about, and I'll tell you why. Allan Passwater is in my congregation, and I guess everybody must know he's a projectionist at the Strand. Anyway, Allan tells me he positively hates running some of the pictures he's required to. He cries sometimes when he has to do that, sobs while the picture's running, he tells me, and he tries not to look, but he has to keep the picture in focus or he'll lose his job, so what else can he do?

"I think it's terrible what a man has to do to keep himself and his family alive these days. It used to be root-hog or die; at least that was honest. But getting back to Allan, I wonder if he and the other projectionists could get together, perhaps talk about striking for decent films. I'd be willing to talk to them about this."

There was applause, and Terhune asked him to talk with them in the name of the BPAF; the community would be grateful.

Kendall Cauffman, publisher of the *Times*, an old man with liver spots, leathery flesh and keen eyes, rose to say that his paper was behind the BPAF 100 percent and that the *Times* would run warnings for parents about bad films if the group being set to preview the films would provide the proper copy.

Minnie wondered who was going to show the films to the preview committee if the projectionists went out on strike. She turned to look at Charlemagne and found him in a deep study. Maybe she should do her naked little dance. Father Bischoff and Andros registered resignation and boredom. Peter was pale and sweaty, staring at the weave of the tablecloth.

"Now," Terhune said, his voice cracking from strain, "is there anyone else?"

Charlemagne got up, dropped his napkin to the table. Heads swiveled. He was in no hurry. With raised eyebrows he surveyed the faces.

"My name is Le Moyne. **Dr.** Le Moyne. My associates and I have listened to you good people, and I want to say we're overwhelmed, yes, overwhelmed, deeply affected."

Turning to his own table, Charlemagne said he knew they would enjoy hearing from his colleagues, but there wasn't time, all he could do was introduce them: "Father Bischoff, who if time would only permit would recount some of his harrowing experiences with patients in a private mental hospital and is an expert exegete in his own right; Minerva—you may recognize the name, if not the face—one of the most able and practicing sexual anthropologists I have ever known; Peter Hartsook, prober of inner worlds, retiring, secret and quiet, as one might expect; and Andros, whose specialty is the structure of extraterrestrial societies."

There was polite applause and some restlessness, and Minnie was afraid Charlemagne was going to let it go at that. But he did not. He smiled, looked around at the faces. "We have heard your problem and I think we have a solution for you." The people stirred with interest. "You think the worst has happened, but it's only the beginning. Let me tell you what's coming."

Kendall Cauffman reached up to his ear, turned his hearing-aid volume control one full notch. "The cupping of bare breasts," Charlemagne went on, "always nicely formed breasts,

I might add, and always belonging to some sexy, deliciously formed women—that you have seen." They were hanging in there now. "Next comes the tongueing of the nipple."

There were gasps. Minnie could not tell whether they were gasps of pleasure or pain. Charlemagne continued: "There are other areas to tongue, and you will, of course, see that, all in glorious Technicolor. Until they run out of places. It will be plain and fancy fellatio and cunnilingus. But that's only the beginning.

"What else is there? Well, there's tribadism, anal intercourse, troilism, onanism, sodomy, sadism, daisy chains, auto-fellatio, bestiality, masochism." He laughed. "Why, when you come to think about it, they've hardly begun to explore the field."

"Mr. Le Moyne," Terhune said nervously. "I don't think—"

"Precisely," Charlemagne said. "Oh, the boys and girls of Bartlettville have an education coming. They will no longer have to depend upon the twisted details learned in the gutter; their knowledge will be accurate and well documented. After the *Kama Sutra* plays at the Strand, their education will be fairly complete." He smiled. "You must give the film-makers their due. They only put out what interests you."

"You said you had a solution," Terhune said sharply. "What is it?"

"Mr. Terhune, I don't think anyone is going to stop the film people from bringing to your fair city all the variations of the erotic theme. Add to what you've already seen, Jew screwing Aryan, Arab screwing Jew, liberal screwing conservative, black screwing white, or vice versa, women and women, men and men, girls and boys, girls and girls, women and girls, men and boys, big dogs, asses, sheep, divide the acts by race and color and erotic preference, add what things the writers and producers might think up on the spot, sprinkle it all with a little child molestation, seduction, incest, rape, sex with inanimate objects —oh, they're on to your appetites!"

"*Sir!*"

Charlemagne held up a hand to stem reaction. "My friends, it doesn't have to be that way. The secret is to make it unlikely they will ever want to send their product to you. Make Bart-lettville bookings unprofitable for them. If there's no market here, the films won't be shown here." Charlemagne smiled beguilingly. "And how to do that? Why, the answer is so simple, it's a wonder nobody has thought of it. It's been under your noses all your lives."

It was quiet. They waited. Minnie wondered how in the world he was going to get out of this.

"The answer is orchidectomy. Yes, ladies and gentlemen, an orchidectomy for every living male in Bartlettville."

There was a long silence. Some people looked around at others, blank and puzzled faces everywhere. Finally, Lillian Praiseworthy, in a small voice, said, "What's an orchidectomy?"

"The cutting off of the balls, dear lady."

They sat stunned, not believing Charlemagne could have suggested this. Minnie was shocked, wondered if he hadn't gone too far. She could see them tarred and feathered.

Charlemagne did not lose his cool. "Let me ask you: Are your genitals dissociated from your heart? Not now they're not, any more than the heart is severed from the head. But the head cannot be surgically removed without killing the host body. Not so the testicles. They can be removed quickly, neatly, surgically. And the male host body will no longer be bothered by sex stimuli. That way, no matter what plays at the Strand the males will not be affected by it. And as for women who exhibit estrus, there is a comparable surgical means to reduce their ardor.

"As a righteous community you surely must know what the Gospel is according to St. Matthew: '. . . if thy right eye offend thee, pluck it out, and cast it from thee: for it is profitable for thee that one of thy members should perish, and not that the whole body should be cast into hell.' Isn't that right, Reverend Clittsfield?"

The reverend nodded reluctantly. " 'And if thy right hand offend thee, cut it off.' "

"Exactly. Friends, this afternoon I was fishing, and from

where I sat on the riverbank near Bartlettville I could look up into the low hills and see cattle there. Some were engaged in sexual intercourse. Any Bartlettville boy could have seen that, and if he were a bright Bartlettville boy—and aren't they all?—he would probably think what works for cattle probably works for people."

Charlemagne paused. "And now Father Bischoff will render his benediction. Father?"

Father Bischoff was startled but pleased as he rose to quell whatever rumblings of reaction were imminent. He clasped his hands before him, raised his head, closed his eyes. "*Nimine ictus cohabitus fulcrum ad ichor dominus est. Dea uturque honorarium plebes invertum sum.* Amen."

He opened his eyes. The people stirred. Minnie hoped Father Bischoff would sit down and they could get the hell out of there, but it was too much, all the faces, all the ears, all the attention.

"Good friends," he said, and Minnie was surprised to see how much like a holy man he seemed to be, standing there, open, humble, full of grace. "We all want to be happy, even priests. If we were truly happy, then we might better administer the comfort and spiritual nourishment you require, receiving from us the salutary remedies that would enable you to rise healed and strengthened from the disasters of life.

"Unfortunately, the priesthood is sterile and unsatisfying because it denies the existence of the one thing that would make us human, just as you would deny the one thing that would make your children human.

"I ask you: Is the body a source of evil? The Council fathers think so. They want us to make an annual public affirmation of our vows of celibacy. And so we are miserable, just as your children would be if they were cut off, so to speak, from those pleasures God has seen fit to equip us to experience. How I wish the Council would open the door to me and my brother priests! But they merely echo the mossy accents of the past. I do not consider sex a sordid submission to weakness, and you

168

must not make that mistake. We must enjoy God's perfections, be happy the way God wants us to be.

"Oh, my friends, I find it so difficult to talk of love and never kiss anyone, only the rings on the fingers of bishops and cardinals." Tears sprang to Father Bischoff's eyes and he did, indeed, have difficulty going on. "I desperately want to share the secrets of my love for God and His mercy in the intimacy of the sex act.

"I didn't want to make myself a eunuch for the kingdom of heaven's sake. Celibacy is no crowning jewel, it's a crown of thorns. I want a woman, a fine-looking woman, round and soft, a woman with ripe breasts. I want to feel what I have never felt, place my hands were they have never been placed, taste with my tongue the sweet juices of love's fulfillment.

"I have a constant erection thinking of these things, but what can I do with it? Where is the woman who will help me? Where is the woman with whom I can share this thing I carry with me now useless but straining for fulfillment?"

Father Bischoff's tear-stained face immobilized everyone; they were helpless before his agony. Now, sobbing, he wailed, "I'm tired of masturbating—I want to screw!" And he sat down, his head falling to his hands on the table, his body shaking with his weeping.

25

"LISTEN," HOCHDRUCK said from the foot of the bed, his hands in the pockets of his neatly pressed business-suit coat and balancing on the balls of his feet, "the reason you've got the shakes is you're letting them run your life, tell you where to go, what to do. If you had any sense at all, you'd get up, pack your suitcase and clear out."

Hochdruck went on with his advice and Peter thought he detected desperation in his voice, which was something new and should have made him feel better, but it didn't. Peter continued to lie in his bed, his bones and muscles vibrating. It was as if he'd been prematurely embalmed; surely it wasn't blood that circulated in his veins. More likely formaldehyde or freon. The violent tremors he rode out by setting his teeth and burying his head in the pillow.

Hochdruck droned on, the air conditioning kept going on and off, Father Bischoff stopped snoring long enough now and then to turn in his sleep and smack his lips, and every once in a while he could hear a car going by on the highway.

When Peter looked, he could see Hochdruck quite well, but he tried to avoid meeting eyes with him. Hochdruck was so damned arrogant, always claiming he had the answers, always moving into Peter's line of sight so Peter would be forced to look somewhere else, to the window, the ceiling, the mirror on the dresser—anywhere. It was fairly dark, but Peter's eyes had long since become accustomed to it. Charlemagne was inert, unmoving, sleeping the sleep of the dead. Peter envied him.

"Look," Hochdruck said, moving to stand between his bed and Charlemagne's, "you know what Minnie and Andros are doing, you could walk right through that door there, catch them at it, see for yourself."

Peter turned away, agitated and despairing. Why didn't Hochdruck leave him alone? But he knew why. The man had access to the secret parts of Peter's mind, knew how he felt about Minnie, was only putting the needle where Peter'd feel it most. But Hochdruck was making up that stuff about Minnie and Andros; there hadn't been a sound from the other room for over an hour.

Hochdruck moved closer, bent over to look at him. Peter closed his eyes. Hochdruck said, "You going to stay? Look what happened, all that talk in the Pheasant Room. You heard what Charlemagne said, and Father Bischoff. You want to go, being witness to crap like that?"

Peter could stand him no more. He threw back the covers and stood up. "Now you're talking," Hochdruck said. Peter snorted, opened a drawer on the night table, took out his journal and ballpoint pen. Hochdruck was disappointed. "That's not going to help." He'd have walked through Hochdruck if he hadn't got out of the way as Peter walked to the bathroom.

When Peter turned on the bathroom lights, the brilliance blinded him momentarily. He urinated, flushed the toilet, then lowered the terrycloth-covered seat and sat down, leaning his back against the water tank, his tremors beginning to recede.

"This is accomplishing nothing," Hochdruck said, jumping up to sit on the sink. "Nothing at all. If you'd masturbate, you'd feel better."

A fit of the shakes seized him again and his teeth chattered. He wished he could get to the outhouse, but it was getting increasingly difficult to do so.

"Of course it's getting more difficult," Hochdruck said. "What do you expect? You had it made until you joined up with these creeps. You had a nice thing going."

Peter forced his mind away from Hochdruck, opened the journal and glanced through some of the early entries, then decided to read them all. As he did so, he was shocked to see the crudity of the early writing and the way he signed his name. He had not written that! Trickery was involved there somewhere, and he looked up to see Hochdruck's smirking face. Hochdruck would know about it, but Peter wouldn't demean himself by asking.

"That's right," Hochdruck said. "You figure it out, hot shot."

It was clear: They'd got hold of his journal and had cleverly imitated his handwriting, replacing what he'd written with distorted, nonsensical things calculated to upset him.

"You know what you should do, Peter? Throw the journal away. What good is it? It's a time waster."

Peter went back, started to read again, studying each entry, trying to remember the circumstances surrounding the writing. He remembered key phrases and words, how he felt in the urinal, in the garage, and it became clear to him he had, indeed, written the words that appeared there. But how could that be?

Hochdruck started a harangue, but with effort Peter shut him out. It struck him that things were changing. For one thing, he hadn't left his body for a long time and it was becoming impossible to escape what was going on around him.

"It's that Minnie," Hochdruck said, sitting in the bathtub. He lay back, yawning. "She's got under your skin. You keep on, you'll be a mess."

It was confusing; Peter didn't know what to think any more. For a while in the Pheasant Room it was the way it used to be, a cocktail and lunch with friends, and he felt good, having gone fishing, being in the sun, shaving and showering and getting dressed. Maybe Hochdruck was right about Minnie's influence, for he remembered how he enjoyed pretending that just he and Minnie were there, that three friends had joined them at the table. He recalled how he wished it had really been that way.

"Too bad she's with Andros, isn't it, Peter? Isn't that what you've been thinking? Well, you can stop. She's made her choice. She's nothing but trouble."

172

Minnie had been attentive, and he hated himself when he drew away, even though she hadn't minded.

"Why should she mind, Peter? She's everybody's meat, isn't she?"

When people started giving speeches, he began to slink away, putting up the old shield around him and burrowing down. Except it hadn't done much good; he didn't get far enough down, couldn't make it all the way to the subterranean reaches. Maybe it was the cocktail, the noise or the smoke.

"It was Minnie, you damned fool."

Whatever it was, he still heard everything, and the things that were said made him nervous.

"That kind of talk, you're going to hear more of it, you keep on with this group." Hochdruck put his hands behind his head, closed his eyes. "Don't say I didn't warn you."

And when Charlemagne got up to talk, he thought he'd vibrate to pieces, all those eyes looking at them. He was only glad nobody seemed to be looking directly at him. Things became chaotic after Father Bischoff's talk, and he became frantic when he couldn't get back into his pod, so he veiled out as much as he could. He thought it was the crush of people that kept him from finding his way to the outhouse.

"I already told you what it was, Peter."

It was Minnie who asked him to help her and Andros get Father Bischoff back to the room, and he was able to do this because it meant getting out of there and away from the people.

"You'd do anything she asked. That's how far it's gone. You going to keep on letting her lead you by the nose?"

But that wasn't the end. People followed them to the room, newspaper people talked to Charlemagne and Father Bischoff, and pictures were taken. He'd gone into the bathroom to get away from the questions, but he couldn't stay because others wanted to use it. He came out, utterly miserable, finally finding sanctuary at the window, looking out and not answering questions, jumping in and out of the tombs when he could.

"I just let you suffer," Hochdruck said, inspecting his fingernails. "Just to let you know how it's going to be from now on."

Once Minnie had come up to him, told him it was all right, everything was fine, not to worry, and that helped, and he stayed for a long time on this side, but he still didn't leave the window, though there was nothing to see outside because it was dark.

"You don't know what I am, Peter. Who talks to you when you're down and out? Me. I'm the only friend you've got."

Things settled down, the people left, and at last everybody went to bed, leaving him alone to go to bed, too, which he did.

Peter turned to Hochdruck, who was pretending to be asleep in the bathtub, and said, "I'd have gone to sleep if it weren't for you."

"Har de har har," Hochdruck said without opening his eyes. "Although it's nice to hear your voice again."

Peter turned away, shifted on the terrycloth, opened the journal to the first blank page following the entries, withdrew the ballpoint pen from his pajamas pocket, settled back. He started to sort out his aims and feelings, wondering as he did so if, at some time in the future, the entry he was going to write would seem as peculiar to him as the initial entries appeared to him now.

Without warning the bathroom door opened and Minnie came in wearing a knee-length marquisette nightie and nothing else. When she saw him, she stopped short. While Peter was startled, he wasn't shaken. He assumed she was some new thing They had thought up to distress him, making her garment so sheer just to agitate him. However, when the currents of air she put into motion reached him, he knew she must be for real, and so he became totally immobilized. He sat and stared and grew cold.

Minnie advanced to stand before him, and when she spoke it was in a low voice because of the sleeping men in the adjoining room. "Peter, is there any aspirin in here?"

He saw the white flesh of her thighs, the jut of breasts and nipples. He could even see her navel. Alarm bells began to go off all over.

She saw where his eyes were. "You don't have to look, you know, if it bothers you." She turned to go to the medicine cabinet, opened it, peered in. "Damn." She closed it, turned back, put a hand to her head. "I've got this headache. Too much excitement, I guess." She looked toward him, smiled and gave a little laugh. "Too much something, anyway." She stretched and yawned, the nightie creeping up the thighs. "What are you doing here?"

Peter wrenched his eyes from her anatomy to look into her eyes. He saw how blue they were, how they fitted her face underneath the jet-black hair which fell around her shoulders, and he knew she was beautiful. Suddenly he churned inside as a variety of forces fought for supremacy.

"Won't you tell me?"

"Watch it," Hochdruck said.

When he did not answer, she said, "Well, you don't have to," and turned, starting to go through the drawers and cabinets underneath the sink. "They give you coffee, water and a hotplate, and they give you ice, but they don't give you aspirin. You know, I'll bet there is more aspirin consumed in motels than any other place in the world." Finding nothing, she turned away in disgust, moving to sit on the thick towel on the edge of the bathtub to consider what to do next.

Peter glanced beyond her to see if Hochdruck was still there. He was, sitting on the rear of the tub registering a look of painful disdain. Minnie turned to see what he did. "Why do you do that, Peter? What do you see around corners and over shoulders?"

"Careful," Hochdruck warned. "She'll seduce you if she can."

"Oh, shut up," Peter said sharply.

"Why do you suppose she came in here dressed like that?" Hochdruck's voice was whiny.

"I'm sorry," Minnie said in a hurt voice. She got up.

"No. Wait." Peter's agitation was mixed with a flowering of

startling affection. His heart pounded and his mouth felt dry. Minnie sat down again. "It's Hochdruck," he said.

"Now you've done it," Hochdruck said in dismay.

"Hochdruck?" Minnie looked at him curiously.

He nodded, gulping and looking down at his journal, realizing what he'd done, saying the unsayable. His throat felt tight and he experienced an overpowering desire to look at her.

"Is this Hochdruck a person?"

"A man." Why did he have so much difficulty speaking to her? She wasn't one of Them, he'd told himself that, so what was the matter? Hochdruck could try all he wanted, but Peter would not back down on that point. He'd talk to Minnie all he wanted—if he could. He felt his cheeks burning with purpose. "I told him to shut up."

"You're digging your own grave," Hochdruck said.

"Is he here now?"

"He's in the bathtub behind you."

Minnie did not turn to look but considered the matter. "Tell me, is he a good person or bad?"

The question was unexpected and took him aback; he hadn't thought about it. Hochdruck himself was probably all right, he worked for Them, had his job to do, persevered, but he certainly hadn't been good to Peter.

"Not a very nice person."

"Liar!" Hochdruck shouted, glaring.

Peter looked up. Minnie's eyes, in their clear blue intensity, gave him an electrical pleasure shock. He felt sweat running down from his armpits, a heaviness in his chest. He swallowed. He was disembodied, floaty, giddy. He didn't want to steal away at all, and this surprised him, and he took heart.

"I may not be back," Hochdruck said.

Minnie had put a hand out to the towel on either side of her, crossed her legs, and now one bare foot went up and down in the air. "What does he do, Peter?"

"Bother me, mostly."

"I gathered that. I had an aunt who used to bother the hell out of me, always telling me I'd go blind if I did things I

176

shouldn't. She'd visit us and when she'd leave she'd press a religious leaflet in my hand together with a dollar bill." She laughed. "I guess she had her good points. I'd blow the money on the sexiest movie in town. Does this Hochdruck do things like that?"

"No. He says things."

"Like what?"

"Like when you and Andros . . ." Peter stopped, shamed by the remembrance. He shouldn't have said it, and now it was said and he felt as if he were going to strangle. His heart lurched first this way, then that. The journal fell to the floor. He was holding the ballpoint pen so tightly his knuckles had whitened.

Minnie bent down, picked up the journal, handed it to him.

Peter's feelings for Minnie crystallized in that gesture, and he felt his eyes beginning to fill with tears of gratitude that she should be there, that she should talk to him, be so kind, overlook his shame, his guilt, his inadequacy. He bit his lower lip. Still the tears came. Flashes of the farm ebbed and flowed; the deep caves loomed yawningly but not invitingly.

Minnie saw how it was with him, gave a little cry, came to sit at his feet, taking the hand that held the pen. "Oh, Peter, it's all right." She pressed her cheek to his knee.

Through blurring tears he could see her head at his knee, her hair shimmering in the brightness of the bathroom lights, hair distorted but clear in his mind, raven hair, and he moved his free hand toward it, drawing back for a moment, then starting falteringly forward again, reaching out until his fingers felt the strands, then pressing his hand to her head, moving it along the way the hair lay, filling with the simple joy of touching again, and wanting to touch again.

Minnie raised her head to look up at him, and now, as she took his caressing hand in her own, kissing the back of it, he saw the miracle of her tears, the delicate gathering of crystal fluid that welled up, trembled on the lower lashes, and then spilled over to the cheeks.

He was so overcome by her concern and his own love for her

that he began to sob, his shoulders shaking. Minnie got up, moved to his side to take his head in her hands, pressing it to her breasts, stroking his hair and murmuring soft things as he wept.

And when it was over, Minnie dabbed at her eyes with Kleenex from the dispenser, after she had handed him some, smiling hopefully as he blew his nose and dried his eyes.

"Don't say you're sorry," she said.

"No." His blood sang and he saw that she was Minnie and that she was more than he'd thought, that magic had been wrought, and she was something in his life which had been so empty.

"I must have needed that," she said. "I don't have my headache any more." She laughed. "Better than aspirin."

He laughed. He hadn't, after all, forgotten how.

"You have a fine laugh, Peter."

He blushed and did not at all feel like running.

"You know, that's the first time I've heard you do that."

He didn't know what to say.

She moved to sit on the edge of the bathtub again. "Tell me more about Mr. Hochdruck."

What could he tell her? He was simply there and he bothered Peter a lot. "He comes around, usually when people aren't there, but not always."

"He's gone now?"

"Yes."

"Is he a real person?"

"Real?" What did she mean?

"If he comes and goes . . . Can I tell you what I think, Peter?"

He nodded, hoping she would always do that.

"I think Mr. Hochdruck is an imaginary person, an hallucination."

She didn't know about how They had powers beyond the ordinary, how They could arrange anything, even make it appear like hallucinations to anybody They pleased. How could he explain it without having to tell about Them? He didn't have to because she went on, her face moody and reflective.

"When I was a little girl, my parents lived for a while close to a dam near Sacramento where my father worked in the power station. It was miles from everywhere and there were no close neighbors, and so I was terribly lonely, with no one my own age to talk to, no playmates. So I invented Kathy, formed her out of my own mind like lots of little girls do, gave her form and substance. She was very much like me—after all, she was me! But she could do things I couldn't, like walking through walls, spying on people and reporting what they were saying, and going anywhere I told her to, like flying up to the clouds and telling me how it felt, what they were made of. We'd have long talks, we'd play dolls, house, have tea in tiny china, go everywhere together. She even talked back to me."

Minnie paused, lost for a while in those years. "I guess I invented her because I needed somebody to talk to, so I wouldn't be so cut off from the world of my own kind. And I think you've invented Mr. Hochdruck for the same reason."

Then she was on her feet, taking one of his hands. "I'm going to bed now, Peter." She gazed at him steadily. "Remember, we all need somebody, you, me, Andros—everybody." She looked at him for another long moment, then smiled, turned and walked out, waving briefly at the door.

26

Bathroom—Entry No. 25

I love Minnie.

I told her about Hochdruck. I didn't tell her about Them. She asked me if she could tell me what she thinks and I said yes and she said it seemed to her Hochdruck came out of my mind.

(That would explain how Hochdruck can come and go at will, how he always knows everything I'm thinking. But it doesn't mean it's true.)

After she left I felt different.

It must be because I cried. I knew that would do something. Or maybe it's because I love her.

It's hard writing I love Minnie, but it's true.

Peter Hartsook

27

DEAR MR. COLBERT:

I am sending this to your office in St. Louis as you requested and hope it reaches you wherever you are.

I want to thank you for the telephone calls. They are very reassuring and let me know you are on the job.

As for your requests for names and addresses and the case histories, I will send you separate letters with the names and addresses (where possible, and if and when), but I do not think you will find them very helpful. I've heard they all live in this part of the country, none west of the Mississippi, where, I presume, you will be when you get the letters. I want you to know this will be very difficult to get and I think it will be expensive. It is only because you think it important that I am pursuing it.

As for the case histories, I talked with Dr. Sheckley again, but didn't get anywhere, so I knew I would have to use money. (How right you were!) I located an employee in the administration building who needed $500 (this is getting expensive!) and she is reading from the files into a tape recorder I provided. She doesn't take them out of the office or photograph them (she doesn't dare!). I had the first tape transcribed and it is enclosed. As you say, it may help you handle them when you make contact (and I still think personal contact will be necessary even though you've told me how you feel about it). I know I would not want to bump into any one of them (so you see I sympathize—Charles is enough!).

Keep up the good work and let me hear from you as soon as you get any definite leads, and let me hear from you even if you don't. Something may develop at this end, too.

Sincerely,

(Mrs.) MARIETTA LE MOYNE

Enc.: Case History

PETER HARTSOOK

Patient was born in Mountbury of predominantly German stock, a second generation removed from immigrant forebears.

Interviews with patient's father and other relatives indicate he was a happy youngster, growing up in a close family with lots of aunts and uncles around. His mother, Hilda, died when he was twelve. She died in labor, and Peter never forgave his father for her death for years. His view of his father then was that he was a blustery, stubborn man who drove Hilda unmercifully. He evidently loved his mother, felt if she hadn't been worked so hard to keep the house so clean and get the meals on time, heavy German meals with touches of old Vienna, according to friends, she'd have had the energy and physical resources to survive the birth of Peter's sister, who died in infancy, and for that he also blamed his father.

To get away from the old memories, Gunther Hartsook, the patient's father, says he closed his shop in Mountbury, where he sold records and phonographs and radios and radio equipment, and moved to Price, where he opened another store and branched out into television sales and repair. He states he thought it would be good for Peter, who he said had turned sour and taciturn, and he declares he was right. Peter went to work for his father, and when Gunther Hartsook retired at fifty-five, Peter took the reins. Patient's father says that through the years the pain of his mother's and sister's passing gradually left Peter, and his son was able to be friends with him. The father never remarried. They never talked about the mother or sister.

Patient married Marcella Ketelby, a frail girl who grew up on a farm near Price, and he entered a happy period of his life. The Ketelbys report he enjoyed the farm and their company. Peter's father believes it must have been reminiscent of the old family in Mountbury, all the relatives, some of whom were farmers. Sometimes Peter would go out to the farm, help with the chores or field work. He seemed to the Ketelbys to be a frustrated farmer.

Marcella hated the farm. As noted, she was not a healthy person. She'd had rheumatic fever when a child, and the illness lingered with her. Patient was her opposite: alive and robust. Marcella's parents believe Peter never understood Marcella's leanings toward sewing and reading, television and the movies, all the sedentary things, and, like his father, he was not very tolerant of her inactivity. In time she developed a severe heart condition and one night, as they were watching television, she had an attack and died. The Ketelbys in no way blame Peter's behavior, but they do admit to his inability to comprehend their daughter's fragile nature.

Patient went immediately into a psychotic state. At the hospital he acted as if he thought the nurses and doctors were jailers. At times patient becomes violent, will touch nothing, will allow no one to touch him, will scream and lash out if they do. Mentions of bodily functions, sensual or sexual things, any strong feelings, trigger episodes, many of them mute states. He is constantly looking for microphones.

The elder Hartsook came out of retirement to run the television business and patient was admitted to Berylwood from Fairview Hospital. Tentative diagnosis: schizophrenia, paranoid type, with catatonia.

28

CHARLEMAGNE BREATHED deeply with noisy satisfaction, a sweep of his arm taking in the cloudless sky, the distant red barn, ring of trees down the glen, the flowers, hills, stumps, birds and everything else in sight, as if it were all his. "A wonderful view, Minerva. Something out of the picture books, that's what it is, and put here for us to enjoy."

"It is beautiful." Minnie looked around. "This was a pasture at one time."

"All the land should so revert."

Minnie brushed a lock of hair out of her eyes. "If only it weren't so hot today!"

They were lying on short grass beneath a large oak, their heads against an old log that had long ago lost its bark, and they were looking down the slope to an open, grassy area that had been invaded by wild pinks, prodigal clover and asters. Beyond it was the barn. Father Bischoff had wandered off to commune, as he put it, his thoughts in the privacy of the far trees even before he moved off. Andros had picked one of the larger trees to climb, one in what had been the barnyard, and he was halfway up making like a chattering chimpanzee. Peter, after having sat silently with them for a time, got up to stroll among the vines, weeds and flowers.

It had been Minnie's suggestion to stop. They had left Bartlettville after an early breakfast, had traveled more than four hours in country that was becoming greener and richer than any they had so far seen, and when they came upon this dell with its quaint barn, Minnie commanded Charlemagne to stop the car.

Charlemagne drove on the shoulder for a few hundred feet to make sure she meant it, then stopped beneath the overhanging limbs of a grove of trees. When they opened the doors of the air-conditioned car they were greeted by blasts of ovenlike air. By the time they had clambered over a rustic fence, ignoring the NO TRESPASSING signs, brushed into a thicket heavy with saplings, walked through the cool bath of shadow that fell on them from larger trees, reaching the small valley Minnie had seen, they were relieved to be able to sit and relax and open collars, for it was truly a hot day.

Charlemagne said, "Being here like this makes me happy I don't have to teach at Oblout any more."

"Being here makes me want to blossom, like the flowers."

"Not that it's a revelation, my dear. I was growing out of it, getting more restless with each passing year. The kids were getting restless, too. I saw it coming. They had more savvy each succeeding year. They bought less and less, and it was getting harder to fool them, which is another way of saying perpetuate the system. Yes, I'm glad I'm out of it, past the hypocrisy. The kids have taken over, stirring the soup and spilling a little in the process, and it's about time somebody did." Charlemagne had removed his shoes and socks, massaged a foot thoughtfully.

"I know what you were. A professor of medieval history."

"Is that what I was?"

"According to Andros. And as far as I can see, you still are. You do lecture a lot, you know."

"I have been told that."

"I don't mind, though, although I'm not sure how the Bartlettville Parents Against Filth feel about it."

"You know what you are, Minerva?"

"I know what I am, a vagrant breeze pleasurably perfumed and lingering in places I like, and I like that, but I have a feeling the silent majority wouldn't think so."

Charlemagne shifted to his other foot. "The neighbors do get restless when you start moving the furniture around, open the draperies and get rid of the room dividers."

"Why do you suppose that is?"

"There's too much social unpredictability in persons who don't draw the shades."

"Tripping out is no crime, private or public."

"Not if you move faster than the men with the labels."

They watched the sweeping flight of a meadow lark. It flung out a series of liquid, high notes across the sloping valley.

Minnie said, "I wanted to go to bed with you last night. It had to do with how magnificent you were with those people." When he turned on his elbow, she silently bore his inspection of her profile. "The feeling wore off."

Andros shouted to them, waving from the top of the barn, where he had jumped from the tree. They waved back. He turned, started to walk around on the roof. Father Bischoff had melted into distant trees. Peter stood still among flowers like a dog sniffing the breeze. They watched him start off in a new direction.

"It must be boiling out there." She added wryly: "I wonder how Mr. Hochdruck stands it."

"He's told you about him?"

"We had a talk."

"Well, everybody needs somebody, and a Doppelgänger will do in emergencies." He grunted. "Odd name to pick. Hochdruck is a German engineering term. Means 'high pressure.' There's also Schmerzen, aches and pains, and Drunter und Druber, old over and under. But Hochdruck beat out the competition, it seems."

In sudden happy inspiration Minnie got to her feet, said she'd had enough sitting, they'd sat in the car for four hours and they'd lain there under the trees for nearly an hour, it was hot and it was time they joined elemental forces.

She hop-danced a few steps, turned on her toes to regard Charlemagne mischievously, raking sweat-damped hair out of her eyes. Settling down, she said, "Shall we strike a blow for unencumbrance? Cast off the fetters? Be free and beautiful?" She drew off her dress, kicked off her shoes, slid out of her panty hose and undid her brassiere, throwing it into the air with a graceful sweep of arm.

She spread her arms to embrace space, closing her eyes and breathing deeply. "The air hasn't fled, Charlemagne. It's here to be felt, to be enjoyed, to be refreshed by." She took off her panties, held them impishly at arm's length, dropped them to the bower floor with a little laugh.

Charlemagne lay there blinking.

Minnie turned and with feline grace ran high on her feet into the sunlight like a ballet dancer, crying, "Come out, come out wherever you are. The air is sweet, delicious, like wine." She pirouetted, ran a few more steps, raised her hands as if reaching for the sun, looking like a worshipping wood nymph.

Andros was making noises on the barn roof. "Hey! Hey, wait!" He scrambled to the cupola, raised the window. And Peter, who'd heard her, stopped where he was and looked across the field in amazement. Father Bischoff materialized from behind a giant oak at the far end of the glade, wiped perspiration from his forehead with a handkerchief as he stared.

"We shall purge our hides, cleanse our bodies," Minnie called out gaily, dashing through flowers, curving around stumps. Andros opened the barn door and stepped out to watch her. She continued, "We shall wash them with the sun, scrub them with the wind."

Andros grinned with pleasure and anticipation as he started toward her, removing his clothes as he came, his eyes glowing with the prospect of a new game. When he reached her he was naked; she took his hand, and together they ran like the wind in a wide circle that took them toward the trees where Charlemagne lay. They turned, bounded up the blossom-studded slope to stand before him, hand in hand, flushed and panting.

"Come on, Charlemagne," Minnie said. "The air's fine."

"It looks like too much exertion to me."

They moved to him, one on either side, taking his arms, pulling him up. Andros would have stripped him, but Charlemagne pulled away, saying, "All right, all right," and laughing as he started to undress. "I will join the romp and divest the day of its cares." And in a few moments he was as naked as they and reaching for their hands.

Andros held off, absorbed in his stare. "Your hair is black down there."

"Senility started on the roof," Charlemagne said, grabbing his hand.

They skipped down the hill, bodies flashing white in the hot sun, laughing, skirting brambles and stumps and irregular ground, slashing through brittle weeds to where Peter stood near the barn looking confused and uneasy. They joined hands to complete a circle and danced around him, telling him to get with it, a dance had been decreed, a dance with the sun as a partner to the madness, bees make way, they were going to be nature's children.

Peter's eyes stayed on Minnie, her flushed face and merry blue eyes, her black hair flowing this way and that in the hot breeze, and when he seemed sure of her he slowly began to take his clothes off. They laughed gleefully, wickedly, and soon they had his hands in theirs, and then they broke and ran around the barn, and Peter ran with them to where Father Bischoff had been standing. But he wasn't there.

"His clothes are here!" Andros cried out, pointing to the garments at the base of a tree.

"But where is he?" Minnie looked this way and that.

"Here," Father Bischoff said, stepping out from behind the bole of a large oak, his face scarlet, his eyes alight.

"Yes, there!" Minnie cried.

And they all ran to him and took his hands and drew him into their circle, the valley filling with their singing and raucous cries, their laughter, breaking and running.

Andros jumped atop a tree stump, assumed the stance of a Hercules, his sweat-sheened muscles glinting in the sun. "Behold, Andros is the sun!"

"We won't worship you!" Minnie led them to converge on Andros, lifting him off, dumping him to the ground, giggling and gurgling, Minnie managing to escape his efforts to pull her down to him. They ran off, Andros scrambling to his feet in pursuit.

They ran to the relative coolness of a wooded ravine, found a patch of ripe red raspberries at its edge and picked some, joking and snickering and feeding them to each other. They slipped on old oak leaves, advanced across the slopes past the barn in mock ferocity, hit out with young branches at the dogs of war Charlemagne said were in front of them. They wove garlands of flowers and when they put them on Charlemagne he protested he was not Lady Chatterley's lover. They played a muscle-straining game of tag, Minnie proving, to everyone's astonishment, to be the fleetest of all. Then they fell in the shimmering high grass in a heap, convulsive with laughter and weak from their exertions.

And that is where they were found by the two sheriff's deputies.

29

THEY LAY where they had fallen in the weeds, at first breathing hard and fast, then slowing, but still not moving, letting the delicious sense of harmony, communion and peace pulse over them.

Peter was on his back, Minnie at his right, on her side, pressed hard to him, her lips near his ear, one arm thrown across his chest to touch Charlemagne, who lay at an angle at his left. Peter knew Father Bischoff was somewhere near his feet because their legs intertwined, and Andros was to Minnie's right, probably pressing to her.

Sweat trickled in the hot sun, and their bodies were washed by a torrent of odors: damp soil, raspberries, honeysuckle, clover. And then, for Peter, there was the tantalizing body smell of Minnie: heady, light and sweet.

It was a farm, there was a barn, and he had expected to smell the familiar things of the Ketelbys', feeling the comfort of family as he did with them, for Charlemagne, Father Bischoff, Andros and Minnie were his family, and yet there was no fragrance of hay, no manure, no sound of lowing cattle, grunting swine, and of course there was no Marcella.

He remembered Minnie running naked across the flower-strewn valley, stopping suddenly to pluck a solitary blossom, the slender curve of her white back bending to the task, to leap up with the prize, her black hair flying in the breeze, shouting with joy, scattering birds with a great scuffling of wings and bright flashes of black and gray, yellow and red.

He remembered how she smiled when she saw him, and how he approached her, trembling with delight, shame being suddenly stripped from him.

He remembered how, when they had suddenly fallen together, Minnie, in a swift, famished movement, went to him, and the memory stirred him even in the enervating heat of the summer afternoon.

How sweet it was to lie together, naked to the world and each other, fears forgotten, wearing only truth and trust!

And then, suddenly, there were the two deputies staring down at them, men in fawn-colored Stetsons and gray tailored shirts with a badge pinned to the pocket, a young, blond bear of a man with freckles and wide brown eyes and an older man with sallow skin, pale-blue eyes and a hardness around the tired mouth.

For a long moment it was a simple tableau: two officers standing and five naked people snuggling in the weeds. And in that instant Peter saw, in wild distortion, that these were the police who came for him when he killed Marcella, and their cold eyes, judging and cruel, flashed like neon.

Minnie stirred and got to her feet, the deputies wide-eyed at her nakedness. Minnie smiled and said, "Aren't you two hot with all those clothes on?"

The younger deputy let go his breath. "Jesus Christ!"

Peter and the others got to their feet. The older deputy squinted. "You're on something."

"We're not," Minnie said.

The deputy watched her, then said, "All right, get your clothes on." And when they didn't move, he said, "I mean right now."

The blond deputy pulled in his stomach, drew his shoulders back. "You heard the man." He didn't seem to be able to take his eyes off Minnie.

Charlemagne sighed, made a wry face and started to move past the younger man. The deputy grabbed Charlemagne's arm. "Where you think you're going?"

"My clothes are up there."

"What's your name, Pops?"

"It's not Pops."

"So what is it?"

"It's Charlemagne."

"I'll bet." The deputy smirked. "Where you from?"

Charlemagne looked from one to the other. "From the Island of Langerhans."

"Where the hell's that?"

"A little to the left of the Island of Reil, right near the Fissure of Sylvius, between the Greater and Lesser Ionics."

The young deputy hauled off, hit Charlemagne right in the stomach. Charlemagne fell to his knees, his face contorting and turning beet red, holding his middle. He vomited. Peter stared in shock.

The young deputy moved to him to get him up and maybe do it again. The older man said, "All right, Al. That's enough."

The deputy named Al looked down at the dry-retching Charlemagne, then turned with a grin to see if Minnie was appreciating his little show, taking steps toward her. When he was near enough, Minnie, with her bare foot, kicked him hard in the testicles. Deputy Al fell like a bull elephant, curled himself into a ball, teeth gnashing, holding his balls.

For Peter, and for all, it was happening in slow motion. The older deputy jumped to Minnie, jerked her arm around behind her.

Andros, recovering from his own shock, took a step toward the deputy holding Minnie, swung his arm and fist in a wide circle, slamming the deputy in the mouth.

The older deputy let go of Minnie, staggered back, blood staining his lips, surprised and dazed, drawing his revolver as he fell, rolling and coming to a stop on his stomach, the weapon pointing at them as Deputy Al, his face white, one hand on his crotch, got up shakily, also drawing his revolver.

The older deputy had the good sense to say, "Take it easy, Al," for Peter could see the deputy might start firing. The older man got to his feet, put his gun away, walked to Andros, looked him in the eye, saying nothing, it becoming a stare-down, the deputy finally moving away to look at Charlemagne, whose face had changed color, from beet red to off-white.

"Goddam hippies," Al said, seething, hobbling around. "Everlasting goddam hippies."

"These aren't hippies," the older man said.

"Goddam pigs," Minnie said in retaliation, spitting. Peter looked at her in surprise. He'd never seen her so angry. She looked beautiful.

The older deputy moved to look down at her, scowling, wiping blood away with the back of his hand. "Like I said, you get your clothes on." He looked around at them. "The whole lot of you."

They started to move around the valley, picking up their clothes, the younger deputy walking straddle-legged for a while, Andros helping Charlemagne, who had difficulty getting himself together.

When Father Bischoff put on his clerical outfit, Deputy Al's mouth dropped open. He said, "I'll be goddamned."

Father Bischoff said, "You may well be."

30

The second case history follows:

SCOTT KLEINSCHMIDT

Patient was born in Wood Park, son of Robert and Agnes Kleinschmidt. His father inherited a meat-packing business in Chicago, where he has offices. Their residence is still Wood Park. Patient is an only child, his parents were more than normally attentive, and Scott was sheltered and protected from the outside world all his young years.

Patient was a precocious child, had a very high IQ, somewhere in the neighborhood of one hundred and eighty, did not have a normal childhood, being insulated from everything. It is reasonable to assume the world was pretty filtered down by the time it reached Scott. His radio, television programs and books were chosen for him by his mother, but Scott managed to sneak copies of science fiction to his room and through them he escaped the world his parents made for him, that world being the violin and the piano, and interviewees agree he grew up hating both. He was shown off at social gatherings, gave concerts here and there as a kid. In school, because of his unusual scholastic abilities, he was prodded, tested and questioned, and great things were expected of him.

When Scott graduated from Wood Park High School, it was with the highest grades ever given there, and he was sent directly to the University of Illinois, where, for the first time in his life, he found out what the rest of the world was like. Roommates relate that he discovered girls, movies and sports, not necessarily in that order, turned out to have normal drives in these directions but lacked experience to enjoy them.

It is claimed that when he realized all the things he'd never had, he knew he didn't want to go to school any longer, but guilt and shame and love for his parents made him continue. He had never failed at anything, and he didn't want to fail then, either for his own sake or his parents', and yet he could not go on.

Patient confided in friends that he was struggling with grave problems regarding school, desires, girls, his parents, his aims, and told them he knew he would probably be in the percentile that would be washed out.

One day in English class he announced his name was Andros, that he had just arrived on Earth from Acheron to do a study of the sexual habits of Earth females. His classmates thought he was joking, but they soon learned he was deadly serious. He was taken to a hospital, his parents were summoned, and patient was ultimately admitted to Berylwood for treatment. Tentative diagnosis: schizophrenia with a highly developed delusional system.

3 1

NEW TRIER COUNTY is one of the smaller counties in the state, one of the few green and hilly areas before the land rises to the west to the high wheat plains. There are monolithic grain elevators beside railroad tracks, the farms are neat and clean, though none of them are small any more, wheat, corn and sugar beets compete with cattle, swine and lambs for profit, and the people wear a mixture of frontier, including high-heeled boots, and conventional city styles.

There are other towns in the county larger than New Trier, but it is the county seat because it is centrally located and the courthouse and county jail were built there more than fifty years ago. The population is listed at 2,500 and it has not increased in twenty-five years. Births have exceeded deaths, but when New Trier youngsters reach the age of reason, they often move elsewhere. It is a staid, steady community, though the advents of radio and television have shaken the roots, changing living standards, rendering residents aware of what is going on in the rest of the country. Not that they approve.

The county jail is a two-story ivied, weathered stone block building with offices, radio room, holding tank and living quarters for Sheriff Len Samuels and his family on the first floor. The second floor houses a formidable cell block for men and an equally repellent set of three cells for women. The basement is used for registration and identification, storage, files and equipment, most of it old and worn. There is a courtyard that barely accommodates four county cars and the sheriff's automobile. It was not large enough to handle the Continental, which had to be parked on the street.

Deputies Bill Grogan and Al McKelty had instructed Charle-

196

magne, Peter, Minnie, Father Bischoff and Andros to sit in the chairs by the stairs while they got ready for them, but the arrestees wouldn't stay sitting down. Andros had to have a Coke out of the machine, and Minnie was interested in the Wanted posters.

"Hey, look," she said to the others, holding up the sheaf and pointing to the picture of an ugly bank robber wanted by the FBI. "Looks like him." She pointed to Grogan. They gathered there, compared, nodded, agreeing. Even Peter.

"I told you all to sit down," Grogan said in a growling voice. "You want I should handcuff you to them chairs?"

"You wouldn't do that," Minnie said.

"Hey! Let's see some handcuffs," Andros said, moving to the counter behind which Grogan was getting ready to work under a fluorescent light with a stubby pencil.

"There's a nice room for you upstairs," Grogan said. "You'll be in it pretty soon, so shut up and sit down."

McKelty came out of the radio room, which snapped and crackled with messages, moving to come around the counter. "You want me to make him sit down, Bill?"

Grogan looked at Andros as if he'd like McKelty to do nothing better, but he said, "Don't bother." He moistened the end of the pencil. "While you're here, you can go first. Empty your pockets."

"I can't."

McKelty was irked. "Why the hell not?"

"Because they're empty already."

Grogan said, "Let's see, kid. Turn 'em inside out."

Andros did. There was nothing in them.

Grogan nodded, the pencil poised. "O.K. What's your name?"

"Andros."

"Andros what?"

"Just Andros. A-n-d-r-o-s."

"Look," McKelty said. "Everybody's got a first and last name. Now Mr. Grogan here is asking you nice and polite. What's your name?"

"Andros."

McKelty looked as if he'd love to clobber Andros, but Grogan shook his head. "We'll let that pass for the time being," Grogan said. "How old are you?"

"One hundred and seventy-five."

Both deputies looked at him, faces darkening.

"That's how many perihelions Acheron Four has made since my emergence," Andros said. "But each revolution of the planet is roughly equivalent to an Earth year, give or take a few days, so it's more or less accurate."

"Shit," McKelty said, turning away in disgust.

"Where do you live?" Grogan asked wearily.

"Usually on the fourth planet of the star Acheron in the Pleiades in the constellation Taurus, but right now—"

"The hell you do!" McKelty roared, turning back, reaching across and grabbing Andros' shirt front.

"I'd be careful if I were you," Charlemagne said calmly, moving to the counter, still trying to rub the ache out of his stomach. "I'm sure you would not want to start an interstellar war." When Grogan and McKelty stared, Charlemagne went on: "Things have been peaceful along the rim worlds, but you're not helping."

McKelty let go of Andros, shook his head in frustration. Charlemagne continued, "Surely you must be aware that other worlds are watching, that we are suspect, being weighed in the balance, so to speak. All our actions are scanned by monitors that flit here and there in the atmosphere." He let that sink in, then put a hand on Andros' shoulder. "This man speaks the truth. If you don't believe him, I'd suggest a polygraph test. That would ease your minds."

"We don't have a polygraph," McKelty said. "Besides, I don't buy all that bullshit."

Charlemagne shrugged. "Have it your way, but don't say you haven't been warned. For the record, I think you'd better tell us what the charges are so they can be transmitted to Central Filtering Complex."

"We were picking daisies," Minnie said. "Is that a felony in this state?"

"What's *your* name?" McKelty snapped at her.

"Minnie the Pooh and pooh to you."

"For openers," Grogan said, "you all were trespassing on Deke Lawler's land, and neither he nor the sheriff like that. There's also lewd conduct, assaulting an officer and resisting arrest."

McKelty pointed to Peter. "How come he never says anything?"

"He's probably in the outhouse," Andros said.

Father Bischoff pressed to the counter. "If you ask me," he said sniffingly, "your only salvation is to sing the seven penitential psalms, people so brimming with hate as you."

"Who pressed your button?" McKelty snarled. "Everybody's the same here, priests, too."

"No Holy Viaticums for you," Father Bischoff said darkly. "Your soul will rot in hell."

"I don't give a shit," McKelty retorted. "You'll be in hell before me."

"What's going on here?"

They all turned to see Sheriff Len Samuels, a chunky, tough-looking man with a cigar in the side of his mouth, stride forward, his gray hair standing every which way, as if he hadn't had time to comb it. He was followed by Deke Lawler, a sleek, gross man with dark, darting eyes and plastered-back black hair. He wore a perpetual worried look. He was sheriff before Samuels.

Samuels faced McKelty. "Is that any way to talk to a priest?"

"Sheriff—"

"I heard it, too," Lawler said, equally outraged. "I never expected to hear anything like that in this jail." He turned to Father Bischoff. "Father, please accept our apologies. I'm sure the sheriff here will see to it that Deputy McKelty apologizes, too."

199

"Sheriff," Grogan said, "they are the ones."

Sheriff Samuels stepped back, astonished. "They are? The priest, too?"

Grogan nodded.

He clamped yellowed teeth down hard on the stub of cigar, not knowing what to think about that, and Lawler muttered, "May heaven protect us."

Samuels said then, "Bill, you come with me and Deke." The three men walked to Samuels' office, went in, closed the door.

In the office, Grogan, who had been chief deputy under both sheriffs, was asked how he came upon these people, and he said he and McKelty, on a routine run past the Lawler place, spotted the Continental, checked the area for the occupants and found them in Lawler's valley. "I called in as soon as I could."

"I know you did." Samuels looked to Lawler. "Took a while to locate Deke."

"I was at Doc Orbst's," Lawler said. "Haven't been feeling up to par lately. They see anything?"

"Don't know yet."

"Well, go on."

Samuels and Lawler were shaken to hear in vivid detail in what state Grogan and McKelty found the people, especially Father Bischoff, and they were further disturbed to learn what happened when they confronted them. In fact, Sheriff Samuels found it so difficult to believe he went to the door to peek out at the girl and came back shaking his head. "She don't look like that kind of a girl. Looks real delicate."

"She might look delicate, Sheriff, but she sure got McKelty."

The sheriff told him he and McKelty should be ashamed of themselves, letting a mere wisp of a girl get the better of them. It was then that he saw the blood crusted on Grogan's lip. "Don't tell me the girl did that, too!" Grogan said no, she didn't, and he told him how it happened. And Samuels had to go take a look at Andros. "Him I see. Could be a fighter."

Lawler, who had been thinking, said if the priest was out there with the others in his valley, doing what Grogan said they were doing, there must have been a good reason. Lawler was Catholic and did not take kindly to thoughts of rogue priests.

Grogan started to tell them what had happened at the jail before Samuels and Lawler arrived, but Samuels cut him off, told him to bring them all in, which Grogan proceeded to do, but not with any cooperation from the lawbreakers.

Once inside, Andros moved around as if the office were a museum room he was examining; Minnie described to Samuels in some detail what she thought of Grogan and McKelty, the county jail and law-enforcement officials; Father Bischoff went to a corner, bowed his head, closed his eyes, put the fingers of his left hand to the bridge of his nose, his right hand fingering his beads, which he was counting. Charlemagne conducted Peter to a chair and stood beside him, cool and detached.

"Please," Samuels said. Lawler went to Father Bischoff and, at a proper moment, interrupted to ask him to come join them. Grogan suggested to Andros that he could look at everything later. Minnie ran out of steam.

When they were all in one place, across the desk from Samuels, he said, "I want to know who you are and what you are doing in this part of the country."

Charlemagne indicated the group. "I happen to be liege lord to these and as such they are beholden to me. Their lives are also in my trust."

Samuels reddened, coughed and shifted in his chair. "That's not answering the question."

Grogan broke in to explain that the Continental belonged to Charlemagne, that he was really Dr. Charles Le Moyne, a member of the faculty at Oblout University, according to his driver's license and papers he had in his billfold, and that he was carrying more than two thousand dollars in cash and had three cashier's checks for five thousand each. Samuels and Lawler were impressed. Then Grogan informed them that the others had no papers at all, no licenses, no identification of any kind.

"Nothing?" Samuels asked, incredulous.

"Nothing," Grogan said.

Samuels shook his head, faced the lawbreakers again. He was

very stern. "I think you'd better tell us why you're in New Trier County."

"We're here for the same reason we'd be anywhere," Charlemagne said. "We wait only the command that bids the trumpets' sound to war so our valiant army can set forth to do battle."

"Stop that!" the sheriff said sharply.

Lawler said, "Just what is your game, Dr. Le Moyne?"

"I guess vanquishing the infidels would properly sum it up."

"Jesus," Grogan said. Lawler scowled at him.

"Is there a Bible in this jail?" Father Bischoff asked. "I wouldn't be inclined to answer any questions without one."

"Of course there is a Bible here, Father," Lawler said. "There are several, unless the sheriff has ordered them removed."

"They're still here," Samuels said. Then, to Charlemagne: "Who are these infidels you mentioned?"

Father Bischoff said, "They are those who have fallen from grace, sir."

"I was asking him."

Charlemagne said, "If it were that easy, Sheriff, they should already be vanquished. Half the battle is searching them out."

"Searching them out?" Samuels leaned forward with sudden interest. Lawler's eyes snapped. "Is that what you do? Search them out?"

"I think," Father Bischoff said, "that it is time for prayer." Though the sheriff tried to stop him, Father Bishoff folded his hands, bowed his head and plunged on. "*Eliquan infamum, moribund pablum moronis est, aqua marina liggetus et myers est funeral prelibatis sum.* Amen."

"Amen," Lawler said, crossing himself.

Samuels was regarding Father Bischoff with narrowed eyes. "I thought the Church had discarded Latin."

Lawler said, "It has in most places, I've heard."

"Forgive me if I seem a little old-fashioned." Father Bischoff said. "I've been trying to break out, but the Council fathers are covered with fungus."

Lawler smiled. "I've never heard it put quite that way. But

202

from what I understand, Father, the trouble is really with the Holy See."

"We're not here to discuss the state of the Catholic Church," Samuels said, annoyed. "What we're here to do is find out what these people are doing here."

"Why is that so important?" Charlemagne asked.

Samuels raised his eyebrows. "Does it seem important?" And when Charlemagne replied that it did, Samuels said, "Then tell me, you mentioned searching and fighting. What do you search and what do you fight?"

"Ignorance, Sheriff."

"Ignorance?"

"Plain or fancy."

The sheriff thought about it. Lawler walked to the edge of the desk, leaned against it, looked down at his big hands, said with elaborate casualness, "What do you think of the *status quo*, Dr. Le Moyne?"

Charlemagne laughed. "Why, there isn't any such thing, Mr. Lawler. Even the beautiful must die."

"Jesus," said Grogan.

"There is a saying on my world," Andros said complacently, as if it were apropos of everything, " 'Rejoice with your life . . . for even as the fresner blooms . . . it is advanced . . . and the remainder cannot be multiplied.' "

"This is getting nowhere," Samuels said angrily, getting to his feet. "What I want to know is what you saw out there when you were in the valley, if you saw anything at all, anything interesting or unusual." Lawler regarded him nervously, but Samuels ignored him, faced them. "Now how about it, folks?"

"I saw a lot of guns," Andros said. "Big ones, little ones, machine guns, bazookas, and a lot of dynamite. It was all in the red barn."

"Oh, my God," Samuels said, dropping heavily into his chair.

"Jesus," Grogan said.

32

The third case history follows:

HOWARD PETERSEN

Patient is the youngest of five brothers and sisters, children of Oscar and Helen Petersen of Chicago. All the other children are married and have children. The family owns the Petersen Type Company of Chicago, one of the bigger rubber-stamp companies, Oscar being president, though Mr. Petersen admits the company is really run by the grandfather and patriarch, Grunneld Petersen. Howard was a vice-president of the company in charge of production.

The Petersen family is Catholic and evidently steeped in tradition, being inbreeders, as they admit, and very tightly knit.

When Howard was a little boy there was the usual conference between the Petersens and another related clan, this time the Nelsons, and it was decided that Howard would one day marry Selma Nelson, and he grew up accepting this decree, they say.

Howard was a good worker, dedicated, honest, and he accepted his role. But while Selma liked him, often said she loved him, Howard many times declared openly that he didn't like her. They spent much time together but not as a courting couple. It was more like brother and sister.

Patient kept delaying proposed dates for the marriage. The families issued an ultimatum that he must marry by age thirty. Howard became disturbed; there were conferences about his behavior. Finally, Howard came out and said he would not marry Selma. However, in the face of the gathering anger of the assembled clans, he gave in. Everything was arranged. It was to be a big wedding at the Church of St. Stephen, where Howard had been an altar boy years before.

On the day of the wedding, in the middle of the service, Howard walked out, got on a plane bound for Rome, claiming to be Father Bischoff, the name of a priest who had befriended him when he was a boy, and in Rome he demanded an audience with the Pope to intervene "for all his brother priests, to improve their working conditions and to change the rule on celibacy."

Patient had no credentials, no papers. He did not have a passport. He was transported home, did not respond well to private psychiatric treatment. His belief in his role as Father Bischoff was unshakable. The family sent him to Berylwood. Diagnosis: schizophrenia.

33

LEN SAMUELS and Deke Lawler had a good thing going. First one would be elected sheriff, and then, because state law prevented a sheriff from succeeding himself, the other would be voted to office. This had been going on for over twenty years and, while there had been other candidates almost every time, the contenders always lost. People were happy with Samuels and Lawler. At least they knew where they stood with them, which was more than they could say for the upstarts, the untested, ambitious challengers.

Both Samuels and Lawler felt they owed something to their constituents, so they were able to present to the public eye regimes without crimes: steady, respectable, uneventful terms in office. It wasn't that there was no corruption, graft, greed or venality. Everybody knew they took bribes and pay-offs, mostly from Alex Gleeb, the closest to an underworld figure that existed in the county. Gleeb ran the few houses of prostitution, bookie joints and card parlors in the county, and had declared publicly that he would never run a racially mixed house, which made people feel better. He had his own strong-arm contingent and was able to keep foreign operators from getting a foothold in the county, which he usually did quietly and efficiently with minimum bloodshed and always with the tacit approval of the sheriff's office. It was a matter of scratching backs.

And so it was that Dalphon Kendall Lawler, popularly known as Deke Lawler, was able to live quietly, if not luxuriously, on his land in the off years, renting out the arable land that he used to have to work before bellying up to the public trough, and keeping unused a small section of pastureland in a pretty little valley where his old barn stood. Samuels had his own estate, one of the finer, more modern homes in the better part of New Trier itself.

It was during Lawler's last hitch that both men became alarmed by incidents and trends elsewhere in the country, the rioting on school campuses, the hippie invasions, hints of and acts of rebellion, and they became fearful that such things might happen in New Trier County, though it boasted no university or college.

Both men found they were in agreement about causes and effects, as a result of long talks at many bars, at their homes, in the sheriff's office, and at public meetings of concerned citizens. For one thing, it seemed obvious to them that the average voter never took time to view issues or look into the political complexion of candidates and were therefore unable to see the obvious contradictions and the increasingly dangerous postures of the new, more liberal office seekers. The average voter was, therefore, uninformed, ignorant of the evils of the new breed of political aspirant. As a result, more and more of the wrong people were being elected; untried and untrue so-called progressives, those who mistakenly believed in permissiveness and stretching the Constitution to cover even those who advocated the overthrow of the country itself. To Samuels and Lawler, it was no wonder that there was lawlessness, violence, an increasing public debt, an invasion of privacy and an erosion of security throughout the land.

Nowhere, they believed, was the situation as terrible as it had become in the judiciary. They held that courts had gone berserk, the federal courts, and the Supreme Court in particular; dominated for so many years by the fanatics of the leftist ideology, these courts were now intoxicated with their power, abandoning both legality and reason. It was obviously only a matter of time before no man in America—or New Trier County— would be safe, Constitution or not.

In one speech before the New Trier Rotary Club, Sheriff Samuels made his position clear. He was quoted in the New Trier *Runner-News*: "Let me tell you something: The courts' peremptory excursion into dictatorship over states' rights and local control of schools is a travesty of major proportions. And this is to say nothing of the press. Ah, yes, the molders of public opinion, the newspapers and television, with their slanted, deceptive propaganda. Why, the whole system of the dissemination of information is corrupt. How cunning they are in their use of psychological mind-conditioning tricks! Make no mistake about it, my friends, the liberals have laid hold of the massive pillars of the news media. I can tell you they happen to have intimate control of them at all levels."

Not to be outdone, when Lawler spoke to the Kiwanis Club and thereby laid the groundwork for his future candidacy, he said, reading a speech he had worked days on: "You gentlemen don't seem to realize we're being sabotaged, all of us, the whole country, all the institutions. It's causing a dangerous rise in our national debt. It's causing the destruction of integrity, ambition and morality. We should have dropped the bomb when we alone possessed the know-how.

"This country is being attacked from within and without, slowly and insidiously. It therefore behooves every red-blooded American to take a stand for law and order, to resist with all his might, all his power, the rats that gnaw at the nation's vitals."

Both speeches were soundly applauded.

When pressed, both Samuels and Lawler could go on in hideous detail, enumerating who, in their minds, were responsible for the awful things that were happening, mostly faceless, nameless people who had wormed their way into high places. These were the gnawing rats, pretending to love the country they were destroying. Or worse, they were unknowing accomplices of gnawing rats, thinking they were making the country better, having swallowed the sugar-coated pills of welfare, education and civil rights.

It was obvious that neither Samuels nor Lawler was going to allow gnawing rats in New Trier County, and the Board of Supervisors didn't want them either, for when the matter of riot training came up for the sheriff, the ex-sheriff and the twenty deputies, the county footed the bill. Not only that, both sheriff and ex-sheriff worked together on a table of priorities, emergency maneuvers, defensive and offensive strategy. But for all that, the county had been invaded by only a few bearded, long-haired transients, usually carrying a guitar and a copy of *Stranger in a Strange Land*, sometimes with, sometimes without a long-haired girl companion in granny glasses and long dresses. After a night in jail these potential troublemakers were sent on their way.

But Samuels was not satisfied with token arrangements. The peril was there for all to see, and, for all people knew, Armageddon might be only a few steps away. So he talked with Lawler about seeing beyond the here and now, a plan for the future, for any contingency, and Lawler caught the fever. As Samuels put it, "Deke, you never have trouble if you are prepared for it." And Lawler agreed. Then Samuels pointed out that Lawler had a vacant barn on his property and suggested they buy surplus arms whenever and wherever they could and stash them in Lawler's barn. Sure, he knew it was against the law, and the Alcohol, Tobacco and Firearms Division of the U.S. Treasury Department had better never find out about it, but this was an emergency.

Lawler knew his wife, Letta, would not be pleased by the prospect, but he also knew that women are notably ignorant in matters of security and self-defense, so he consented.

Together Samuels and Lawler went to auctions, sales of surplus war materiel, and, using the county's good offices, sent away for items they could get in no other way. They had, in the process, amassed a formidable arsenal: a barnful of M-1 carbines, hand grenades, Garands, Springfields, hand guns of every size and description, both domestic and foreign, a few machine guns, antitank rockets, bazookas, explosives, fuse cord, sniper scopes and some radio gear for field operations.

They also organized an undercover group they called the Vigilans, and Gleeb and his men figured prominently in the table of organization. They never had a meeting or any training, but the Vigilans, which was wholly volunteer, was expected to rise to the occasion if and when attack was imminent.

Having so made New Trier County safe from invasion, Samuels and Lawler did not relax but had lately come to live in fear that their arms cache might become a matter of public knowledge. It was already a matter of public speculation. This in itself, they reasoned, would not be bad, even if it was illegal; in fact, it might prove a deterrent to those thinking of insurrection. But there was the opposition, the gnawing rats and their ilk. What about them? What if they were to discover that in a barn in Lawler's valley were the instruments with which revolution could be successfully waged?

And so it was that the arms depot became a matter of vital concern. The only answer was constant vigilance. That was why deputies always made sweeps by the land, night and day, making sure the weapons remained undiscovered and undisturbed.

That was why the disclosure by Andros that he had actually seen the guns, the ammunition and the dynamite when he crawled through the cupola and down through the barn shook the sheriff and his heir assured. Charlemagne and his party were from the outside. Were they part of the conspiracy to destroy the country? Were they a contingent of or representatives of the gnawing rats? Samuels and Lawler could not be sure. They certainly were evasive enough. It would be just like subversives to enlist the aid of a priest to color their operation protectively. And that naked romp in the valley, was that a cover for Andros? Again they were not sure. Spies were known to be devious and clever. They would have to be checked out very carefully. But what to do in the meantime?

The answer Samuels and Lawler decided upon was to pretend that nothing was amiss, not to lodge them in the county jail, where their incarceration would be a matter of public record, but rather to invite them to Lawler's home until information on them, which Samuels would request, came through. At Lawler's home they could be watched and evaluated. If they were agents of some kind, it would soon become evident. If they tried to flee the county, for example, that would be an admission of guilt. Not that they would ever get out of the county.

Both men were sure of that. The question remaining was: Would the people accept the invitation? If they did, it hinted of complicity; if they did not, Samuels would be forced to lock them up until it was clear just who and what they were.

As it turned out, Charlemagne, on behalf of his group, happily accepted Lawler's offer, and there were sighs of relief all around.

34

THE FIRST thing Lawler did when they reached his home was to introduce them to his wife, Letta, and inform her his guests would be with them for dinner and the night. Mrs. Lawler, a large, cheerful woman, was surprised but not displeased; though she hungered for it, her husband seldom brought people home for dinner, except Len and Kitty Samuels or, when he was in office, a few of his deputies and their wives. Mrs. Lawler immediately set to making beds in the roomy, sprawling country house and preparing a beef and kidney pie for eight, and she hummed as she worked.

The second thing Lawler did was to take his guests out to the barn, ignoring their questions, trudging up the slope in the late-afternoon sun ahead of them, wheezing with labored steps, his bright sport shirt clinging to his back with the sweat of effort by the time he opened a small door set into a larger one and directed them inside.

The interior of the barn had been emptied of everything removable, and everywhere, in the stalls, in the loft, on the floor and in slings hanging from crossbeams, were weapons: rifles, hand guns, carbines, machine guns and bazookas. There was such a profusion of weapons that it was impossible to calculate the number. Some were in cases, some were wrapped, and others just lay or were stacked together. There were also cases of ammunition, cartridges, explosives and miscellaneous equipment piled about.

As they moved about, impressed, Lawler held his breath, observing them, his eyes blinking brightly with expectation.

Minnie said, "Isn't it against the law to have all this?"

When Lawler didn't answer, Charlemagne said, "It certainly

isn't against the law of survival," and he moved to a rack of hand guns and picked one up.

"A Bergman M-10," Lawler said, moving to him and watching his face. "Danish pistol, nine-millimeter."

"Very pretty," Charlemagne said. "Very deadly, too, I presume."

Andros picked one up, Lawler saying, "A Luger M-08, toggle-joint lock, Maxim type."

"Careful where you point that thing," Charlemagne said.

"They're not loaded," Lawler said.

Andros pointed it to the windowed cupola high in the roof, pulled the trigger. The pin clicked on an empty chamber. Andros said, "Bang!" and grinned.

Peter was absorbed in a shotgun, not touching but staring at it. Minnie moved to him and asked, "That gun interest you?"

"My father," Peter said. "He had a gun like this. Used to go hunting." He went back to being lost in remembrances.

"It's unholy," Father Bischoff said, his distaste for it all showing in his face.

Charlemagne said, "How would you feel about it if it was a church we were defending?"

"God is our fortress and needs no defending. Guns are weapons of the devil, turn man against man."

Minnie sat down on a case of ammunition and looked dejected. "I think all this is awful. It makes me sick."

"That's taking a depressing view," Charlemagne said cheerfully. "After all, it's a way of getting rid of the surplus population. It's been going on for years, Minerva, and Mr. Lawler may be planning to take the matter into his own hands. After all, men have killed perhaps a hundred million of their fellow men in the last fifty years, so it's only natural. Think of where we would be today if all those people and their children were alive and crowding our streets."

"That's no reason it has to continue."

"A plague upon our times," Father Bischoff said. "The sins of the fathers."

Lawler didn't know what to make of them.

Charlemagne said to him, "It's a magnificent collection, Mr. Lawler, an omnium gatherum of weaponry. But what is it for?"

"Defense."

"What do you plan to defend, the whole country?"

Lawler said harshly, "You've read about the riots, haven't you?"

"Ah," Charlemagne said with an understanding nod. "An antidote to rebellion." He approached a cartridge case, picked up a scrap of paper on top of it. "It seems to me, though, you have enough materiel here to outfit a division."

"Just enough to discourage anybody who tries anything in New Trier County, that's all."

Charlemagne turned his back, brought out a pencil and began to draw on the scrap of paper on top of a barrel. He clicked his tongue. "It's too bad. Really, it is. Such a waste."

"Waste?"

"So unnecessary, Mr. Lawler."

"What are you doing there?" Lawler came to look at what Charlemagne was drawing, but Charlemagne quickly concealed it. Lawler looked him in the eye. "I sure don't get you."

"There are so many better ways of discouraging open resistance against established authority, ways that would not litter the streets with dead."

"Is that a fact," Lawler said with complete disbelief and lack of enthusiasm.

"And yet be just as effective." Charlemagne moved to a packing case, continued his work with the pencil. Lawler craned his neck to see. "If you want my opinion, Mr. Lawler, there are several principles being violated here." Lawler moved closer and was now able to see what Charlemagne was drawing. "When those who speak out against the established order are killed, they become martyrs. The believers who inevitably follow martyrs often don't speak out first. They kill first. And then it follows that there is open warfare and a lot of people are needlessly murdered."

"What *is* that thing you're drawing?"

Charlemagne turned, put the drawing in his pocket. "I'm sure a man like yourself, a man who believes in law and order, a peace officer—you and Samuels do take turns in office, judging by the pictures and posters in the county jail, isn't that right?—dedicated as you must be to keeping that peace, would not favor a general bloodletting. Am I correct, Mr. Lawler?"

Lawler considered it. "No, I'm not in favor of killing anybody, never did like that, never had to do that all the years I served and hope to serve, but I don't see how you can get around it if they're out there tearing up things, burning banks, bombing buildings."

Charlemagne brought out the drawing, added a few more details. "Of course."

"Will you tell me what that thing is?"

"This?"

Lawler nodded.

"Well," Charlemagne said reluctantly, "it so happens this is a trebuchet."

Lawler stared. "A what?"

"A trebuchet, Mr. Lawler. Seeing all these weapons put me in the mood to draw it."

Lawler examined it.

"It's a medieval weapon, but it is an effective one." Charlemagne laughed. "The way you were talking reminded me of it. You see, it was used in medieval times to discourage open rebellion, the kind you mentioned. It had a fine record along that line in its day. It's a pity it isn't used any more." Charlemagne crumpled it up, threw it down.

Lawler picked it up, straightened and smoothed the sheet. "How could a thing like this stop a rebellion?"

"Mr. Lawler, the trebuchet was the heavy howitzer of the medieval artillery. Its verge, or beam, was an entire tree, preferably a freshly cut one." He referred to the large wooden mangonel on wheels he had drawn. "You see, it operates very much like a trapshoot. A sling is attached here to the beam, and when this weight here at the end of the trestle is drawn up to the top by a windlass, it's ready to go. A tug on the lanyard, the weight goes down and the beam goes up, and—*voilà!*—the sling is swung in an arc and the projectile is on its way to the target."

Lawler was fascinated.

"One should not be deceived by its looks," Charlemagne said. "This little outfit could heave a hundred-pound rock five hundred yards."

Lawler was busy thinking of possibilities.

"In the old days," Charlemagne said musingly, "live prisoners were sometimes thrown into castles with this device. Or maybe dead horses. But for modern purposes—a riot, say—such an engine could throw a hundred pounds of nuts and bolts into the next street." Again he laughed. "It would beat pounding heads with batons, wouldn't it?"

Lawler could see that what Charlemagne said was right, that blood begets blood, and that, while he and Samuels seemed to have no recourse other than the gathering up of weapons to make a stand against what forces might be mustered against them, this instrument could clearly be an alternative. As such it would not result in death, in killings, and for that the people of the county would have him to thank if revolution did come. That his guests were not gnawing rats or their agents was now apparent. If they were they would not have been so open about such a clever weapon. And even if worse came to worst and this thing failed to quell the uprising, he and Samuels would always have the other weapons to fall back on.

"What is thrown is purely at the operator's option," Charlemagne was saying. "A hundred pounds of butter, grease or even ice cream."

"Or manure?" Visions danced in Lawler's head.

"Or manure. The variations are endless. And one more thing: The construction and ownership of a trebuchet isn't against the law. It can be wheeled anywhere, if one would use axles and modern-day automobile tires. The winch is no problem in this day. Instead of the old wooden sleeve bearings, one could use metal ones, even ball or roller bearings. Yes, it certainly would be a challenge, Mr. Lawler."

Lawler's eyes were gleaming with the possibilities. "Then it would be possible to build one, do you think? I mean right here, on this farm?"

"Build one? Here?" Charlemagne registered surprise. "Why, I suppose you could do so very easily, come to think of it. Do it in a few days, as a matter of fact. But of course you'd have to have the proper tools, a few saws and woodworking equipment. You know, one might do worse than emulate our forebears."

"Oh, I have those things you mentioned. Around the farm things are always getting out of whack, though I haven't done much lately. But . . ." Lawler struggled to ask it. "I was wondering—could *you* build it? *Would* you build it? You seem to know so much about it."

Charlemagne smiled. "Why, Mr. Lawler, it would be my pleasure."

Jail Minnie could have taken. At least in jail you know where you are and what you're doing or not doing. And you have someone to blame, something to gripe about: the knucklehead jailers, bull dykes in the main; or the food, ordinary and tasteless, or cellmates, mostly moth-eaten entrepreneurs of the streets or girls coming down from a high with wild faces, screaming meemies with rings under their eyes and red worms on their arms, girls in need of more than a good shower and Ice Blue Secret. God, yes.

But this little slice of Americana was getting to her, and she hated herself for allowing it to happen. Smile. Say nice things. Pretend. She didn't feel like it. Oh, the beef and kidney pie had been really great. And Mrs. Lawler had been pleasant and not too nosey. And the house had been thrown open to them. So what the hell, why was she so bitchy?

She knew why. It was Charlemagne. Charlemagne knuckling under. Charlemagne going along with law and order. Charlemagne hunched over the desk at one end of the room with Lawler and Andros, drawing up plans with a felt pen and a ruler and figuring weights and lift and levers and sizes of this and sizes of that. And Andros with a slide rule, yet, going along with it. Old Lawler looking like the cat that ate the bird, all smiles, head bobbing, drinking too much of his elderberry wine. Christ, he was getting loaded!

The other end of the room: Mrs. Lawler in front of the television set watching the movie and trying to ignore everybody. Peter wandering around looking at things. Father Bischoff fallen asleep in a platform rocker and snoring.

And what a room! Wall-to-wall shag rug. A crystal chandelier. Trophies in a glass case. A hat rack made of horns of animals with some of Lawler's Stetsons hanging there. An overstuffed chartreuse divan (where she was sitting). Matching chairs (into which Peter plopped once in a while). A large coffee table. An ormolu clock. An overstuffed zebra-striped plastic hassock. All stuff her commune would have tossed out in two minutes. God Bless America!

And what books! Mostly *Reader's Digest Condensed Books* with a sprinkling of books like *Red Cancer in the State Department*, *Wachtower Book of Recipes* (Watchtower Book of Recipes?), *Audel's Guide to Engineering*, *Law Enforcement for Peace Officers*, *The Diminishing Light of Freedom*, *Law or Anarchy?*, *Girl of the Limberlost*, *The Torch and the Cause* and *Training for Power and Leadership*.

On the coffee table was a cigarette box in the shape of a dog which Andros gleefully discovered would deliver a cigarette like a turd, with an imprinted message on its side: I CAME FROM NIAGARA FALLS. There was also a large redwood outhouse with a little man inside which Andros had found would turn to pee toward him when he opened the door. Andros, the natural voyeur, nearly wore it out. Lettering on one side said SOUVENIR OF YELLOWSTONE NATIONAL PARK.

Anyway, the divan was comfortable.

A tapestry in the form of an old sampler offered a smidgen of philosophy:

> A friend is not a man
> Who is taken in by sham;

218

He is a man who knows your faults
And doesn't give a damn.

Instant crap.

I *am* in a mood.

I know your faults, Charlemagne. You get carried away. You're worse than Andros the way you can't help yourself when you get excited about something, really get turned on. But can't you see that that awful collection of death in the red barn is enough? Do you have to be an accomplice, add to it? You're no Professor of Medieval History. You're a Professor of Mediocrity. You don't have feet of clay. You have feet of plastic. Oh, Charlemagne, how can I love you and hate you at the same time?

When she'd had a few minutes alone with him after dinner, she asked Charlemagne, "Do you really mean to build that goddam thing?"

"It's better than going to jail."

"Is it? I'd rather be in jail."

"We came, Minerva. We saw. We conquered. Are you forgetting the bastions?"

"You're forgetting them, Charlemagne, giving in like this, slobbering all over Lawler."

He looked at her sharply, and she thought for a moment he was going to tell her something, but all he said was "*Il est plus honteux de se défier de ses amis que d'en être trompé.*"

"Oh, come off it, Charlemagne. You know I don't care to hear that shit."

"It's La Rochefoucauld, my dear."

"I couldn't care less."

"It means it is more shameful to distrust one's friends than to be deceived by them."

So what the hell did that mean? Hurt, she turned away, her cheeks burning.

A cuckoo clock cuckooed eleven o'clock.

Four china plates painted with flowers gathered dust in a wire rack over the trophy cabinet. She could have thrown them, one by one, at Charlemagne. The trophies in the case were for marksmanship and bowling. The ones for softball had the patina of age. In the center was a large loving cup with an inscribed legend:

DEKE LAWLER
New Trier County's
MAN OF THE YEAR
1968

Well, folks, your man of the year is getting so plastered he'll soon have to be carried to bed.

To one side of the trophy cabinet was a trivet with the words: *Kissin' s Fine but Cookin' Lasts*. On the other side was a rack with a hideous display of salt and pepper shakers. On a pedestal in a corner was a lava lamp, its colored blobs writhing in slow motion.

The pillow on the divan beside her had balsam in it.

I am too much for this world, she thought, closing her eyes. I have passed beyond it, I am out of alignment to the order of things and the ways of the people in this room. I am a giant absurdity full of emptiness. Charlemagne, who kept us together with his concern, has defected and is now working for the other side and seems to have taken Andros with him, leaving the rest of us rudderless and adrift.

She felt a hand on her shoulder and awakened with a start to find Charlemagne standing before her, Mrs. Lawler behind him. She has kindly eyes, she thought. She shook her head to get the sleep out, and as she did so all the events of the past hours rushed in. She'd rather have stayed asleep where she was.

"Everybody's gone up to bed but you," Charlemagne said. "You were a sleeping Diana. Nobody wanted to wake you." Why was he being so nice?

Minnie got to her feet, looked toward the desk. "Where's Charlie Sunshine?"

"We had to carry him to bed."

Mrs. Lawler said, "You will have to excuse Dalphon. He's not used to so much company."

"He seems to be expecting a lot of it," Minnie said tartly. "He's got a barnful of things to greet them with when they arrive."

She was astounded to see the hint of tears in Mrs. Lawler's eyes and she was sorry she'd said that.

Mrs. Lawler said, "I'd be happy if the earth would open and the barn sink into it." She seemed to mean it. "Before he and Len started putting the guns in there, Dalphon was a happy man." She turned away, got out a hankie to dab at her eyes. "Excuse me."

Minnie turned to Charlemagne. "You're not helping, Carolus Magnus."

Misunderstanding, he reached out to take her arm. She moved away.

"I'll show you your room," Mrs. Lawler said. "I hope you don't mind a featherbed. Our children used them, but they're all gone, married now."

"I'll love it," Minnie said, moving to follow her. Yes, she'd jump into it, let the feathers fall on her, swallow her up, and there she'd stay, suspended forever in feathers like a bug in amber. There are worse ways to die.

35

In the Room at Lawlers'—Entry 26

We took our clothes off in the fields today and it was great and I felt free and it made me love Minnie even more because it was her idea.

The things that happened in jail after we were arrested I didn't like, but I didn't worry. I don't worry when I'm with Minnie and the others.

Mr. Lawler has many guns in his barn, one of them being a .410 shotgun, the kind my father used when he went hunting, and when I saw it I thought about those days.

Mr. Lawler's house is a large one and his wife seems awfully nice.

I guess we will work on that thing Charlemagne wants to make, though I'm not sure about Father Bischoff. Minnie doesn't seem to like the idea.

I haven't seen Hochdruck since that time in the bathroom with Minnie. Good riddance, I say.

I even watched television a little tonight and nothing happened. The horizontal hold needs adjustment. If I have time I may fix it.

Peter Hartsook

36

LAWLER SAT in the office of the sheriff. At least his body was there. His thoughts were with the lumber he was going to order delivered and with the tires, wheels and assorted necessities for the construction of the trebuchet. His thoughts were with these things even as he read in the paper the account of the fuss stirred up by his guests at the Bartlettville Inn.

He didn't care about that, although he realized that at another time he might have been angered. What was really important was that he had a headache, he was pretty well hung over, and he wanted to get back to the farm for lunch and to work it all out of his system under the hot sun that afternoon. But Samuels had called him and he'd had to stop in; otherwise Samuels would have come out to the farm. Right now he didn't want that.

Samuels, noting his mood, lifted his feet off his desk in order to slide his swivel chair closer to where Lawler was sitting. "It was Grogan showed it to me. Should have had it, but somebody always gloms onto the paper before I see it, so we didn't have it. Would have slapped 'em all in jail without this folderol. Don't see why Sheriff Parsons didn't do that over there, the way they acted. But that's not all. We've got some information on them. Came in this morning. . . . You don't seem to be listening, Deke. You hear what I said?"

Lawler put the newspaper down on the edge of the desk. "You got a line on them, you said."

"Found out they're straight out of the loony bin. Of course that comes as no surprise to me, the squirrely way they acted when they were here." Samuels squinted, leaned toward Lawler. "What's the matter with you, Deke?"

They couldn't have been that. Samuels must have got the information wrong. Lawler had had crazy people in jail when he was in office; they even had a padded cell for the really wild ones. The people out at his house were nothing like that. But he didn't want to get into an argument with Samuels about it.

"Elderberry, I guess."

"You tied one on again?"

"Doesn't agree with me, that elderberry."

"I keep telling you wine hangovers are the worst kind." Samuels leaned back. "Anyway, you can set your mind to rest about them, forget about trying to find out what they're up to because they're up to nothing. They're from the booby hatch and that explains everything." He chuckled. "Come to think of it, Deke, that wouldn't make a bad cover." He paused. "Give you any trouble?"

"None at all." Lawler squirmed. He had planned to say something to Samuels about the trebuchet, but now he didn't think it would be a good idea. In due time Samuels would see how clever Dr. Le Moyne really was. "Look, Len, I've got things to do."

"Who doesn't?" Samuels' hand dipped into the mess of papers on his desk, expertly extricated a typewritten sheet. "Here's the poop. They escaped from a place called Berylwood. You've probably heard of it. Ritzy private funny farm. Some alcoholics, but mostly nuts. Oh, the girl isn't off in the upper story, but the rest are. The older one, Dr. Le Moyne, he was committed by his wife. He's the one who engineered the escape, taking the other three with him: Hartsook, Petersen and Kleinschmidt. One of those last two is the real name of the priest."

"Before he took his vows."

"No, I mean that's his real name."

"Priests take different names."

"Deke, he's not a priest. He only thinks he is."

"I can tell a priest when I see one." Samuels was a Protestant, wouldn't know about such things. Besides, there was something wrong about the information Samuels had. Father Bischoff had said grace and a few prayers, and everybody had complimented Letta on her beef and kidney pie, and then they'd got right down to work on the plans for the trebuchet. They were all right, Lawler was sure. Nothing loony about them at all.

"O.K.," Samuels said. "Have it your way. Anyway, from what they were able to find out at the other end, Mrs. Le Moyne wants her husband back in the sanitarium so he can get treatment. There's a doctor, a Dr. Therin Sheckley, at the sanitarium. He wants everybody brought back when they're found, including the girl. Thinks a lot of her. They say he'll pay for travel, including the girl, so it's no skin off the county's nose. Oh, another thing. There's a private investigator named Colbert on their trail. Nobody knows just where he is right now." Again Samuels paused to take stock of Lawler. "You all right, Deke?"

"Just a little shaky is all, Len."

"You ought to watch that. Well, anyway, it was just a routine, confidential inquiry. I think I'll get in touch with Dr. Sheckley and Mrs. Le Moyne today. If you want, I'll get a county car out there, take them off your hands, though God knows I don't want them here in the jail any longer than I have to."

"They're no trouble where they are, Len."

"If these people send a car out it would take two, three days. If they fly out and fly them back, they could be here in a few hours. I'll ask them how they want to handle it."

Lawler was sweating. Samuels was going to spoil everything. "Look, Len, you mentioned something about cover."

"What about it?"

"Well, suppose, after all, they are what we thought?"

"You said they weren't giving any trouble."

"That's just it, Len. Look at it this way: If they're crazy, they'd be acting funny, wouldn't they?"

"What do you call the way they acted with Grogan and Mc-Kelty and the way they were here at the jail?"

"Yes, but now they're not acting that way."

"What are you getting at?"

"Isn't that a little odd? How do we know they're not operating out of that place—what was the name of it?"

Samuels referred to the report. "Berylwood."

"Berylwood. So they come here and get caught and they act crazy, so we notify the people back there. Naturally, the people back there would want them back right away to get the report, send them on to their next mission."

"I think they're whacky, Deke, and the sooner we get them out of the county, the better."

Lawler said casually, "I'd rather be sure, though, Len. Wouldn't you?"

"You mean you're still not sure?"

"Not completely." Now for the lie. "There were a couple things they did. They didn't seem important at the time."

"What things?"

"I'd rather not say right now. I just think we'd better hold off informing those people, let them stay at my place a couple more days."

"That's an imposition, Deke. And that's a lot of work for Letta, making meals, having guests like that, even though the county's reimbursing you for it."

"A thing as important as this, I think we ought to let them stay where they are, keep an eye on them for a couple more days. After all, they've been there for only one night. They haven't had a chance to reveal anything."

Samuels frowned, toyed with it. "I suppose you're closer to it than me, so if you think it'll solve something, I suppose it's all right. Let's see. Today's Wednesday. How about Friday? If you don't have the goods on them by Friday, I'll call those people and we can urge them to fly out here. I don't know how we're going to explain keeping them this long, though."

"Let's not worry about that."

"O.K.," Samuels said, getting up. "Two days. I'll expect to hear from you Friday morning one way or the other. And you be careful out there, O.K.? You can never tell what people like that are going to do."

"I'll watch it."

"And, oh, Deke," Samuels said as Lawler started for the door, "lay off the elderberry wine, huh?"

Long boards from the lumber yard, wheels from the junk yard, tires from the recap man, a big straight tree shorn of limbs and being shaved of bark by Peter, Andros working the chain saw, which made so much noise Minnie wanted to scream. Charlemagne and Lawler chattering over the plans spread on the raw lumber, talking stresses and strains, angles and lengths. Hard-hat time, it looked like, but there were only bare heads, Andros and Peter working without shirts in the hot sun and Minnie feeling like a fifth wheel.

"Just a spare," she said. "You hear? I'm just a spare. Use me when the others go flat." But of course no one could hear her above the staccato blare of the saw. Peter paused once in a while to smile at her, but as far as Andros was concerned, she was dead. He had another toy. Well, the hell with him. It was Charlemagne who took the heart out of her. She never thought he'd jump off that cloud, but there he was, Charles Le Moyne, the building contractor, cheek by jowl with old Dalphon, Deke the Bleak.

She'd watched them all morning while Lawler was in town getting the materials, standing in the way most of the time, when they felled the tree and moved things around, and now she was just tired of the whole thing, so she set off in search of Father Bischoff, who had rejected the entire enterprise and had moved off to higher ground to commune with God.

She found him masturbating in the bushes.

When he saw her, he stopped, his face becoming a panicky white, then red. His penis became limp even before he turned away to stuff it back into his pants.

"Don't stop on account of me," she said, moving to a grassy slope on still higher ground. She sank down, lay down, turned on her back, looked up at the sky, a fine shade of blue. She wondered if Father Bischoff would run for his life or come to talk to her. "Sorry I spoiled it," she said to the air.

Then he was there, looming over her, looking down at her

with agonized eyes. She felt a compassion for him, wondered why she chose to lay there and thinking she knew.

"Hello there," she said.

"Sometimes," he said in a tight voice, "sometimes the pressure gets so great . . ."

"I know." Yes, she knew as surely as she knew her own need. "But I really don't think a bird in the hand is worth two in the bushes."

His face was all grimaces, sweaty tensions. My God, he was sweating; it was popping out all over. What misplaced values, circumscribed life had brought him to this? Seeing him so made her churn inside, a companion to his frustration. It should not be.

"Listen," she said, "it's my fault."

"No."

"It is. If I hadn't come by, you'd be through by now and we could sit here and enjoy each other's company and you'd be feeling much better." She sat up. "So go ahead and do it. Then we'll talk."

"I—I couldn't."

"Then I'll do it for you." She reached for the zipper.

"No!" He stepped back in alarm.

"Why not? What difference does it make whose hand it is?"

He stood perspiring so copiously and looking so miserable she thought he might pass out. But she was glad he did not run off. Battles were being fought all over inside him, she could see that. So she got up and started to remove her clothes, saying, "Before you keel over with sunstroke, get out of those roasting things." She laughed. "We'll be children, young innocents, basking in the sun." She knew he wasn't moving, just watching. She did not look at him.

When she was naked, she tossed her head to get the hair out of her eyes, sat down on the grass and looked out across the valley through the bushes. On a lower level a few hundred yards away the others were working on the trebuchet. Beyond that, far across the valley, stood the red barn looking rural and innocuous. She felt a cooling breeze, leaned back on her hands, closing her eyes.

She heard his stirring behind her, his labored breathing. Then he was at her side. She opened her eyes, turned to see he was bare, smiled and said to his suffering eyes, "That's better now, isn't it?"

He was grinding his teeth in torment, unable to answer. He was also trembling and breathing hard.

She took his hand. "Tell me who you are." His pulse was racing.

"Who?" His voice was high. He wet his lips. His jaw quivered.

"Are you Father Bischoff?"

He nodded, uncertain, being swept along.

She smiled. "I don't think so." She indicated his clothes with a nod. "I think the real Father Bischoff is over there." She held his nervous eyes with her steady ones. "Father Bischoff or not, are you a truth teller?"

"A truth teller?"

"Do you speak the truth to friends?"

"Yes," he croaked.

"Then tell me: What do you want to do?"

His eyes widened in alarm, his mouth became slack. He tried to pull his hand away. She wouldn't let go.

"Don't you see? It's all right."

He commenced shaking. She held on to the hand, put an arm around him, drew him close. Suddenly, as if all the wires that held him together snapped at once, he collapsed at her side, starting to cry, closing his eyes as she held his head to her shoulder. He sobbed, shaking.

"Let it all come out," she said gently, tears forming in her own eyes. "I love you and Charlemagne loves you and Peter loves you and Andros loves you."

His body was shaking violently now and his sobs were so loud they surely would have been heard by the working men if it had not been for the chattering chain saw.

As his wracking sobs dissipated and his shaking subsided, she continued to hold him close. Then gently, so gently, she stroked him, murmuring lovingly, until finally he stirred and she saw that she had aroused him.

He drew back to look at her, and she saw the wonder and discovery in his eyes. His mouth was moist, his lips parted. He moved to her, kissed her hesitantly, then warmly. The sigh he gave was a concession to innocence soon to be lost, and Minnie felt a quickening within herself, a response to the demand she sensed in him.

It was not a complete abandonment, a giving up of identity, even though it was a merging. It was more of a tenderness, a slow exploration, an uncertain step, and then another, an increasing firmness until that moment when they forgot the hot sun, the breeze, the buzzing of the saw, a quick step off the planet and back again, and then a few minutes of lying there not saying anything.

When Father Bischoff raised his head and looked at her, she saw that the fear and agony she had so often seen in his eyes had vanished. They were warm eyes now and full of love.

"Minnie," he said gravely.

"Father," she said, equally grave.

He smiled and she knew it was all right.

He moved from her, lay looking down at the valley. She wondered what he would say, knowing the crush of thoughts and feelings that surely must now possess him.

He turned to her. "We'll get married."

She resisted an impulse to laugh. "No."

"I don't mean we *have* to get married. I mean I *want* to marry you."

"No. I'm not the marrying kind." She put a hand on his arm. "I don't mean to be flippant. I just don't want to marry anyone."

"I love you, Minnie."

"And I love you . . . Father?"

"Howard. You can call me Howard if you want."

"Howard. Howard Bischoff?"

"No. Just Howard."

"Anyway, marrying somebody is when you want to set up housekeeping, maybe have children."

They sat for a long time watching what was taking shape in the valley.

He said, "I do feel different."

"I'm glad."

He was lost in thought for a long time. Then he said, "I thought, if it happened, I wouldn't want to be a priest any more, and I wanted to be a priest, so I could never let it happen. But now . . . I think I could be a priest, all right. I don't mean to go to a seminary. I mean minister to people."

"The great unwashed."

"Just people, no matter who they are."

"You'd be good at it. You could be a priest-at-large."

"Something like that." He turned, looked at her solemnly. "You should be a priest."

"Me?"

"You're always doing something for somebody."

She looked away. "I do, sometimes. I'm pretty bitchy, though. I don't seem to have any patience any more. I don't think I could be a very good priest. I don't think I'd even want to be one."

"No," he said, settling back. "Just be what you are: Minnie. That's being the most wonderful person in the world."

37

Everything was taking shape, they were working together, Peter was needed, and he was glad to be able to add his muscles to what there was to do, even fixing the horizontal hold on the television, resolving the focus and improving the contrast controls just as in his own life there was less residual distortion and Berylwood seemed years ago and Hochdruck was only a word his uncle used to say, his uncle being an engineer, a boiler inspector, as Charlemagne had pointed out the other night, hitting on it by accident, and then repeating it over and over, and Peter finally seeing that this was true, yes, it was, he'd been invaded and taken over by German terms heard from his uncle when he was a kid.

They called him Jellybeans then because he was so round and fat and happy, and he remembered that along with a lot of other things he thought he'd forgotten.

Charlemagne was perched high on the trestle, applying grease to the verge shaft opening. Andros was trying to settle the stones in the weight receptacle. Father Bischoff was working with the cables on the winch and windlass, looking unclerical. Lawler was in the house. How many times had they hauled rocks for the receptacle? There must have been a ton of rocks of all sizes in there. Soon it would be run up to the top and then released, to drop like the lead weight it was, the beam sweeping up to pull the nylon sling in an arc, throwing the projectile. It was going to be something to see.

Jellybeans. Not because he was sweet but because he was fat. Where had all the fat gone? Maybe, he told himself, to my head.

Peter shifted in the grass to let the hot sun bake another part of him. The sun felt good and so did the sweat it created. He'd been looking around at the farm, the sun being just right, the air hanging heavy with moisture, and he was pulled back to the Ketelbys. He thought about Marcella until things wavered and he got off, but it wasn't anything like before, no slide down anywhere, not even a glimpse of the outhouse, no need for foils or shrouds. He was sure They weren't through with him yet, but he'd been having the feeling lately that if They ever tried anything again, he'd be ready for Them. I've got a little muscle now, and there's less fat, less Jellybeans, and there's Minnie, and it all isn't over yet, not the way they'd been talking, all the California things for her, and all his little-boy things, not getting to Marcella, not wanting to get to Marcella, but knowing they were going to get to Marcella, and not knowing what would happen when They did.

But sitting where he was he knew it was just natural history working itself out, a heart pumping blood for so many years and no more, a liver living its life span in its host having to take what happened, all the food, the drugs, the alcohol, and not being able to do anything about it, unprotesting. If you protested, you killed your host. So Peter would ride it out, let it happen as it would. Like Father Bischoff was doing, not able to do enough now after being against it at first, Father Bischoff smiling and not saying Latin but real prayers at meals and looking to the future and good times, Father Bischoff resurrected like Andros busy with his hands and arms and feet, stripped down and sweat-filmed, throwing himself into it with Peter, hauling rocks, bark-stripping, planing and nailing and doweling, flashing his white teeth, and nobody saying foolish things any more, and Charlemagne reminding them there wasn't much time because Lawler said there wasn't much time, and Peter not caring but playing the game of getting it done.

He was nearly all there; he felt it like a growth in his body, not alien but benign, a stirring like pregnancy in a deep, unidentifiable cavity of his body, up from death and burial, exhumed and shaking the clods of grave wax off grayed and larded, stiffened and atrophied muscles and skins, blood alive and running and everywhere inside things stirring.

Best, though, he wasn't afraid any more.

Lawler hung up on Samuels, not wanting to prolong it, saying what he had to say, then moving out of the house, not wanting to talk to Minnie or Letta, taking his guilt with him but reasoning there was no other way.

He started up the slope to the trebuchet, seeing it as a crude thing on wheels, mostly lumber but bearinged and greased, soon ready to go, and hoping it lived up to expectations, and quivering inside with the thrill of having a weapon no one else had, one sure to please Samuels when he saw what could be done with it, and also seeing it as the answer to a scourge soon to come. There would be no laying waste to New Trier County now. There would only be discouragement to the despoilers, the wreckers, the teeth-baring kids with their sticks and stones and insults and vulgarisms, their filth and flames. The county would be safe. Lawler had seen to that. They would thank him for it.

Samuels would be calling the doctor and Mrs. Le Moyne, telling them to fly out, and that was all right, it didn't matter what the guests were now, crazy or not, agents or not, they'd soon be out of the county, and he and Samuels would have the thing, the trebuchet. He felt twinges of pity and guilt, but what else could he do? His guests would leave after the demonstration; they'd get in their car and he'd bid them goodbye, and even Letta would think they were on their way to California, and he knew she was even now preparing sandwiches for them to take along and she'd wish them well, as he would, too, but he'd call Samuels right away; they wouldn't get very far before county cars would be after them, catching up with them before they crossed the county line, take them back to jail.

As Samuels said, they'd probably protest; they might even try some of the funny stuff they did before, but it wouldn't matter, Samuels and Grogan and McKelty and the rest of the deputies and jailers wouldn't pay any attention to them this time, it was all decided; they'd just put them in cells and keep them there until the doctor and Mrs. Le Moyne came after them, the doctor alone or both or representatives, it didn't matter who or how, to escort them back to Berylwood one way or another, and they'd never see them again. It was better that way.

He liked Le Moyne, who treated him as an equal, even though Lawler had had no college, but in a thing like this, in war, one had to put emotion aside, do what had to be done, not let sentiment interfere. There were lives and businesses and a whole county to protect.

Le Moyne, his feet resting on those bags of marbles, a glass of Lawler's elderberry wine in his hand, had told him many interesting things about the medieval period, and he was able to make Lawler feel as if he were living those times, and when Lawler gazed at the mangonel he almost believed it.

"Look at it this way," Le Moyne had said at one point when they were resting briefly, "this thing is really an onager, and that means wild ass, and they used to call it that because it kicks like a jackass when it's fired, as you will see. But it generated a lot of respect in its day, did its job as it will here, doing what has to be done. Do you understand that?"

Lawler said that he did, and he did. People might laugh when they looked at it, but as Le Moyne said, once they saw it in operation, they'd see what it was good for.

The way Le Moyne went on, talking about dukes and kings, blood-red blades, charges and battles, good knights and bad, it was almost as if Le Moyne himself believed no time had passed and he was back there in the Middle Ages on what he called his Holy Crusade, righting wrongs. Lawler did not argue with him. Let him have his beliefs; he could take them with him. Lawler and the county would have the trebuchet.

"It's going to be a fine day," Mrs. Lawler said, watching from the door as Minnie arranged things in the trunk of the car.

"It sure is." Minnie didn't have to look up at the clear sky to tell that; it was a fine day indeed because this was the day they were getting out of there, moving on their way again, shuffling off, not to Buffalo but to San Berdoo and freeways and smog and neon and sunshine and Santa Anas that could blow you off the road. Minnie wondered if Mrs. Lawler had ever itched to jump up and strike out for somewhere far away from New Trier County.

"A real nice day for traveling. Good you've got air conditioning."

"It comes in handy all right." Mrs. Lawler was always saying something kind, comfort-producing, and Minnie wished she wouldn't do that. She guessed Mrs. Lawler didn't want to make waves; life had become too short to hassle over. But it had left her with nowhere to go, she and old Lawler married all those years and having all those kids and still not able really to talk to each other, just snatches of safe talk, cryptic bits, hints of hostility, blind stabs here and there, but never touching each other with it, not really.

"I'll make something you can take along, eat on the way."

"You don't have to do that, Mrs. Lawler."

"No trouble."

Mrs. Lawler went back into the house and Minnie went back to fiddling around with the luggage. A few days there and already it was like tearing up stakes after years, and there was excitement in it, and Minnie knew they all felt it, not so much because of that ridiculous machine they made in the pasture as because it was practically over and they'd be off to God knows what, and she hoped they wouldn't get hung up again on anything so silly.

She could not understand Charlemagne's going along with Lawler, and it had almost come to a split right down the middle of what they had, Charlemagne talking in circles as he usually did to others, never to Minnie, and Minnie cursing him out for it, and Charlemagne laughing and trying to put his arm around her as if it all were a big joke. She'd always thought he was firm and rooted and definite, even if he did speak obliquely—that was part of his charm—but on the matter of the trebuchet talking to him about it was like punching marshmallows. She had finally given up trying to get any sense out of him about that.

The others had plunged in to help, even Father Bischoff, but mostly, she thought, because Father Bischoff had a lot to think about, new ground to cover, new stances to perfect. They obviously didn't share her hatred of weapons. In that area Mrs. Lawler agreed with her, but Minnie thought it wasn't so much because of the weapons as because of Lawler's obsession with them.

She guessed it had been good for them, giving the rest of them something to do. As for herself, she'd been left to talk to Mrs. Lawler or watch television, and she saw it hadn't changed, still the same old shit, and she'd done her nails instead, her hair, sunbathing, reading a little, finding a few marijuana plants and having to laugh about that but not pointing them out, and not having the ambition to do any processing, though she'd have loved to get stoned for a change, the elderberry wine Lawler made being good only for nausea, Charlemagne complimenting him on it and obviously lying through his teeth. Why, Charlemagne?

The past nights were mostly talks with Peter about California and what they'd find there, and being glad to see his interest, and telling him things she remembered, then listening to him about how it was when he was a kid, good vibes there, she was getting to like Peter a lot now that he was talking, so unlike Andros the animal who was disgusted because she wouldn't relieve the sexual tension any more, and it seemed over between them. Father Bischoff smiling at her, being sweet, and not wanting to jump off the planet again this soon, satisfied he'd made it once and relishing the experience, and she not moved to entice him. It was hiatus time and all the sex cells lay dormant, which is the way they should lie between lays.

The trebuchet stood on a level area halfway up the valley, all angles and corners, alien to the rolling landscape, a gigantic insect from another world, its verge arm thrust upward as if

237

ready to pluck some vagrant bird out of the sky midflight. It looked ungainly and entirely unfinished, but that was because the lumber was new and freshly worked and it had been so hurriedly put together. Grease, liquefied by the hot sun, made long streaks down the wood, running from bearings and sleeves.

It waited only to be tested, those who had built it standing nearby full of pride for their work. The weight of the rocks in the wooden cage at the end of the beam where it was levered had been carefully calculated. The mass that the projectile should be had been reckoned. The proper tensions of both right and left cables, which would direct the flight of the payload, had been worked out by Andros on the slide rule, checked and rechecked by Charlemagne. All that remained was the question of what to arm it with.

Lawler did not fancy scattering nuts and bolts about the pasture five hundred yards distant, and he said so. He joked that there wasn't enough manure around to use, adding that he'd reserve that option until he saw the face of the enemy.

"Greek Fire," Charlemagne said. "We'll send Greek Fire across the valley." When Lawler looked at him dumbly, Charlemagne told him it would be fitting to use an even older weapon, a Greek ball of fire often used in battle, explaining it was made of pitch, resin, grease, metal filings and something inflammable, such as oil or naphtha.

Lawler, who said he never missed a Fourth of July fireworks display, declared that a ball of fire was a great idea, and so they foraged around collecting suitable ingredients from the house, garage and barn, abandoning pitch and resin in favor of a large mound of oily rags, old rope, scrap metal for weight, pieces of wood, paraffin, a little gunpowder. They worked in the hot sun putting it all together, weighing each part, then tying it and twisting it into a homogeneous mass, then winding it with baling wire and crimping it tight into a ball so it would not disintegrate in the air.

When it was in place in its sling on the long platform which began just back of the windlass, Andros and Peter operated the

238

winch which pulled the weight upward. They paused as each cog was reached and ratcheted so Charlemagne could be sure everything was going right. Slowly the beam arm was lowered until at last the end of it lay on the platform so the nylon sling could be attached. Then, with Andros, Charlemagne stepped off the five hundred yards to a point down the valley where Andros made a wide circle with powdered chalk. That was the target area.

Viewing the circle from where he stood beside the trebuchet, Lawler found it difficult to believe that the projectile could possibly reach it, but Charlemagne assured him it would.

A last inspection. Everything was secured. The lanyard was ready to be pulled.

Lawler unscrewed the top of the gallon of gasoline. He poured it over the ball of material and they saw, to their satisfaction, that it was soaking in. Then Lawler put the cap back on, moved to the lanyard.

It was the moment of truth. Lawler stood with the rope in his hand looking at Charlemagne. Charlemagne stood at the sling, a match ready to strike. Andros and Peter stood to one side of him, Father Bischoff on the other. They looked toward Lawler, saw the eagerness in his face, his expectancy, his sweat.

"Ready?" Charlemagne asked.

"Ready."

Charlemagne struck the match, threw it. The ball burst into flame with a whooshing sound.

For a moment Lawler stared at it. Then he pulled hard on the lanyard. A lever clicked. A pawl was released. The weight started its descent, the verge being whipped upward, snatching the nylon sling and the ball of burning material. The verge bent as the weight plummeted, whipping the sling in a wide arc, the air whistling with its passing. One side of the sling slipped off the beam as it neared the end of its violent swing upward, sending the ball of fire streaking free, high in the air, the verge hitting its stop post with a dull *thunk* as the ball, trailing a wake of black smoke, whined out in a long arc.

The ball of fire soared, graceful and beautiful, reaching the

239

top of its arc. But it was not headed for the chalked circle. It started downward like a glowing meteor, burning brightly and emitting a high, keening note, plunging down toward the barn, hitting the roof near the cupola and leaving a gaping hole there. A moment later the sound of its entry reached the ears of those at the trebuchet. Lawler still held in his hand the rope of the lanyard, watching, not believing, as billows of smoke came through the hole in the roof. Through the windows of the cupola yellow flames could be seen.

"God!" Lawler muttered. He dropped the rope and started a stumbling walk toward the barn far across the valley. Even as he did so there was the sound of small-arms and rifle fire as shells began to explode and there were dull thumps that shook the whole barn.

When Charlemagne, Andros, Father Bischoff and Peter reached the house, they found Letta Lawler standing on the patio, gazing out at the valley with a curious expression.

"Did you call the fire department?" Charlemagne asked.

"No," she said. "No, I didn't do that."

They turned and were joined by Minnie to see that Lawler had stopped halfway to the barn, standing in the tall grass in the late-afternoon sun, watching the barn burn. He kept raising and lowering his arms. Never once did he glance toward the house.

"Do you want me to call them?" Charlemagne asked Mrs. Lawler.

"No," she said, turning and moving into the house. "I'll do that." Before she picked up the phone in the kitchen, she said, "Don't forget to take the lunch with you."

"Thank you," Charlemagne said.

"Thank you," she said with a wry smile, dialing.

Charlemagne had to go out and get Andros because he wanted to watch the fire.

They lost no time getting into the car, not saying anything, Minnie wanting to catch Charlemagne's eye but not being able to and not knowing what she would say when she did.

On their way, Andros twisted around to see, unable to take his eyes off the burning barn, which was now sending a black plume of smoke hundreds of feet into the air. Every now and then there was an explosion.

At one point they passed two fire engines going in the opposite direction. The engines were soon followed by two sheriff's cars, sirens screaming, red lights whirling.

When they had passed beyond the county line, Charlemagne slowed the car to the legal limit.

Minnie could contain herself no longer. "Charlemagne," she said, putting a hand on his shoulder, "I love you."

38

En route—Entry No. 27

En route. That's funny. En route to where? Even Charlemagne doesn't seem to know exactly, except we're going in the direction of California and are supposed to end up there.

Everybody seems to be feeling pretty good. Glad to get away from having other people around and be with the family again.

Riding in the car and trying to write isn't easy. That's why this is so jiggly.

The weather continues good. We've been very lucky about that.

Nobody seems to mind what happened, but everybody thinks that even though the barn is gone, Mr. and Mrs. Lawler will be happier. Maybe ever after.

I hope the horizontal hold stays put.

I suppose I should be thinking about what we will be doing when we get to California but

39

THE ROAD had become bumpy even for the Continental, so Peter stopped writing and sat with the ballpoint pen in his hand, his hand resting on the journal, looking out at the fleeting fences and fields.

Riding for hours, they had seen the terrain gradually change from furrowed fields to wide expanses of less tillable land. They had come from an area where trees had been cut and burned off and bogs drained years ago to make way for crop rotation and fallow years, and they were entering a part of the country where few trees had ever stood and the land was such as to discourage seeds.

Peter sat next to the window and, though the air conditioning was going, he could feel the heat of the sun through the tinted glass. Minnie sat between him and Andros, her head back against the cushion. She had fallen asleep. Andros was slumped in his corner, napping.

At length Minnie stirred, sat up and looked out, viewing the barren fields with dull eyes. After a while her eyes dropped to the journal in Peter's lap, and she said, "What do you write, Peter?"

Peter closed the journal. "Things. Impressions."

"It's a journal," Andros said, waking up and yawning.

"Can I read it sometime?"

"Sometime, maybe."

Andros said, "Anybody can keep a journal."

"Dr. Sheckley said I should do it."

"Are you glad you started it, Peter?"

"Yes."

Andros turned to survey Minnie's profile. "So that's it. Prick-time."

"I've always wanted to keep a journal," Minnie said wistfully.

Charlemagne lifted his eyes from the road to look at her in the mirror. "What would be in it, Minerva?"

"All her conquests," Andros said.

Minnie turned. "There have been no conquests."

"What are they then?"

"They're not conquests."

Father Bischoff stirred himself to say, "Andros thinks of them that way when he does it."

"That's a lie!"

"We're coming alive," Charlemagne said, "and that augurs well for the driver. Keeps him awake."

Andros said to Father Bischoff, "Just because you never had any, that's no reason to take it out on me."

Father Bischoff turned to regard him with an amused expression. "Who says I never had any?"

"The closest you ever got to it was your good right hand. You said so yourself."

"That shows how much you know."

Andros turned to survey Minnie's profile. "So that's it. Prick-happy Minnie's been at it again."

She turned to say hotly, "Just because I wouldn't take care of you on the farm you don't have to be insulting. It so happens you were more interested in other things. Besides, I could see our relationship was losing its meaning for you. No woman likes to be a mere convenience."

"Then it is true?"

"Yes, it's true. It was very nice, too."

"I'll be damned," Andros said, trying to laugh but doing so without conviction. "So that's why you ignored me."

"You're not the only one in the world who can screw," Father Bischoff said. "That probably comes as a shock to you."

"Well, well," Charlemagne said.

"What about the Council fathers?" Andros asked. "God

244

knows we've heard enough about them. They go out of office or something?"

"Fuck the Council fathers," Father Bischoff said.

"Well, well," Charlemagne repeated.

"You're hell-bound, Father," Andros said.

"If so," Father Bischoff said calmly, "I'll be in good company."

Andros thought about it. "I guess we're all hell-bound after what we did to the barn."

"No," Charlemagne said. "We assailed the bastions and bright shine the helms with jewels set in gold. It was gleaming shields and glittering spears. We have upheld the honor of the race."

They rode in silence for another hour before Peter said, "Minnie, will I like California?"

Minnie, nearly asleep again, said, "I don't know." She forced herself awake to study him for a long moment. "Yes, I think you will, Peter."

"Why did you look at me like that?"

"To see what's inside."

"Crap," Andros said.

"You don't have to listen to us," Minnie said. "Just put your head down and go back to sleep."

"Talk about something else, for Christ's sake. Talk about California is all we hear."

"If we're going there," Peter said, "I want to know about it."

"Peter," Father Bischoff said, "I think that bug in Andros' head has migrated to his rectum."

Andros snorted. "Now that you've screwed, you're so brave, fuck the Council fathers and all that, but you don't have guts enough to call an ass an ass."

"I don't want to use everything up at once. I'm just letting them fly when I think they're right for punctuation and proper emphasis. I also don't believe in casting pearls before swine."

"I'd rather hear about California," Charlemagne said. "It

would be an improvement over this bickering. Go ahead, Minerva."

Minnie tipped her head back, looked low out of her eyes at the onrushing road between Charlemagne and Father Bischoff. "I don't know what to say I haven't said already. I guess California is different things to different people. Sometimes, when I think of it, I see miles of people, other times miles of roadways, and still other times miles of beauty, some of the most breathtaking in the world. Then sometimes I see the ridiculous contrasts. Some people I know build stereo outfits from scratch and others make Indian moccasins. Some women buy a two-thousand-dollar gown at a Beverly Hills salon while others take it all off for nude group therapy at Elysium. So what? I don't know what to make of it all, there's so much of it.

"Maybe that's the secret, just letting it be, enjoying it, like the heat of the desert, the dryness there, the chill of the late-afternoon breeze off the ocean, things like that. Did you know you can get stuck in the ice and snow and slush in the High Sierras? I guess what I'm saying is, whatever you want, you can find it there. Palm trees, icicles, manicured lawns, the Golden Gate Bridge, the long curving sweep of beach from Ventura to Santa Monica and beyond, so many people, so many golf courses, polo at Santa Barbara, skin diving at San Diego, skiing at Mammoth, lawn bowling at Laguna. Pick your passion."

"Nothing there for me," Andros said morosely.

"We're going to Los Angeles," Charlemagne said.

Minnie blinked. "The megalopolis, freeways looking like ribbons somebody's tied the package up with. But I didn't know we were being that specific."

"We've always been going to Los Angeles, Minerva."

"Is that a fact?" There was an edge of hurt. "I don't see why you couldn't have said so."

"La Rochefoucauld—"

"Oh, Charlemagne, please!"

"Oh, you make it all sound great," Andros said, "all that California shit. But from what I've heard, it isn't like that, it's more like smog and the press of stinking bodies. Where do you suppose the deodorant commercials were born? In L.A., that's where. Right with the fags, the ghettos, the crummy building construction, the winos, the crappy architecture, the crime rate . . ."

"You can see ugliness anywhere if you want to."

"I can tell you this," Andros said with chilling quietness, "Andros isn't going there." He turned to eye the scenery, thereby cutting them out.

Father Bischoff said, "Andros does have a bug up his rectum."

They stared at Andros, Charlemagne darting glances in the mirror, Andros being impassive, wearing an I-don't-care-what-you-think look.

Charlemagne asked, "Any reason?"

Andros ignored him.

Minnie said, "You need to get your rocks off, so you're taking it out on everybody."

Andros turned with disdain. "Now who's being insulting?"

"That's insulting?"

"Damn right."

"It got a rise out of you, though, didn't it? You weren't talking."

"O.K., O.K., so you got to me. That doesn't mean I'm going all the way to California."

"Why the hell not?"

"I don't know. So shut up."

"Roland," Charlemagne said. "You're Roland, my right-hand man. I need you at my side, slide rule and all. We all need you. We're an imperfect body without you."

"Roland died."

"Roland is dead, in Heaven God hath his soul. That's true, but there is death for all—me, you, Minnie, Peter and Father Bischoff—but none of us is dead yet. Still, I see you're dying a little."

"I just don't want to go all the way out there, that's all."

Father Bischoff said, "You mean you'd let us go on by ourselves without you?"

"That's right."

"Minnie," Father Bischoff said, "isn't there something you can do for him?"

"No."

"I wouldn't accept it even if she tried, so let's just drop the whole thing, shall we?"

Minnie put a hand on his arm. "Andros . . ."

He shifted his arm away. "Keep your hands to yourself."

"I'm sorry." Minnie had never seen him in such a state. "Just tell me something: Is it me?"

Andros took his time answering, and when he did his voice was tired. "No, it's not you, Minnie."

"What is it, then?"

"I don't know. Just shut up for once."

"But we're your friends, for God's sake! If you can't talk about it with us, what good are we?"

"Then let me be, if you're friends. Just let me be."

"All right," she said. "Be."

40

JAMES COLBERT was worried about whether Mrs. Le Moyne was going to get there in time. He'd called his mother, Flo, in St. Louis, she being in charge of the office when he was on the road, and she said she'd been unable to contact Mrs. Le Moyne. That was bad because he'd located Charles Le Moyne and party, and now, if Mrs. Le Moyne could not come to Onanda, what good would all the work he'd done be?

Of course he could continue to follow them wherever they went, but there would still be the problem of letting Mrs. Le Moyne know and setting it all up again. The agreement was that all he had to do was find them, show Mrs. Le Moyne where they were, actually walk in with her (he hoped she didn't demand this) and then his work would be done. He was not about ready to take on four insane patients and a slut all by himself. He would not even let himself contemplate such a rash, unwholesome act. He prided himself on moving in and out quickly in such unsavory cases. Usually the situations rotted away once clean air hit them.

The waitress served him his eggs, and he examined them, no fertile ones, and after carefully inspecting and wiping the knife, fork and spoon, he proceeded to cut the once-over-lightly eggs into neat squares. As he ate his breakfast he kept his eyes on mirrors and windows. He never liked to be taken unawares, never liked it when a quarry came in to sit nearby. He prided himself on many things, anonymity being one, and he did not think Lamont Cranston could have been more dedicated about the evil that lurks in the hearts of men, though he did wish for his invisibility. Too often he'd been forced to endure the end of a case; he'd often wished he could just simply disappear, move on to other things that needed doing. Sometimes, when he was in a crowd, he felt invisible because people did not notice or speak to him, but this was because of his unique talent for blending in. He'd rather have it that way, for if you were unremarkable you were also unassailable and therefore less vulnerable to shock, carnality or passion.

There was no hurry now. His people were in Onanda at the Grand View Motel on one side of the court and he on the other. For all he knew they could be eating at that moment at the motel restaurant. For himself, he never ate where his people ate. He did not like the association. Neither did he like the chance that he might be recognized or talked to or in any way jeopardized. He was a meticulous man and he knew it; he was also a cautious man and he knew that, too.

He'd had a difficult time trailing the fugitives. He knew there were relatively few routes to California, direct routes, and he did not think they would linger; they weren't on a sightseeing trip. Yet, checking gasoline service stations and hotels and motels was delaying and time-consuming. The nut in the priest's outfit saved the day. Once that was established and linked to the car, it became easier. The case histories he thought might help provide some hint of direction or purpose, but they had not. There was nothing in the names either. But that was the way with his work; he considered everything, every angle. It was plod, plod, plod, step, step, step. That was the way it was with avenging angels, and that was the way it was with James Colbert. The mills do grind exceedingly small. And he and his mother were proud of his part in it.

He had hit the jackpot in Bartlettville, and he was pleased they had stayed there as long as they had, because that made up for time he'd lost. The people at the motel told him more than he wanted to know, and his suspicions about the girl were verified. She was sinful, completely amoral; stocks were not good enough for her because she was a witch, a sexual witch, the kind that destroys men. Her actions alone made him more determined that ever to find them quickly and end what she might do.

The Bartlettville *Times* was a help, especially the pictures, which supplemented those he was carrying. They were doomed, the people were, there was no question about that; he would find them and end it all, shut that Le Moyne's filthy mouth. He quite agreed with Sheriff Parsons about the Bartlettville Parents Against Filth meeting, and he only wished the sheriff had been there so he might have arrested them, even though the sheriff admitted there seemed to be no real grounds, no legal grounds, but they surely could have created some.

He was a day behind at that point. Sheriff Parsons had been kind enough to phone him on the road to tell him he'd received a strange call from Sheriff Samuels in New Trier County about arresting five people who resembled the five Colbert was looking for, but when Colbert went to the county jail and talked with Samuels and his deputies about it, they knew nothing, which was odd. He was not altogether convinced they were telling the truth (and Colbert was so conversant with the truth he was sure he recognized it when he heard it); he could not see why they would lie. He checked the New Trier *Runner-News*, but the newspaper had no news stories about his people and the reporters and editors knew nothing, had seen nothing.

He'd taken off then, going far along the road, clear to Arizona, without finding a trace, and he concluded they had not gone that far. Either that or they had taken another route, which hardly seemed likely, so he backtracked with the map, ready to take alternate routes if he found nothing. But on the other side of Albuquerque he'd located a service-station attendant who remembered the car and the people.

From there it had been an easy matter to keep going down the road until he found the car in Onanda.

James Colbert finished his coffee and, after a careful look around, got up and paid for his breakfast with two new dollar bills, the kind he invariably demanded at banks (let them handle the dirty money; God knows where it might have been), and received change, which he wrapped in his handkerchief before putting it into his pocket. He didn't mind the cashier's startled gaze, and he might have explained, as he often did, but since she did not ask him to, he did not.

Out on the street, he walked amost mincingly, convinced his special step gave him more control of his body, an appearance of ease and no-purpose, which he thought was disarming. He was actually quite athletic, being able to run three miles in twenty minutes. He had an intricate system of exercises that he went through every morning and evening which kept him in shape.

Onanda, he saw, was a bright, sunlighted little town, a way station to and from the West, given to flamboyant motels that competed for the traveler's dollar. It seemed to him there were quite a few tourists, and he supposed they were Odyssites, whatever they were. The signs he saw in windows everywhere, with a tiny credit to the Onanda Chamber of Commerce, read:

WELCOME ODYSSITES

ODYSSITES
YOU'RE OUTA SIGHT!

ONANDA LOVES
The American Odyssite Society

After making sure none of his people were around, Colbert checked at the office. There had been no calls for him. He thanked the clerk, looked at his watch. It would be 11:10 in St. Louis. If Mrs. Le Moyne had got in touch with his mother, she would have called him by this time. He would call her late in the day. He might even try to get Mrs. Le Moyne in Oblout himself.

Once in his room he emptied the handkerchief into the washbasin, ran hot water over the coins, washed them with soap and water, then put them out on a towel to dry. Then he washed his hands. Next, he removed his clothes, took a shower. After that he brushed his teeth, used a mouthwash for gargling, then dressed, went to the sun porch with his binoculars and focussed them on the rooms across the way. The doors were open to the two sun porches and he could make out people moving about.

He put down the binoculars, picked up the 35-mm camera and checked it. He'd taken thirteen shots with the telescopic lens, still had plenty to go. Mrs. Le Moyne would have the proof he'd done his part; if she failed to heed his summons, it would be her fault, not his. If he were to lose his party now, he'd still collect. He let his eyes move about, looked down at the pool. He saw the girl in the bikini and even as his throat became clotted with bile, as it always did when it responded to his body's glandular treachery, he realized with shock who she was: Minnie. She was sunning herself on a beach towel.

Colbert commenced shaking and sweating in the welter of his ambivalence. Taking a deep breath, he examined her anatomy, trying to maintain all the detachment he could; he had to be sure, compare her with the girl he'd seen in the rooms across the way, and he became sure. The same dark hair. The same . . . bust . . . figure. Her eyes were closed, but he knew they were blue. A dark blue. He wet his lips and, with trembling hands, hating himself for what his profession sometimes required of him, focussed the camera for a series of shots.

41

ABOUT THIRTY miles southwest of Onanda, the Diablo Mountains begin, heralded, as one approaches them via a sinuous road, by a massive butte named La Bestia because it is almost impossible to climb, rising as it does almost straight up two thousand feet from the valley floor.

It was here, centuries ago, that Indians lived in cave pueblos high in the cliff faces, sheltered under great sandstone ribs of earth, leaving their homes periodically to hunt in the canyons created by the sawtooth walls of the mesa which jutted out into the canyons, bringing home wild turkey, bighorn sheep, deer and cottontail rabbits, living on cactus, beans, corn gruel, chokeberry and yucca when flesh was unavailable.

The most popular canyon then, as now, was Esqueleto Canyon, wide and strung with gray-green sagebrush, gnarled, stunted clumps of juniper and piñon trees, and sparse grass. Visible from the canyon floor are ruins of the old stone and adobe dwellings in the cliffs that the ancient rock climbers created.

Desolate, deserted and unvisited for years, except by prospectors and their mules, the canyon became famous when, thirteen years ago, Anton Tuplifski was set down on its floor by Venusians, who had transported him by flying saucer to their planet and returned him to Earth to spread the glad tidings of a world without death, a world without pain, a world at peace, and with promises to return on the same day some future year. It seems that Tuplifski, an old, weatherbeaten Russian-born prospector, had been snatched from that very valley floor by these same marauding Venusians some two weeks earlier. His mule was also taken on board the space ship, but the Venusians kept the mule. After his release, Tuplifski trudged over the hot, red, dusty ground to Onanda, where he told his amazing story to anyone who would listen.

Tuplifski, unfortunately, was not well received by his fellow Earthlings, and his story was widely discounted. But there were some who knew he was telling the truth because they, too, had been captured by space people and taken on long trips to other planets. It naturally followed there was a great comparing of notes, accounts of the various odysseys were written and exchanged, and Esqueleto Canyon eventually became a shrine and gathering place for those who had left Earth for brief periods on the outer reaches, and they began to gather there each year on the anniversary of Tuplifski's deliverance from the Venusians, hoping it would be the year of the aliens' second coming.

Tuplifski died, but a bronze plaque to his memory was erected at the site, and it was appropriately dedicated at the ninth annual convention of the Odyssites, as they called themselves, most of whom had completed an interstellar (or at least interplanetary) odyssey of one kind or another, or were sympathetic to those who had. And so they formed the American Odyssite Society, with a constitution and bylaws, and an agreement to abide by Robert's Rules of Order at the annual election of officers.

Their stopping in Onanda had been by chance, but it was at the behest of Andros, who had become increasingly intransigent about going any farther toward California, that the trip to Esqueleto Canyon was agreed to by Charlemagne, mostly as a gesture to him, an inducement to change his mind and continue the journey.

Minnie was taking a sunbath by the pool, studying through nearly closed eyes the man on the sun porch who was taking pictures of her, when Charlemagne called down to her that they'd be joining the Odyssites at the mountains. She had noticed the man before, with binoculars, observing them, and it hadn't bothered her, but picture-taking was a little different. However, she did not mention it.

Twenty minutes later they were moving out of Onanda in the Continental, joining others who were bound for the same

255

place, and in aggregate they raised a great cloud of dust as they sped along the snaking road to the giant butte. At the base of the cliff they parked among hundreds of campers, trailers, buses, pickup trucks and cars of earlier arrivals.

When Peter got out of the car, he stood looking up at the butte, which was truly a massive, impressive sight. "I've never been this close to a mountain," he said in an awed voice.

The others looked around, saw the cosmopolitan flavor of the bumper stickers, from JESUS—YES and AMERICA, LOVE IT OR LEAVE IT to NIETZSCHE IS PIETZSCHE and GOD IS DEAD BUT DON'T WORRY MARY IS PREGNANT AGAIN. However, most of the stickers simply read ODYSSITE THIS YEAR and had been received by members several months previous.

They started out of the parking lot, moving to a midway, which consisted of carnival concessions, ice-cream trucks, soft-drink, hot-dog and hamburger stands, kiddie rides and games-of-chance booths, and it was crowded; Andros was reluctant to leave it. As they walked on, dead brush and flung popcorn crackled underfoot, not yet having been matted, seeing only ordinary people everywhere, Earthlings in trousers wearing beards and miniskirts and maxis, human beings with and without children, but mostly with children who were already covered with red dust and carrying ice-cream cones, popsicles or candy sticks; they also saw young lovers and wizened ones, a few hippie types and a number of motorcyclists looking for girls.

They drifted with the crowd under colorful pennants flying everywhere, beneath banners welcoming the Odyssites, strolling and stirring to the crush of the crowd, the air fragrant of people and pine, passing loudspeakers hung in trees and paging first Mr. Williams and then the mother of Sue Grafton, who'd been found lost and was crying, past long wooden trestle tables yet unused, red and blue and white crepe-paper bunting, to tent museums where artifacts from a thousand and one worlds were exhibited, all for a price, displays of manners and dress from Mars and Venus and stars as far away as the Lagoon Nebula. But nowhere was there an exhibit of the manners, customs or dress of Acheron Four, and Andros was disappointed.

As they walked in the hot sun, an occasional cool breeze brushed their cheeks. Juniper smoke hung in shreds in the air, and displaced horned toads ventured bravely forth from beneath bushes, making dashes for what looked to be safety.

Suddenly Minnie said, "Don't look now, but there's a man following us and he's taking pictures. He's the one from across the way at the motel."

They came to a casual stop, turning to observe James Colbert, who looked away and started to take pictures of an enlarged organism from a planet in the contellation Scorpii.

Peter said, "I've seen him at the motel."

"I'll talk to him," Andros said belligerently, and he would have started off but was restrained by Charlemagne, who suggested they wait to see what else he would do.

Father Bischoff said, " 'Fret not thyself because of evildoers, for they shall soon be cut down like grass.' "

Minnie laughed. "He doesn't really look evil."

"Come on," Andros said impatiently.

They walked on.

The crowd was gay, music blared, laughter was everywhere and the registration table was to the right of the assembly area. An older man with a worried look was in charge. He wore an official's badge on the crisp, white shirt that seemed curiously out of place, and it said he was Mr. Douglas. Others connected with registration sat at the long table with books for signing, cards and badges and forms before them.

They registered, became members for five dollars each, and were awarded round badges with their names lettered thereon.

Then, because they wanted Andros to take part, Mr. Douglas surveyed him pleasantly, saying, "I assume you've had an odyssey?"

"I'll say he has," Minnie said. "All the way from Acheron Four."

"And where is that?"

Andros told him.

"The Pleiades, eh?" Mr. Douglas smiled. "Well, we haven't

had anybody from there yet. But of course the universe is infinite." He studied Andros. "You'll want a space, of course."

"A space?"

"An area. A numbered area. It'll be printed in the program so people will know where you are." He referred to a list. "We've got four areas left. You can set up at any one of them. The cost is a little higher this year: twenty-five dollars. But of course it's for a good cause, isn't it? And it does help pay for the lights." He laughed a little nervously. "Where's your stuff?"

"Stuff?" Andros was becoming annoyed.

"Exhibit stuff. You know: artifacts, pictures, pamphlets, books about your experiences. You know. Might even make back your entry fee, you sell enough of them."

"I don't have anything like that."

"Tape recordings of the native language, movies of rites, samples of life and dress—Odyssites always have these things."

Charlemagne, seeing Andros' dissatisfaction, interceded. "I'm afraid you don't understand, Mr. Douglas. You see, Andros here is from Acheron Four himself. *He* is the exhibit."

Mr. Douglas was unimpressed. "I see. Well, maybe you could give a lecture in your native tongue, but I wouldn't guarantee you'd get a very big crowd."

"It is forbidden by Universal Ukase to speak the language of Acheron on minor planets."

"Hmm. Well, that does make it difficult." He shrugged. "In that case, all I can suggest is you take an area, number sixty-three, say, and be there at seven—that's when the Odyssites really get rolling—and see how many people turn up. There's never been an Acheron Four entry before, so that's in your favor."

"Actually," Charlemagne said, "Andros here is an Earthman. The extraterrestrial is very small and is lodged in his brain. It directs all his thinking, all his movements."

"Four millimicrons long," Andros said. "Acheron Four is really a very small planet."

"Maybe you could put on a native dance, give out with a mating call. Could you sing a native song?"

"I just want to tell about my home planet."

"Dull stuff," Mr. Douglas said. "No offense intended. The big thing this year is Treflu from the planet Zragachathron in the constellation Monocerotis. He's got some girls from the Temple of Forbidden Things, and I understand they don't have any hair. They're going to demonstrate reproduction. It's a parthenogenetic thing, so it won't be offensive to Earth people. Treflu has assured us of that." He chuckled. "Going to have a look-see myself. They've taken three spaces. So you see what you're up against."

Andros was sure people would come to see him. "As far as I can see," he said, "I'm the only true E.T. here. I don't need fancy dancing girls or reproduction rites, artifacts or pictures."

Mr. Douglas said everyone has his own idea of what needed to be done and he would not stand in the way of an honest presentation.

Seeing there was no dissuading him, Charlemagne bought area sixty-three and made sure Andros' name would be in the program. They inspected the area, finding it to be a small boothlike cubicle with overhead lights that would be turned on at night.

To the right was a cubicle already set up and run by a little old lady in sneakers wearing a babushka and magnifying glasses that gave her a bug-eyed-mistress look. Her name, she said, was Penelope Potter, and Mrs. Potter would be selling wildly colorful oil paintings she said she had made on a conducted tour of the eleven satellites of Jupiter the previous year. Mrs. Potter was also taking bookings for the next conducted tour, the Jovians willing, for two dollars each. A brochure would be sent out two months prior to departure time. When she discovered they were not potential customers but friends of Andros, who would have the adjoining booth, she lost the gleam in her bug eyes, but she did lend Andros a camp stool so he'd have something to sit on.

To the left was a cubicle reserved for a man named Simpson, who they were told would that night offer for sale the congealed blood of the ferocious lizards of Genthus III. The plasticlike baubles, which were to sell for a dollar each, contained specks of sperm which was reputed to have an aphrodisiac effect on Earthlings exposed to it. Some of the space balls of blood were already in boxes in the cubicle ready to be opened, and they could see that the lizards of Genthus III had bright blood indeed and in all shades.

Andros declared he would be willing to discuss the flora and fauna and culture of Acheron Four, "But that's all. I'm not hawking anything, except the need for understanding between the cultures of divergent star systems." Nonetheless, Minnie and Peter worked out an attractive sign that read: ANDROS, EARTH'S REPRESENTATIVE FROM ACHERON FOUR—FREE. They then decorated the cubicle with colorful bunting.

Charlemagne, trying to ease what he thought might be disillusionment, told Andros Earth people are fickle at best. "They're easily led, easily distracted by bright lights and lures. They wouldn't know the truth if it came up and bit them hard on the nose."

"Don't tell Andros about Earth people," Andros said. "He is fully conversant with all types."

Father Bischoff offered to pray for him, and Minnie said she'd do a sexy dance if Andros wanted, but Andros said this would violate the spirit and letter of Acheron Four's culture, which was a passive one. "Nothing must be done to enhance Andros' image," he said. "Andros will speak for himself."

The opening of the cubicles was signaled by the playing of a militant tune from Castor Two over the loudspeaker system, and people began to stroll by. But Andros drew no listeners. Adults passed by with the programs and took due notice of him, but they did not tarry, being more drawn to Mrs. Potter's artwork and a chance to visit Jupiter's moons, and to Simpson's trays of shiny, transparent bloodballs of lizard sperm. A few children smiled and several girls expressed interest in Andros himself, but that was all.

They stayed with him, trying to engender interest among the passers-by, but there were too many flamboyant displays to see, and at last Andros, grown sullen, said he wanted to be left alone. So as night came and the lights strung over the cubicle came on, they moved on.

Father Bischoff found two Methodist clergymen, a Baptist minister and a rabbi of the reformed Jewish faith, with whom he struck up a conversation, and they moved off to discuss casuistry and other vital theological problems.

Charlemagne, Peter and Minnie saw some food-dyed purple pigs which purportedly came from Ursa Major, found Treflu's reproduction demonstration no more than a lecture on flatworms, though Treflu himself was magnificent in his robe of many colors. The girls from the Temple of Forbidden Things seemed very much like body-painted children with plastic bald pates. They sat through a Moody Bible Institute film which explained that God was 100 percent behind even the brainless diatoms, and they saw fire-eaters from Regis who looked just like fire-caters from Ringling Brothers, Barnum and Bailey, and at last they returned to Andros to find him sitting alone and uncommunicative.

Charlemagne suggested that Peter and Minnie take in more of the displays while he talked to Andros, who was obviously disturbed and at low ebb. So they took their leave of them.

They sat in the car because Minnie's feet were tired, sitting without speaking because their ears had been so recently assailed by talk, by sounds and shouting, and by screaming children. They were far from the heart of things, the press of the crowd. The amplified voices and music were only faintly heard where they were, quiet in a moonlighted graveyard of parked cars.

Minnie had said the moon was full and that was all, and Peter had ducked his head to look through the windshield and found that it was, and he shivered because he remembered the earth rise on the moon and guilt suddenly clotted in his throat and his stomach knotted. He expected waverings and distortions, but nothing happened. He relaxed again. He was tired. They had been on their feet for a long time.

Peter was not used to walking. He had never walked much, even as a child in Mountbury; there were always relatives around to take him places if his father was not available. His father gave him a bicycle but he used it hardly at all. When they moved to Price he spent most of his time either in school or working in the store, having no interest in exploring the countryside. He never really stretched his muscles until he helped out on the Ketelby farm.

In country like this there would be little use for a bicycle; the distances were too great. He wondered what the people of Onanda did before the automobile, if Onanda existed then. He supposed they used horses, but here even for horses things were a long way off. He decided he liked this country very much. The air was dry, drier even than dry days in Price, and the scenery was like in the movies. He was glad now he'd seen so many films with Marcella. She'd been crazy about Westerns. It was too bad she could not have seen it like this in real life. She would have loved it. When he first saw the mountains he would not have been surprised to see Indians watching him from the mesa top, or Gary Cooper suddenly leaving a cavalry charge out of Esqueleto Canyon. He had never thought he'd see the West, yet here he was in the heart of it.

"What was she like?"

Peter turned. He could plainly see Minnie's large eyes. At night you couldn't tell they were blue. "What was who like?" He knew whom she meant, it was coming, the whole thing about Marcella, as he knew it would, and he felt muscles tightening everywhere.

"Your wife."

He turned away, inundated by memories. He swam in them for a while. Then he said, "She wasn't like you."

"Is that good or bad?"

"Different. She was . . . different." The many faces of Marcella flashed in his mind; he was surprised to find he could accept them without feeling. She was dead. It was a simple fact: Marcella was dead.

"What did she look like?"

Peter shifted on the seat. "Oh, she wasn't as tall as me, she had blond hair, fair skin. Her eyes were a mixture—blue, green and brown. Flecked."

After a while, Minnie said, "Did you love her?"

Quickly: "Of course I loved her."

She was silent.

Now slowly: "I really did love her. She was thoughtful and kind, never had a bad word for anyone. She would have made a wonderful mother."

"You never had children?"

"No."

"Did you want children?"

"We both did. But Marcella's health wasn't up to it, the doctor said. We were supposed to wait until she got better."

"What was wrong?"

He found himself sweating but not as shaken as he thought he'd be. "She had rheumatic fever when she was a child and she'd had a couple of heart attacks. Minor ones."

Minnie moved so her head lay back on the cushion. "I don't know whether I'd want a kid or not." She laughed softly. "I really should make up my mind." She swiveled her head to him. "Do you think I'd make a fit mother?"

"Oh, yes! You're so healthy!"

She turned her head back. The moonlight was in her eyes. "I turned down a couple of the little buggers. I figured the world was in bad enough shape without my adding to it. I suppose that's a big cop-out."

"You're young yet."

"So are you, Peter, for God's sake, though sometimes I get the feeling you think your life is all over." She sighed. "It really isn't, you know." After a while she said, "What actually happened to Marcella?"

Guilt spilled though him. He could not answer.

She turned. "Peter?"

He still could not say it. It was as if his mind were in a vise and the jaws were closing.

"You're not in the outhouse, are you?"

263

"No."

"Then tell me."

"I can't."

"You can."

He allowed his mind to go free, back to that night. "She—" he took a breath—"Marcella had a heart attack and died. That's all."

"I'm sorry. . . . But it does happen, you know."

"I know. We . . . we were sitting there, sitting there after dinner in front of the TV, watching TV. It was a Western with Glenn Ford. You see, Marcella liked Westerns. She liked all kinds of movies, adventures, romances, historical, musicals. . . . I guess she saw in them things she could never do herself, She wasn't supposed to do anything . . . strenuous. So she did sewing and she read a lot, visited with friends. We had someone come in, do the house. She was . . . frail."

"I'm sorry I've been so nosey, Peter. You don't have to say any more. I can see it's racking you up."

"Frail," he said, tears springing to his eyes. "So frail." The pictures began dancing. "And I . . . I . . . " It hit him and he lurched violently and headed for the outhouse, except he didn't go there; there was no way to get there, and he sat where he was, gagging.

She stared at him, seeing his working mouth, his wide eyes, his neck muscles working, and seeing the tears spilling out.

His eyes stung. The pictures were really slamming at him now, one after another, hard and fast, the terrible pictures, Marcella lying there naked, and then the police, and . . .

Peter screamed with the remembered pain of it, grabbed frantically for the handle to the car door, finally finding it, flinging it open and spilling out of the car, falling to the ground, lying there, moaning softly because the pictures wouldn't stop coming.

Minnie uttered a cry, got out on her side of the car and ran around to him, reaching out to him.

When Peter felt the dead Marcella touch him, he shrieked, leaped to his feet and started off, running blindly, past cars, not

264

knowing where he was going, stumbling over things, running away, trying to escape the persistent images that had control of his mind. Marcella was dead . . . dead . . . dead . . .

He ran and ran until he was far from the cars, and it was quiet, and he didn't care about anything, anything at all. He fell to the ground, pushing his face into the dust, clutching at it with trembling hands, wishing he were dead like Marcella.

"Peter."

He did not know how long he'd lain prone. He had not heard Marcella's approach. Fire ignited inside him, blazed in his head. He moved around, saw her a few paces away. It wasn't Marcella. It was Minnie.

"Go away," he said harshly. "Go away!"

"No."

He got to his feet. He had to make her go away so he could die. "I killed her!" he shouted. "I killed Marcella! God in heaven, I killed her, killed her, don't you understand that?" He found himself laughing and crying uncontrollably, doubling over in agony.

"I don't believe that."

"I'll kill you!" he roared at her, straightening. "The same way! By God, I'll do it! I will!" He took a step toward her, capable of the violence needed to remove her from his sight, from his psyche.

"No."

He was only a few feet from her, saw her throat, unprotected in the moonlight, the rise of breast. He was guilty. He'd killed one, he could kill another. He wanted her. Her body. Just like he wanted Marcella's. He did hunger for it. He would kill her the same way. His breath was rasping; he knew that his eyes were wild, that he'd lost control. His body was responding to automatic inner urgings.

Then, abruptly, everything gave way; all the seams opened and his strength ran out, and he could not even stand on his feet. He collapsed, weak and panting.

He lay there. He felt her hands beneath his head. It was lifted to her lap. She stroked his forehead. His cheek. He felt tears falling on his face like drops of warm rain.

After a while: "I still don't believe you killed her."

"I did, Minnie. I really did." The thought was wrested from where it had been hiding. "Just the way my father killed my mother." He felt sorry for his father. He'd had to live with it the way Peter had. But his father had been stronger. "You see . . . you see . . ."

"You don't have to talk about it."

". . . I really hated her."

"Oh, come on now, Peter."

He now spoke slowly, haltingly, ruminatively. "Not at first, because of the farm. I liked the farm and the Ketelbys, her parents. She was diminutive and petite and I thought she was feminine. She was, but as I said, she was frail, and she became more so. I didn't know she was going to die. So help me, Minnie, I didn't. Any more than I knew I hated her. I tried to live with the things she couldn't do, but I wasn't really doing that.

"I kept wanting her more and more. Why? Maybe I was really wanting to kill her. That's when the guilty feelings came, and then the pictures, and the knowledge that others were watching us even as we watched what was on TV.

"I was often angry with her but I could never let her know that. It would have disturbed her, made her worse. So when we'd fight about sex it was always a short fight and I'd give in, except I was finding it harder to do this. . . . So on that night she didn't want to . . . she wanted to keep on . . . watching TV . . . and I . . . I lost my head . . . I actually tore her clothes off and had her there . . . and she died . . . underneath me."

Peter felt nothing, just a vague numbness. He could still see the moon. Nothing wavered. He didn't want to run off anywhere, and he wondered how this could be. He heard Minnie say softly, "How awful!"

He sighed and went on. "I don't know who I called first, the police or the doctor. I do remember having her dressed by the time everyone got there, but I didn't think it would do much good since They'd been watching through the TV."

"They?"

"Yeah." He grimaced. "No. Not They. Not really. Me." He gave a low laugh. "That's funny. That's really funny."

"What is, Peter?"

"They and Me. I really mixed them up, couldn't tell the difference." He faced her. "Anyway, I killed her, Minnie."

"No."

"Stop saying no! I really did it, Minnie. If I hadn't forced her into it she might have lived longer." He looked away. "I think I can live with that now, though."

The moon was suddenly blotted out by Minnie's head, and he saw her large eyes illuminated by the moonlight's reflected effulgence. Her face came nearer and her lips brushed his. "I'm glad," she whispered.

He reached up, pulled her head down to his, wanting to feel her lips again, and after he had, he said, "It's strange, kissing someone again."

"It's like being born again, Peter."

"It is." He drew her down again, kissed her, then let her head rise up. "How did you know that?"

She laughed. "I'm always being born again."

He looked at her steadily. "You're not frail."

"No."

When Peter and Minnie returned to the Continental they could not find it because cars had started pulling out for Onanda and other destinations, creating a giant dust pall that reduced visibility. They walked through it, moving out of the way of oncoming headlights, until they finally located the others, who were already there, waiting.

Father Bischoff was sleeping fitfully, sitting up in the front seat. Charlemagne sat with his feet out the door on the driver's side, socks off, massaging his feet. Andros was in his usual place in the back.

267

Seeing their glances at the snoring Father, Charlemagne said, "The good padre may be a bit hung over in the morning. He was playing chugalug with his pro friends."

Father Bischoff shifted. "The rabbi," he mumbled. "Oh, that rabbi! Such a drinker!" He drifted off again.

It wasn't until they got in beside Andros that they noticed the blood on his face, his swollen cheek and eye, and the way he sat ignoring them.

"What's happened to you?" Minnie asked.

When Andros did not answer, Charlemagne, who was putting on his shoes, said, "He's in a state. All wrought up."

They could see that for themselves now, the way his lips were pressed together, his eyes narrowed, as if he were in deep thought. Peter said, "What happened, Charlemagne?"

"He got into a fight. Claimed to be the only true Odyssite at the convention, and a few took exception, including Treflu. He knocked Treflu out, actually, but then he was jumped by some of Treflu's friends." Charlemagne closed the door and started the engine.

"He was in a mood, you know, and it didn't improve after you left." He drove the car out of the parking lot, following a galaxy of red lights moving toward the exit to the winding road to Onanda. "I wasn't there at the time, otherwise it might not have started; I'd gone to the john. When I got back, Andros was gone. Then I heard the ruckus, and there he was in the middle of it. The convention police were going to arrest the whole lot of them, but I talked them out of arresting Andros."

"A little money," Father Bischoff said thickly, opening his eyes to mere slits. "All it takes is a little money." He sank back again, his head falling heavily to one side.

"Yes," Charlemagne said. "I paid them off."

"Andros," Minnie said, "I'm sorry you were in such a foul mood. I hope you'll feel better tomorrow."

Andros did not move, looking past Father Bischoff's head to the line of red lights on the road. It was as if he weren't there.

Peter said, "Andros . . . "

Andros stiffened, then turned to Minnie and Peter. They

could see only his outlined head. He said, "Don't call me that."

"Why not?" Minnie asked.

"I'm not Andros."

Peter blinked. "You're not Andros?"

Minnie said, "I know you're Andros. I saw your face when we got in."

"I did, too," Peter said. "You're Andros all right."

"No."

"Well, then," Minnie said, "if you're not Andros, who are you?"

"Scott."

"Scott?"

"Scott Kleinschmidt."

"Do you think that's an improvement?"

Peter said, "But what happened to Andros?"

"He decided to abandon my body."

"A wise thing," Father Bischoff said, rising up. "A wise thing and good for the country." He giggled, put his head down on the cushion, making lip noises.

They were then silent, riding along, absorbed in it. Then Charlemagne said, "Whose body did he take over? Treflu's? One of his helpers?"

"I didn't notice," Scott Kleinschmidt said, yawning. It seemed he might go to sleep. Then he thought the better of it. "Since Andros no longer runs me, I make my own decisions. I've decided to come along to California with you."

"Oh, Andros!" Minnie said. "I think that's wonderful!"

"I told you, the name is Scott."

"Scott," she said. "I'll have to get used to that."

Father Bischoff raised his head for the last time on the way to Onanda to say, "*Coito ergo sum.*"

"Amen," said Charlemagne.

42

In the Motel in Onanda—Entry No. 28

I'm writing this in bed with Minnie beside me reading the journal up to this point as I said I might let her do sometime. She "oh's" and "ah's" every now and then and says something, such as how different the entries are, and I agree, telling her I was surprised about that myself.

When I look at them I know they were me even though I found that at times hard to believe and still do, but I don't dwell on it, it's in the past and I think it would be a mistake to sit down and try to figure it out. It's better to be like Minnie, take things as they come.

Minnie confided to me that her last name is St. John. That should be Father Bischoff's name! Isn't that right, Minnie? (She'll be reading this in a few minutes.)

Scott (I keep wanting to write Andros) is feeling better. (He and the others are in the other motel room.) He says he's got a lot of things to think out. I told him he's not the only one, and not to expect too many answers, if any at all. Charlemagne says he's proud of Scott, his being able to take the loss of Andros like that. He says that's just like an alien, deserting a man without thanks after using him all that time. "I'd never trust one enough to provide room and board," he said. I suppose he was joking, but you never know with Charlemagne. I know I'd never go that far. If there is ever to be a meeting between us and people from another planet, suspicion and distrust would hardly be the way to begin the relationship.

The scenery has changed so much (and I like it!) I can hardly wait to get to California to see if it's different yet. Minnie says I will love it, and I hope she is right.

I thought of calling my father, but I agree with Charlemagne, who says he thinks it's a little too early for that. We're going to get set up out in California and then I'll call him. I frankly don't know what to do with the business, if it's still mine and if he's still working at it the way Dr. Sheckley said he was.

Charlemagne says we're leaving in the morning. "Oh, not at the crack of dawn." If I know Charlemagne, it will be after lunch. And if there was a good fishing hole nearby, it wouldn't be until the day after that.

Well, I see that Minnie is getting to the end of what I'd written before, so I'll just cut this off right here.

43

"LIFE," CHARLEMAGNE said with the air of one who knows, "is a welter race."

They were in the motel coffee shop eating a late breakfast. Minnie stopped buttering her toast to look at Charlemagne uncertainly. "A welter race?"

"And," Charlemagne continued, "it is made so by the ineluctable presence of others."

Minnie said she had no idea what a welter race was.

"Look at it this way, Minerva. If you were born alone, the only human being on the planet, you'd have only yourself to blame if things went wrong. Isn't that right?"

"Nobody gets born alone, Charlemagne."

"Exactly. Right away we've got to start with extenuation. Somebody has to be there to provide the birth."

"How else?"

"And that's the host mother."

"Really, Charlemagne!"

"And already we're in trouble. We find the world isn't ours exclusively. We have to share it with someone else: Mother. So we're down one. Crippled for life before we even take the first breath."

"It's getting worse," Peter said. "We'll be standing on each other's shoulders before long."

Father Bischoff said, "Are children a necessary by-product of the sexual act? I ask you."

"Now," Charlemagne said, "you multiply the mother by the obstetrician, the anesthetist, the diet kitchen personnel, the diaper people, insurance men and all the credit-card numbers waiting to ensnare you, and it becomes a miracle anybody ever makes it to three score and ten."

"I have some uncles who did," Peter said. "They were all long livers. They may even be alive yet."

"Look in their eyes, Peter, the next time you see them. Know what you'll see? People who understand the charts, the weights, the track. They've calculated the risk, the odds, the weather. They've got it all doped out, don't think about it any more, they've run the welter race so many times they couldn't do anything else."

Scott, his right eye bloodshot and the surrounding tissue blackened, his left cheek blue and swollen, picked at his eggs and chewed carefully. He put a finger tentatively to an incisor, pushed this way and that because he thought it felt loose. "I never cared for races *per se*. Maybe that's because I never attended one."

"We're in the middle of one right now," Charlemagne said. "Everybody is. It's the race to make the money before the payment becomes due."

"Scott never had to do anything like that," Father Bischoff said. "He was born with a silver spoon up his behind."

"It makes a difference," Peter said. "I really think it does."

"I'm ignoring the attempts at wit," Scott said, "because I'm remembering getting the forms and working out my own line of possibility and probability for races at places with magic names like Santa Anita, Belmont, Hialeah and Aqueduct, but it was all on paper, post positions, past performances, jockeys, weights and tables, every factor imaginable. It was so complicated it was fun, but I never made any money at it, real or imaginary."

"The race is run right," Charlemagne said, "when survival is the goal. You've got to get out of that starting gate way ahead."

Father Bischoff, who was suffering a monumental hangover, said, "Speaking of survival, I'm not sure if I'll live. Every time I say anything, the top of my head comes off."

"Then shut up," Scott said. "It would give all of us the relief we need after last night."

"I only hope the rabbi isn't feeling any better. I suppose that's not very Christian of me."

Charlemagne finished his eggs, sat back with a satisfied expression. "As for our own race, it's time to don our golden spurs and move on. Otherwise we shall be devoured by worms, wyverns, dragons and devils from the deep."

"You can count on me," Scott said. "I won't renege. A promise is a promise. The sooner the better."

"Well, I'm not ready to move out," Minnie said, a little piqued. "I won't be ready until we try out the body paint like we agreed last night." She saw no brightening interest in the faces. "Otherwise why did I go out and buy it this morning?"

"It will keep, Minerva."

"I don't think so." She lifted a sack from the seat beside her and upended it on the table. Small paintbrushes and bottles of water-based dayglo rolled about. "There." And when there still was no reaction, she said, "Don't you see? It's a challenge. We've got to do better than those little girls from the Temple of Forbidden Things, for God's sake!"

Charlemagne said, "They lacked imagination, all right." He picked up several bottles in turn. "Is this all they had? Fuchsia, cerise, cerulean, lemon?"

"Those are the interesting ones. There are basic colors, too: pink, green, purple, yellow ocher. And here's black and white."

"We'll use them tonight."

"The muse is fickle."

"Tonight, Minerva."

"Now who's letting the welterweights get to him? What's the big rush when there's art to be done? Where's that letting go? Do we have an appointment out there?" She looked around. "Nobody here for creativity?"

Scott fiddled with the bottles. "They are bright colors."

"We'll paint you first, Scott."

"Now wait a minute! I didn't say I wanted to be painted!"

"Peter?" Minnie turned.

Peter flushed. "I don't want to be painted either."

Peeved, Minnie started to scoop the bottles back into the paper bag. "Welshers, that's what you are, the whole lot of you. Last night you couldn't wait to get started. Today you're all somebody else."

"We could paint you," Peter said.

"I don't want to be painted."

"I'd help," Father Bischoff said. He signaled the waitress, got more coffee as Minnie put the last of the bottles into the sack and put it down on the seat. "The food and coffee seem to be helping."

"I think it's the thought of the body painting," Scott said.

"That, too," he admitted.

"Well, I suppose, if there's no other way," Minnie said, as if she'd thought it through.

"All right," Charlemagne said, resigned to it. "It's body painting first. But after that . . . "

"It won't take long, especially if everybody works at it."

"Work, she says." Scott grinned, stretched, leaned back, yawned. He grimaced with pain. "Damn." He took a long drink of his coffee, swirled it around in his mouth. It seemed to help. "Where are we going to live?"

"Live?" Minnie's look was blank.

"Out in California."

She looked at Charlemagne. "There's always a beach house."

Charlemagne said, "Is that a last resort?"

"Oh, no. They're really fine places, beach houses. Expensive, too. There are a lot at Malibu, Santa Monica—that's Route One, the scenic highway right by the ocean. That would be a wonderful place to live! I'd forgotten! There's the ocean right out the back door—or the front, if you want to think of it that way—and there are long stretches of sand, sun and fog, and company. There are always people walking on the beach, any time, day or night."

"Is that a fact?" Scott stirred, interested. "Even at four in the morning?"

275

"Even then. Also, it's not far from things—the Valley, Hollywood, downtown."

"You know," Peter said, "I've never seen the ocean."

Charlemagne said he could see them in a beach house. "It could serve as a base for our forays."

"Forays?" Father Bischoff frowned. "Don't you mean frontal attacks? There's a lot to be done out there."

"Who cares?" Scott sat back and closed his eyes. "People walking along the beach. That's important." He grinned. "Especially if they're girls. Yes, girls and sun." His eyes popped open. "I think I could lie in the sun for a whole year, doing nothing but listening to the surf."

"Why not?" Charlemagne asked.

Father Bischoff wanted to know if it was very far from the Strip, and Minnie told him it wasn't. She said, "At first the distances might seem long to you, but they get shorter the longer you live there."

"I'd like to see the Strip. I really would."

Charlemagne rubbed his hands gleefully. "On with the rucksacks, I say. There's a place for each of us out there. And if there isn't, we'll make a place. After all, the world was made for conquering."

"It certainly wasn't made for drinking," Father Bischoff observed.

When they had finished their coffee and a long discussion of the Odyssites and the events of the previous night, they moved out of the coffee shop and returned to their two connecting second-floor rooms, Peter and Minnie going into the one that had suddenly become theirs, Minnie to prepare for the body-painting exercise, Charlemagne hurrying into the bathroom of the other, and Father Bischoff collapsing into the room's only easy chair. Scott started to pace the floor.

Father Bischoff said, "I wish you wouldn't do that."

"It helps me work things out in my mind."

"It doesn't help me."

Scott stopped abruptly, and Father Bischoff darted a look at him, expecting something inflammatory, but Scott was looking out the opened door to the sun porch across the way where James Colbert was watching them with binoculars.

"Look at that son of a bitch. He doesn't give a damn whether we see him or not."

"He was doing that all day yesterday and this morning before we left for breakfast. Didn't you see him?"

The toilet flushed and Charlemagne came out, moving to join Scott at the doorway, pushing his shirt into his pants. He stopped to give Colbert a middle finger salute.

When Colbert did not react, Scott said, "How about that!"

"He must be looking at something else." Father Bischoff put his hands over his eyes and started a gentle massaging action. "Must be interesting, whatever it is."

"Two of a kind, you and that voyeur," said Scott.

Father Bischoff withdrew his hands, squinted toward the doorway. "Losing that bug in your brain hasn't helped your disposition. Not that it was any great shakes to begin with. Besides, what's wrong with watching?"

"Not doing." Scott snorted. "Somebody ought to go over there, shove those binoculars up his ass."

"I'll pray for you while you're gone. Maybe he'll black your other eye just to balance things out."

Charlemagne shook his head. "It's high time we got on our way, I can see that."

"I could outdrink a little old rabbi," Scott said.

"That's what I thought."

Minnie came through the connecting door, naked and angry. "A girl can't take her clothes off without being ogled at." She gestured to Colbert, but he had moved inside.

"That never bothered you before," Scott said.

"Thanks a lot."

Charlemagne, with calm reason, said, "Did you think of closing the door, drawing the draperies?"

"I like fresh air."

44

JAMES COLBERT turned off the water and stepped out of the shower stall feeling a lot cleaner. He could not imagine what had possessed him to continue looking through the binoculars at that brazen bitch when she started to take off her clothes. Did she suppose no one was watching? She did not. Surely one day she would be one of the damned. Although Colbert belonged to no religious sect, he believed in a wrathful God; he felt there was, in the hereafter, retribution for the reprehensible, the nature of the suffering being directly proportional to the magnitude of the crime committed. Colbert often spent idle hours speculating what punishments fitted what shameful acts.

He dried himself, happy to be able to look forward to the end of this assignment. Soon Mrs. Le Moyne and Dr. Sheckley would be there, and then it would be out of his hands, his responsibilities would be over and he could get back to St. Louis. He must not forget to destroy the photograph of Minnie that he had worked over with the pin. It was not that he was ashamed of what he'd done (after all, it was rather like dispensing justice); it was simply that they would not understand it, least of all Dr. Sheckley.

Colbert was still upset, even though the pin pricking had eased the tension. It was bad enough that he had been so absorbed in watching Minnie—that meant he was not keeping his eyes on the others and they might have seen him—but what was worse, when that fornicatress had turned and stared at him, naked, *he had not been able to take his eyes off her!* It was right after that that he got out the colored pencils and a pin from one of his shirts and did to the photograph what somebody should do in person.

Colbert shuddered. He would be glad when this case was over, really over, and he could get back to Flo, pure, unsullied, dear Flo. (Why couldn't more women be like Flo?) Mrs. Le Moyne had called three hours ago from Albuquerque, having flown there from New Trier, where she said she talked to Sheriff Samuels. (Now he understood that the sheriff had lied to him after all, but he could not, for the life of him, figure out why.) Colbert could not make much sense out of what Mrs. Le Moyne said, but he thought she said she met Dr. Sheckley in New Trier (or was it on the plane?) and they would be traveling together to Onanda (how could she do that after all the terrible things she'd had to say about him?). It was such a mess he'd have to take two weeks off to get himself straightened around and all the muck drained out of his system. At least two weeks.

Earlier, he'd had a few minutes of panic when he thought his people were getting ready to leave, but it was only for breakfast. Himself, he'd been up for hours, had eaten his breakfast long before. He knew they wouldn't be up very early, considering all that had happened the previous night. And those Odyssites, those dirty, deluded people and their screaming children! God deliver him from having to rub shoulders with their kind again!

As it was, he'd had time to set up his portable darkroom in the bathroom and develop and print the pictures, making several of Minnie in the bikini and two each of all the rest: those in the room (taken from the sun porch), at the convention, in the booth, as they wandered around, the fight (a good series there), and the phony priest when he disgraced the clerical things he wore by drinking to drunkenness (some fairly good, though rather static, shots).

The previous night, fearing that his people might leave Onanda when they returned from the convention, he'd followed them home, but they'd quickly closed the drapes, so he knew they were staying. He could imagine what that Jezebel was doing behind the curtains. Thinking about it, he'd had to shower twice and take two Seconals before he was able to drift off to sleep.

He slipped into his blue terrycloth robe, stepped into the room and then to the sun porch to pick up the binoculars and look across the way. He was surprised to see no one stirring, but he could see they hadn't checked out or anything, clothes being strewn about.

Colbert was on the point of inspecting other rooms to see if things were as they should be when he heard a shuffling sound behind him. Surprised, he turned. His heart gave a flip-flop. There, facing him in his room, were the very people he had expected to see across the way—all five of them! Peter, the last one in, was closing the door.

"There's no one at home over there," Charlemagne said pleasantly, "because we're here."

Colbert was too startled to do or say anything, caught off-guard as he was, and feeling suddenly naked and helpless in the bathrobe, and now seeing in shock that Minnie was wearing a robe, too, a short one.

His heart trip-hammering, his mind still numbed by the magnitude of the intrusion, Colbert did have one thought: get to the telephone, summon help. He sidled through the sun-porch doorway and slowly began to sidestep toward the phone. Nobody seemed to notice.

"Well, well," Scott was saying, moving about, looking at the paintings on the walls, the clothes Colbert had so meticulously arranged in the closet. Father Bischoff, who had been standing in the middle of the room looking dazed, plopped into the easy chair and let out his breath. The girl continued to look at Colbert curiously; he reddened and looked away. The shortie robe she was wearing barely concealed anything.

Charlemagne came to sit on the bed, preventing Colbert from being too overt about the phone. Charlemagne said, "You've been so curious about us we decided to come over and satisfy it. Isn't this personal contact better than field glasses?"

Colbert, standing at the head of the bed, his back against the wall, held his breath. He was in a dither. The telephone was

280

right there on the night stand within easy reach, yet he found he could not lunge for it. He said, "You have no right to come bursting in here," but he didn't like the edge of panic in his voice.

"I'll be damned," Scott said. "He can talk. I thought all he could do is look." He laughed and moved onto the sun porch.

"You're not being very neighborly," Charlemagne said.

"What have we here?" Scott picked up the binoculars from where Colbert had left them on the small sun-porch table.

It had gone far enough. Colbert left his place by the bed to retrieve the binoculars. But he was too late. Scott tossed them over the railing. Colbert lurched out to the sun porch to look over the railing. There, at the very bottom of the pool, were the binoculars. He began to feel sick. He turned to Scott. "Those were expensive binoculars!" Now he would go in and call the police. Let them try to stop him! He turned to do it.

"Is that so?" Scott smiled, picked up the 35-mm camera. "What's this?" He swung his arm back.

Colbert lunged for the camera, but again he was too late. With a sinking heart he saw the delicate instrument arc through the air and fall with a small liquid *plunk* into the pool. He reached for the railing to steady himself, feeling he would truly be ill now. The camera had cost him more than three hundred dollars!

He swallowed with difficulty, turned his white face to Scott. "You'll pay!" he said hoarsely. "You'll pay for that!" But he knew it was impossible; he'd never collect. You can't collect from crazy people.

"Ha!" was all Scott said before he turned and moved into the room, Colbert pressing himself hard against the railing to give him more than the room he needed. He could not stand the thought of one of them touching him. In fact, he might just stay out there on the porch; he wished there were some way he could lock the sun porch from the outside. His eyes followed Scott and beyond to where Charlemagne was sitting on the bed, the attaché case on his lap, open.

Colbert, his blood running cold, stepped inside.

281

"Case histories," Charlemagne was saying. "Very interesting, Mr. . . . ah, oh yes, here it is: Mr. James Colbert, Private Investigator. That explains how you managed the case histories. And here are letters from Marietta Le Moyne. Even more interesting."

"That's all confidential," Colbert said, moving to the bed but not daring to take the case. Charlemagne was crazy, too. If binoculars and a camera could be thrown into the pool without a second thought, only God knew what other things they were capable of.

"Very resourceful, that Marietta," Charlemagne said, glancing through the letters. "She certainly is paying you enough. Are you worth it?" Colbert met his eyes without flinching. "You should be ashamed of yourself, though, you really should, spying on people the way you do."

"A false brethren, he came in privily to spy out our liberty," Father Bischoff said, but his heart wasn't in it.

"Mr. Colbert," Charlemagne said, getting up, "you could have come to us. We'd have cooperated, told you what you wanted to know. You didn't have to resort to this pettifoggery."

They were all crazy, all right.

"Aren't you ashamed at all?" Minnie asked, moving to him. When he said nothing because he was trying to forget she was there in that shortie robe, she added, "Not even a teeny bit?"

"Filth," Colbert found himself saying, spitting it out. "Slut."

"Listen," Peter said, coming forward, belligerent. "That's no way to talk to Minnie."

Charlemagne took Peter's arm to stop him. "You know, Peter, it always saddens me to find a man with acid in his veins."

Colbert had taken heart, stared at Charlemagne. "You're crazy." He looked at the others, his eyes a little wide. "You're all crazy, the whole bunch of you."

"We're not," Peter said.

"I don't think that's any way to talk about one's neighbors, Mr. Colbert," Charlemagne said. "In a way, we're closer than that, considering that my wife hired you." He made an amused face. "That doesn't surprise me, though, Marietta hiring you. She was always a desperate woman, even when there was nothing to be desperate about."

There was a loud "Whoop!" from the bathroom, and Colbert knew instantly what it was, and he died a little remembering the picture he had planned to flush down the toilet. Perspiration jumped out on his forehead.

They moved, intercepting Scott as he came out with the pictures in his hands, excited. "Look at these!" he said, moving to the bed to spread them around.

Colbert eyed the door. If he could get out . . . But he could not go out. Not in his bathrobe.

"Not bad. These are not bad." Charlemagne moved the pictures around. "I've never really liked photographs of myself, but these are candid and they're all right." He looked up. "Congratulations, Mr. Colbert."

"I don't like me," Minnie said.

"Oh, they're really good of you," Peter said.

Minnie picked up the picture Colbert wished had vanished into thin air. "What's this?" she said, frowning. The others gathered around. It became suffocatingly quiet.

The memory came washing back to Colbert, the way he used colored pencils to make the flesh tones, a black one to make the triangle of pubic hair, erasing the bikini with the overlay of color, making her nipples red, the surrounding circles salmon pink, her lips scarlet, and using the pencils to make her eyes appear open and deep blue. And then he'd taken the pin and stabbed clear through the positive paper in the genital area. And, oh, the satisfaction of that initial pin/prick! And another pin/prick lunge! And doing it again and again, moving up to the breasts and stabbing there with the prick/pin and then pricking the mouth and the eyes, pricking, pricking . . . He found himself shaking with the remembered ferocity of his feelings, sweat running down from his armpits.

They were looking at him now with their crazy eyes, their

accusing eyes, four mad men and a harlot, all of them as bad as she because she'd brought them all down—and he was compelled to step back by the sheer force of the evil that was in their eyes.

Minnie let the photograph fall to the bedspread, then started slowly around the bed toward him. "Why?" she asked (as if the slut didn't know). "Why did you do that?" (Such innocence; how they can feign it!) She moved closer (he could feel the evil emanations) and he saw that her eyes were a clear, deep blue (devil's eyes, witch's eyes) and he was filled with a violent love/hate and a violent attraction/repulsion.

"You took off my bikini," she said (trying to get him to think about it). "Didn't you like it?" (I know why you had it on.) "Did you want to see my body?" (No, I didn't want to just see it!) "Is that it?" She started to loosen the belt of her robe (is there nothing filth like this won't stoop to?) and Colbert was sure he would vomit. Yet he did not. She dropped the robe and he closed his eyes (but he saw her as she would be, naked, in his mind's eye). "Look, Mr. Colbert. Take a good look. *Look!*"

His eyes fluttered open and he saw. He gagged. She moved toward him. He backed farther until he knew he could retreat no more. She glided toward him until she was only a foot away, smiling with her evil Circe mouth. Her hands reached for his robe tie. Sweat ran everywhere and blood pounded mightily. He felt his robe fall open.

It was suddenly suffocating. All oxygen had fled the air.

Her body touched his.

He uttered a guttural sound, lurched sidewise.

His head hit a shelf projection. He saw bright stars in an infinite firmament before he fell unconscious to the floor.

"It's nothing serious," Charlemagne said, examining Colbert's head where it had made contact with the shelf projection. "In fact, I don't even see any swelling." They were clustered about the bed, where Colbert had been laid out; his blue terrycloth robe had been hung over the back of the nearby dressing-table chair.

"That's a relief," Peter said. "It was such a loud *whack* I thought it might have killed him."

"Not a thick head like his," Scott sneered.

Father Bischoff came in from the bathroom, a dripping wet washcloth in his hands. He moved to Colbert, folded the cloth and put it on his forehead, pressing it there. Water trickled to Colbert's ears. "Don't anybody confuse this with holy anointing."

Minnie, who had taken one of Colbert's hands into her own, was rubbing the wrist and forearm with her other hand. "You know, I think he was more frightened than anything else."

Scott nodded. "He sure had the jim-jams, all right." His eyes wandered to Colbert's crotch. "You know, he doesn't have a bad one. Size-wise, I mean."

"Well hung and hung-up," Charlemagne said. "One of life's little tragedies."

"He looks like a baby, the way he is," Minnie said. "He's got baby fat, and such soft skin. I wonder if he shaves."

"He could use a toupee," Scott observed.

They became silent, absorbed in their contemplation of the unconscious Colbert, so peaceful in sweet sleep, which imprisoned his furious rage and fright, his soft lips smiling in moist innocence, his pink skin glowing, health peeping through pores everywhere.

Father Biscoff said, "He'd make a good cadaver."

"True," Charlemagne said.

Father Bischoff added hastily, "But I'm not suggesting anything."

Charlemagne considered the body in a peculiar, intense way. Then, having thought it through, he said with a gleam of malicious elation, "It would be a shame to leave him like this."

Minnie's eyes began to blink in sympathetic vibration. She turned to Charlemagne with an intake of breath. "Yes!"

Charlemagne laughed, sure of it now. Exultant: "Like

Gonelon's, his torment should be fearful and extreme, his sinews racked from head to heel, every limb wrenched from sockets clean!"

Father Bischoff, Scott and Peter stood watching, not understanding and more than a little uneasy.

Charlemagne turned to them. "But that's no good, don't you see? He'd never know. *Poof!* and it would be over."

"It's got to be something else," Minnie said.

"Something more fitting and proper, more suitable to the times and the place." Charlemagne chuckled at their chagrin. "Something excruciatingly delightful!"

Minnie clapped her hands with delight.

Scott stopped his gaping to grab it and say, "Yeah! We could even paint on a toupee!"

"To each his own." Charlemagne looked this way and that at the body, very clinical in his study of it. "We will divide this cadaver." He said it almost regally.

"He won't be a cadaver much longer," Peter pointed out. "Then what?"

Father Bischoff beamed with inspiration. "Why, we tie him down! We can do worse than take our lead from the Inquisition."

"A good precedent," Charlemagne said heartily. "We don't want him jumping around, spoiling the artwork."

In the five minutes it took Minnie to get the paints she had bought, they had tied Colbert's arms and legs to the corners of the bed with belts they found among his things in the closet. Spread-eagled, he was a tempting target, ripe for their attack with brushes.

Father Bischoff staked out an abdominal area, Scott chose the chest, Peter the feet, Minnie the legs and Charlemagne the arms. But before they could assault those areas with dayglo, Colbert's eyes opened.

Colbert stared at them all dully, with befuddlement, as if unable to separate them from the dreams he'd been having. Then

286

he tried to move and found he could not. His eyes went wide and he opened his mouth.

Scott, who was holding the folded washcloth Father Bischoff had brought in, dropped it on Colbert's mouth to stifle his outburst and was ready to follow it with his hand. Colbert jerked his head from side to side until the washcloth was thrown off.

"Easy does it, Mr. Colbert," Charlemagne said equably, dipping brush bristles into a bottle of fuchsia. "You don't seem to realize you are about to become a human mural."

"Yes," Minnie said, fairly oozing enthusiasm, "we're going to outdo the Odyssites."

Scott said, "One good turn deserves another."

"Dayglo," Charlemagne said, stirring his color, "is much better than colored pencils."

"You . . . *swine!*" Colbert finally spat it out, writhing against his fetters.

"Swine?" Father Bischoff blew what he thought was dust off the area of flesh he'd taken. "We're not pigs. If you are reaching for expletives, I could give you some far better than that."

"Help!" Colbert shouted.

Scott shoved the washcloth into Colbert's mouth, and Charlemagne paused to look down at Colbert like an angry parent. "Really, Mr. Colbert, you ought to learn more control than that." He nodded to Scott.

Scott removed the washcloth.

"Help!" Colbert shouted.

Scott again crammed the washcloth into Colbert's mouth.

Charlemagne shrugged. "So be it."

Scott came in from the sun porch. "Look," he said, "how much longer?"

"Just because you've done your part, don't be so itchy bitchy," Minnie said. She was sitting between Colbert's legs, her own feet beneath her, surveying the smooth curve of cerulean she was painting up Colbert's inner right thigh and deciding to broaden it. As she touched the brush to the flesh, Colbert squirmed and made noises behind the washcloth. His eyes were wild.

Minnie said, "Now, now, Mr. Colbert, you're holding things up again." She waited. Colbert quieted—it seemed not so much in compliance as with fatigue.

Peter, kneeling at Colbert's left side, worked where Scott had painted two crude brown shields over Colbert's chest, making lacy black lines which simulated a brassiere, running them down to the bedspread. "This is fun," he said. "It's the first time in my life I ever painted anything."

"It brings out the best in people," Charlemagne declared, working to make purple corkscrew shapes on the left arm. "I'm not so sure with Mr. Colbert, however. I don't think he appreciates our collective creative effort." He paused to lean over and speak candidly, his face inches from the face of the spread-eagled man. "Just think of yourself as the ceiling of the Sistine Chapel, Mr. Colbert. Do you think you could do that?" Colbert's answer was to toss his head violently, yank at his fetters and make growling sounds into the washcloth. "I guess not," Charlemagne said, sitting back, waiting for the paroxysms to subside before daring to get back to his work.

Father Bischoff, from Colbert's mid-section, said, "I was always interested in art," and he sat back to regard critically the pink-cheeked cherub he had just completed painting on Colbert's stomach.

Minnie leaned forward to inspect it. "Why, I think that's wonderful, Howard! You have a real knack."

Scott, who had been examining the work, came to stand near Colbert's pelvis. "What about pins? Aren't we going to stick pins in him?"

Colbert thrashed about, heaved and pulled.

"I don't dig the pin bit," Minnie said.

"We could use a broomstick."

Charlemagne got off the bed to move around it to get at Colbert's other arm. "Nothing must vitiate what has been done here. That means no pins or broomsticks. It's too bad we don't have Mr. Colbert's camera. We could record this work for posterity."

Minnie was examining the genital area. "You know, this part here is going to be a real challenge."

Charlemagne agreed. "Perhaps it would have been better if we'd shaved off the pubic hair."

Minnie didn't think so. "If we'd done that I could not now make it a lovely pink fuzz." She washed out the brush and reached across Colbert's leg for the pink dayglo.

"I was always partial to cherubs," Father Bischoff said happily, beginning to make another over the liver. "They look like such angels, but they always have a mischievous air about them."

Minnie's ministrations to the pubic hair were having unexpected dividends. Colbert's limp organ was beginning to come to life. "Good, Mr. Colbert," she said encouragingly. "You just keep it coming." She frowned. "But I'll be frank. I don't know what to do about your scrotum."

"Blue," Scott said with a wicked laugh. "He's got to have blue balls."

Minnie considered it. "No. I think blue is a depressing color for testicles." She washed out her brush again. "On the other hand . . ." She looked around for the blue bottle.

"I still think he's got quite a cock," Scott said.

"And I'm going to get to it." Minnie worked with the blue brush on a scrotal sac that kept crawling this way and that. "I'm saving it for last."

"I think you should have it," Peter said. "You deserve it."

"My feeling exactly. A thing of joy should be a beauty forever."

Colbert started squirming again, tugging, stretching and making dire noises in his gag. But the belts held firmly.

"There," Father Bischoff said with satisfaction, giving a final touch of brush to the second cherub's quiver, bow and arrows.

Minnie studied her project at close range. "A real problem

here. A black shaft? An orange one?" Colbert's penis responded, and Minnie said, "That all helps, Mr. Colbert." She decided, picked out the black bottle and began applying the paint to the now fully extended shaft, which pulsed heavenward. When she finished, she wasted no time. "Just hold it right there. Mr. Colbert," she said, hurriedly washing the brush and opening a bottle of cerise dayglo. "The crowning touch!"

They paused to watch her brush it on the head. Colbert began to shake and moan. "Take it easy, Mr. Colbert," she scolded. "That's not cooperating." But the organ's excited pulsations made it difficult for Minnie to apply the vivid red color to the corona. When she finished, she sat back with a sigh of satisfaction and tried to regard her work with the objectivity she thought it demanded.

"Well," she said, "I don't think we've improved on nature, but we've certainly made it more colorful."

45

Minnie, I'm coming to you!

Therin Sheckley's life was once the sum of a number of certainties and predicated upon a number of reasonable probabilities, a fairly good case for cause and effect. But now he was no longer sure of anything. Since the advent of Minnie, the whole firm latticework of premises and conclusions by which he ran his life had been jiggled like a random kaleidoscope pattern. Even with Minnie being gone so long from him, the mere thought of her brought a rush of blood to his head and groin and rendered him tremblingly sensitive to his need of her.

Life has become miserable without you.

Life had become increasingly contradictory and paradoxical. He had not believed he could have ever physically left Berylwood to bring back an escapee, not to mention four escapees (he did not have the time; he could not leave the rest of his patients; he could not leave Elizabeth), yet here he was, doing it. He had not thought he would ever allow himself to be in the same car (even the same room, if it could be helped) with Marietta Le Moyne, yet here he was chauffeuring her to a Southwestern U.S. town he'd never heard of before.

Marietta was, for the moment, quiet, and he was glad of that. Her lips were drawn tight, her eyes searching passing billboards as if she expected to catch her husband hiding behind one of them. Or perhaps she was lost in the world of recrimination she was chief resident of, since she had dwelt on it a good share of the time since they left Albuquerque. Therin viewed her as a vengeful woman, a harridan driven to regain what she thought was hers. He supposed she would go to any lengths to get the money Charlemagne had taken out of their savings; he wondered if she would even have murdered for it if she thought she could get away with it. He could not blame Charlemagne; it pained him to think he would have to bring him back with the others, start the observation period all over again, but there was no alternative.

His hands were damp on the wheel; he knew his lips were as thin as Marietta's (being driven, as she was, but for a more wholesome purpose); his eyes were on the unfolding road because he wanted nothing to happen to prevent him from reaching Onanda and the Grand View Motel. Thinking about it, a little buzz of excitement captured the pit of his stomach.

Can you feel my nearness, Minnie? Are you aware of my speeding toward you?

Therin wrested his thoughts from Minnie and made himself again consider the woman beside him in the car, following Colette's advice ("Look for a long time at what pleases you, and longer still at what pains you"), and wondered if it was possible that his low evaluation of Marietta could be unconsciously colored by the projection of his own unacceptable and unrecognized faults. Of course he could come to no real conclusion because there were no third parties to judge the matter objectively. It was true he didn't like her (she was not only vengeful, she was also bitchy and sharp-tongued) and if the things about her he didn't like were really the way he was, then if he were nasty to her, he would, in effect, be castigating himself in a classic projected self-hate syndrome. On the other hand, if he were nice to her, would this not be a form of narcissism? He snorted with amusement at his spiraling thoughts.

"What?" Marietta gave up the scenery to look at him.

"I didn't say anything."

"You made a noise."

"Yes, I suppose I did. Actually, I snorted."

"How much farther?"

To the next snort? he wanted to ask, feeling free-floaty with love and giddy because Onanda was somewhere out there ahead, and Minnie was at the end of the road, waiting. But he looked at the odometer and reported, "About twenty-five miles."

Marietta turned back to the passing scene, which was mostly desert and ran to Kleenex snow and beer cans.

Yes, Minnie, I'm near you and coming nearer.

Therin still did not understand Minnie, which he supposed was part of her fascination for him, though he did know that she was terribly involved with his psyche and that what he was would not be complete until he had done a penetrating dissection of her (which was what he should have done before).

He could not understand how she could have left him, never looking back, never writing, never phoning. He refused even to consider it rejection. He was sure they had kidnaped her, changed her so he was no longer loved by her (her adjustment to them, plucky as it was, must have been miserable for her). He hoped, however, to recapture something of what they'd had together (even though he'd be covertly putting her through analysis, since he could not afford to become so emotionally distraught again).

Not much longer, love.

He was a knight on the white charger bringing love, and thinking of love made Therin wish there were real answers to love and behavior in loving relationships. Patients had the easier time of it; they were not aware of all the uncertainties, all the unknowns. They could still believe (ah, the vain, deluding joys of belief!); but where was the linchpin that kept professionals (the answer men) firm and secure?

In his own life Therin was perfectly willing to experience total polarity, yet he knew it would be foolish deliberately to invite misery into it. While he knew that in suffering there is meaning, Therin was willing to forgo some of that meaning in exchange for a little peace and quiet.

When he had considered how generous he should be with Elizabeth (when he married her), he decided not to be generous at all, and for a very good reason. As a psychiatrist, he

293

knew that generosity is often construed as a maneuver for placating a superior (or as a compensation for a feeling of inferiority), and he did not want his generosity to her viewed as a sign of weakness or neurotic dependency. In his profession, that would have been bad. He had never discussed it with her because this would have been an admission of manipulation or overt stinginess which could have had converse interpretations, and this would have made the behavior self-defeating.

And there was tenderness. Tenderness, he knew, could be interpreted as aim-inhibited sexuality or it could be suspect as a reaction-formation against sadistic leanings. And so he was not tender with Elizabeth either, thus defeating any would-be inference-makers.

But he had to stop at kindliness, which he knew was really a sublimated libidinal urge. After all, if he treated Elizabeth with no feelings at all (the only really safe way), she might as well not be there; and so he said to hell with it (as far as kindliness was concerned), and always saw to it he was kind to her, though this was hard after Minnie came.

Having worked out generosity and tenderness (both negatively) and kindliness (positively) early in his marriage, he proceeded during the years of his life with Elizabeth to work things out in other areas. He had succeeded so well and his life had been so evened out that it had become curiously unsatisfying and aseptic.

Until Minnie arrived, that is.

Minnie knocked all that askew. With Minnie he found he never thought about generosity (or his decision about it); he was simply generous in every way with her (how could this be?). He never thought about tenderness either; he was simply tender always with Minnie (was he becoming schizoid himself?). What was more, he found himself full of humility and surrender when he was with her, and this certainly was not at all like Dr. Therin Sheckley.

With Minnie the birds sang.

But since Minnie had gone, birds didn't sing any more. Or they seemed not to. And that was why he *had* to have her back.

294

He needed Minnie to balance Elizabeth's austerity, hauteur and fundamentalist logicality and his worry about psychological inferences, for with Minnie, with her carefree, childlike ways, he could kick up his heels and lose himself in her (and to hell with everything else). He needed her so he could explore the parts of himself that had for so long lain hidden.

He supposed his eagerness to find and speak with Minnie was the reason he did not understand what went on with Sheriff Samuels.

After all the bleak days at Berylwood, throwing himself into his work (to forget her), trying to listen to others (and not his own heart and juices), the call from Sheriff Samuels was a life brightener, indeed, and he began to breathe again, for Samuels had said the five people Therin was looking for were in New Trier and he should fly out and get them; he'd hold them for him.

There never was any question about going. He was on his way within the hour. Before he left he tried to call Marietta Le Moyne, but he could not reach her.

He was so taken with the thought that he would soon see Minnie again that the ordinary things of life paled by contrast; that was why, when he arrived in New Trier (by rented car from the airport some fifty miles distant), he found himself unable to be more than mildly surprised to find the sheriff closeted with Mrs. Le Moyne. But when the sheriff told them there had been a mixup and that through a mistake the five persons they had come to get had been released, he was stunned.

"I'm sorry," the sheriff said (not looking sorry at all, Therin thought), "I really am, you folks making that trip all the way here and then not finding them. I tried to get in touch with you to stop you but you were already on your way."

Therin was crushed, unable to say anything. But not Marietta Le Moyne. She burst out with such a colorful denunciation of law enforcement in general and law enforcement in New Trier County in particular that Therin could not help being impressed. He was glad, too, for he could not have done it. It was not that he did not believe in raising one's voice (after all, he did preach getting all those feelings out), it was simply that doing so would not have been Therin Sheckley.

Therin walked out with Marietta, leaving Len Samuels and his deputies red-faced and discomposed. He was sick at heart and bewildered, only half listening to her tirade against jerk-water-town sheriffs and how she ought to refer the matter to the district attorney or the state's attorney or whatever they had in this godforsaken county, a matter for the grand jury, no less, Therin thinking it didn't matter, Minnie wasn't there, he didn't care about taking anybody to task about it, all he wanted was Minnie and now she was out there somewhere on the way to California.

"Doctor," Marietta said, stopping to face him on the side-walk, "you don't look well."

"I'm not."

"You need a cup of coffee."

He protested, but once Marietta had made up her mind, there was no getting around it. She took his arm and practically dragged him down the street.

They sat for a long time in a booth in a small coffee shop not far from the jail, Marietta still rankled and going on about Sam-uels, but Therin was too lost in gloom to pay much attention. Eventually she got around to wondering why they both should be there, deciding it must have been insurance and declaring it was further proof of the sheriff's ineptitude.

Suddenly Marietta straightened. "I completely forgot about Mr. Colbert!" She slid out of the booth before Therin could gather wits enough to ask what she meant. He saw her enter a phone booth at the coffee-shop entrance and speak animatedly to someone at the other end of the line and he wondered if she had contacted Colbert and, if she had, where he could possibly be and how she managed to do that if Colbert was on the job.

Marietta came back, jubilant.

"They're in Onanda!" she said, taking her seat.

"Onanda?" He had no idea what or where that was, but his spirits improved with the news.

"At the Grand View Motel." She referred to a slip of paper

upon which she had written several things. "Room two-**eight-two**."

"They're in room two-eight-two?"

"No. That's Mr. Colbert's room."

"I see." But he didn't see at all.

She saw his befuddlement. "I called St. Louis, his office. There was a message there for me from Mr. Colbert. I tried calling the motel but he's not in his room." She snorted with scorn. "About time he did something to earn his money."

The pleasant buzz that had started with Samuels' call had returned to his stomach. Onanda, his mind kept saying. Onanda. It had a happy sound to it.

She got right to work on it. "We'll fly to Albuquerque. That's the nearest city. We'll rent a car, drive to Onanda from there." Her eyes were fairly snapping. She saw his dubious expression. "It's cheaper, our going together, Doctor."

"Of course."

So they turned in their rental cars at the airport, flew to Albuquerque, where Marietta called Colbert, found that everybody was still there, picked up a rental and started out, Therin praying they would not be too late.

Minnie, we're here!

Almost before Therin had completely stopped the car in a parking space near the office at the Grand View Motel, Marietta was out her side and starting for the stairs, walking without stretching, as if she had not just ridden three hundred miles. Therin envied her her nerveless dedication, wished he were not so anxious and dry of mouth.

At the bottom of the stairs Marietta turned to wait and he hurried to join her there, thinking perhaps she was, after all, not so wholly cold and impersonal as he thought, until he realized she did not want to face Colbert alone. Remembering how Colbert had acted in Dr. Tillheimer's office, he couldn't blame her.

He walked with her up the stairs, trying to get hold of himself, but it was difficult. He looked around at the doors, wondering which one would lead him to Minnie. If she was still there. After all, it had been hours since Marietta had talked to Colbert, and perhaps, as at New Trier, they had moved on.

No, you're here somewhere; I feel it!

They reached Room 282 and Marietta knocked.

There was no answer.

So Colbert had taken off to follow his charges, and he and Marietta would have to move on together again.

"Goddammit!" Marietta lifted a clenched hand, hammered with the side of it on the door. "Colbert! Answer the door!"

At least she is finding release, Therin thought with a sigh.

Oh, Minnie, Minnie, Minnie . . .

There was a faint, muffled sound from inside. Marietta froze, her fist upraised. They heard the sound more plainly now. Marietta opened the door and they went in.

Colbert was on the bed, his arms and legs secured to the bedposts, naked, painted in bright poster colors which did not seem to be dry. Colbert's eyes were bugging out and he was making throaty noises through a pink washcloth in his mouth as he writhed.

Marietta ran to the bed, pulled the washrag out, saying, "What's happened to you?"

Therin reached the bed, began unbuckling the belts as Colbert said hoarsely, "They did it! They did it!" With a hand that Therin had freed, Colbert reached for a blue terrycloth robe on a nearby chair and draped it over his mid-section.

"They're crazy," Colbert said, pulling so hard at the remaining belts that Therin had difficulty in unfastening them. "They're filth! They've got to be locked up! And that girl, that horrible girl, she's—she's the worst of all." He was breathing hard as Therin undid the last belt. "They've got to be locked up, put away!" His eyes were on fire. "Some dark place, some remote dungeon, out of the sight of all decent men—somewhere deep, a wet place, where no light comes . . ." Colbert was shaking.

"Mr. Colbert," Marietta said harshly, "get hold of yourself. Now tell me: Where are they?"

"Eight-sixteen." Colbert reached for the phone. "But they won't be there for long." He had the receiver to his ear.

"What are you doing with the phone?"

"Calling the police. I'm swearing out a warrant."

Marietta reached over, put a finger on the cradle phone stud, breaking the connection. "What good will that do? We can't take them back if they're in jail."

Therin felt a cold, damp wind of apprehension blow over him at the thought of Minnie in jail.

"They're beasts!" Colbert spit it out. "They're uncontrolled beasts! They've got to be caught before they leave. There's no time!"

Marietta said coldly, "If you want to get paid, you'd better forget the police and go over there with us."

"Over there?" Colbert became panicky again. Then pugnaciously, in a quavering, overwrought voice: "Not without protection. Not without the police."

"Legally," Therin said, "there's nothing the police can do. Our people will have to be convinced it would be best to return for treatment."

"There's no time for talk!" Colbert wailed.

Marietta saw logic that had escaped them. "If I know Charles, he won't want to go back. But if he's faced with arrest, I'm sure he and the others will think the better of it." She turned to Therin. "You call the police, Doctor."

"Why should he do it?"

"Because you're in no condition to, Mr. Colbert. Now hand that phone to Dr. Sheckley."

"All right," Colbert said reluctantly, "but I still think they should be made to suffer for what they did to me." He handed the phone to Therin and started for the bathroom.

"Where are you going?" Marietta asked.

"I'm going to wash this stuff off, get dressed."

"There isn't time," she said sharply. "You said that yourself."

"But I can't go like this!"

"If you want to get paid you will."

Colbert sank to the bed dejectedly. "Why did I ever get mixed up in this?"

Therin, the phone in his hand, said, "What am I supposed to say to the police?"

"The truth," Marietta said. "Tell them who you are and explain that you need help subduing some escaped lunatics."

46

FATHER BISCHOFF, his packing completed, had sat in the easy chair for so long without saying anything that Charlemagne, who was putting the last of his things in a suitcase, turned and asked him what was wrong.

"Nothing," Father Bischoff replied airily, getting up, his face constricted in thought. "I've been thinking about body painting, that's all." He moved to Charlemagne, his mood serious and well-intentioned. "I have come to the conclusion that decorating bodies could become a full and glorious ritual, complete with instructions, ceremonies, exorcisms and scrutinies."

Charlemagne walked around the room, opening drawers and cabinets to make sure they were empty, Father Bischoff following him. "Father, it's a wonder the men of the Council never thought of that."

"Oh, it's far too much fun; the Council fathers would never permit it. But in my church—"

Charlemagne turned to him with surprise. "Your church?"

Father Bischoff nodded briskly. "Yes, that is what I was thinking about. It's the only way. Ritual in my church will have all the old litanies, the dark, metaphysical things that churches used to have."

Scott, who had come in from the bathroom in a clean undershirt, with a glance at them moved to the dresser, where he'd laid out a fresh dress shirt. "Look who's starting a church. A fucking priest."

"It wouldn't be modern at all," Father Bischoff went on, ignoring Scott. "Everything is modern today, and I think that's what's wrong. My church will regress. Who wants logic in church anyway? Is the encyclical *Mediator Dei* logical? My church will be a return; it will be full of the old occult wisdoms, mysticisms, arcane things from the old books, fetors from shackled devils, charms and spells. In my church fornication will not be a sin."

Peter and Minnie came leisurely through the connecting door dressed as they all were: for the road. Peter put down the suitcase he was carrying.

"Well?" Minnie said.

"O.K.," Scott said, "so you're ready ahead of us for once. We'll make a note of that."

"You look very nice, Minnie," Father Bischoff said with glandular overtones.

"Look out," Scott said. "He'll grab you for his church, make you the Holy Mother."

"Babies will not be our goal," Father Bischoff retorted belligerently.

Scott hooted derisively.

"All right, all right." Charlemagne snapped his suitcase closed. "Let's show a little unanimity—at least before we get into the car."

Peter said uneasily, "It's rather late in the day to be starting out, isn't it?" He did not look pleased with moving out. Minnie drifted to the window.

"That's a plus factor," Charlemagne said. "I've heard this is the time to travel across deserts."

"It could be beautiful at night," Minnie said.

"Where we're going, large is the plain and widely spread the world." Charlemagne lifted the suitcase off the bed. "Do we have everything?"

"What we don't have yet," Minnie said, "is over there. Isn't that Dr. Sheckley?"

They all gathered at the window and looked across the way. They saw Colbert in his bathrobe waving his arms as he talked to Marietta Le Moyne and Dr. Sheckley, who stood arguing with him. Then, as one, the three started for the door.

"That's him, all right," Scott said.

Charlemagne said in dismay, "And that's my termagant wife.

Let me tell you, no Moslem god ever brewed more spleen."

"What are we going to do?" Minnie asked in alarm.

Charlemagne thought about it. "There are always idols to smash, images to smite, Minerva."

Scott said, "Shouldn't we just get the hell out of here?"

"No. We'll wait. They'll be over directly, I imagine." Charlemagne left the window to sit heavily on the bed. "The way I see it, the battle is inevitable." He regarded the others as they, too, left the window, and he saw their trepidation. "Lift up, my lords," he said heartily. "Ready your burnished blades to fight!"

But they were not cheered, moving rather as people under a cloud to weigh this new crisis, fearful of the outcome.

Dr. Sheckley and Marietta came in without knocking, moving in not at all on tentative feet but as two people who'd had, as life's goal, this moment and were not about ready to let it escape but moving in to embrace it at last, knowing their advantage. And in their wake, in his blue terrycloth robe, came Colbert, wary and nervous.

They found Charlemagne standing by the bed not looking at all ready for the thrusts to come, Minnie in the easy chair watching them steadily with a bland and guileless expression, Father Bischoff half reclined on the far side of the bed regarding them through hooded eyes, and Scott with his rump hoisted to half stand, half sit at the dresser looking combative.

Colbert, with a wet palm, pushed the door closed and stood near it, ready to run if the tide should turn.

"Charles," Marietta said pleasantly, purringly, "we've come for you."

A tremor of deep concern passed over Charlemagne's features, but he quickly brought himself to heel and peered at her face. "Whatever happened to your nose?"

"It's been fixed."

"That's not your own hair."

"Of course it's not."

"Your face isn't the same."

"Oh, stop it, Charles!"

Dr. Sheckley nodded absently to the others, stepped lightly across the room to stand before Minnie, looking down at her white face, his eyes aglow. "Minnie," he said breathlessly.

Minnie managed a smile but she did not get up. "Hello there, Therin."

Dr. Sheckley reached out, took her hand. "I've missed you. You have no idea how much I've missed you."

"Therin . . ."

"The house has been so empty." Dr. Sheckley became choked up.

"I'm sorry. You were very nice, and it was great fun, but—"

"You've *got* to come back." When she blinked to keep back tears and looked away, he patted her hand. "You really must, you know." Dr. Sheckley did not seem so sure of it, however, and he peered at her intently to perceive her true feelings. He saw them and did not want to believe them. "Minnie." He held hard to her hand, not wanting to let go because it was an anchor, a bridge to what had been, and he did not want to lose that.

"I'm sorry," Minnie repeated.

"Charles," Marietta said, and there was an admonitory edge to the word. She had taken a stand before her husband, her arms folded, a lethal gleam in her eyes. "You're going with us. You're all going with us and there's no argument about it. Isn't that right, Doctor?"

"What?" Dr. Sheckley turned to her, dazed.

"I don't think so," Peter said with rash confidence, getting up from the suitcase and going to Minnie and Dr. Sheckley, looking the doctor straight in the eyes. "We're going to California, Doctor. All of us."

Dr. Sheckley stared at him with disbelief.

"That's right," Scott said, leaving no doubt and moving from the dresser.

"Thank you both," Charlemagne said, taking heart. Seeing Dr. Sheckley's bewilderment, Charlemagne smiled and said,

304

"Peter speaks, and Andros, it seems, has chosen other habitation."

"I always belittled that little bug," Father Bischoff said mournfully. "Now I rather miss him."

"You see," Charlemagne said, "we're a *Gestalt*. One speaks for all."

"And we're wasting time," Father Bischoff said, hoping to get the rally moving. "There's a church to be founded."

"And Father Bischoff here," Charlemagne went on gamely, "is going to start his own church, which will be a throwback, an ecumenical pasticcio, so to speak, with a major emphasis on body painting."

Colbert shuddered at the door.

"Stop this nonsense!" Marietta said in an ugly voice. "It so happens that you all are patients of Berylwood." She eyed Minnie reproachfully. "All except you. And frankly, I can't see what the doctor sees in you."

"Lord," Father Bischoff said, rolling his eyes, "deliver us from this cruel torment."

"You shut up," Marietta snapped. "You're no priest and we all know it." She drew in her breath. "My husband had no business helping you all escape, and for that he is culpable, or rather he would be culpable if he were not insane."

"Marietta—"

"You shut up, too, Charles. It's out of your hands now. We're here and we intend to see to it that you all are returned safely to the sanitarium. Now the question is: Are you going to come quietly? There are several policemen on their way here to see to it you do as we say, so you can see there isn't much point to continuing this dreadful charade."

"Mrs. Le Moyne," Dr. Sheckley said, moving to her, "I don't think we should be so hasty. From what I see here—"

"Doctor," Marietta said, eying him coldly, "you may be a psychiatrist, but I know Charles, and if these others are anything like he is, force is going to be needed." She turned to view them all with disdain. "And when the police see what you have done to poor Mr. Colbert here, I think they will want you out of Onanda as quickly as possible."

Marietta turned and moved to the door as if to thwart any escape, standing beside Colbert, who glared at them all from this safe distance.

Dr. Sheckley went to Minnie to look down at her, searching her face and not knowing what to say to her. Minnie was not looking at him but at Charlemagne. She was worried and uncertain and even Charlemagne seemed overwhelmed by Marietta. When she caught Charlemagne's eye, the glance she exchanged with him was eloquent of the emergency.

"We're not going to go," Scott muttered, visions of a beach house slipping away. "Are we, Charlemagne?"

Charlemagne did not move. He stood now looking at the floor.

Peter said bravely, "Of course we're not going," but it was obvious he was trying to shore up resistance already manifest.

"There's a church, and I . . . " But Father Bischoff was so overcome he could not go on.

At last Charlemagne raised his head to lock eyes with his wife across the room. "We're not going, Marietta," he said quietly.

Marietta drew in an angry breath, but before she could say anything, Colbert flared: "Then you and your friends will rot in jail here. I'll see to that. As soon as the officers get here—"

"Shut up, Mr. Colbert," Marietta said with undisguised contempt.

"Lord have mercy!" Father Bischoff lowered his head and crossed himself.

Marietta strode to Charlemagne and it seemed for a moment she would slap him as they stood face to face. Then Charlemagne looked over her shoulder to the door and Marietta turned. Three policemen were coming in.

The first man was Sergeant Elton Redduck, a burly, suntanned, non-nonsense man who looked born to his uniform. He came in cautiously, regarded them all carefully. He was followed by Patrolmen Robb and Bailey, both younger men. They did not venture as far into the room as Redduck.

306

Redduck said gruffly, "All right, what's going on here and which one of you is Dr. Sheckley?"

"I am," Charlemagne said with calm assurance, stepping forward and shaking Redduck's hand. "I'm glad you got here in time."

Dr. Sheckley turned to stare at Charlemagne in astonishment.

Marietta recovered her voice. "He's not Dr. Sheckley." She pointed to Dr. Sheckley. "He is."

Redduck's eyebrows went up and he looked from one to the other with rising doubt.

Charlemagne laughed regretfully. "You'll have to forgive them, Sergeant. You know how it is with mental cases."

"Mental cases!" Marietta saw the ominous direction things had taken. She said distinctly and carefully, "This man is my husband and his name is Charles."

Charlemagne clucked sententiously, shocked by the suggestion. "A simple case of transference, Sergeant. I don't know why it is that women patients persist in falling in love with their psychiatrists."

"Now listen here, Charles," Marietta said vehemently, blowing her cool. She shot a look of panic to Dr. Sheckley.

Sergeant Redduck stood uncertain, beginning to fume.

Father Bischoff came forward. In his unctuous best he said, "May I say something, Sergeant?"

"Of course, Father." The sergeant relaxed.

Marietta said, "Sergeant . . ."

"Let him speak."

"Thank you," Father Bischoff said. "You surely must realize these are sick people, and your dilemma is itself understandable, but this man here is the doctor. You have my word for that." He gave out with an exhausted sigh. "We've come a long way, halfway across the country, and we've finally caught up with them and we're tired. But, try as we have, we cannot convince them they must go back with us to the sanitarium to continue their treatment."

"He's lying!" Marietta said loudly, coloring in anger. "He's not even a priest!"

Charlemagne shook his head. "It is truly sad."

"She's telling the truth," Dr. Sheckley said, recovering and coming forward. "Let me show you my credentials." He got out his billfold.

"Sergeant," Charlemagne said patiently, "that is what this is all about. This patient, Mr. Kleinschmidt, stole my billfold and papers and refuses to return them to me."

"That's a lie!" Marietta cried.

"Just who are you?" the sergeant asked, giving her his full attention.

She drew herself up. "I am Marietta Le Moyne."

"She's right about that," Charlemagne said. Then, in a lower voice, to Redduck: "She's also an advanced case of schizophrenia with paranoid overtones. I'd be careful with her, if I were you."

"Don't let him fool you!" Colbert said, advancing from the door. "He's one of the patients!"

"Who are you?" Redduck asked.

"James Colbert. I'm a private investigator."

"It's his delusion," Charlemagne said unhappily. "Actually, his problem is he's an exhibitionist, isn't satisfied with the body God gave him and is given to trying to improve it by painting it. Remove your robe so the sergeant can see, Mr. Colbert."

Colbert went white, started to back away. But Minnie, who had got up from the easy chair, walked over to Colbert and pulled the robe tie. The robe fell open, exposing to the sergeant's gaze the colorful artwork it had been concealing.

Redduck blinked rapidly in amazement.

Colbert uttered a moan of anguish, tried to cover himself, but Minnie kept holding the robe open. Colbert twisted himself violently away, but Minnie hung on to one arm. Suddenly the robe ripped apart and half of it came off in Minnie's hands. Colbert stumbled toward the entrance. Patrolmen Robb and Bailey made a grab for him as he went by, but they succeeded only in getting hold of what was left of the robe. Colbert, uttering a whimpering cry, jerked to one side, the rest of the robe coming off. He shrieked, grabbed for the door, opened it and ran out, Patrolman Robb in swift pursuit. Colbert's cries faded.

For a long moment no one said anything; then Dr. Sheckley and Marietta, rightfully fearful that the same thing might happen to them, moved on Redduck to impress him with their case, exhorting him not to be too quick, things weren't what they seemed to be, but having a difficult time because Peter, Scott and Father Bischoff kept denying their charges. Charlemagne stood back, aloof.

Redduck was finally forced to shout them all down, and when it was quiet he turned to Charlemagne. "Who are these other people?"

Charlemagne indicated Scott and said, "That's Dr. Scott, my assistant," and then, referring to Peter and Minnie, "and that's Peter Kleinschmidt, brother to the patient, and that's his wife, Minnie. They were so worried about Peter's brother they insisted on making the trip with us, thinking they might intercede somehow, influence a recalcitrant patient. Father Bischoff over there is Mr. Kleinschmidt's priest. He came along for the same reasons."

Dr. Sheckley had locked eyes with Minnie in a sort of last-ditch nonverbal appeal for help. But he saw the truth at last in the depths of Mediterranean blue and he was forced to turn away, his face becoming at first drawn, then resigned. He turned to the policeman. "Sergeant, this is ridiculous. Except for the girl, all these people are patients of mine."

Charlemagne nodded sympathetically. "It's the paranoid overtones coming through. Did you hear it, Sergeant? We're all patients. Next, you'll be a patient. It's really pitiful." As the sergeant turned to take a step toward Dr. Sheckley, Charlemagne said, "I'd be careful, if I were you, Sergeant. Kleinschmidt hasn't killed anyone yet but he has decided homicidal tendencies."

Dr. Sheckley snorted. Redduck drew back but said to him, "I think you'd better return those credentials, Mr. Kleinschmidt."

"Don't you do it!" Marietta cried. "All will be lost if you do!"

Charlemagne shook his head. "Even the dreams of the deluded die hard."

Redduck eyed Dr. Sheckley, decided he didn't look too dangerous, stepped toward him. Dr. Sheckley retreated, his face determined, his billfold clutched before him. "Now, now, Mr. Kleinschmidt," Redduck said soothingly. "You know you shouldn't have stolen those credentials."

Dr. Sheckley twisted to one side as Redduck came close enough to grab the billfold. Redduck lunged, grabbed the billfold; but Dr. Sheckley, angered by it all, would not let go. They struggled.

"Dr. Scott," Charlemagne said, "I think the sergeant could use some help."

"Certainly, Doctor." Scott moved to Dr. Sheckley and now all three were fighting for the billfold.

Patrolman Bailey, standing guard at the door, watched with anxious eyes but did not dare leave his post.

"Charles," Marietta hissed, "you're not getting away with this."

"You'll feel better after a good night's sleep, my dear."

With Scott's help, Redduck finally wrested the billfold from Dr. Sheckley and moved to Charlemagne with it. Redduck looked back to Dr. Sheckley, who seemed small, defeated and dazed. "Quite a fighter," he said. "I see what you mean." Charlemagne reached for the billfold but Redduck did not give it to him immediately.

Marietta said levelly, "Sergeant, this is going to be the saddest day of your life when you discover what a terrible mistake you're making."

"Sure," Redduck said.

"As a matter of fact, if you'd take the time to open the billfold and look inside, you'd find Dr. Sheckley's driver's license and photograph, which ought to prove who's who."

Minnie gave a little gasp. Dr. Sheckley turned to her and saw her frightened concern. She looked to him and now there was pleading in her eyes. Dr. Sheckley smiled wanly, then moved to Marietta, saying, "It won't work, the game's up, sweetie, might as well confess." Taking her arm, he turned to Redduck. "You've got us. We'll go quietly."

"Well, now," Redduck said. "That's more like it." He handed the billfold to a surprised Charlemagne and moved to Marietta and Dr. Sheckley.

Marietta's face was contorted with new anger at this new aspect of Dr. Sheckley as she tore her arm away. "You bastard! What the hell do you think this is accomplishing?" Her furious eyes flicked to Minnie and back. "That bitch got to you, is that it?"

"It's no use," Dr. Sheckley said calmly. "They're on to us. We're cuckoo and you know it."

"Oh!"

Just then Patrolman Robb came in, breathless. "Chased him over to the other wing, Sarge. Tried to get in a room over there. He's down in the car, locked in the cage section."

"Good," Redduck said.

Charlemagne said, "Sergeant, I'd be pleased if you'd take them to jail for a short while until we straighten things out here. And I'd be pleased if you were gentle with Mr. Kleinschmidt."

"No, you don't!" Marietta cried out in utter outrage. She advanced to Charlemagne, started to pound at him with her fists. "God damn you, Charles!"

"Poor thing," Dr. Sheckley said with a chuckle.

"Now, lady!" Redduck said, moving in, taking her flailing arms captive. "That's not going to do you any good." When Marietta turned her head and bit his hand, Redduck shoved her roughly toward the two patrolmen. "Put the cuffs on this one."

"I'm sorry about all this," Charlemagne said, brushing his suit.

"Things like this happen," Redduck said. He turned to Dr Sheckley. "Now you, sir."

"Of course, Sergeant."

As they went by Charlemagne, Redduck said, "See you down at the jail."

Dr. Sheckley said with a wry smile, "Goodbye, Doctor."

Charlemagne nodded solemnly, "Goodbye, sir."

"Charles!" Marietta screamed from the door. "As heaven is my witness, you'll pay for this."

The patrolmen pushed her ahead of them out the door.

Before going out, Dr. Sheckley turned for a brief last look at Minnie. She stood wringing her hands, biting her lips and trying to keep back tears.

47

THE WILD clouds of late afternoon had disappeared and with them the sunset-coppered castellated battlements that were buttes far distant but looking close because of the clear, dry air.

Now the Continental whispered through the night along a road that occasionally threaded its way between low-lying hills that had a few hours before been covered with yellow wild-flowers, gnarled mesquite and sagebrush, but for the most part ran so straight through such a mind-staggering vastness that it seemed it would never end. Indeed, the travelers had a feeling they might be trapped forever on it.

Charlemagne drove the car at nearly one hundred miles per hour, but still the distant, dark shapes of unknown mountains never seemed to get any closer.

Minnie, who had been napping between Peter and Scott, had awakened and now sat still, peering out at the moonlit wastes that did not seem to be moving by at all, and felt unreal and alone.

Charlemagne flicked his eyes to the rear-view mirror. "A noble-born woman, instructed in the faith, has awakened." The words, the first to be spoken for a long time, caused the others to stir.

"I feel . . . remote." Minnie yawned and stretched.

"A man is never remote as long as he is alive and knows it."

"Maybe so, Charlemagne, but I knew people who were remote and lived right there in the middle of everybody. Besides, I feel sorry for Dr. Sheckley."

"He'll be all right. Remember, he didn't have to do it."

"I know and that's why I feel sorry."

Peter said sleepily, "Where are we?"

"I think we're between here and there," Scott said, blinking with lethargy and eying the dismal desert.

"If I were up to it," Father Bischoff said with a weary smile, "I'd offer a prayer for Dr. Sheckley. The gods have been good to us and should be thanked."

"Blasphemy, if I heard right," Charlemagne said. "Unless you're speaking of the triune."

"I'm speaking of those old, worn-out gods, the ones that served so well before we tried to find out His name and address."

They were silent. In the far distance blossomed a corona of light that seemed eerie and displaced until it divided like an amoeba into two spots of light and moved in accelerated enlargement toward them, at length flashing past with a whine of air, the red jewels of its tail diminishing in the night and eventually blinking out.

They were once again alone.

"I had a dream," Charlemagne said.

"It's dangerous, dreaming while you're driving," Peter said.

"Nevertheless, I did have a dream."

Minnie said, "Well, what was it?"

"I dreamed St. Gabriel came to me and said, 'Up, Charles! Assemble thy whole imperial might. With force and arms unto California ride.' It seems the land there is besieged by alien tribes."

"Oh, Charlemagne!" Minnie replied with a giddy, involuntary laugh.

Father Bischoff said, "What did you reply to the angel?"

"I said, 'God, how weary is my life!'"

"Weary!" Minnie slipped forward on her seat, the better to speak to him. "Why, your life has just begun, it's hardly started, it's all spread out there ahead of you!" She squirmed to sit back to add soberly, "In fact, it's hardly begun for us all, I'd say."

"Amen," said Father Bischoff.

314

48

Beach House—Entry No. 36

Today is my birthday and, judging by the way things are
going around here, it's going to be a different birthday than I've
ever had. They're planning a party and everybody's supposed
to be here for the special announcement, but I don't know if
they will be, especially Minnie, and I feel so tense I thought I'd
come up here to the second floor bedroom of this big house and
try to get myself together by writing this entry.

From the desk in this room I can look down into the backyard, where there is a fountain, a wide patch of grass that Scott
keeps mowed (grass looks out of place so near the ocean), a
rock garden and a big area of cement with a table and chairs
(which is where the party's supposed to be).

Right now the only people down there are my father and
Bernice, and they're talking by the gate that opens to the beach.
The ocean can't be more than a hundred yards farther on. It
really looks great today, the waves, the beach and the sky. A
great day for a birthday!

Things haven't changed much since my last Beach House
entry, and events don't happen with the same frequency that
they did when we first arrived in California, but time does
move on.

Of course we have fewer worries. For one thing, we have
ceased being afraid Mrs. Le Moyne is going to follow us out
here and make trouble. Although Charlemagne says he isn't really interested, he listened when my father told him that Dr.
Sheckley had told him Mrs. Le Moyne had managed to sell the
house in Oblout and had flown to Spain. I don't see how she
could have done this since the house must have been owned

jointly, but my father and I did not press Charlemagne, who we guess must have settled up on the sly with her. But of course you never know with Charlemagne.

My father says he believes Dr. Sheckley holds no grudges. He says the doctor does not discuss it, and I can't blame him. But the doctor did get his billfold back, so he can't be too angry about that. It was in the mail waiting for him when he returned to Berylwood. If I were Dr. Sheckley, I would chalk it all up to experience. I think that is what he must be doing.

Mr. Colbert seems to be better. My father said Dr. Sheckley told him confidentially Mr. Colbert has been a difficult case but he's responding to treatment now that Mr. Colbert's mother does not visit him any more.

I'm glad my father decided to sell the business in Price and come out here. He even jokes about it, says, "Pete, I got a good Price for it," and laughs. It makes me feel good that he calls me Pete. He hasn't done that since I was a kid. On the other hand I can't remember us ever being so close as we are right now that we're opening the store out here. My father and I even manage to get suntanned together, and that's one thing we never did before either. I guess we're living in a more relaxed way. He says, "That's what California does to you, Pete," as if he was the one who always lived out here and invited me to come out. Life is surely amazing!

The thing that worries me is Minnie. At first she was always with us, but lately she's here and then she's not here. I suppose she feels this is her base and we can expect her back any time—after all, she's a free agent—but this time she's been gone nearly two weeks and we all miss her and worry about her. I think I miss her most of all, and if she isn't here I'm not sure how good the party will be.

I suppose, if I've got to be frank, Minnie's actions are the result of Bernice. Bernice, as you know from previous entries, I met when my father and I were out looking for likely places to rent for the store. We've become friends. All right, if I'm going to put it straight, we're lovers. I don't know whether or not

Minnie is jealous, but she certainly has acted strangely ever since I introduced her to Bernice.

I have plans for Bernice (the announcement today is that we're going to be married, though everybody knows that already), but as I told her, my father and I first have to open the store before we actually tie the knot.

Bernice surprised me when she said she wanted to help with the store, what could she do. So she's doing the decor. I never heard of decor for a television sales and repair store, but Bernice said she had some ideas she'd like to try out. I know my father likes Bernice because he said for her to go ahead, and then he turned to me and asked me if it was all right. I looked at Bernice and when I saw her and the way she was looking at me, I said it was all right. I guess I fell in love with her right then.

Father Bischoff's out there now, talking to my father and Bernice. I'm glad he took time off from his work in his church on Sunset Boulevard, but I knew he'd be here.

And now Charlemagne's out there, too. The party's beginning to shape up. As usual, Charlemagne's done it up right, putting that cake there on the table. What a big one! I'm sure we won't be able to eat it all. Maybe the sea gulls will swoop down for crumbs (do sea gulls eat things like that? I'll have to ask Charlemagne).

Father Bischoff calls his church the Symbolic Church of the Ancient Brotherhood. He's been successful raising money and he's happy dispensing his services to the young mostly because of the psychedelic interior and the odd rituals, taking a different mystical direction each week. But that's like Father Bischoff. Maybe his success is because he doesn't preach against fornication, if anything, he encourages it. He sets a good example for it, my father says.

Scott's coming through the gate from the beach now, really brown from the sun. He runs three miles on the beach every morning. He has a lot of friends, too. They were filming a television commercial here on the beach a few days ago, and Scott managed to get in it. It was a soft-drink-company commercial.

317

He enjoyed it, says he might even try to get more work in that line. But I think he's waiting for Charlemagne to ask him to go to Spain with him, and I think Charlemagne's planning to do that.

Charlemagne's bid to be technical adviser for that film *Song of Roland* finally came through. We learned they had written to him at the university about it and he did have it in the back of his mind, but he had his doubts about it when he learned the film company was going to make it in Spain, but he feels if he does run into his wife over there it will be a miracle. He says he plans to keep his eyes open and his hand on his lance. He has an office at the company in Hollywood, but he lives here, as we all do. He will be leaving in a few weeks and will be gone for about three months. We'll keep the home fires burning.

I'm glad Father Bischoff's and Scott's relatives have all been here and gone. It was pretty crowded here for a while and there was a lot of arguing this way and that about going home and taking up the reins, but both Father Bischoff and Scott have learned to say no.

I had to stop writing for a minute because of what I saw down there.

Minnie came in (yes, she's here!) and she stood for a while just looking at Bernice. And then Bernice turned and looked at her. And then Minnie ran to Bernice and embraced her and kissed her cheek!

I do love Minnie. And Bernice. I love them all!

And now, wouldn't you know it, Charlemagne is opening a big bottle of champagne!

He's poured glasses for all, and they're lifting those glasses to me up here because they know I'm here and can probably see me, and they're toasting me! Their lips are saying, "Happy birthday, Peter."

Excuse me, but I've got to get down there.

0060